KU-215-572

Maggie Craig was brought up in Clydebank and Glasgow, the youngest of four children of a railwayman father and a mother who worked in the typing pool of John Brown Land Boilers. Maggie was working as a medical secretary when she met her Welsh husband, Will, when he was doing part of his apprenticeship in a Clydeside shipyard, and she and Will subsequently sailed the world on oil tankers before settling in Glasgow and starting a family.

Maggie now lives in an old blacksmith's house in rural Aberdeenshire with Will and their two children. She is the author of DAMN' REBEL BITCHES, which tells the story of the women of the Jacobite rebellion. Her two earlier novels, THE RIVER FLOWS ON and WHEN THE LIGHTS COME ON AGAIN, are also available from Headline.

Also by Maggie Craig

The River Flows On
When The Lights Come On Again

The Stationmaster's Daughter

Maggie Craig

HEADLINE

Copyright © 2000 Maggie Craig

The right of Maggie Craig to be identified as the Author of
the Work has been asserted by her in accordance with
the Copyright, Designs and Patents Act 1988.

First published in hardback in 2000
by HEADLINE BOOK PUBLISHING

First published in paperback in 2000
by HEADLINE BOOK PUBLISHING

10 9 8 7 6 5 4 3 2 1

All rights reserved. No part of this publication may be reproduced,
stored in a retrieval system, or transmitted, in any form or by any
means without the prior written permission of the publisher, nor be
otherwise circulated in any form of binding or cover other than that
in which it is published and without a similar condition being
imposed on the subsequent purchaser.

All characters in this publication are fictitious and any resemblance
to real persons, living or dead, is purely coincidental.

ISBN 0 7472 6391 4

Typeset by Avon Dataset Ltd, Bidford-on-Avon, Warks

Printed and bound in France by
Brodard & Taupin

HEADLINE BOOK PUBLISHING
A division of Hodder Headline
338 Euston Road
London NW1 3BH

www.headline.co.uk
www.hodderheadline.com

To railway children everywhere:
from a Blue Train kid

And to Sandy, Kathleen and Pat –
who were also lucky enough
to have the stationmaster for a father

Acknowledgements

I should like to thank Margaret Stewart for most generously giving of her time to tell me about her childhood in Partick. The memories she shared with me were an invaluable source of information and inspiration.

I am indebted also to Louise Logan for searching through the legal texts in order to be able to furnish me with advice on a point of law.

Thanks are also due to my son. Ably assisted by his sister, he made sure that I kept my nose to the grindstone throughout a long and enjoyable summer. He also made me laugh a lot – which was just as important.

PART I
1935

Chapter 1

Although more perceptive people saw all the other shades within the glossy strands, Caroline Burgess was a redhead as far as most folk were concerned. When she was a child, both she and her brown-haired mother had learned to smile dutifully at the jokes about the milkman and the postie. Her father Archie, who invariably referred to her hair as her crowning glory, teasingly told her it was the colour of newly fitted copper pipe.

Esther Burgess was fond of declaring she would die happy if she had hair the same colour as her daughter, and Carrie herself loved it. Looking pretty in pink was out of the question, of course, but she could wear lots of other colours her friends couldn't. Take, for example, the pale green cotton sundress she had on today. The material had been a bargain for precisely that reason. The shade wouldn't suit everybody.

Sitting up straight in the striped deck-chair, she smoothed the cool cotton down over her knees. She didn't think anyone would be able to tell the garment wasn't a bought one. Esther was a good dressmaker, who took great delight in running up a frock or a skirt out of a few shillings' worth of fabric. She and her daughter had found the cloth for the sundress at one of their favourite shops, a fabric warehouse in Montrose Street up in Glasgow.

Carrie leaned forward to pick up the hand mirror lying on

top of the book she'd brought out with her into the garden of the station house. She was happy with her hair, but she could have done without the freckles which went with her typically Scottish colouring.

Despite the broad-brimmed straw hat she wore as protection against the May sunshine, she could swear she'd acquired half a dozen more of the annoying little dots since she'd come outside fifteen minutes ago. Not a very desirable state of affairs – especially with Matthew Campbell due any minute.

He was on back shift this week, and her mother had agreed the two of them could spend some time together today before he went along to the booking office to start his duties. With a bit of luck, Carrie thought, she might be able to convince Esther that Matt could call past *every* day this week. She sighed contentedly. Newly left school, with nothing to do for the next few months but wait for her exam results, the summer stretched before her with what seemed like endless promise.

With a furtive glance towards the back door of the solidly built stone cottage in case her mother might be watching, she fished a slice of lemon out of the jug of lemonade she had made earlier that afternoon in preparation for Matt's visit. Replacing the beaded crochet cover protecting the drink from the insects buzzing about the garden, she applied the fruit to her nose and cheeks. She heard a throaty chuckle.

Starting guiltily, she looked across her father's potato drills to the fence which separated the long garden from the equally long platform of the railway station. Several faces were grinning at her over the palings. The squad of railway navvies was obviously coming off day shift.

Her eyes lit on Ewen Livingstone. He was standing a pace or two behind his workmates, apparently fascinated by something lying on the platform. Bare-headed, he carried his navy working jacket slung over his shoulder, his index finger

4

crooked through its hanging loop. His mop of fair hair appeared not to have seen a comb for a week. As usual. He raised his head and Carrie looked quickly away.

'Lemon juice against the freckles? Sure, we could all be doin' with some of that today, Miss Burgess.'

It was the ganger of the Permanent Way men who had spoken – Martin Sharkey, a middle-aged man almost as wide as he was tall. Sweeping off his bunnet in salute, he wiped his broad and shining forehead with the back of his hand.

'It's a devilish warm day, eh?' Consciously or not, his eyes went to the jug of lemonade. Jumping to her feet, Carrie lifted the chunky green glass pitcher and the tumbler she had put out for Matt and walked over to the fence. Weaving a little to avoid her dress catching on the potato shaws, she picked her way daintily round the edge of the vegetable patch on one of the paths her father had constructed to divide his garden into its different areas.

'Would you like a drink?'

With a sweep of the hand which held the tumbler, she indicated that the invitation encompassed the whole group. She was going to be in trouble if they all accepted, even if each man took a gulp from the same glass. What the heck, she could always fetch the second jug she'd made, left in the scullery to keep cool. The P-way men had a tough job, out in the open all day and subject to the vagaries of the climate. In the case of the west of Scotland, those were considerable: freezing fog, ice, slush and snow; scorching heat and torrential downpours; the fine misty rain which could go on for weeks, penetrating coats and jackets and shoes.

Sometimes, as the old joke went, you got them all at the same time – although that wasn't really a joke at all. Everyone had experienced days when Mother Nature flung all four seasons at you at once.

5

'No, thanks, lassie,' said one of the men, 'but it's kind o' ye, all the same.' He tipped his bunnet politely and headed off down the platform. Three of the other men followed his lead, leaving only their foreman standing by the fence – and Ewen Livingstone. She darted another glance at him. Was she imagining that faint look of reproach on his pale face?

Sharkey surveyed them both thoughtfully. 'I'll be getting on too, Miss Burgess, but Ewen here will take a glass of your lemonade. Won't you, son?'

They stood for a minute or two gazing after the ganger, watching as he caught up with the rest of the squad. Heavy-footed in their working boots, the men clattered over the bridge to the other platform and then were swallowed up by the cavernous exit at the end of it. It framed a steep flight of stairs which led down into the hustle and bustle of Partick.

Carrie pulled back the bolt on the platform gate. Invisible from the railway side, it was an integral part of the picket fence. Like the villain coming up through the stage floor at the pantomime, she had often enjoyed surprising an unsuspecting passenger by suddenly emerging from the riot of rhododendron bushes – interspersed with the occasional silver birch or rowan tree – which tumbled along both sides of the garden.

'Will you come in for a wee minute?'

Carrie hoped she didn't sound as reluctant as she felt. She'd been avoiding him for over a month, since the railway social club *ceilidh* at Partick Burgh Hall. She owed him an apology for that night when, not to put too fine a point upon it, she had used one young man to make another jealous. She repeated the invitation, forcing herself to look Ewen in the face.

Compared to him, she had to admit her own freckles paled into insignificance. His, darker than his tousled locks, marched across his cheeks and nose in the summer months. Yet underneath them, his complexion was as smooth and creamy as her own.

'Do you want me to?' Ewen asked gravely.

'Of course,' she said, turning about and leading the way back to the deck-chairs. If she got the exam results she was hoping for – and her teachers had said they would be astonished if she didn't – she was heading for nearby Jordanhill College after the summer holidays to start her teacher training. Last month she had met a recently qualified member of the profession at a tennis party up on Partickhill.

The young woman had insisted that one of the most important qualities required when facing a classroom full of children – all potential wee horrors if they spotted the merest hint of weakness – was the ability to act the part. Judging by this performance, I'm halfway there, Carrie thought ruefully.

Some of the tension in the atmosphere dissipated when they reached what Esther Burgess referred to as the lawn. This was to differentiate the square of grass near the back door of the station house where the family sat out in the summer months from the drying green on the other side of the pebbled path which bisected the long back garden.

'I'm manky and mucky,' Ewen said, declining Carrie's invitation to sit in the second deck-chair, set opposite her on the other side of a small home-made garden table. He took a long stride to avoid standing on the flowers which bordered the lawn, threw his heavy jacket on to the grass and sat down on the edge of the drying green. The ground there was raised by several inches, bordered and supported by upended railway sleepers.

'This makes a fine seat.' He stretched his legs out and crossed them at the ankles, the white chuckies which formed the path crunching under the pressure of his heavy boots. He looked around him with every appearance of pleasure, and

7

Carrie felt herself relax a little. Was it possible they could slide back into their previously relaxed friendship as though nothing had happened?

'This is almost like being out in the country,' he said. 'Ye certainly wouldnae think we were between a passenger station and a goods yard.'

'It's the trees and the rhododendron bushes.' She gestured towards the latter. It being May, the extravagant pinky-purple blossoms were just coming into their full glory. 'They screen us off from everything. Even the noise and soot sometimes.' The constant danger of the pernicious black flecks puffed out by steam engines settling on clothes drying on the washing line was the bane of her mother's life. Carrie tried a tentative smile. 'If the wind's blowing in the right direction, that is.'

'Aye,' he replied. 'I don't doubt it.' If he had noticed that wee smile, he hadn't responded to it. His eyes drifted once more over the garden: the vegetables, the raspberry canes, the neatly trimmed grass. 'Your daddy works hard,' he observed. 'Making everything grow. The tatties and the vegetables and the wee flowers and everything. It must be rare having all this right outside your own door.'

'You're not near a park or anything?'

His eyes came back to her face. 'There's no' much grass in Keith Street, hen.'

She knew instantly that the reminder of the difference in their circumstances had been entirely deliberate. Before she could think of some suitably neutral comment, Ewen spoke again, his face thoughtful. 'Apart from the Quaker graveyard, of course.'

'What's that?'

The delivery was faultlessly deadpan. 'A graveyard wi' deid Quakers in it.'

'Walked right into that one,' she conceded, expecting him

8

to grin in triumph. He was nothing if not quick-witted, and he had caught her out like this several times. No smile appeared, however. He continued gazing at her with that pensive and extremely disconcerting look on his face.

'I m-mean,' she stuttered, 'why is there a Quaker g-graveyard in Partick?'

He tilted his chin, angling his face towards the sun. 'Och, there was a group o' them here once. In the olden days, like. When Partick was a wee village. Seemingly there were some folk called Purdon among their leadin' lights. That's why we've got a Purdon Street.'

He was full of wee snippets like that, what he himself called 'another piece of useless information'. Carrie had no idea where he got them all from. She supposed he must read a lot.

'Where is Purdon Street again?' The answer didn't matter. Keeping this harmless conversation going as long as possible did.

'Where the steamie is,' he replied, using the colloquial name for the building which housed the public baths and wash-house. The station house had its own little laundry room off the kitchen, equipped with a clothes boiler, two deep sinks for steeping and rinsing clothes and a mangle for squeezing the water out of them. Many of Partick's overcrowded tenement homes, like those throughout Glasgow, had no such luxuries. On washday the housewives who lived in them pushed prams piled high with their families' dirty clothes to the steamie.

Ewen pretended to catch himself on. 'You wouldnae know where that is, of course. The street the Carnegie Library's on the corner of, then. That's more your kind of level.'

Carrie didn't miss the edge to his voice. So much for having a harmless conversation, slipping back seamlessly into their old easy comradeship. Trying to get her courage up to offer

9

that apology, she studied him over the flowers. He sat framed between a clump of marguerites and the group of red hot pokers Archie Burgess had planted in a circle next to them. The flaming hue of the spiky flowers matched the red neckerchief Ewen wore knotted at his throat, traditional garb for Permanent Way men.

'Catches the sweat,' he had once told her cheerfully, 'and it comes in handy for tying tae the end o' a wagon if you need to leave a warning signal for the man coming behind you.'

She couldn't help noticing he had a hole in the sole of each boot. Embarrassed for him, her eyes slid to his navy reefer jacket, lying on the washing green beside him. That was also traditional gear, as were the brown corduroy trousers he wore. Whether the men bought their working clothes themselves or had them issued free of charge by their employers every two or three years was a perennial bone of contention between them and the railway company.

The jacket was pretty threadbare. The elbows were soon going to be through. Couldn't his mother sew some patches on for him?

With a pang, Carrie realised she didn't even know if he had a mother. The two of them had talked a lot since Ewen had come to work on the railway – almost two years ago now – but somehow their conversations had never really touched on the personal. She had picked up the subtle signals that he preferred it that way.

She hadn't even known he lived in Keith Street until he had mentioned it just now, only that his home lay in one of the crowded streets along towards Partick Cross, on what her mother called the wrong side of Dumbarton Road. Ewen Livingstone belonged, quite literally, on the wrong side of the tracks.

His cheerful description of the state of his working clothes had been perfectly accurate. His trousers and blue collarless shirt were pretty manky. He had his sleeves rolled up and she saw that his muscular forearms had caught the sun. The fine hairs on them were golden, like those at his throat where, under the red neckerchief, the first two or three buttons of his shirt were undone.

'So, do I get a glass of lemonade? Or do I have to roll over and die for Scotland first?' The pale eyes were quizzical.

'What? Oh, sorry.' Carrie hastily lifted the pitcher and poured. 'Is that Bobby you're talking about? Does he roll over and die for Scotland?'

Ewen nodded, but there was a gleam in his light eyes – she had never been able to decide whether they were grey or blue – which told her he knew very well that she was grabbing at any possible topic of conversation except for the one that really mattered.

Bobby was a mongrel of indeterminate parentage but impeccable manners, intelligence and training. His owner Donald Nicholson was a man of few words, but his dog was a great favourite in Partick. Being invited to take him through his various party pieces – giving his right paw, giving his left paw and so on – was considered to be a great social coup. It was a sure sign that his rather taciturn master approved of you.

'Aye. I seen him and Donald when I was on the way tae ma work this morning.'

Resisting the temptation to correct his grammar, Carrie handed over a tumbler of lemonade. He gave her a glimpse of his old smile as he took it out of her hands.

Ewen Livingstone wasn't handsome exactly, although his features were pleasant enough. It was the face-splitting smile and the mischievous twinkle in his eye which made him attractive. Up until the *ceilidh* a month ago, both had almost

11

always been in evidence whenever Carrie and he had met: when he jumped nimbly up on to the platform after working down the line somewhere; when he stopped on his way to and from work to exchange a few words with her.

Caroline Burgess would have been an extremely unobservant young lady indeed if she hadn't realised fairly early on in their relationship that Ewen Livingstone had a wee fancy for her. She would have been lying if she'd claimed to have no feelings for him in return. There had been at least two occasions when she had been in imminent danger of being kissed over the fence. She wasn't entirely sure which one of them had been the first to take a step back . . . or whether or not she was grateful for the physical barrier provided by the wooden palings.

Then, shortly before Christmas last year, Matthew Campbell had arrived at Partick, transferred from Hyndland, the next station up the line. Carrie had taken one look at the new clerk and forgotten all about the young P-way man.

Matt was everything Ewen wasn't: tall and handsome, well-spoken and well-dressed, and with a quiet maturity and sophistication which appealed strongly to Carrie. At twenty-four, he was seven years older than she was. That age gap worried Carrie's mother, but Matt's grave courtesy and respectful attitude were beginning to win her round.

The invitation to afternoon tea extended by his mother had also helped. Esther Burgess had been mightily impressed both by the spacious main-door flat at the posh end of Gardner Street and by Matthew's father. According to her, Charles Campbell was the dead spit of Ronald Colman, and charming with it. Her daughter was inclined to agree with her there, but she had found Matt's mother rather cold. Spotting her curl of the lip at the way Esther raised her pinkie when she drank her tea hadn't exactly endeared Shona Campbell to Carrie either.

12

Mature and courteous Matt might be, but it had taken him long enough to ask her out. A month ago an exasperated Carrie, convinced the attraction between them was mutual, had decided to do something about it. The railway social club do had seemed the ideal opportunity, especially when she found they were seated at the same table.

He asked her up for the first dance, saw her politely back to her seat at the end of it – and proceeded to stay firmly in his own for the next half hour. Sitting on the opposite side of the round table from him, the noise of accordion and fiddles had made conversation impossible. Then Ewen came bounding up, the fair waves of his hair flying, looking for all the world like Bobby the dog when he spotted one of his favourite humans. He had one girl by the hand and was looking for another to make up a threesome for the Dashing White Sergeant. A plan began to form in Carrie's mind.

It crystallised during the procession of the dance round the hall. Meeting young Mr Campbell, persuaded on to the floor by a colleague to make up a set of two men and girl, Carrie was not at all displeased to be greeted by a ferocious glower. To make sure she was on the right track, she stood up with Ewen for the next dance, a Military Two-Step. Getting up with him the third time for a waltz might have been pushing it a bit – but it did achieve the desired result.

As she came back into the hall from the powder room after the brief interval, Matt stepped out from behind one of the pillars which supported the balcony of the ballroom and took a firm hold of her hand.

'You're dancing every other dance tonight with me,' he told her. His voice was low and husky, his beautiful brown eyes intense. She had made a joke about loving masterful men, but secretly she had been thrilled. To her shame, seeing Ewen's face fall as he came eagerly towards her and then registered that she had her hand in Matt Campbell's had given her only the merest twinge of regret at the time.

She was thoroughly ashamed of herself now that the first heady flush of being Matt's girlfriend had subsided and she was beginning to think straight again. Taking a drink of lemonade, she set her glass down on the table, carefully not too close to her book. She looked up and saw Ewen's light eyes go to her head.

'Are you wearing that for a bet, Miss Burgess?'

The cheeky comment didn't bother her. The brim of her straw hat was rather large. The 'Miss Burgess' did. They had long since gone on to first name terms with each other. If this unusual formality was a measure of how much she had hurt his feelings, she was truly sorry for it. Stalling for time, she removed the hat and laid it on the table. It covered most of the surface, so she took the book on to her lap.

'You've ayeways got yer heid stuck in a book, haven't you? Romantic poetry, nae doot. A' hearts and flowers. Nothing whatsoever to do wi' real life.'

Thirty seconds ago she'd been feeling sorry for him, but now Carrie bristled. 'They're not romantic, as a matter of fact,' she said with an unconscious lift of the chin. 'You might even like some of them.'

He shrugged. 'Read me one, then. I'll bet ye cannae find anything that'll mean something to me. That would mean something to any working man.'

She was more than happy to pick up the challenge. She knew exactly which poem to choose. 'Listen to this,' she urged. 'It's by Robert Louis Stevenson. It's called "From a Railway Carriage".

'Faster than fairies, faster than witches,
Bridges and houses, hedges and ditches;

14

> *And charging along like troops in a battle*
> *All through the meadows the horses and cattle:*
> *All of the sight of the hill and the plain*
> *Fly as thick as driving rain;*
> *And ever again, in the wink of an eye,*
> *Painted stations whistle by.'*

She broke off, unnerved by the fierce and sullen silence with which Ewen was listening to her. 'It's about a train journey, you see –'

'I'd worked that out,' he growled, giving her one of his do-you-think-my-head-buttons-up-the-back looks. Drawing his legs up in front of him, holding his lemonade in one hand, he bent his head forward and stared down at the stones on the path. 'Read the rest of it,' he commanded, his voice muffled slightly by the posture.

> *'Here is a child who clambers and scrambles,*
> *All by himself and gathering brambles;*
> *Here is a tramp who stands and gazes;*
> *And here is the green for stringing the daisies!*
> *Here is a cart runaway in the road*
> *Limping along with man and load;*
> *And here is a mill, and there is a river:*
> *Each a glimpse and gone forever!*

'Well?' she demanded when she had finished.

Ewen straightened up. 'No' bad,' he admitted grudgingly. 'He's got the rhythm of the train in his words. That's clever, that.'

She closed the book and reached for her lemonade. Ewen tossed the last of his own drink back with a gulp and placed the glass on the path, tilting it against the railway sleeper

15

border so that it wouldn't fall on to the stones. Then he raised his head and fixed her with a penetrating gaze.

'Go on then,' he said softly, both elbows now resting on his knees, his hands loosely clasped between his legs, 'spit it out. You'll feel a whole lot better afterwards. You're quite right, Carrie. Ye do owe me an apology.'

She supposed he didn't have to be a mind-reader to work out why she had invited him in this afternoon. And despite his rough speech and lack of education, he was by no means unintelligent.

'About what happened at the *ceilidh*,' she began and then paused. What was the best way to phrase this? 'I-I'm sorry –' What was she sorry about? That she had hurt his feelings? But men didn't like being reminded of their vulnerabilities, did they? 'I'm sorry about what happened.' She faltered under his steady gaze. 'I mean –'

'Go on,' he said in an infuriatingly encouraging tone. 'I might even throw ye a biscuit if ye manage tae get tae the end o' a sentence. Like rewarding Bobby for giving me a paw.' He gave a short bark of laughter. 'Don't glare at me like that. Ye'll get wrinkles to go wi' your freckles.'

'Ewen Livingstone –'

He rose abruptly to his feet and came towards her, thrusting his hands deep into the pockets of his corduroy trousers as he stood on the path in front of her.

'I'll say it for you, will I, Carrie? You're very sorry you used me to make Matthew Campbell jealous. You're very sorry you got up to dance with me three times for that express purpose. No' because you actually wanted to dance with me. Perish the thought, eh?'

His eyes were boring into her across the red hot pokers. Like red hot pokers. He muttered something she didn't catch, except to realise it was an exclamation of some sort. He took

16

a couple of paces away from her, his angry feet making quite an impression on the path. She'd have to get the rake out and smooth the pebbles over after he'd gone. He stomped back to stand on the other side of the flowers.

'And – although I might just be flatterin' myself here – you're very sorry that I'm only a railway navvy and you're the stationmaster's daughter. Is that no' the sum of it, Carrie?'

Dismayed, and upset that he was so upset, she stood up and went to him, the poetry book sliding unheeded into the canvas seat of the deck-chair. The skirt of her green dress swished against the marguerites as she took a long step between the flowers and over the earth of the border.

'Ewen.' She laid her fingers on his bare forearm but he shook her off, pulling his hands out of his pockets and waving them angrily.

'I suppose you thought you were as well to keep me dangling. On standby, like. Till someone better came along. Someone like Matthew Campbell.' The name was spat out. 'A young gentleman more suited to your superior social status.' He enunciated the final three words with careful and precise sarcasm. 'Is that it, Carrie?' he demanded, nostrils flaring. 'Have I got it right?'

He wasn't much taller than her, but he had his head – fair waves more unruly than ever now – tilted back at a haughty angle. The posture enabled him to look down at her. She studied his face and wondered if he did have it right. Had she refused to let herself care for him because of the difference in their social positions? She didn't want to think that about herself.

'Ewen . . .' she said again. She had no idea what she was going to say to him. He didn't give her any help, simply kept staring down at her with cool and unforgiving eyes. There was a noise behind them: footsteps coming round the side of the house.

'Sorry I'm a wee bit late,' called a cheerful voice. 'Oh!'

It was Matthew. Carrie threw him the swiftest of glances over her shoulder. She was in no doubt now about the colour of Ewen's eyes. They had darkened to an icy winter blue.

'In the name o' God,' he whispered. 'I didnae think you'd do it a second time. I really didnae think anyone would stoop that low.' He took his frosty gaze off the rapidly approaching Matthew Campbell and bent it once more on Carrie. 'I've obviously had far too high an opinion of you, Miss Burgess. I'll not make that mistake again.'

18

Chapter 2

Now she had two angry young men to deal with. Far too late, Carrie realised how it must look to both of them: that she had engineered this meeting. Nothing could have been further from her mind. Martin Sharkey had all but pushed Ewen into the garden, and their ensuing conversation had simply put Matt's imminent arrival out of her head.

Engineered or not, the encounter was fast turning into a confrontation. Matt and Ewen were looking at each other in a way that made Carrie's blood run cold: sizing each other up.

However much your parents tried to protect you, you couldn't grow up in Glasgow without learning to recognise the warning indicators of an outburst of male violence. It had to do with the stance, the locked eyes, the crackle of tension in air suddenly become icy, the very silence which preceded such explosions.

Those weren't scarce these days. There were so many men out of work. Frustrated and dispirited, with too much time on their hands, they stood about for hours at street corners, ready to take offence at the smallest slight, real or imagined. Sometimes one man simply had to glance at another the wrong way. Then the challenge would ring out. 'Are you looking at me, Jimmy?' And you would find yourself having to hastily cross to the other side of the street to get out of their way.

Matt's question was worded differently, but the aggression was exactly the same.

'What's he doing here?'

He took a few slow and deliberate paces towards them, halting a couple of feet from the back door. Beside her, Carrie felt Ewen slowly shifting posture. His eyes, she knew, were fixed on Matt.

An image of dogs about to launch themselves into a yelping and biting scrap slid into her mind. She could practically hear the growls, see the bared teeth and cocked-back ears.

If only she hadn't been so stupid and so selfish the night of the *ceilidh*. She had caused this hostility between two young men who might otherwise have scarcely noticed each other. She knew there were girls who would love to have two boys fighting over them, but she wasn't one of them. She hated this sort of thing.

Like her father, she was a natural peacemaker. Archie Burgess belonged to that other group of men, the ones who would wade in, often at considerable risk to themselves, to break up a fight. In her father's case it was usually a dispute between two late-night drunks at the station. She had anxiously watched him do it on more than one occasion. He always did his best to reassure her afterwards.

'Did ye no' see their arms, lass? No bones in them. Flailing about like the India-rubber man. Drunks are harmless that way. That pair hadnae a hope in hell – excuse my French, hen – of landing a decent punch.'

Despite his protestations, she noticed he always swore her to secrecy about his role in breaking up these fights as far as her mother was concerned.

Her mother! Carrie shot an anxious glance towards the back door of the station house. For some reason she'd never been able to fathom, Esther Burgess had a down on Ewen.

This certainly wasn't going to endear him to her. Moving swiftly, Carrie side-stepped neatly over the chuckies – gosh, Ewen had churned them up – bent down and scooped up his shabby navy jacket from the edge of the drying green.

She called once more on her acting skills, consciously making her tone of voice as even and pleasant as possible. 'I invited Ewen in for a glass of lemonade, Matt.'

'You what?'

He hadn't shouted, had barely even raised his voice, but the tight set of his mouth gave him away. He had been charm itself to her since they had started walking out together, but she had known, somehow, that he might have a bit of a temper . . .

Ignoring his question – under the circumstances that seemed the wisest course of action – she held the jacket out to Ewen.

'He was just going when you came in.'

For the second time that afternoon, she laid her hand on Ewen's arm. The springy golden hairs felt slightly damp, the skin underneath them clammy. He didn't shake her off this time, but she had to exert considerable pressure before he took the death-ray glare off Matthew Campbell.

'What?'

She extended her arm, offering him his jacket again. 'I said, you were just going. Weren't you?'

She had the impression he had to re-focus in order to understand what she was saying. His whole concentration had been on Matt. All her fault, Carrie thought miserably. She had made the two of them hate each other.

Feeling more guilty than she ever had in her life, she saw that hate wasn't too strong a word. Judging by the look on Matt's face, Ewen's feelings were more than reciprocated. Surely she wasn't worth all this?

She wasn't certain if Ewen sensed her anxiety, but she felt the bunched muscles under her fingers relax a fraction and he took the jacket from her. 'I'll relieve youse both o' my presence then.'

Matt's lip curled at that 'youse'. That wasn't fair. Ewen hadn't been given the opportunities the two of them had. She wasn't going to part from him on bad terms either. They'd been friends for too long. As though he were a bomb which might go off if she wasn't standing right next to him, she darted forward to the deck-chair, grabbed the book of poetry and whizzed back to the path in about three seconds flat, thrusting the book out to him.

'Why don't you borrow this, Ewen? Give it back to me in a couple of weeks.'

His eyes flickered briefly down to the book, then returned to her face.

'No, thank you, Miss Burgess. I wouldnae want to deprive you o' it.'

'Go on, Ewen,' she urged. 'You'd enjoy it. There are some great poems in here.' He might be childish enough to keep up this 'Miss Burgess' malarkey, but she wasn't going to retaliate.

'Thanks for the lemonade,' he said firmly, and headed off in the direction of the platform gate. Avoiding Matt, still standing close to the back door, he cut across the lawn, apparently intending to leave without so much as a backward glance.

'Oh!' Carrie nearly stamped her foot. 'Don't be so bloody stubborn!'

He stopped and turned, feathery eyebrows raised in disapproval. 'A lady like you shouldnae swear.'

'Well, take the blooming book then.' She held it out again.

Matthew laughed, and sauntered forward to join them both on the grass.

'Not much point in lending him a book, Miss Burgess,' he said. *Miss Burgess?* Good grief, they were both at it now. Honestly, men could be really pompous sometimes.

'Don't you know your wee friend can't actually read?'

Like a train seeing an unexpected red signal up ahead, the conversation ground and screeched to a halt – and a deep and ugly flush stained Ewen's creamy skin.

In the silence which followed, Carrie heard the chug-chug of a locomotive shunting wagons over in the goods yard. Nearer at hand, a blackbird was singing. Somewhere within the mass of rhododendron bushes, she thought. Their singing was at its sweetest at this time of year, when they were building their nest and raising their young.

'He can't write either. It's in the staff records. He can barely manage to set his own name down. You should see his signature in the ledger.' Matt's voice was full of disdain. 'Or what passes for his signature. A child of five could do better. He might as well have made his mark.'

Carrie stared at him, scarcely able to believe her ears. Was this the same man who had been so attentive to her over the past month, who only last week had presented her with a single white rose?

'That's how I see you,' he'd said softly, 'as pure and beautiful as this perfect flower.' It had been an early blossom, a bud on the point of unfurling. She was a rosebud too: a girl poised on the brink of womanhood, ready to open up to the right man, the man who would love her for the rest of her life. The words had thrilled her. So had the long, deep kisses which followed them.

She couldn't understand how the man who was capable of such romantic words and gestures could be standing here now saying these cruel things. She didn't doubt they were true. One look at Ewen's stricken face, deathly pale now that the painful blush had faded, was enough to verify that – as was the way he was refusing to meet her eyes.

Why hadn't it occurred to her that he might not be able to read? She knew, because of his rough accent and bad grammar – and because he'd told her so himself – that he hadn't had much education. He'd left school at fourteen and alternated between casual labouring jobs and long periods on the dole until her father had taken him on as a surfaceman the day after his seventeenth birthday.

'Thanks for the lemonade, Miss Burgess,' he repeated, and strode off once more in the direction of the platform gate.

'Leave it, Carrie.'

Matthew's assumption she was going to do as he said was enough to propel her towards the corner of the house.

'Ewen! Wait!'

He was already on the platform. She was sure he would have pretended not to hear her if he hadn't realised that the gate wasn't properly closed. Hearing the squeak as it swung open behind him, he turned and pushed it to. His hand was coming over the spars to push the bolt home when she reached him.

'Ewen,' she said, placing her fingers over his. 'I'm sorry . . .'

'Take your hand away.'

'Ewen . . .' she repeated helplessly.

'Please take your hand away.'

Lost for words, and not knowing what else to do, she did as he asked. He fastened the bolt in place. Then he met her eyes at last. His own looked completely washed-out, bleak and desolate.

'Goodbye,' he said. 'Goodbye . . . Carrie.'

'This lemonade's a bit warm. Is there any more in the scullery? And did you speak to your father about the rostering for the weekend?'

24

Matt was standing by the deck-chairs, apparently quite at ease. More angry with him than she would have believed possible, Carrie chose her words carefully, trying to keep a hold on her temper.

'You didn't need to show him up like that. You made him feel small. You hurt his feelings.'

He shrugged. 'So what? He's a railway navvy. The lowest of the low.' He lowered his long frame into one of the chairs.

'Whatever happened to the brotherhood of the workers, Matthew?' she asked lightly. 'And have you forgotten that my father started off as a shunter?'

Matt was strong in the union, and the all-encompassing National Union of Railwaymen at that, which welcomed members working in all the railway trades: from salaried clerical staff right through to manual labourers. It had been a conscious political decision, he had told her, in line with his socialist ideals.

Unusually for a stationmaster, Carrie's father was also an NUR man, staying loyal to the union which had welcomed him when he had first become a railway servant. That had been back in the days of the old North British Railway Company, for the past twelve years and more part of the mighty LNER – the London and North Eastern Railway.

'Your father worked his way up,' insisted Matt. 'And you're a stationmaster's daughter and I don't think you should forget that.'

Carrie stared at him in disbelief. 'Just because I'm a stationmaster's daughter doesn't mean I consider myself a cut above everybody else!'

'Well, you should.' He paused and studied her, then smiled and held out his hand. 'Come here.' He reached for her, but she stepped back, evading his grasp. It was more than

25

anger. She was disappointed in him.

'Carrie, people like Ewen Livingstone are never going to work their way up. They're not capable of it. He's not on your level and he never will be. Now,' said Matt, looking up from the deck-chair with a winning smile, 'since you *are* the stationmaster's daughter and I'm your young man, am I working this Saturday or am I not?'

As well as *ceilidhs* and dances, the railway social club organised frequent excursions. On Saturday there was one to Oban, the west coast terminus of the West Highland line. Not everyone could go, of course. The stations still had to be manned. Matt had drawn the short straw as far as the booking office was concerned.

Carrie's voice was clipped. 'I did ask Father, but he feels he can't change it. He'd be accused of playing favourites with his daughter's boyfriend.'

Organising the shifts for all the men who worked underneath him was one of Archie Burgess' biggest headaches. When he drew up the rosters for each month he had to make sure everyone had their fair share of day shift, back shift, night shift and rest days. Some men had preferences for one shift over another. They had a considerable amount of respect for their stationmaster, but that didn't stop them making their feelings crystal clear when they didn't get the shift or rest day they had put in for. As Matt had.

'So you're not going to try to persuade him?'

Tight-lipped, Carrie shook her head.

'You could if you really wanted to. You can wind your father round your little finger.'

She'd never heard his voice so cold, nor seen such a scornful look on his handsome face. Was he expecting her to back down over this? She wasn't going to. It was a pity Matt couldn't come to Oban, but she wasn't prepared to put any more

26

pressure on her father. He had enough stresses and strains in his job already.

During the previous winter he had started to experience crippling chest pains. Despite his demands that they stop making such a fuss about nothing, his womenfolk had insisted on calling in the doctor. He had given Archie a thorough examination and told him he needed to watch his diet and relax more. Try to forget about the job when he was off duty. Easier said than done when you more or less lived above the shop.

Matt stood up. 'So you won't speak to him about it?'

'Please try to understand,' Carrie said. 'It could cause my father a lot of trouble. He's got enough on his plate as it is.'

'Right. Fine.' Matt folded his arms across his chest. 'Are you going up the hill to play tennis tomorrow tonight?'

'Yes, I am.'

They'd had this argument yesterday. He had quizzed her about who else would be there, particularly which boys. That was quite flattering in one way ... but a bit irritating in another.

'Even though I don't want you to go without me?'

Carrie tossed her coppery head. 'You can hardly expect me to give up all my friends for you. To sit at home twiddling my thumbs whenever you're working.'

'I thought people in love only needed each other.'

She let out a sigh of exasperation. 'Matt, that's rubbish and you know it.'

'So, basically, what you're saying is that Ewen Livingstone's feelings matter and mine don't.'

'Matt,' she pleaded, 'that's not at all what I'm saying.'

'That's what it sounds like to me.'

He stood in front of her: tall, elegant – and completely unbending. He *was* waiting for her to back down. Well, he was going to have a very long wait. The faint look of incredulity which flashed across his handsome features when she said nothing almost made her laugh – almost.

'I'd better get to work then,' he said eventually. 'We wouldn't want the stationmaster to think I was trying to get away with anything just because I'm his daughter's boyfriend. Would we now?'

That was two men who had walked out on her today. She was doing well. And she and Matt had parted without making any arrangement to meet again. She heard the back door open, and turned towards the sound.

'Caroline, pet, you're not forgetting that there's more lemonade in here?' Esther Burgess looked curiously at her daughter standing alone by the deck-chairs. 'Carrie? I thought Matthew was paying you a visit today.'

'He's been and gone, Ma,' she said brightly. 'Didn't want to be late for his work. Why don't you come out and have a glass with me?'

Definitely a touch of the actress. At this rate, she thought with grim humour, I'd have been better applying to the Royal Scottish Academy of Music and Drama in Buchanan Street than teacher training college.

Chapter 3

'Caroline Burgess! You never walked through the streets of Partick dressed like that!'

Carrie laid her tennis racquet on the gate-leg table, folded now against the wall of the big square living room of the station house. Glancing down at her divided skirt, she smoothed a hand over its white piqué folds. It was certainly short, stopping a good four inches above the knee, but it wasn't exactly indecent.

Her legs were beginning to acquire a healthy glow. She went to great pains to protect her face from the sun, but light brown legs and arms were fashionable, even if she did sometimes think it wasn't so much a tan as all the freckles joining up with each other. When she looked up again at her mother, her face was glowing with mischief.

She'd had a good time this evening, indulging in a little innocent flirtation with the boy she'd partnered for a game of mixed doubles. It had all been light-hearted fun and taken seriously by neither of them.

Her tennis partner had cheerfully offered to see her home, but she'd told him just as cheerfully not to bother. She was perfectly capable of walking home on her own, especially at this time of year when there was daylight until late at night. Also, although she didn't say this to the young man, she didn't want anyone reporting to Matt that she'd been seen with another lad. Partick was a busy place, only a few miles from the teeming centre of Glasgow, but it was still the village it had once been as far as gossip was concerned.

'I did,' she said now in response to her mother's question. 'I got a couple of wolf whistles, too.'

'With legs like that I'm not surprised,' said her father, emerging from behind the broadsheet pages of the *Evening Citizen*. Ensconced in one of the upholstered dark-red armchairs which flanked the neat tiled fireplace, he lowered the newspaper on to his lap and stretched out his legs on the hearth rug. The grate held its customary seasonal vase of dried flowers, placed there by Esther Burgess every spring and ceremoniously removed in September or October when the first fire of the autumn was lit.

'You get your shapely pins from your mother, you know. Only I'm the only person who ever sees hers. It's a damn' shame.' Relaxing before he went back up to the station to do his nightly rounds, his jacket off and his dark waistcoat unfastened, Archie's eyes twinkled as he surveyed first his daughter and then his wife. The latter stood in the narrow passageway which led from the living room to the back kitchen and wash-house, a tea towel in her hands.

It did Carrie's heart good to hear her father joking like this. In overall command of the railway station, one of the busiest on the Glasgow suburban network, dealing with the rostering of shifts was only one small part of his workload. He had to oversee every aspect of both the passenger and freight traffic sides of the business – and deal with the extensive staff which carried it out.

There were all the different grades of clerks, both on the passenger and the goods side. The porters had their own hierarchy, from the leading porter down through to the lad porters. One of their main duties in the winter was to tend the various coal fires throughout the rambling station buildings: in the waiting rooms on either platform, in the ladies' waiting room on the up platform, in the booking office, the station-master's office and their own little room. That was situated on the opposite side of the booking hall from the office where the passenger clerks like Matt worked.

Then there were the signalmen who worked in the box a hundred yards or so beyond the end of the long platform. The goods yard, over on the other side of the station house, had another set of offices full of busy parcels clerks and sidings which echoed all day to the puffing of engines and the calls of drivers and shunters, not to mention the surfacemen. The Permanent Way squads had a brick-built bothy in the goods yard, also heated by a coal fire.

Archie Burgess loved his job, but as he himself drily put it, his staff didn't always work together in perfect peace and harmony. All of their disputes – major or minor – eventually ended up on the big solid desk in his office.

He looked relaxed enough now. With mock solemnity, he tapped the side of his nose with his index finger and threw another wicked look at Esther, his eyes deliberately sliding down to her legs. 'Definitely shapely,' he said. 'Like the rest of her. I'm the only man who can testify to that, as well.'

'Archie Burgess!' Blushing, his wife advanced into the room and flicked the tea towel at him.

'Careful, Mother, you'll have his eye out.'

Father and daughter grinned at each other. It was one of Esther's favourite admonitions. It went along with *Don't eat an apple last thing at night, it'll lie on your breast till morning* and *Always wear clean underwear every day in case you get run over by a tram.*

Carrie had once asked why you would be worrying about the state of your pants and brassiere if you were lying in the middle of Crow Road with a broken leg. Without a trace of irony, Esther Burgess had drawn herself up to her full – and deeply unimpressive – height and stated that she personally would be black affronted if any member of her family turned up in Casualty at the Western Infirmary wearing grubby underwear. What kind of housewife would the doctors and nurses think she was?

'Aye, dangerous things tea towels, eh, Carrie?' said her father now, the impish look still on his face. 'You'd think folk would handle them with more care, wouldn't you?'

'Och, you!' The cloth was flicked once more in Archie's direction. He lunged forward, grabbed it and pulled. Despite a valiant effort to maintain her stern expression, his wife ended up on his lap, laughing into his face. Carrie laughed too. She loved it when her parents horsed around like this. They were like a couple of weans sometimes.

'You both think you're so smart, don't you?' demanded Esther.

'Nope,' said Archie cheerfully, squeezing her waist. 'We know we are. It runs in the family, you might say. For all those who had the good fortune to be born a Burgess.' He winked outrageously at Carrie.

Opening her mouth to retaliate, Esther was pre-empted by the noise of a train thundering past on the railway line outside, yards from where the family sat. The house, and everything in it, trembled in sympathy.

As a child, Carrie had provoked some hilarity when, a puzzled frown wrinkling her small forehead, she had asked friends of her parents why their house *didn't* shake at regular intervals. Having lived with it all her life, she found the vibration entirely normal and oddly comforting – like listening to the trains at night while she was lying in her bed.

As the noise disappeared into the distance Archie glanced

across at the clock which stood, still gently trembling, on the mantelpiece.

'The first Home James,' he murmured.

It was his name for the empty carriages which went through at this time every night, three sets in all, so as to be in the right place for the start of passenger traffic the following morning. With no passengers to consider, they could rattle along at quite a lick, hence the nickname: 'Home, James, and don't spare the horses.'

Carrie moved towards the door. Her father timed his final visit of the day to his domain after he heard the third set of empty carriages pass. That would be in exactly – she checked the clock herself – twenty-nine minutes' time. She'd better get a move on if she wanted a private chat with Matt. She saw her mother's eyes go once more to her bare legs.

'The other girls walked home in their tennis skirts too, Ma,' she said innocently. 'Even the ones that live up on Partickhill.'

The girls who lived up on Partickhill hadn't very far to walk, the tennis courts being close to their homes. From the expression on his face, she could see that had occurred to her father, but what mattered to her mother was that she took the behaviour of those who lived up the hill as a yardstick for her own daughter's behaviour. If they had walked home in their tennis skirts, then it must be all right.

Carrie lifted her racquet from the table and put her other hand on the doorknob. 'All right if I pop along to see Matthew for ten minutes?'

'Aye, on you go, hen,' said her father, the twinkle still in his eye and his wife still on his knee, his arms loosely about her trim waist. They'd be kissing as soon as she went out of the door, thought Carrie fondly. 'I'm sure he'll be glad to see you. And since he's on back shift, there won't be many other people about.'

33

'You're not going to the station in your tennis skirt?'

'No, Ma, of course not.'

She was tempted, mind, simply to see the look on Matt's face. No, better not. Mr Matthew Campbell, clerk grade three, could be surprisingly strait-laced at times. About some things, at any rate.

The second Home James was approaching as Carrie went out on to the platform, and she stayed where she was for a moment, turning only to secure the bolt of the gate. The instruction to stand well clear had been drummed into her from an early age. As the van glided past, the guard spotted her and raised a hand in greeting.

She stood and watched as the train swung on towards Hyndland, the two paraffin lamps on the back glowing in the May twilight. Checking those were visible was an old railway-man's habit, one she had acquired from her father. If there were two red lights to be seen at the rear of a train all was well. Not only would a following train be able to see it stopped at a signal or a station, it also meant no carriages had become uncoupled, as had been known to happen. Archie Burgess had a fund of railway horror stories, many of them revolving around runaway trains somehow cut loose from their engine and driver.

Despite the whooshing noise made by the heavy door as it slid open over the hard floor of the booking office, Matthew didn't hear her come in. He was concentrating too hard on whatever it was he was doing, perched on a tall stool to one side of the arched ticket window checking tickets off in a huge ledger. Several piles of them, held together by elastic bands, lay on the counter in front of him.

Studying him as he worked, Carrie's fingers itched to brush back the stray lock of hair which was falling forward on to his

34

brow. Like Ewen, he had wavy hair which could sometimes be a little unruly, but there the resemblance stopped. While Ewen was all light eyes and pale skin, Matt was much darker, with soulful brown eyes. He was taller too, and elegantly slim, although with a strength in his arms which made Carrie dizzy.

He heard her at last, and looked up. Sliding off the high stool, he came on to his feet. Even the way he stood was elegant, one foot extended a little to the side, hands casually in his pockets. He was always smartly dressed, a knife-edge crease in his trousers and a neat collar and tie around his neck even when he was off duty. He was a fastidious kind of man.

He stood looking at her gravely, not a trace of a smile on his face. It was obviously up to her to break the ice.

'If I say that I'm sorry, will you say that you're sorry?' she asked.

'Maybe,' he said cautiously.

Walking towards him, her heels tapping on the linoleum, she slowed her steps, swaying a little and swinging her arms as she approached him, trying to get him to drop the serious expression. She was sure she could see a tiny lifting at the corners of his mouth. She stood up on tiptoe to kiss him. She had closed her eyes, but felt his lips curve into a reluctant smile.

'Hussy,' he murmured, but he pulled his hands out of his pockets and fastened them about her waist instead.

'Kiss me back,' she mumbled against his mouth. Her knees turned to jelly when he obliged. Sometimes, though she blushed to admit it, it was she who wanted to go further, not him. Like last week at the pictures. He had given her the choice of the Tivoli or the Rosevale – nothing but the best for the stationmaster's daughter, he'd said. She'd chosen the Tiv – and the special seats at the back designed for courting couples, with no central armrest to get in the way.

He had called her a hussy then too, but once they were ensconced in one of the special seats he had been quite enthusiastic about the idea . . . They hadn't paid much attention to the film.

'*Are* you sorry then?' she demanded as soon as she had got her breath back.

'You promised you'd say it first.'

She pulled back, enough for them to focus clearly on each other's faces. 'I'm sorry if I upset you yesterday.'

He raised his dark eyebrows into two beautiful curves. 'Don't you mean you're sorry you invited *him* into the garden?'

'If that's what upset you, then yes I'm sorry about it. Are you sorry for upsetting me?'

'Och, Carrie,' he blurted out, 'of course I'm sorry! Of course I am. I love you, Caroline Burgess!'

That impassioned outburst required the reward of another kiss. And then another. He was smiling at last, but she fixed him with a stern look.

'Are you sorry for being so nasty to poor Ewen, as well?'

'Of course. But it is true what I said, Carrie. Honest Injun. He can't read or write. I think he only managed his signature because someone else had written it out for him to copy – your father, I think. It looks like his handwriting.'

Continuing to hold her loosely, he swung round and indicated a shelf on the opposite wall which held document boxes and ledgers. 'It's in there somewhere. I could show it to you if you like. There's Livingstone's name written out neatly and then what's obviously his own attempt at it. It's all over the place. Takes up nearly half a foolscap page. Do you want to see it?'

'No,' she said swiftly. 'There's no need.' The mental image of that crudely formed signature was enough – as was the thought of the struggle Ewen must have had to make it. 'I didn't disbelieve you,' she told Matt, 'but you hurt his feelings, and embarrassed him in front of me.'

'I know,' said Matt humbly, 'I don't know what came over me.' He regarded her solemnly for a moment. Then, unexpectedly, he pulled a face: self-mocking and apologetic. It made him look very boyish.

'Well . . . I do know what came over me. I was jealous when I saw you with him, and I lashed out. Reached for whatever weapon came to hand. Please forgive me.' He lifted her hands, bent his head and kissed both sets of fingertips in turn. 'It's only because I love you so much,' he said, looking up at her with liquid eyes.

'It's not my forgiveness you should be asking for,' she replied, refusing to allow that look to melt away her resistance.

Matt dropped her hands and straightened up. His voice was clipped, his words terse. 'You can't honestly expect me to apologise to him personally?'

'That's exactly what I expect.'

The dark eyebrows weren't curved now. They were down over his eyes in two straight lines. Then they lifted again.

'You're a hard taskmaster, Miss Burgess.' He heaved a theatrical sigh. 'But if that's what it takes for you to forgive me . . .'

She jumped in before he could change his mind. 'Tomorrow morning? If he's going on the Oban trip?'

'Wouldn't that be even more embarrassing?' Matt's frown was questioning now, not bad-tempered. 'For him as well as for me? Surely it would be better to wait for a suitable occasion. When I can have a quiet word with him with no other ears flapping.'

'I suppose that's reasonable. How do I know you'll do it, though?'

'You'll just have to trust me.' His hands tightened on her

waist. 'Don't you trust me, Carrie?'

'With my life.' They kissed again, but she wasn't letting him off the hook too easily. 'You were awful nasty to him.'

'I was jealous,' he repeated. 'He fancies you.'

That was a statement of fact she couldn't argue with, but she did her best to reassure him. 'He's not even nineteen yet, Matt.'

'And you're not even eighteen. He's much more your age than mine. Do you fancy *him*?'

'I'm very fond of him. As a friend,' she added hastily, seeing Matt's brows draw together once more.

'I don't like you having friends like him.'

'Matt, I told you. You can't expect me to give up my friends for you.'

He bit his lip. 'I know that. I know I'm being unreasonable. It's just that . . . well, I love you so much . . . I want to have you all to myself.'

She lifted her hands from where they had been resting on his chest and put her arms around his neck. 'You've no need to be jealous of Ewen Livingstone,' she assured him. 'Or anyone else for that matter.'

'You do love me, then?'

'Of course I do,' she said, touched by his uncertainty.

'Then prove it,' he said. 'Marry me.'

Chapter 4

'Marry you?' Carrie dropped her hands and took a step back, out of his arms.

'Is it such an unexpected question?'

'Yes . . . no . . . I mean . . . I don't know . . .'

'Don't tell me clever little Miss Burgess is lost for words.' He reached out and tapped her nose with one teasing finger. He seemed to have completely regained his good humour. 'I thought you loved me too, Carrie. What's so odd about me asking you to marry me? You know we've already discussed it.'

Discussed wasn't exactly the word she would have used. The subject had been raised. They'd only known each other properly for a week when he had first mentioned it and she had laughed, assuming he couldn't possibly be serious. She told him now what she had told him then.

'Matt . . . I'm too young to get married.'

His smiled faded. 'So you don't love me, then?'

'Of course I do!' This was becoming exasperating. It was supposed to be women who constantly needed reassurance about these things. She saw his face cloud over. Oh, dear. Now they were back to square one. Taking a mental deep breath, she began trying to explain.

'Matt, you know I'm going to Jordanhill after the holidays. That's going to take me three years for a start –'

He interrupted her. 'Why are you going to the college, Carrie?'

She looked blankly at him. 'To train as a primary teacher, of course. You know that.'

'No, that's not what I mean. Why are you bothering to go to college?'

'Why am I bothering?' she repeated. Truth to tell, both questions had taken her aback, as had the first answer which had popped into her head. *Because my parents want me to.* That didn't seem an entirely satisfactory answer. Nor was it one which Matthew would readily accept. She thought about it. Why *was* she going to Jordanhill?

'Because,' she said slowly, 'it's an interesting and worthwhile thing to do.' She looked up into his face, formulating her answer as she went along. 'Because it'll give me a training. Because it'll allow me to have a career.'

'Which you'll have to give up when you get married.'

'Ye-es,' she agreed reluctantly. She could see exactly where he was headed.

He pressed the point. 'You know that teachers aren't allowed to stay on if they get married.'

'The female ones.'

'Well, of course the female ones, Carrie,' he said irritably. 'Why would men have to give up because they get married?'

She decided to let that one go. The argument which would undoubtedly ensue would only lead them up a blind alley.

'What's your point, Matt?'

'You know very well what my point is, Carrie. If we're going to get married eventually, then you going to Jordanhill really isn't worth it. It unnecessarily delays something which is going to happen anyway.'

He paused, waiting for her to agree with him. When she didn't, he posed a question. 'Tell me something. Are you

40

going to come out as a primary teacher and marry me straightaway?'

She drew her breath in sharply. 'I think you're assuming a bit too much here, Matt. I haven't agreed to marry you at all yet.'

'We love each other, don't we?'

She nodded. Yes, she loved him, but this badgering was beginning to get her a wee bit irritated . . .

'And people who love each other get married?'

She nodded again.

'So,' he went on, 'are you going to marry me – let's see now . . .' he screwed up his face in concentration '. . . in the summer of 1938?'

'I think I would have to work as a primary teacher for a few years, Matt,' she said levelly. 'Otherwise it would be a waste of all that training, wouldn't it?'

'How many years?'

'Matt, how would I know? That would depend.'

He persisted. 'Three years? Five?'

'More like five years,' she allowed.

'So that would be until 1943? Eight years from now? Is that right, Carrie? You ought to be good at arithmetic if you're going to teach it to wee ones. Have I got my sums right?'

'Perfectly correct,' she said tightly.

'I'll be thirty-two in 1943, Carrie. And you expect me to wait for you until then?'

'I don't expect anything,' she burst out. 'I haven't worked any of this out!'

She moved closer to him, hands raised to touch him – or in a plea for him to see things from her point of view – but he took a step back, retreating from her.

'Oh, Matt, try to understand!'

'Maybe *you* should try to understand, Carrie.' His voice

was low and throbbing with passion. 'Do you think I'm made of stone? Do you think I can stand to kiss and hold you, to be as close as this to you, and not be able to go any further? For eight long years?'

So that was it. The same old story. She lowered her arms. This was why she had broken up with her last boyfriend. His hands had wandered a bit too far and when she had slapped them away, he had issued the ultimatum. If she wasn't prepared to allow him to take certain liberties then that was it. Carrie frowned. It hadn't seemed to her to be like that with Matthew. Haltingly, she tried to put it into words.

'But, Matt . . . sometimes I feel . . . Well, it always seems to be me who wants to go a wee bit further . . . not you.' She blushed, but struggled on. 'Sometimes I've thought that you don't . . . that you don't really want me . . . in that way.'

'Not want you in that way?' He looked genuinely incredulous. 'Och, Carrie, of course I do! I want you in every way.' He moved closer. The look in his eyes was sending chills racing up and down her spine. 'But I want us to be together properly. Honourably. I've got far too much respect for you for it to be otherwise. And love,' he added, his voice like velvet. 'Lots and lots of that, Carrie. If you'll only let me give it to you.'

She couldn't doubt his sincerity. She raised her hands once more towards him. This time he grabbed them and held them against his chest.

'I'm twenty-four. I thought I was never going to find a girl I wanted to spend the rest of my life with. Then I met you.'

'Oh, Matt,' she breathed.

He curled his long slim fingers around her own. 'I want you to be my wife, Carrie. A wife to set up home with, to have children with, to be happy with for the rest of my life. Don't you want any of those things yourself?'

'Of course I do – but not yet. I'm –'

'Too young,' he supplied flatly. 'Too young for me, you mean. That's what your mother thinks, isn't it?'

He was always so quick to take offence, far too sensitive for his own good. All the same, she was touched that he had allowed her to see that side of him. Most boys, she felt sure, hid their deepest feelings, even from the girls they cared about – maybe particularly from the girls they cared about.

He loved her. If she'd had any doubts before, this intense conversation had swept them all away. So she would coax and cajole and get him into a better mood. It took her ten minutes, but she got her reward in the end: a series of passionate kisses which left her breathless and trembling.

'Maybe I'll not let you have any more until you agree to marry me,' he said when, with one eye on the clock and conscious of Archie's imminent visit to the booking office, they reluctantly separated.

'And they say women are moody,' she teased, delighted to see him in a lighter mood.

'So you'll let me try and persuade you to marry me?'

'I don't suppose I can stop you,' she said happily.

He crooked a finger under her chin. 'Such a lovely face you've got, Caroline Burgess. Like a beautiful wee fairy creature a very lucky man might find at the bottom of his garden.'

'Oh,' she murmured. 'That's so sweet. Do we have time for one more kiss?'

He walked her back along to the platform gate, his arm warm and possessive about her shoulders as they skirted the flower beds which punctuated the platform at regular intervals. They were interspersed with half whisky barrels, doing sterling service now as flower tubs, filled with geraniums and fuchsias and tumbling nasturtiums. Cast-offs from one of the whisky bonds down at Dumbarton, they'd been transported up to Partick in the guard's van. Laughing at something Matt said, Carrie stumbled and almost fell into one of them.

'Mind your papa's flowers.' Slipping his arm around her waist, he drew her closer into him. 'You'd think Mr Burgess had enough to do in his own garden without all this,' he observed as they continued along the platform.

'Are you kidding? He wants to win the Best Station Garden competition again.'

'It's a lot of work,' mused Matt.

'Well,' she said, punching him playfully on the arm, glad they had left behind the intensity of the last half hour, 'his staff could give him some more help. How about you, Mr Campbell?' Although everyone took great pride in gaining a prize in the competition, it was really only Archie, the leading porter and one of the signalmen who were prepared to put their backs into the work required to win one.

'Is that a hint, Miss Burgess?' His laugh was a pleasant sound in the twilight. 'I'm far too impatient for gardening.'

'Impatient? You?' They had reached the gate and she slipped out from under his arm and turned to face him. 'When you can wait so long for certain other things?'

'Not by my own choice,' he said smoothly. He raised his hand to her cheek and gently drew his knuckles down it. 'I'd take you anytime.'

He meant every word of it. She could see that in his dark and dreamy eyes. And she was excited by the direct way he'd put it . . .

'In fact,' he murmured, bending forward and placing his mouth very close to her ear, 'I'd like to make love to you right now. This very minute.' He placed his hands on her shoulders and pushed her against the fence, where the rhododendrons leaned over and formed a halo above her head. 'I'd lay you down under these bushes,' he whispered, 'and I'd pull a handful of petals off and sprinkle them in your hair . . . your very beautiful hair.' He cupped her face in his hands, threading his fingers through the red-gold strands.

'Oh, Matt,' she breathed, 'that's so roman—'

He stopped the words with another kiss. Carrie didn't understand the feelings he was arousing in her. Lost in the pleasures of his mouth, his hands buried deep in her hair, she knew only that they felt good.

Back on her own side of the fence a few moments later, she paused, listening to his footsteps ringing smartly back up the platform. The smell of the Virginia stock which her father had planted in his beloved garden floated to her on the velvet darkness of the night. She was a lucky girl. She lived in a nice house, with a beautiful garden. She had parents who loved her – and each other – and she had Matthew. He wanted her so much. Yet he was prepared to wait for her. She was sure she could win him round about her going to Jordanhill. He would be proud of her.

The third Home James rattled past. Carrie heard the front door open and the sound of her father's footsteps. Regular as clockwork. She slid the bolt on the platform gate, ready to usher him through. His head was bowed as he came round the corner of the house and for a few seconds he was unaware that she was observing him. She almost cried out. His mouth was set in a tight line, one hand lay in a fist on his chest and she didn't like the pallor of his skin. It had a bluish tinge. Then he looked up and spotted her, and his face relaxed.

'Been keeping young Mr Campbell off his work then, have we?'

'I'm afraid so,' she said, moving forward to greet him. 'Are you all right, Daddy?'

'I'm fine, hen.'

'You've got the pains again?'

'Only a wee twinge or two.' He took a breath which struck her as being somewhat cautious, an impression confirmed when he gave a relieved smile. 'That's it past. Don't make a fuss now, there's a good lass. There's no need to say anything to your mother.'

Carrie put her hands on her hips. 'I'll not tell Ma if you'll agree to go and see the doctor if it happens again.'

Archie's lips twitched. 'That's blackmail.'

'It's for your own good, Daddy,' she told him sternly, reaching once more for the gate.

'You're a fine lass,' he said. He patted her arm and went through on to the platform. He paused briefly. 'I couldnae have let Matthew Campbell off the morn. You appreciate that, don't you, pet?'

'Of course, Daddy,' she assured him. 'He knows that too. Ma's going to come with me instead. It'll be a nice outing for her.'

'Aye. And we'll keep what happened just now between you and me and the gatepost?'

'For the moment,' she said steadily. 'You know the conditions of our agreement.'

He laughed and went off to start his rounds.

Matthew gave his stationmaster a report on the evening's activities and went off duty, running lightly down the covered stairs to Dumbarton Road with a spring in his step. Carrie was all his, and she had forgiven him.

He strode along the pavement in the direction of Gardner Street but crossed the main road and went down a side street well before he got there. With a furtive glance behind him to check there was nobody about, he plunged into the dingy close he'd come to know well over the past couple of years.

He'd had the foresight to tell his parents he might be required to do a little overtime tonight. He took the stairs two at a time.

There wasn't much conversation in the top flat he visited, but there was uninhibited company – and at a very reasonable price. A man needed an outlet, didn't he? What he had told Carrie was perfectly true. He wasn't made of stone.

Tackling the climb towards his home at the top of Gardner Street some time later, he felt mellow and relaxed. He had handled things well tonight. That was one advantage of being that bit older than Carrie. He'd been as excited as she had been, but he'd managed to hold himself in check. That hadn't been easy. She was so lovely . . . and there was something terribly innocent about the way she responded to him. That was as it should be, he thought solemnly. Carrie was a nice girl, in a different league from the tart with whom he'd spent the last half hour.

That didn't mean he wasn't longing to do with one girl what he had just done with the other – but only once they were married. He wasn't planning to wait eight long years for that particular pleasure either. He lifted his chin to the night air and smiled. Persuading her to change her mind about Jordanhill was a challenge. Despite his recent encounter, the thought of the type of persuasion he might bring to bear to influence that decision was evoking some very pleasurable stirrings. It was good to be young and virile.

He glanced over to the left, where Partickhill Road began. It was one of the discreet streets where the big houses and handsome villas of the neighbourhood stood, including his own former family home. He'd spent his early years there and visited his grandfather regularly until the great disaster had struck six years ago.

The move to North Gardner Street, which had taken place well before the stock market crash, had been meant to be temporary. From what he had managed to glean, his father would have been more than happy to continue living in his own father's house, but his wife and the old man hadn't got along. Naturally, in the fullness of time, when his grandfather died, Matt and his parents would have moved back to the ancestral home. Some other family occupied it now – dreadfully *nouveau riche*, his mother said disparagingly.

Walking towards his own front door, Matthew reflected, as he often did, on how very different his life might have been if the family fortunes hadn't taken a tumble.

He wouldn't have been working on the railways for a start. He'd probably have fallen into some cushy number in the newspaper business owned by his mother's family. That was all gone now – or as near as dammit. He'd been eighteen in 1929 and although Shona Campbell had been distinctly unimpressed by his choice, going out and getting a job had seemed the heroic thing to do. He wasn't so sure about that now. It was all a bit of a struggle, and he worked damned hard. To make his life even more difficult there was also a log jam of older men in front of him, blocking his path to promotion.

Matt extracted his key from his pocket and walked up the short path. If the Crash hadn't happened he probably wouldn't have had to pay for his pleasures either. In an indiscreet moment last Christmas, when they'd both had far too much to drink, his father had told him of the life he'd known as a young man living in a big house which employed plenty of pretty young parlour maids. To be sure they made a fuss sometimes, but that was all part of the game.

Full of malt whisky and *bonhomie*, Charles Campbell had bestowed some paternal advice.

'But we don't marry that sort, my son.' His arm around Matthew's shoulders, his speech was only slightly slurred. He held his liquor well. Only the frankness of the subject matter indicated how much he'd had of it. 'We marry good girls – pure girls. The sort who have to steel themselves to put up with it. The kind who lie back and think of England. Or in our case Scotland.'

In bed in the darkness of his room, Matt smiled. He couldn't imagine Carrie was going to lie back and think of Scotland. He was going to have the best of both worlds: a good girl and a passionate one.

Chapter 5

Esther Burgess woke up the following morning with a hum-
dinger of a sore throat, putting paid to her plans to replace
Matt as Carrie's travelling companion for the day. Swollen
glands and a croaky voice didn't stop her issuing her daughter
with the usual set of dire warnings, though.

No going off on her own when they got to Oban. It would
be better if she chummed up with a couple of nice girls. Even
then, they weren't to wander too far away from everyone else.
Be careful crossing the street. People drove so fast these days.
She wasn't to take any shortcuts or go up any deserted lanes.
Terrible things could happen to young girls out on their
own . . .

'They're going to Oban, Esther, no' Chicago. I doubt Al
Capone'll be there. Nor the white slave traders neither,' said
Archie in exasperation, silencing his wife by the simple
expedient of sticking a teaspoon of cough medicine in her
mouth. 'And the lassie'll miss the train if you go on at her any
longer and we cannae have that now, can we?'

Both his wife and daughter had a tendency to leave catching
trains until the very last minute. They would stand at the
window, cup of tea in hand, watching for the train to come
into view before they even left the house. As soon as they
spotted it they hastily set down the cup, sped to the door and
flew out through the platform gate. It drove him mad. The

stationmaster's wife and daughter should set an example to other passengers, not use their special privileges to catch the train by the skin of their teeth.

This morning, however, Carrie eschewed the platform gate for the more sedate and official route to the station: through the front garden and along the public footpath which led up from Crow Road. Matt was coming out into the booking hall as she got there. He smiled when he saw her. It was a sunny, 'good morning' kind of a smile.

Wanting to keep the mood going, she skipped up to him like a little girl. A shaft of sunlight slanted down from the long windows between the booking hall and the platform outside. It caught all the dust motes and Carrie's shining hair, curling smoothly under at the ends. She hadn't slept very well last night, waking early and lying there worrying about her father's health. Realising at half-past five that she was unlikely to get any more sleep, she'd got up and washed her hair. It had dried just in time.

'You look lovely.' Matt's admiring glance took it all in. A neat little red hat with green trimming and a sporty pheasant's feather set off Carrie's forest green lightweight wool costume. The white of her blouse made an ideal contrast, the red and green embroidery on its front placket complementing her ensemble perfectly.

'Give us a kiss, handsome.'

'In front of everyone?'

'Be a devil.'

'If you insist, Miss Burgess,' he murmured, suiting the action to the words. Neither of them noticed a shadow falling across the column of sunlight as, outside on the platform, Ewen Livingstone moved away from the windows which looked into the booking hall.

The special excursion train was already at the platform,

itself thronged with people. Leaving Matt to get on with the task of seeing them all off, and spotting her father coming down the platform to do the same, Carrie moved over to a group of girls she knew. Like herself, they were all the daughters of railwaymen. Working on the railways was like being part of a big family. Everyone knew everyone else, even across the different companies.

There weren't nearly so many of those as there once had been. The Grouping of 1923 had absorbed the many smaller companies operating throughout the British Isles into four large ones: the London and North Eastern Railway, the London Midland and Scottish, the Great Western Railway and the Southern Railway. That didn't go far enough for many people, who looked forward to a nationalisation of the whole of Britain's railways. This, they thought, would improve both safety and the working conditions of the employees.

Scotland was divided up between two of the Big Four: the LMS and the LNER. Many thought of the latter as an Edinburgh company. Its headquarters were certainly in the capital, at Waverley Station. However, it was active in other parts of Scotland too, including Glasgow and the west of Scotland. It had inherited Archie Burgess's domain from the old North British Railway Company.

The girls accepted Carrie readily into the circle in which they stood, adjusting their relative positions so she could fit in, and commiserating with her over her mother's sudden illness.

'D'you mind if I come with you?' she asked.

'Nae bother,' said Mary, daughter of a senior parcels clerk. 'We'll see if we can all get a compartment together, shall we?'

'Is Douglas not with you?' asked Carrie, referring to Mary's steady boyfriend, a junior signalman at Partick.

'Aye, but we decided we'd travel with our own friends and meet up when we get to Oban.'

'Douglas doesn't expect you to spend all of your time with him, then?'

'Och, no! We both like to spend time with our friends as well.'

That sounded like a sensible idea, although Matt wouldn't have approved of it. He seemed to think that when you became boyfriend and girlfriend every other friendship had to go out of the window. Another of the girls echoed Carrie's thoughts.

'I thought Matthew Campbell and you would have been going together today.'

'Unfortunately he's got to work.' Carrie pointed him out further up the platform, trying to get the chattering and excited day trippers to stop talking long enough to get themselves on board the train.

'I thought the stationmaster's daughter would have been able to pull some strings about that.'

The words had come from outside the happy circle. The girl who had uttered them stood behind Mary.

'Janice,' said Carrie politely. 'I didn't see you there.'

The shrug of the shoulders was very offhand. 'That doesnae surprise me.'

'Miaow, miaow,' mouthed Mary silently to Carrie. Since childhood there had been an awkwardness between Carrie and Janice Muirhead. Her father was a railway signalman too. Decent and God-fearing though he seemed to some people, Mary wasn't the only person to tell Carrie he was also a bit too free with his hands when his children stepped out of line.

Carrie and Janice had been in the same class at primary school. They had played happily together until Janice had invited Carrie to come home with her after school one day. Esther, who knew all about Davie Muirhead, had forbidden her to go. She hadn't told her daughter the real reason why until much later. The younger Carrie had attributed the refusal

54

of permission to her mother's disapproval of the Muirhead home being on the wrong side of Dumbarton Road, and had blurted out an embarrassing and stumbling apology to Janice, inadvertently communicating that view to the girl. Ever since, Janice had looked on her as a complete snob.

'Don't mind her,' said Mary, steering Carrie towards a carriage door and throwing a smile at an exasperated Matt, who was doing his best to persuade people in a holiday mood and hell-bent on enjoying themselves that it might actually be a good idea if they got on to the train. Departure time was less than two minutes away. He relaxed a little when he reached the girls.

'Shoo, ladies,' he said. 'Your carriage awaits.'

With a sly look at Carrie, Janice turned and bestowed a dazzling smile upon him.

'Anything in trousers,' muttered Mary as they clambered into the train. Janice had taken herself off elsewhere. 'She'll get herself a reputation if she's not careful.'

'She already has,' said one girl darkly. 'Why d'you think she had to take a fortnight off work before Christmas last year?' She looked round the compartment. 'According to what I heard she was recovering from an operation. One that wisnae carried out at the Western Infirmary either,' she added meaningly. 'More likely on old mother MacLeod's kitchen table.' She was referring to a woman in White Street who had a bit of a reputation herself – one for helping girls who got themselves into trouble.

'No!' someone breathed, eyes sparkling with malicious interest. 'You're not serious.'

'I am,' insisted the girl who had spoken first. 'The thrashing her daddy gave her when he found out didnae help much either. Took his belt to her, apparently.'

Mary and Carrie exchanged a look and Carrie hastily

changed the subject. She hated this kind of gossip. She also felt sick at the thought of what poor Janice had endured. To have that happen to you, and then for your father to beat you at the end of it . . . She couldn't begin to imagine what it must have been like growing up in a house like that, especially when she thought of her own loving and gentle father. Davie Muirhead was a brute. No love at home, so Janice went looking for it elsewhere – and found the wrong sort. The sort that got a girl into trouble.

Doors slammed. A whistle blew. They were off. Excited chatter ran through every compartment and carriage. The sun was shining, it was a day off and everyone was in high spirits and determined to have a good time.

The train trundled through Hyndland, slowly passing the extensive grounds and grey chimneys of Gartnavel Hospital. Then Carrie caught a glimpse of the twin spires of Jordanhill College, her destination after the summer. As long as my exam results are all right, she reminded herself. It didn't do to tempt fate by being too cocky.

Once they left the cranes of Clydebank and Dumbarton's shipyards behind them the train picked up speed. For a few miles the track stuck close by the river in its lower reaches, the water broadening out as it approached the Tail of the Bank. There were more shipyards on the other shore, at Port Glasgow and Greenock. After they passed the pier at Craigendoran, from where ferries took passengers all over the Firth of Clyde, the north side of the river became much more rural, with green fields, farms and cottages heralding the start of the Highlands.

As Carrie had half expected, it wasn't long before her companions' conversation worked its way round to Mr Matthew Campbell.

'He's quite a catch, Carrie.'

'Aye, he's dead good-looking,' chipped in another admiring voice.

'Absolutely gorgeous,' agreed Mary.

Carrie laughed and glanced out of the window. The train had slowed again. They were chugging through Helensburgh Upper, crossing the Highland Boundary Fault Line, she thought, geography lessons still fresh in her mind. The scenery was growing wilder and more dramatic by the yard, but when Carrie turned from her contemplation of it she couldn't help smiling. The expectant faces turned her way demonstrated that her friends were more interested in quizzing her about Matt than in admiring the beauties of their homeland.

'Is Matthew romantic, Carrie?' Mary asked. 'He looks as if he would be, does he no'?' She looked around at her companions for confirmation. That gave Carrie a couple of seconds to collect her thoughts.

She certainly wasn't going to tell them what he had said about strewing the rhododendron petals in her hair. That would remain beautifully and deliciously private between him and her. However, she told them about his gift of a single rose, and gave them a slightly censored version of the words he'd used when he had presented it to her. That sent them all off into paroxysms of delight.

'Oh, that's dead romantic! See my Douglas? Buying me an extra pickled onion with my bag of chips is his idea of the height of romance.' Mary exaggerated the pronunciation of the word, making it *ro-mance*. Striking a dramatic pose, she twisted round and leaned back over Carrie's lap, making goo-goo eyes at her all the while. 'Obviously when it comes to romance, none o' us has even lived compared to Miss Caroline Burgess!'

Carrie laughed again, revelling in the good-natured banter.

* * *

Archie Burgess wore an impressive official hat to indicate his status as stationmaster and esteemed servant of the LNER. It bore the company badge and rather a lot of gold braid. He was inclined to refer to the latter, somewhat irreverently, as scrambled egg. Looking longingly out over Oban Bay, on the opposite side of the street from the shops she was currently being dragged round, Carrie was beginning to think that her brain might be in danger of turning into that very substance.

Understandably enough, Mary had gone off with Douglas when they had disembarked from the train at the busy fishing and ferry port. Poor Douglas had looked quite confused when all the girls in turn had sternly instructed him to make sure Mary got as many pickled onions as she wanted if he was buying her a bag of chips for her lunch.

Appetites sharpened by the journey and the sea air, Carrie and another of the girls whose company she'd enjoyed on the way up had decided to eat first and then go for a walk along the prom together. However, as they came out of the restaurant after their meal, the other girl was approached by a young shunter who shyly asked her to accompany him on a walk. The invitation was politely extended to Carrie too, but she had gracefully declined. She had no wish to play gooseberry and knew very well that this particular young man's eye had been on her friend for quite some time.

Watching them go, she was almost knocked into the road by a raucous group of girls. Was she on her own? They couldn't have that. Despite a protest that she really didn't mind, Carrie found herself being swept along with them.

Her current companions, one of them Janice Muirhead, seemed to consider shopping the main purpose of life – when they weren't giggling furiously or fluttering their collective eyelashes at any of the groups of young men from the day trip who were also wandering around together. Oban being a relatively small place, that was happening all too often.

Coming out of yet another souvenir shop, Carrie began to mentally invent excuses for taking her leave of them. She really would like to walk along the front, get some good sea air into her lungs. Or maybe she could climb up to the coliseum-type structure which dominated the town. She had broached the prospect tentatively ten minutes ago, but it had been brushed aside. Climb up to that big monument? Whatever for?

There was a sudden outburst of giggles and greetings. They sounded like a group of chattering monkeys Carrie remembered from a visit to the zoo last summer. Then she heard a well-known male voice responding to the high and excited female ones.

'Good afternoon, lassies!'

It was Ewen, one hand politely tugging his bunnet in greeting.

'What are you up to, Ewen?' yelled one of the girls. His normally sunny disposition made him a great favourite with everyone.

'I'm away off for a walk,' he said. 'Any o' youse yins want to come wi' me? We could go right along to the Ganavan sands.'

'How far's that?'

'Och, I don't know exactly. Probably about a couple of miles.'

The suggestion was greeted with shrieks of horror.

'Walk all that distance? Not on your nelly! Sorry, Ewen. Anyone fancy afternoon tea instead?' That provoked an enthusiastic response.

Carrie cleared her throat. 'I'll come for a walk with you.'

'Miss Burgess,' he said formally, 'I didnae notice you there.'

The noisy chatter around them ceased abruptly. Carrie was

59

all too aware that Janice Muirhead had narrowed her eyes and that all the girls were regarding both Ewen and her with open curiosity. Everybody knew she and Matthew Campbell were walking out together.

'If y-you'll have me,' she stuttered, and wished the words unsaid when she heard Janice snigger. 'I'd like a decent walk.'

Let them think what they want, she thought defiantly. Why shouldn't I go with him? He is a friend of mine, after all. For one awful moment she thought he was going to turn her down. He looked very serious, almost forbidding. Then he gave her an odd little bow.

'I'd be honoured, Miss Burgess.'

She chanced a quick glance at him as they passed the Columba Hotel. He looked uncomfortable, half-throttled by an unaccustomed stiff collar and tie. His jacket had been pressed and brushed, but it was even shabbier than his working one. It was also a bit neat for size. His shoulders had filled out a lot in the past year.

'Where's the boyfriend today, then?'

'Rostered to work. Somebody has to.'

'Oh, dear, what a pity. I'm so sorry he's missing this very pleasant outing.' Carrie gave him a dirty look. He must have known that Matt was working today. He'd been very much in evidence on the platform before the excursion train had left. They strolled on, past the small jetties from where boat trips left.

'Take the young lady to see the islands and the seals,' offered one man, smiling broadly at Carrie, but addressing his next comment to Ewen. 'Is your lassie not bonnie enough to deserve a wee treat?'

Carrie shook her head apologetically. She'd caught sight of the price chalked up on a blackboard tied to the rail of the esplanade. It wasn't unreasonable, but she doubted very much Ewen would be able to afford it.

'No, thanks,' she said brightly. 'We're needing to stretch our legs.'

They moved on, but before they had gone very far Ewen slowed his pace, looking back over his shoulder. 'Would you have wanted to go?'

'Nope. I'd much rather walk.'

'Let's walk then,' he said tersely.

'Look at that church on the other side of the road!' she said a few moments later. 'The architecture's really modern, isn't it?'

'It must be the new Catholic cathedral,' he growled. 'St Columba's. Seemingly they only built it a few years ago.'

Another piece o' useless information. If he had been in a better mood, she would have teased him about that. It didn't seem advisable at the moment.

They had left the bustle of the town behind them. To their left, the bay was opening out and on their right the road was lined with large and imposing villas. Many had been converted into small hotels, but several were clearly still family homes.

'Lovely houses. Like the mansions up on Partickhill.'

He made an odd noise. It sounded to her like a snort of derision. She thought she knew what that meant: disapproval of the moneyed classes.

'Are you a socialist?'

'I'm no' anything,' he said shortly. 'What's politics ever going to do for the likes o' me?'

She opened her mouth, ready to come out with one of Matt's pronouncements about the need for working-class solidarity. Perhaps not. In any case, considering Matt's upper-middle-class background, she did sometimes think his comments were a bit rich. Even in her own relatively privileged position, Carrie knew a lot more about the realities of working-class life than he did.

She looked out at the sea. It was a beautiful rich blue, sparkling in the sunlight. The big island which sheltered Oban itself had come to an end, but the view in front of her was studded with islets and rocks. Was that Mull in the distance? With his capacity for picking up information, Ewen probably knew, but it didn't look as if she was going to get a civil word out of him today.

A wave of tiredness swept over Carrie. Her sleepless night was starting to tell on her. It was more than simple fatigue. Despite the beauty of her surroundings, she was beginning to feel quite depressed. Earlier in the day she had resolved to put her worries to one side, but now she felt them all crowding in on her again. The surly silence of the young man walking beside her wasn't helping one little bit.

'Are words on ration today, Ewen?' she demanded. She heard the belligerence in her tone. She didn't give a damn if he heard it too. 'Why did you ask me to come for a walk with you if you're not prepared to hold a civilised conversation?'

'I issued a general invitation,' he said stiffly, 'before I saw you were wi' the lassies.'

She stopped dead in the middle of the pavement. 'So you'd rather I left you alone?'

'I didnae say that.' He had stopped too, and they turned to face one other.

'You've hardly said anything!'

'Maybe that's because I don't want tae say too much!'

'What's that supposed to mean?'

He started to speak, then stopped himself. She bunched her hands into fists. 'Ewen Livingstone,' she demanded through gritted teeth, 'if you've got something to say, then say it and let's get it over with!'

'You want to hear what I've got to say, Miss Burgess? You want to bloody hear?'

'Don't swear. It's not necessary if one has an adequate vocabulary.'

'I beg your pardon, I'm sure,' he flung at her. 'I'm no used tae spending time wi' ladies like yourself!'

'Oh! Just tell me what you've got to say. Right now!'

'All right then, I will!' he yelled, then looked around him in embarrassment and lowered his voice. They were standing close to an ice-cream kiosk where several people were waiting to be served.

'Why are you bothering to walk with me?' he asked in a quieter voice. 'Are you still using me to make Matthew Campbell jealous? Hoping the other girls will report back tae him that you went off wi' me? Or do you really fancy a wee bit of rough?'

She drew her breath in on a hiss. 'That's an awful thing to say!'

He folded his arms, lifted his chin and gave her a magnificently disdainful look. 'Aye, well, sometimes the truth is awful, Miss Burgess.'

'Oh, for Pete's sake,' she wailed. 'Stop calling me Miss Burgess. And stop being so horrible. I thought we were friends.' She straightened out her fingers and lifted her hands in a gesture of helplessness. Then she brought them down hard, slicing through the air. 'Oh, just stop it!'

He raised his fair eyebrows. 'People are looking, Miss Burgess.'

'Let them bloody look!'

'Don't swear. It's no' necessary if one has an adequate vocabulary.'

'You'd drive a saint to swear!'

In the middle of Oban esplanade, and to her utter horror,

Caroline Burgess burst into tears. She never did that sort of thing. If she had confused herself, she had completely unmanned Ewen. The supercilious look vanished from his face and he took an urgent step towards her.

'Och, lassie, there's no need for that. Don't greet, hen. I didnae mean to upset you. I'm awful, awful sorry. Don't cry, Carrie. Please!'

Chapter 6

'Better now?'

Carrie nodded, and managed a watery smile before giving her nose a final blow with an extremely sodden handkerchief. He had pulled her to an empty bench further along the esplanade, sat her down and listened to all of it. She had apologised profusely for her bad behaviour at the *ceilidh*, begged him to believe she hadn't intended the confrontation with Matt in the garden to take place, and told him how worried she was about her father and his health.

'A lot better,' she said. 'And thank you for rescuing me back there, too.'

'Rescuing you?'

She nodded her head. 'Yes. If I'd had to look at another mustard pot with *A Present From Oban* painted on it or a whisky glass decorated in lurid colours with a picture of a bagpiper I'd have had the screaming abdabs in the middle of Oban High Street.'

'The screaming abdabs, eh?' he murmured. 'I'd love to have seen those. Personally I love all those calendars wi' cute wee Scottie dogs on them. You know? One black, one white, and with *Frae Bonnie Scotland* written underneath them.'

She gave him a curious look.

'I can pick out some words. I've tried to teach myself to read, but I cannae say I've made much of a job of it.'

'How come you didn't learn at school?'

He rubbed the side of his nose and looked embarrassed. 'Well, I didnae go to school very much, to tell you the truth.'

'I'll bet you regret that now,' she said pertly, beginning to recover.

'You'll never know how much,' he said. His voice was quiet but unmistakably sincere, and she wished she hadn't made the smart comment.

He relaxed his posture. While she'd been recounting her tale of woe, he'd been sitting with one ankle up on the opposite knee, occasionally leaning forward and giving her hand an awkward pat.

'Look,' he said, 'how would it be if I volunteered to help your daddy with the gardening? At the station or at your hoose. I don't know anything about the technical stuff, but I could do some o' the hard labour for him. I suppose it's past the time for digging, but maybe I could do the weeding for him, that kind o' thing.'

'Would you really?'

It was a generous offer, especially when she considered the long hours he already worked.

'Aye. Of course I would. Your daddy's been good tae me. He gave me a job when other people wouldnae.'

She smiled gently at him. 'D'you know something, Ewen Livingstone? You're a very nice person.'

'I like your daddy. I like his daughter too.' He reached out and took a strand of her hair between his thumb and index finger. 'When it comes to you, maybe it's a bit more than liking.' His rough voice had dropped to a whisper, as soft as the sound of the waves slapping against the sea wall beneath their feet.

He began to stroke the smooth tress he held, his touch as light as a feather. 'You've the bonniest hair,' he murmured.

'Ewen . . .' Please don't say any more, she thought. There was too much between them: background, education, status. Not to mention a certain Mr Matthew Campbell. Whether he saw it in her face or got the silent message, Ewen took his hand from her hair and turned his head away to look out over the sea for a moment. Then he got to his feet.

'Still want to walk along to Ganavan?'

She smiled up at him, relieved at how well he had taken her rejection. 'I can't think of anything I'd like better.'

'Can you walk and eat at the same time?'

'I'm willing to give it a try.'

'Then I'll go back to that kiosk and get us both an ice-cream.'

'Is that Mull over there?'

'Aye. Mull of the Mountains,' Ewen said easily, stretching out his legs and crossing them at the ankles. They were sitting on a bench overlooking the Ganavan sands. 'One of the Inner Hebrides.'

Caught by the poetry of the name, Carrie repeated it. '*Mull of the Mountains*. Is that where your family's from?'

Partick was full of folk from the Highlands and Islands. The flow south in search of work had been going on for generations. There were the girls who came to the city's great teaching hospitals to train as nurses and the tall, strapping men who peppered the ranks of the Glasgow police force. Islanders with the sea in their blood manned the merchant ships and passenger liners which sailed all over the globe. They crewed the ferries and the Clyde puffers too: the tough little boats which transported coal and everything else between the Lowlands and the islands and settlements of the rugged West Coast.

The shipyards on both sides of the river provided work for

many. There was a high concentration of Highlanders both in Govan on the south side of the Clyde and in Partick, which sat opposite it on the north bank.

Carrie was pondering something. 'I didn't think Livingstone was a Highland name.'

He assured her that it was. 'Although there's a Gaelic version of it too. We don't come from Mull, though. We belong to Appin, and a wee island called Lismore. They're both up there somewhere. Someone pointed them out to me on a map once.' He had his hands thrust in his pockets, but he lifted his chin to indicate the general direction, and told her that the famous Dr David Livingstone's family had also come from the same area.

'Do you go back to visit?' Carrie knew lots of people did. The flood of people took place in reverse, at least on a temporary basis, during the summer months.

'No. I wouldnae be exactly welcome there, you see.' The bench creaked as he shifted his position on it. 'Don't ask,' he said in response to her look of surprise. 'You don't want tae know.' There was the oddest mix of expressions on his face. 'You don't know what to say now, do you?'

That was too much of a challenge to resist. 'You're a man of mystery, are you?'

His face lit up. 'Aye, I like that. A man of mystery.' He was studying her, surveying the smart little felt hat, his eyes travelling up the pheasant's feather and back down again.

'Very up-to-the-minute,' he pronounced. 'Now, do you call that style Tyrolean or Robin Hood?'

'Either really.'

She was intrigued by the way he was forcibly changing the subject, but also greatly amused by this unexpected interest in fashion. When he ventured the opinion that she was wearing the hat at exactly the right angle, Carrie laughed.

'Is that another of your pieces of useless information? How

68

you should wear a Tyrolean hat? I can't think you're going to find much use for the knowledge yourself.'

He smiled. 'A woman I know likes to buy the fashion magazines when she can afford them. She reads the articles out to me.' His smile grew broader. 'Whether I want to hear them or not.'

'Is she a friend of your mother's?' Now she was unashamedly fishing for information.

'She was.'

'She *was* a friend of your mother? What happened, did they fall out?'

His expression grew sombre. 'My mother died three years ago, Carrie. Not long after my sixteenth birthday.'

She laid an impulsive hand on his shoulder. 'Oh, Ewen, I'm so sorry.'

'Don't be. She loved me and I loved her.'

That answer had bounced straight back at her, and it had sounded a touch defensive. Regretful that she had unwittingly put her foot in it, she asked him what she thought was a practical and unemotional question. 'So do you live with your father?'

He hesitated. Then, with the air of a man who had just made a decision, he said quietly, 'I never knew my father, Carrie. My parents weren't married. I'm illegitimate.' He gave her a crooked smile. 'I'll not soil your ladylike ears with the technical term.'

'Oh,' she breathed. So that's what the big mystery was, and no doubt also the reason for her mother's disapproval of him. Being born out of wedlock was a terrible thing, a subject for gossip by adults and name-calling from your fellow children. It brought a stigma with it, one you would carry to the end of your days. Ewen's tight lips and paled skin seemed to indicate that he had experienced his full share of jibes and taunts.

Her heart filled with sympathy for him. People could be so cruel. Was he wondering now how she was going to react? She hoped he knew her better than that. It was hardly his fault that his parents hadn't been married. That had always been her belief. Why should the sins of the fathers be visited upon the children?

'Would you like to talk about it, Ewen?' she asked briskly. 'I mean, I'll listen if you want to tell me, but don't feel that you have to.'

The grim expression on his face relaxed. 'You're real sweet, Carrie Burgess,' he said softly, 'but no, I don't really want to talk about it. Is that all right?' he asked, his brow furrowing.

'Of course it is.' Anxious to put him at his ease, she went back to practicalities. 'So who do you live with then?'

'I live by myself.'

'By yourself?' She had never heard of anyone of their age living alone. There were plenty of young married couples, of course, but not single people in their teens. 'Who looks after you?'

'I do,' he said proudly. 'I can cook. And clean.'

But not sew, she thought. That explained the lost buttons and the lack of elbow patches on his working jacket.

'Does your mother's friend help you out sometimes?'

'Aye. Her and her mother-in-law. They've lived together since Jimmy died.'

'Jimmy?'

'Son tae one, husband tae the other,' he said briefly. 'He was killed in a shipyard accident. They'd only been married a few years when it happened.'

'How sad. But I suppose his wife and his mother must comfort one another in their loss.'

Ewen burst out laughing.

'What's so funny?'

He had to wipe his eyes before he could speak. 'They never stop fighting, that pair.'

'What do they fight about?'

'Everything and nothing. Both o' them could start an argument in an empty hoose. Sometimes it's over me. I go round there every Sunday for ma dinner and they fight over whose turn it is to cook it, whose turn it is to serve it, which one o' them is the best cook. You should hear the things they call each other. I think "black-hearted bitch" is one o' my personal favourites,' he mused.

Carrie was gazing at him in amazement. 'So why do they stay together?' she asked.

He looked shrewd. 'Because they're actually very fond of each other and they both really loved Jimmy – although his grieving widow miscalls him too, with the old lady shouting at her about no' speaking ill of the dead. You were quite right. They do comfort one other, but they'd die rather than admit that.'

Carrie shook her head. 'Folk are odd, aren't they?'

'They certainly are.'

They sat in comfortable and companionable silence for a while. Then she posed another question. 'Is that how you know all the things you do? Because your mother's friend reads her magazines out to you?'

'Well, I always listen when she does that. Or anybody else, for that matter. There's one or two o' the surfacemen who buy a paper every day. Sometimes we get a real good discussion going about something in the news. And I've got my own wireless set. I've learned a lot from the programmes on that. I saved up for it,' he told her with quiet pride. 'Took me ages. By the time I'd got enough money together I'd grown out o' ma good jacket.'

'So you had a hard choice to make?'

'Aye. The wireless or holey elbows. No choice at all, really,' he said with a grin. 'I talk to people a lot as well. It's amazing

71

what you can learn from other folk.' He took his hands out of
his pockets and sat up straight on the bench, his face alive
with enthusiasm. 'Before I met you and the lassies today,
someone was telling me all about McCaig's Tower. You know,
the big monument up on the hill?' They couldn't see it from
where they were sitting, but he waved an arm back in the
direction of the town.

'I thought it was called McCaig's Folly?'

'Ah, well, but my informant' – he looked sheepish – 'that
is, the wee wifie who sold me the gammon roll I had for my
dinner, well, she says that a whole heap o' people don't agree
with it being called a folly. This Mr McCaig apparently had it
built to provide work for unemployed stonemasons. So it
wasnae a foolish thing to do at all.'

'No,' Carrie said reflectively. 'It was a good thing.' Like
him, she could more than see the point of anything which
provided work. 'I'd love to walk to it. There must be a great
view from up there.'

'There is. That's where I was this morning. It's a steep
climb, mind.'

'So you wouldn't fancy going up again?'

'I don't think we would have the time, hen.'

Dead on cue, a church bell somewhere in the distance
began to sound the hour. Warm and relaxed and enjoying his
company, Carrie lazily counted the chimes, her eyes closed
and her face turned up towards the sun. Five o'clock. Then,
with a start, she straightened up abruptly. Five o'clock! Their
train home was due to leave in thirty-eight minutes' time!

She was a stationmaster's daughter. She knew the trains had to
run on time. Come hell or high water. So why was she standing
in front of the buffers of a curiously empty and echoing
Oban station gazing in dismay at empty tracks? The special

72

excursion train – Carrie consulted her smart little wrist watch – had left for Glasgow precisely eleven minutes ago.

'My mother's going to kill me.'

Especially, she thought with a silent glance at Ewen, if she finds out how much time I've spent with you today. He might not be Al Capone or a white slave trader, but he was equally as undesirable in Esther Burgess's eyes.

'I doubt it.' The object of her mother's disapproval seemed to be in an infuriatingly cheerful frame of mind. 'Anyway, why don't we check the timetable for the next train and then you can phone home? Your da's probably still on duty, and if he's not someone can pop round to the station house with a message for your parents. Then they won't be worried when you're not on the special.'

It was a sensible suggestion. Carrie should have thought of it herself.

'Will you check the timetable, then?' she asked, waving towards the wall to the right of the booking office where large white posters displayed the details of arrivals and departures. 'I'll see if somebody here will let me phone Partick.' Her eyes lit on the booking-office window. The shutter was down. That was a bad sign. 'Unless they've all gone home for their tea, that is.'

'Eh . . .' said Ewen, sending her an odd little smile. 'I think *you'd* better check the train times.'

'What?' Then she realised. 'Sorry,' she mumbled, blushing at her *faux pas*.

'Och, you're the very soul o' tact, Miss Burgess,' he said in mock-outrage. They strolled over to the wall. They were in no rush now.

'How long till the next train?'

She showed him, pointing it out.

'Look. Here it is. Glasgow Buchanan Street. You said you

can pick some things out. See the capital G for Glasgow? Here it is again for Garelochhead.' She ran her index finger back up the poster, underlined the words and said them slowly, breaking them up into their component syllables.

'Glas-gow Bu-chan-an Street. Now you.'

'Me?'

Ewen looked startled, and a little nervous, but he did as she had done, using his finger to trace along beneath the words, sounding out the names.

'Very good. And you said you know your numbers.'

He peered at the figures. 'I know some o' the numbers.' He sounded anxious.

'Go on,' Carrie encouraged.

He pronounced them carefully. 'Seven . . . two . . . No, it's twenty-two. Seven twenty-two?' He turned to her for confirmation, a little frown between his brows.

'That's right. Seven twenty-two.'

He swung back to the wall. 'But what's this after the seven twenty-two?' She waited, willing him on. His face cleared. 'Och, I know. *PM*. That's right, isn't it?'

She beamed at him. 'Well done!'

'If you tell me I'm a clever boy I might well no' be responsible for my actions, Caroline Burgess. You'll be a dab hand with the infants when you start teaching. Do I get a jelly baby or a dolly mixture for getting it right?'

'I think we're going to need more sustenance than a bag of sweeties if we're not going to be back home till some time around midnight.'

They left the station and went into the street to look for a blue and white *You May Telephone From Here* sign. She had tried knocking on the door of the booking office and the stationmaster's office, but to no avail. There was nobody about.

'Terminus stations,' suggested Ewen. 'They probably do all

go home for their tea here. Why should they hang around if nothing's going to happen for another couple of hours?'

A seagull the size of a pampered cat hopped across in front of them, scavenging for scraps of fish left on the jetty which abutted the railway station. The tang of the sea and its bounty was strong. Carrie was preoccupied, worrying about how late it was going to be before they got home.

'My mother *is* going to kill me,' she said mournfully.

Ewen looked amused. 'You're your parents' darling,' he said. 'I imagine you'll survive unscathed.'

He was always doing that, coming up with words she wouldn't have expected him to know. Uneducated he might be. Unintelligent he certainly wasn't.

They headed towards the shops on the seafront; but there didn't seem to be any signs indicating a public telephone. However, there was a chip shop open.

'Can I offer you a fish supper, madam?'

The aroma was certainly enticing, but Carrie chewed her lip. 'Maybe we should keep looking for a phone.' The words were scarcely out of her mouth before she was struck by an unwelcome thought. Matt was still on duty. More than likely she would get him when she called. He wasn't going to be exactly overjoyed when he found out she was stranded in Oban with Ewen Livingstone.

He was saying something, pointing out that nobody was going to be worrying about them yet. Why not enjoy their tea first and then continue the search for a telephone? They'd still be getting the message through a good two hours before the excursion train pulled into Partick without them. It was another sensible suggestion. And, a little voice whispered, it postponed having to make any explanations to Matt.

'Let's eat,' said Ewen decisively. 'In God's fresh air and in God's own country. We can sit on a bench and enjoy the view.'

'Shall we go Dutch on the fish suppers?'

'I offered to treat you.' His wide mouth was set in an uncharacteristically tight line.

'I'm sorry,' she said hurriedly. 'That would be lovely. Thank you.'

'We poor people are proud, you know,' he went on, still frowning at her.

Trying to work out how to smooth the feathers she had unwittingly ruffled, she cast around for the right words. To her relief, she saw his face break into its more customary smile. He'd been teasing her.

Ewen waited out on the street while Carrie went into a hotel to phone. Her heart sank when Matt's voice answered. He should have been off duty for half an hour by now. He wasn't pleased to hear that she'd missed the train. He was even less pleased to find out how late she was going to be home.

'Don't worry,' Carrie said brightly. 'I'm not on my own. There's a couple of us here.' Well, she thought, a couple can be taken to mean a few people, not just two. She crossed her fingers, but the charm didn't work. There was frost in his voice, crackling up to her over the hills and mountains and lochs which separated them.

'Who *exactly* is there with you, Carrie?'

She told him – and heard the sharp intake of breath all the way along the hundred miles of phone line.

'And where are you now?'

'In a hotel.' Now that a cat was out of the bag, she was beginning to feel a bit calmer. She hadn't intended for this to happen, after all.

'Is it a respectable sort of place?'

It was on the tip of her tongue to tell him that the hotel foyer was full of painted *houris* and men who looked as if they might be white slavers or dope fiends. She thought better of it.

'Of course it's respectable, Matt. It's perfectly respectable.' The folding door of the telephone booth was slightly ajar. She pushed it completely shut and looked out through the two glass panels which adorned its upper half.

'There's a receptionist who looks as if she's about a hundred and fifty years old, and the only other person in the place is an old lady with a wee dog on her lap and a fox fur around her shoulders. It's completely hideous, but she looks the very soul of respectability.'

'Don't be flippant, Carrie,' he said irritably. 'Now, listen to me.'

After she came off the phone, she held it in her hand for a second or two and addressed it as though it were the young man to whom she had just been speaking. Correction. The young man who had just been speaking to her. Or perhaps *at her* would be a better choice of words.

'Want me to salute you as well, Matt?' she enquired wrily of the heavy black receiver.

'Everything all right?' Ewen asked as she emerged from the front porch. He was stroking a fluffy ginger cat which was balancing precariously on its dainty paws on the narrow-topped wall which surrounded the hotel's front terrace. 'Did you get through to yer faither?'

'He'd gone for his tea. I got Matthew Campbell.'

'Oh. Him.'

'He speaks highly of you too,' she snapped back, still smarting from the interrogation to which Matt had subjected her, not to mention the set of instructions he had barked out. How could he be so lovely sometimes and so horrible at others?

She was to sit in the hotel until the train left. By herself. Then she was to travel home. In a different compartment from Ewen Livingstone. Preferably a Ladies' Only compartment.

With a wave of the hand, she indicated the hotel behind them and told him that Matt wanted her to wait there until it was time for the train. Ewen scowled.

'I sincerely hope you told him to go and fu—'

Carrie's eyes opened wide and he hastily amended it to 'go and raffle himself'.

'I told him no such thing,' she said sharply, annoyed that he had so very nearly used such an awful word in front of her. 'Matthew Campbell *has* asked me to marry him, you know.'

'He's what?'

'You heard,' she said tightly.

The ginger tom had been revelling in Ewen's stroking. When it abruptly ceased, the cat looked momentarily disgusted. Then he jumped down off the wall, ran along beside it and slunk stealthily around a corner and out of sight. Ewen, his expression grown thunderous, didn't appear to notice.

'I presume you told him you're far too young to get married?'

Now she had another man trying to run her life for her. This was too much.

'What I told him is none of your business, Ewen Livingstone.'

The shutters came down over his cool eyes. 'Right. Fine. Well, away back into that hotel and sip tea. They probably wouldnae let the likes o' me in, anyway. I only hope ye don't die o' boredom. I'll see you at the train.'

He was struck momentarily dumb when she announced her intention of travelling home, alone, in the Ladies' Only compartment. She saw it in his face, though: disbelief, insult, upset. He managed a parting shot before he stomped off.

'If you let him boss you around like this now, what's it going to be like after you're married? Have ye thought of that, Carrie?'

Chapter 7

This was ridiculous. She was the only person in the Ladies' Only compartment. There weren't many people on the entire train, which made it all the sillier that Ewen was sitting a few compartments along from her, probably also on his own.

Elbow propped on the wee table which jutted out from below the window, Carrie contemplated the scenery. It was as spectacular and dramatic on the way down as it had been on the way up. The trouble was, its very grandeur inspired her to think, thoughts racing off in a hundred different directions.

As they emerged from the narrow defile of the Pass of Brander she was confronted by the expanse of Loch Awe. The water was sparkling still in the long summer's evening. She gazed gloomily out at it.

The train sped on. She glimpsed an impressive-looking castle through the trees as they turned round the head of Loch Awe before making brief stops at Dalmally and then Tyndrum Lower. Opposite the station there, a small boy sat on the lower slopes of a gentle hill. He waved at the train. She returned the greeting, moving her arm in a wide and prolonged arc so he would be sure to see her.

Crianlarich was the next stop, then Ardlui at the top of Loch Lomond. After that, it wouldn't take very long to leave the hills behind, re-crossing the Highland Line back into the

Lowlands – at which point she herself would have to face the music.

Her mother would be up on the ceiling, but that would wear off once her daughter was safely back in the bosom of her family. Besides, Carrie knew that Esther trusted her really. Her father would pretend to be angry to support his wife, but there would be a twinkle in his eye. What she'd never hear the end of was the stationmaster's daughter managing to miss her train. Her father would tell that story forever and a day. Matt, however, would be hard pressed to see the funny side of any of today's events.

It was a short hop from Tyndrum to Crianlarich, where there was always a longer stop for the engine to take on water, time enough for the passengers to stretch their legs for ten minutes. Carrie stepped out on to the platform at exactly the same moment as Ewen did. They looked along the carriage at each other. He'd taken his jacket off, and had also removed his stiff collar and tie.

'Is there a tea room here?' she asked quietly.

'Famed both far and wide,' he replied. 'Great home-baking, so I'm told.'

'Would you let me treat you this time?'

'A gentleman never lets a lady pay for herself,' he responded loftily. They discovered, however, that they were too late. The renowned tea room was closed for the night, so they had to content themselves with sauntering up and down the platform in the deepening twilight of the Highland night.

That was the plan anyway. The midges had a different idea. The blood-sucking insects, attracted by the smell of warm human skin and the feast which lay beneath it, swarmed around them in seconds. Attacking every piece of exposed skin, their irritation value bore no relationship to their tiny size. They stood it for a couple of minutes, then retreated, Carrie delaying only long enough to fetch her things from the Ladies' Only compartment.

'We couldnae get a cup of tea,' said Ewen with a laugh, still slapping at the beasties which had followed them back into the train, 'but the midgies are getting a drink from us.'

'Wee horrors, aren't they?' she agreed, engaged in the same ritual dance as himself. 'The curse of the West Highlands. My father says that if you kill one of them, ten thousand of his pals come to the funeral.'

'Do you not know how to get rid o' them?' Ewen asked. 'You mix up a paste of sugar and water . . .'

Carrie sat down. 'White or brown?'

'Brown. Demerara's the best.'

'Right.' She was listening carefully. Ewen worked out of doors. He was bound to have learned from the older men a foolproof method of keeping the dreaded midgies at bay. Sitting across from her, perched on the edge of the long upholstered seat, he was miming the mixing-up of the sugar and water, warming to his theme. His hands rose to pat his cheeks.

'Then you spread the paste on your face and arms – and any other exposed parts of the body.'

'And does that keep them away?' she asked eagerly.

'No – but it rots the wee buggers' teeth!'

Laughing at his own joke, he flung himself back into the seat then looked momentarily dismayed. 'Oh, excuse me, I didnae mean to swear in front of you.'

'It's not the swearing I mind,' Carrie said swiftly. 'It's the terrible joke.' This was the way she liked him, friendly and relaxed and talkative. He didn't mean anything by his swearing. It was normal in the company he usually kept. She knew he didn't do it to shock.

'A real luxury this,' he murmured, 'to be sitting on the cushions.'

'Surfacemen usually travel in the guard's van?'

'Aye. We have some good laughs, but the view's no' very good.' He gestured with his thumb towards the window. 'Certainly no' as good as from here. Did you see that dead interesting-looking castle at the head o' Loch Awe and the wean sitting on the hill back at Tyndrum?'

'Yes to both. Did you wave to the wee boy?'

'Aye, of course I did.' He twisted round, angling his body so he could stretch his legs out in the well between the two bench seats. A contemplative smile touched his mouth. 'D'ye think he was clambering and scrambling – all by himself and gathering brambles?'

Carrie sat back in her own seat. 'You liked the poem, then?'

Ewen was checking the disposition of his feet, eyes downcast. Were his eyelashes a little fairer than his hair? She thought she could see some gold in there among the feathery strands. His jaw line was beginning to shadow with the faintest suggestion of stubble, but the skin on his cheeks, as she'd observed before, was as smooth as a baby's. He looked up, and straight at her.

'I loved the poem.'

The train juddered, and pulled slowly away from the platform. Surely it was that jolt which was making her suddenly breathless?

He threw her an odd little glance, then heaved a sigh of deep contentment. 'I could take a lot of this.'

She thought, perhaps, that it might be as well not to enquire exactly what he could take a lot of.

'Do you like the pictures?'

His eyes lifted again, to the space above and behind her head. Underneath the luggage rack made of steel struts and string mesh where Carrie had carefully laid her jacket and hat and where the back of the seat was bolted on to the wall, there

82

were three frames. The one in the middle surrounded a mirror. It was flanked on either side by small posters showing the beauties of Britain, underlined by the message, *It's Quicker By Rail*. On Ewen's side of the compartment there were pictures of Bamburgh and Edinburgh Castles. Carrie's held views of Loch Long and Loch Lomond.

'Aye, they're dead artistic. I love the way they do them.' He lifted a hand in frustration. 'Och, I don't know the word to say what I mean.'

'The style of them?' she suggested.

'That's it. The style. They paint them in a particular style, don't they?'

Ewen examined all of the pictures in turn. There was real appreciation in his eyes. 'I love paintings,' he confided. 'I often go along to the Art Galleries on a Sunday afternoon to look at them.'

'Not looking for talent?' she teased. Glasgow's municipal art gallery, housed in a magnificent red sandstone building over the River Kelvin, on the fringes of Partick, was well-frequented on Sunday afternoons by young members of both sexes. It was a well-known meeting place.

'Why would a man go looking for talent when he's already found perfection?'

He gazed at her, the expression in his eyes exactly the same as it had been when he had been studying the pictures. This time the jolt Carrie experienced had absolutely nothing to do with the motion of the train. He might have been stumped for a word a minute ago, but at other times he could be all too eloquent.

'Ewen . . .' she said, her face troubled. 'Please don't.'

He continued to study her for a moment or two. Then, palms upward in a gesture of hopelessness, he lifted his hands.

'I know, I know. I shouldnae have said it. Like I shouldnae

have said what I did this afternoon. Don't bother giving me the wee speech about wanting us to stay friends. I think I know it off by heart by now.'

He looked away from her and leaned his head against the window. 'I don't want you to be in any doubt about how I feel about you.' His voice was quiet but firm. 'I want you to know you have a choice. That I'm here if you need me.'

She thought that was one of the saddest things she had ever heard. He would never be her choice. Judging by the way he was choosing not to meet her eyes, he knew full well she was going to reject him again, yet he was laying his feelings bare to her. His painful honesty and vulnerability brought a lump to her throat.

He was staring out of the window now – or at his own large hand which he had pressed flat against the glass. It was a strong hand, used to hard work, his splayed fingers blunt and powerful. Matt's fingers were strong too, but tapering and slender with it.

The train, labouring up one of the steep gradients which characterised the West Highland line, had slowed. Without shifting his position or looking at her Ewen posed a question. 'D'ye want tae change back to the Ladies' Only compartment at Garelochhead?'

'Not if you promise to behave yourself.' She sounded as brisk as her old gym mistress.

She could see one side of his face, and half of the quick smile her words had provoked. It was a lot more than rueful. After a moment or two he sighed and lifted his head. 'I promise. Cross my heart and hope to die.' He raised his eyebrows at her. 'Right then. What would ye like to talk about now?'

Carrie had politely asked the driver before they left Oban if he would do a request stop at Partick for them. Archie Burgess took care to thank the man personally but didn't delay the train any longer than was strictly necessary. They had a timetable to adhere to.

With a wave to the guard and that automatic glance at the rear lights as the train swayed out of the station to complete the final brief stretch of its journey to the city, he walked smartly down the platform towards his erring daughter and her friend. One of them at least betrayed a little anxiety as the stationmaster approached. Ewen was shifting from one foot to the other, waiting for the dressing down.

Standing four-square outside the booking office, Archie did his best to oblige. Carrie wasn't going to undermine his authority in front of his staff, so she acted the meek and penitent daughter and tried not to respond to the answering gleam in her father's eye. She had been relieved to see him waiting for them, especially as Matt was there too, looking far angrier than Archie Burgess did.

He must have been scanning the carriages as they came in. He had his fingers wrapped round the handle of the open door of the Ladies' Only compartment, and stared when he saw Carrie and Ewen emerge from one further up the platform. As though he couldn't believe his eyes, he peered into the empty compartment. That made Ewen chuckle. Not a wise move. Especially as Carrie couldn't entirely contain some amusement either.

After a few questions which Ewen answered nervously but apparently to his stationmaster's satisfaction, Archie gave him a formal rebuke and dispatched him off home. He took his leave of Mr Burgess respectfully, gave Carrie a cheerful wave and completely ignored Matthew, who turned to watch him go with cold eyes.

'Right then, young lady,' barked Archie in a very creditable imitation of a stern patriarch. 'We'll be for home. Your mother wants a word with you too.'

Matthew coughed. Carrie knew what he wanted. She supposed there wasn't any point in putting it off. 'Could Matthew and I have five minutes alone together, Father? Please?'

Grumbling in a token sort of way, Archie told his daughter he'd be waiting for her by the platform gate in exactly five minutes. 'Not a second longer, my girl!'

She turned to Matt. He was so handsome, especially when he looked as he did at the moment, all smouldering eyes and unruly dark hair. Walking over to him, she lifted her face and offered him a kiss, but he jerked his head back.

'Matt? What's the matter?'

His voice was low and impassioned. 'You've spent all day with *him*. That's what's the matter!' He gestured towards the station steps which Ewen had descended a few minutes ago. He'd be walking along a quiet and deserted Dumbarton Road now, heading home to an empty house in Keith Street.

'Matthew,' she said carefully, taking a step back. 'I did not spend all day with him –'

'That's not what I heard.'

She stiffened. 'Not what you heard? From whom, might I ask?'

'It doesn't matter who told me, Carrie.' Matt was holding himself as rigidly as she was. 'What does matter is that you apparently sneaked off with Ewen Livingstone straight after lunch.'

'Sneaked off with him?' She repeated each word with angry precision, both her voice and her temper rising.

'Yes. I understand the two of you weren't seen for the rest of the afternoon.'

Her chin went up. 'What are you implying, Matt?'

86

'I'm not implying anything.'

The coldness in his voice suggested the exact opposite. 'Don't you think I'm entitled to an explanation of your behaviour?' he demanded. If it hadn't been directed at her, she might have found his haughtiness and air of wounded pride quite magnificent – if a touch theatrical. Her father hadn't subjected her to this kind of an interrogation. She saw no reason why she should take it from Matthew Campbell.

Suddenly she realised who'd supplied him with his information: someone who'd been there when she'd accepted Ewen's invitation to go for a walk, someone who might well have made it her business to notice that the two of them had failed to make the train for the return journey.

'Janice Muirhead told you, didn't she?'

His face betrayed the answer.

'I'll bet she enjoyed that,' said Carrie lightly.

He gave her one of his disdainful looks. 'You're wrong, as a matter of fact. I practically had to force it out of her.'

'Oh, I'm sure you did! Tell me,' she asked with careful sarcasm, 'would this be the same Janice Muirhead we're talking about? The one you recently described to me as a complete trollop? I believe those *were* the words you used.'

'My opinion of her moral character doesn't matter, Carrie. Judging from what you yourself said to me over the telephone, her information was accurate.'

'Don't be so pompous, Matt. You sound like a policeman giving evidence at the Sheriff Court.' Carrie paused, and made a conscious effort to calm herself down. This was escalating into the mother and father of all arguments, rather more than a lovers' tiff. 'I did not *sneak off* with Ewen straight after lunch,' she said, striving to excise the anger and irritation from her voice. 'We bumped into each other in the early afternoon and I was so fed up trailing round the shops with Janice and her friends . . .'

'You didn't get fed up with Ewen Livingstone's company,' he interrupted. 'You were enjoying yourself with him so much that you missed the train home. How could you do that, Carrie? You've got a watch, haven't you?'

Keeping her temper was beginning to require a great deal of effort. That patronising question hadn't helped. 'Ewen and I walked along to the Ganavan sands. It's quite a distance. We got talking and completely forgot the time. But we're both home safe now. Isn't that all that matters?'

She moved towards him, laid a conciliatory hand on his arm. 'It's you I love, Matt,' she said softly.

He looked down at her hand, resting lightly on the sleeve of his dark jacket. 'Is it?'

'You know it is.' Her voice grew gentle. He had sounded very uncertain when he had asked that question, as if he really was unsure of her. That was why he was acting this way, overreacting wildly to her having spent time with Ewen because of that uncertainty.

'I love you, Matthew Campbell. Only you. How many times do I have to tell you?' She willed him to lift his gaze from her hand, and eventually he did.

He gave her a shamefaced smile and a swift kiss on the lips. 'What were you and he talking about?'

'Och, I don't know. Different things. Lots of things.'

He persisted. 'What sort of things?'

'Matt, I can't remember all the things we talked about, but you've got nothing to worry about. Honestly. It was all perfectly innocent.'

She had a sudden mental picture of Ewen leaning his tousled head against the window of the compartment, awkwardly confessing his feelings for her. That was one confidence she certainly wasn't going to betray.

'D'you know what I think, Carrie? I think you don't want to remember, that you don't want to tell me what you and he were talking about.'

'I told you, we talked about a lot of things. We were with each other for quite a while.'

That was the truth, but it had been the wrong thing to say. Matt's eyes flashed with anger. 'You'd have spent a lot less time with him if you'd travelled home in the Ladies' Only compartment,' he snapped. 'Why didn't you do that?'

'Because it was boring sitting on my own.'

'But I had expressly told you not to sit with him, Carrie. Why didn't you?'

'Matt,' she pleaded, 'it shouldn't be about one person telling another one what to do. Isn't it about love?'

He moved his arm, shaking her hand off. 'Aren't you going to promise to obey me when we get married?'

She'd never given that much thought before. It might be what you said when you made your wedding vows, but surely most modern husbands didn't really expect obedience from their wives? Her father didn't. He and his wife discussed family matters, often argued the toss about them. Archie didn't always win those arguments. He wasn't the kind of husband who expected to.

A rogue thought flitted through Carrie's brain. What kind of husband would Ewen Livingstone be? Fun, she thought immediately, always willing to look on the bright side and make jokes and the best of a bad job if the going got rough. She couldn't imagine he would expect his wife to obey him either.

The young man who stood in front of her with such a forbidding expression on his face was also assuming rather a lot.

'I haven't actually agreed to marry you, Matt.' She could hear for herself how haughty she sounded. Well, she was feeling pretty haughty. 'Had you forgotten that?'

'No, I hadn't forgotten. I don't understand why you won't say yes, but I hadn't actually forgotten,' he said bitterly. 'How can I when you keep telling me you're too young for me?' They were glaring at each other now.

'In fact, Carrie, if you're not prepared to make that commitment to me, and if you really can't understand why I'm so upset about you spending all this time with Ewen Livingstone, I'm wondering if we shouldn't perhaps think of calling it a day.'

She took a deep breath. 'I think maybe you're right.'

He hadn't expected her to say that. She saw him rock back on to his heels. 'Is that what you want?' he asked stiffly.

'I think it's for the best, yes.'

They held each other's gaze for a few long seconds.

'Goodbye, Matthew,' she said. 'Thanks for all the places you've taken me to and all that. I do love you, you know. That's the simple truth.' She stomped off up the platform. Her father was holding the gate open for her. Carrie swept through without a word.

'Everything all right, lass?'

'Oh, Daddy!' she burst out, and went into his arms.

Chapter 8

'Hello there.'

Carrie sat bolt upright in the deck-chair, although the words had been no more than a murmur. It was Ewen, leaning over the fence and the blossoming white flowers of the potato shaws. She walked over to him. She didn't want to have to shout this conversation in a voice loud enough for half of Partick to hear.

'Where are your workmates?' Peering over the palings, she cast a swift glance up and down the platform.

'Already gone,' he assured her. He seemed to understand her desire for discretion. 'I saw you sitting out when we came up on to the platform, so I pretended I'd left something behind at the bothy and had to go back for it.' He shifted the canvas bag in which he carried his tools from one shoulder to the other. 'Did you get an awful row from your ma on Saturday night?'

Carrie shook her head. She'd washed her hair this morning and dried it in the sun. The shiny strands felt like satin on her smooth cheeks. 'Not too bad.'

'I havenae seen you for a few days, though I've been looking out for you since Monday.'

He hadn't seen her because she'd been staying inside as much as humanly possible. Esther had more or less ordered her out today. Since Sunday morning Carrie had busied herself

91

tackling every conceivable task which needed doing around the house. There wasn't a garment unmended, a sock undarned, a shirt lacking a button or a mirror or piece of brasswork unpolished throughout the Burgess home. She had even got out the canteen holding her mother's EPNS fish knives and forks – a prized wedding gift used only on the most special of occasions – and cleaned and polished every single one of them. As Esther had done the very same job herself not two months before, motherly patience was beginning to wear a little thin.

'It's tiring me out just watching you,' she had said firmly as the family sat down to the midday meal Carrie had insisted on preparing – as she had done every day that week. 'You haven't sat still for days. You're going to sit in the sun with a good book this afternoon. You need some fresh air. And a wee rest.'

'Best do as she says, lass,' Archie had chipped in. 'She's fearsome when roused. Take it from one who knows.'

Carrie had smiled mechanically at her father. After dinner was finished, she took a very good book outside with her, one she'd bought some time ago and hadn't got round to reading yet. She'd been looking forward to it. She was on page fifty before she admitted to herself she wasn't taking in a single word.

'I was worried about you. I thought maybe she'd kept you in or something,' said Ewen, his anxious voice recalling Carrie to the present. His concern almost made her laugh. The thought of her mother as some kind of fierce dragon-lady who'd lock her in her room on a diet of bread and water was the first thing she'd found remotely amusing since Saturday night.

'No,' she said, 'she's been all right about it.'

Her mother had been about to hit the roof when she found out that her daughter had spent several hours alone in a railway compartment with a boy of whom she disapproved. However, when she realised Carrie was unable to tell the story herself because she was crying bitterly over her argument with Matt, she had reacted in the same way as her husband and offered the sobbing girl the comfort of her arms.

'Oh, that's good,' Ewen said, his face clearing. 'I found a reception committee waiting for me when I got back home.'

'The two ladies you told me about on Saturday?'

'Aye. Mr Sharkey's son Pascal – you know him, don't you?' Carrie nodded. Pascal Sharkey, a friendly and likeable lad, had been taken on as a clerk earlier in the year. 'He noticed I'd missed the train and mentioned it to his father who unfortunately told the Terrible Two when he bumped into them later on that night. What a row I got for worrying them half to death!' Ewen grinned. 'Then a beaker of cocoa and about four pieces o' the old lady's shortbread. And her shortbread's worth having, let me tell you. I'd have taken the scolding anyway, and no' just for the sustenance. Saturday was a rare day, wasn't it?'

'It was,' Carrie agreed, studying his open face and thinking about it. It *had* been an enjoyable day. The fact she was no longer walking out with Matthew Campbell didn't alter that.

Last night was the first one she hadn't cried herself to sleep over the break-up, but Matt shouldn't have tried to boss her around like that. No girl with any spirit could stand for that sort of treatment. Practically ordering her to sit in the Ladies' Only compartment, for goodness' sake! It wasn't on. She could understand that he'd been jealous, but surely once he'd calmed down he must have realised himself how high-handed he'd been? Only it was Thursday now and he still hadn't come to apologise, so it didn't much look like it.

'Are you all right, Carrie?'

Ewen was looking very concerned. She'd better make an effort. It wasn't his fault. Not directly, at any rate.

'I'm fine.' She gestured towards the platform gate. 'Are you coming in?'

He fixed her with a level look. 'That depends.'

'On what?'

'On when you might be expecting Matthew Campbell to turn up today.'

She looked him straight in the eye. 'I'm not expecting him today. Or any other day for that matter.' It was time she faced facts. If Matthew hadn't come round to apologise the day after their quarrel, he was hardly going to do so five days on. 'We broke up on Saturday night.'

'Oh, really?' Ewen's eyebrows all but disappeared into his fair hair. 'Well, hen, I'd like to say I'm sorry about it, but I cannae be that two-faced, I'm afraid.' He was regarding her with a speculative air. Realising what it meant restored some of her pertness.

'There's no need to look at me like that, Ewen Livingstone,' she said sharply. 'I'm not looking for another boyfriend. Not at the moment, anyway.'

'Would a friend be acceptable?'

'A friend would be fine.'

'Right then,' he said briskly. 'I've something I want to ask you, but no' here.' He glanced at the raised arm of the signal at the end of the platform. 'There's a train due. Can we go some place where every railwayman in the west of Scotland cannae see us?'

'There's a bench round the other side of the house.'

'That's a bit more than a bench,' he said a minute or two later, looking at the wooden seat which sat against the windowless gable of the house.

'My father made it,' she told him proudly. Archie had built a rustic arch over the seat. Taking cuttings from a wild rose which grew elsewhere in the garden, he had

94

trained the small pink blooms to climb up it.

'A bower,' Ewen said. 'That's what you call this. Is that no' right?' He looked questioningly at her.

'I suppose you would call it a bower. It's one of my favourite spots in the garden,' Carrie confided. And, she thought silently, despite the romance of the bower she had sat here with Matt on only one occasion. On grounds of practicality he had insisted that they move. The little briar roses attracted too many bees. Carrie had never minded the hard-working insects. If you kept still, they didn't bother you, simply got on with their work and flew on to the next flower.

She sat down at one end of the slatted seat and indicated to Ewen that he should join her, but he stood for a minute or two looking down at her.

'I shouldn't really sit here, of course,' she joked, becoming slightly uncomfortable under his prolonged scrutiny. 'Redheads don't suit pink!'

'You suit pink roses very well. A beautiful bower for a beautiful maiden,' he concluded softly.

She ought to have reminded him what had just been said about them being friends and nothing more, but instead she said gently, 'You've the soul of a poet, Ewen Livingstone.'

He snorted. 'I'm no poet, but this fellow was.'

He reached into his canvas bag and fished out a package, loosely tied up in brown paper. Curious, giving him an uncertain little smile, Carrie opened it and took out the book which was inside: *A Child's Garden of Verses* by Robert Louis Stevenson. She looked quickly up at him.

'Och, Ewen, that's awful nice of you, but I've already got a copy of this.' She wondered that he hadn't realised that.

'It's not for you. It's for me.'

'For you?'

He gulped and swallowed hard. 'I thought,' he began. 'I

mean, that is ... I wondered if ... we could use it. You and me.'

The admiring look had left his face. He was very earnest, and obviously nervous. He swallowed again and came out with it.

'Teach me to read, Carrie,' he said. 'Please teach me how to read.'

Chapter 9

'You're going to what?'

'Teach Ewen Livingstone to read,' she repeated. 'We've already begun, although I'll have to get some proper teaching materials. We started this afternoon with Robert Louis Stevenson's poems for children, but they're too difficult for him at the moment.'

The struggle to cope with even the first line of what he referred to as 'the train poem' had dampened Ewen's spirits somewhat, but Carrie had chivvied him along. He had to learn to walk before he could run. His teacher was a novice too, but she would find out the best way of going about things. Or die in the attempt. That last comment, coupled with her obviously growing interest in the project, had brought the smile back to his face.

Carrie wished her new role as Ewen's teacher could have had the same effect on her mother. Esther Burgess, serving spoon poised over the large willow pattern bowl which held what was left of the potatoes, was unusually stony-faced.

The lines on her forehead grew deeper as she looked across the table at her husband. 'Did you know he was illiterate?' she demanded. Carrie winced at the word. It was such a cruel one.

Archie heaved a deep sigh. 'Aye, I knew. He didn't have much schooling. What with one thing and another.'

A look passed between husband and wife.

'That's what worries me,' said Esther, grimly spooning out potatoes on to her daughter's plate without stopping to ask if she wanted them. 'That boy's got a terrible background. You do know that, don't you?'

About to cut into one of the potatoes – grown by her father in their own garden and, she firmly believed, the most delicious food on earth when birstled in the pan with a knob of butter before being brought to the table – Carrie laid down her knife and fork in exasperation.

'Oh, Mother, that's not his fault, is it? And he's trying to improve himself. That's why he's asked me to help him. He's got ambitions. All he needs is a bit more confidence in himself.' She leaned forward over the table, the better to make her point.

Esther shook her head. 'Carrie, when it comes to his family history you don't know the half of it –'

'I know all of it,' she said coolly. 'He told me when we were at Oban. About being illegitimate, I mean.'

She heard her mother's sharp intake of breath, and saw her parents exchange another look. Ridiculous! Was she supposed to pretend she didn't know what the word meant? She wondered how Esther would have reacted if she'd used what Ewen had called the technical term . . .

'Surely you can't blame any child for being born out of wedlock? It's not the child who makes that choice.'

'She's got a point, Esther. Aye, I'll have another tattie.' Archie handed his plate across the table to his wife. 'And you have to give the laddie credit for wanting to better himself.'

'But why does Carrie have to help him do it?' wailed Esther.

'Because I'm the only person he can ask. He doesn't want anyone else to know he can't read and write. You will keep it a secret, won't you?' She looked pleadingly at both of her parents.

'Of course, hen,' said her father. He laid a hand over hers. 'It's a good thing you're doing. That lad could go far if someone would only give him a hand up. He's got something about him – a kind of spark.' He gave his daughter's hand a squeeze, released it and applied himself to his potatoes. 'That's why I gave him a start.'

Carrie smiled into her father's tired eyes. 'I know, Daddy. He's got great respect for you. He's offered to help you in the garden or with the station flower beds, if you would like.'

'In his own time? Och, that's kind o' the boy. I'll maybe take him up on it, lass.'

Perhaps, Carrie thought silently, Ewen's offer could kill not two but three birds with one stone. He would feel happier if he was making some recompense for the time Carrie was going to spend teaching him. Her father would be relieved of a physical burden and a considerable amount of mental stress and strain, and the resulting benefits to Archie's health would endear Ewen to Esther. Her mother's next words shattered this pleasant little idyll.

'So Ewen Livingstone will be calling at the house every day, and we're not to tell people why. You know it won't be long till the tongues start wagging, don't you? What will Matthew Campbell think?'

Carrie picked up her knife and fork again, doing her best to give a nonchalant shrug of the shoulders. 'Why should I care what he thinks? Mmm, these tatties are really tasty, Daddy. Are they the Maris Piper or the Pentland Dells?'

'So you don't care about Matthew any more,' Esther persisted. 'I suppose there's some other reason why you've been crying yourself to sleep every night since Saturday, then? And doing every wee job possible around the house so you don't have to go outside and run the risk of bumping into him?'

'I'm not saying I don't care about Matthew,' said Carrie, finding it more difficult than she expected to meet her mother's shrewd look. 'But I wasn't prepared to be bossed around by him. I told you that, Ma. He owes me an apology.'

'He was concerned about your reputation, Carrie. That says an awful lot for a young man.'

Funny. Now that Matt was no longer walking out with her daughter, Esther seemed inclined to forget all the objections she'd had to him. Even the age difference which had bothered her so much before seemed not to matter now.

'My reputation was perfectly safe, Mother. I know you'll find this hard to believe, but Ewen behaved like a perfect gentleman – at Oban, and while we were on the train.'

Esther snorted in disbelief. Before an infuriated Carrie could respond, Archie intervened. 'I was going to offer to take the plates through and bring the dessert, but I think I'd better no' leave you pair alone in case I come back and find blood on the walls!'

Carrie's expression of self-reproach was a mirror image of her mother's. She leaped up out of her chair. 'You both stay where you are. I'll see to it.'

When she came back through she set down the Eve's pudding which had been keeping warm in the oven of the Baby Belling, carefully placing the enamel ashet on a cork mat in the centre of the table. Then she fetched the jug of custard she'd made and set it down on another one. Handing out the dessert bowls, her back temporarily to Archie, she received a silent message from her mother. Loud and clear. *Let's leave this for now. We don't want to worry your father.*

Carrie gave her a reassuring and apologetic smile. On that point, the Burgess women were in wholehearted agreement.

Ewen proved to be a quick learner, soaking up everything she could give him – and more. Carrie spent some time each evening preparing for the following day's lesson. It was never enough, and she often had to rack her brains to think of something extra.

That was how they came to institute the words of the week, which he had to learn to recognise in their printed form and also to practise using as much as he could in speech. The unlikely conversations which resulted caused them both a fair amount of hilarity, for example when he reported another surfaceman's reaction to his observation that one of their comrades was looking a wee touch *delicate* today. Had he perhaps spent too much time in the pub the night before *consuming intoxicating beverages*?

Martin Sharkey, himself blessed with the silver-tongued eloquence of the Irish, had been mightily amused by Ewen's announcement, after carrying out a particularly dirty job, that he was off to the tap in the bothy to *perform his ablutions*.

Initially the words of the week were taken from the big English dictionary Archie Burgess had bought when his daughter went to secondary school, but later they came from a smaller version Carrie gave Ewen for his nineteenth birthday.

She'd wanted to surprise him by knowing the date – asking her father to look it up in the staff records – and she did. Esther had agreed – with considerable reluctance – that he might have his tea with them that evening. Three weeks on, she wasn't showing much sign of relaxing her disapproval of him, but Archie had insisted.

'Well, Esther, we'll be having tatties and vegetables out of the garden with our meat, I suppose, and the laddie *has* been helping me grow the stuff!'

For to Carrie's surprise, and vague unease, her father had accepted the offer of help in the garden with some alacrity and without the necessity for her to issue any dire threats. So

Ewen, stiff and nervous and having performed some very vigorous ablutions at the scullery sink, came in and sat at the table with them. He was voluble in his thanks for this unexpected birthday treat and a little over-enthusiastic in his praise of Esther's cooking – trying that bit too hard to please his hostess – but it all passed pleasantly enough.

They dispatched a substantial meal of tender rump steak stewed with onions and carrots from the garden, accompanied by floury potatoes, buttered cabbage and peas from the same source. Carrie had shelled the latter that afternoon, sitting in a deck-chair on the lawn watching her father and Ewen toiling to keep down the weeds. Despite the disparity in age and status, the two men seemed to get on well together. Much of the conversation which floated across to her was a spirited discussion on the merits of various football teams.

While Esther cleared the plates away, Carrie disappeared into the front room and came back proudly bearing aloft the cake she'd baked and iced earlier in the week. She placed it in front of Ewen, laughing at the expression of amazement on his face as he followed its descent on to the table. To her further amusement, she saw that he was counting its tiny candles, making sure it really was for him.

Digging into the deep pocket of her green sundress, she extracted her present of a dictionary, carefully wrapped in navy blue paper and decorated with a silver bow. She had thought the combination pleasingly masculine. With a flourish, she put that in front of him too.

'For me?' he asked wonderingly, looking up at her as she stood beside him. 'Both o' them?'

'Well, it is your birthday,' she replied, lips twitching. 'Haven't you ever had a cake or a present before?'

She regretted the words the moment they were out of her mouth. Ewen's good-natured face crumpled.

'No' since my mother died.' Apparently overcome, he bent his head and covered his eyes with his hand. Every member of the Burgess family froze in silent sympathy. Even Esther's face softened.

Archie recovered first. 'It's all right, lad,' he said, giving Ewen an embarrassed pat on the arm. 'We understand. Give yourself a wee minute.'

Carrie bent towards him and slid a swift and sympathetic arm along the hunched shoulders. 'I'm so sorry, Ewen,' she whispered, her lips almost touching his ear. 'I didn't think.'

'It's me who should be sorry,' he said a minute or two later. 'Making an exhibition o' myself.' He sat up and squared his shoulders. 'I cannae apologise enough, Mrs Burgess. Mr Burgess.' He managed to look them both in the face.

'No need for apologies, laddie,' said Archie. Esther, watching as her daughter took her arm from Ewen's shoulders, said nothing. Carrie herself was totally focused on him, her one aim in life at this precise moment to make him feel happier again. Lifting the small navy and silver package, she handed it to him.

'Open your present,' she instructed cheerfully. 'I want to see if you like it.'

His reaction didn't disappoint her. 'An English dictionary! Och, Carrie, that's great!'

She smiled broadly in relief. He sounded really pleased.

Chapter 10

'You seem to be sitting awful close to me.'

'Well,' responded Ewen, his face carefully blank, 'we are reading off the same book.' He indicated it with his index finger. 'I've got to sit close to you to be able to see the words.'

Carrie pursed her lips and looked suspiciously at him. 'Didn't you have to do an eye test when you joined the company?'

They were in their usual place, on the bench round the corner from the kitchen door. It was a hot and still day, with scarcely a breath of wind to disturb the warm air. There were at least two bees busy in the roses which tangled through the trellis above their heads. She could distinguish the different notes of their humming. Like her, Ewen didn't seem to be bothered by the proximity of the industrious little creatures.

'I don't recall,' he said loftily, using one of the current words of the week.

'Pull the other one, Livingstone, it's got bells on,' she said, resolutely ignoring the smile which greeted this sally.

She'd felt very tender towards him since his birthday, touched by the emotion he'd shown that day. However, she was beginning to wonder if she'd conveyed the wrong impression by bestowing that impulsive hug upon him.

'Everyone's got to pass an eye test before they're even

considered for a job on the railway,' she said. 'You know that as well as I do.'

Ewen struck a contemplative pose. 'Well . . . no' cloakroom attendants or kiosk assistants, Carrie.'

'You're neither of those,' she pointed out, poking him in the chest to emphasise her point, an action which served merely to broaden his smile. 'You're in the sort of job where you have to be able to see if a signal's changed colour or if there's a dirty great locomotive bearing down on you.'

'Looks like you've answered your own question, then.' The freckles danced across the bridge of his nose as he wrinkled it in a teasing grimace. 'Miss Smart Alec.'

'So,' she demanded, the shimmering curve of her hair swinging as she stuck her chin out, 'there's another reason why you're sitting so close to me?'

'Aye,' he said cheerfully, not a bit abashed. 'I like sitting close to you.'

She should have told him off there and then, got to her feet and forcibly put some space between them, but instead she stayed where she was and spoke soft words into the few inches of warm air which separated them.

'You're incorrigible, Ewen Livingstone.'

He was studying her face. At rather closer range than Carrie found comfortable. 'If I'm a good boy, will you explain to me what big words like that mean?'

'Come off it, pal, you know plenty of big words.'

'What, like wheelbarrow? See when you teach me to write, can that be my first word?'

Carrie raised her eyebrows. 'Wheelbarrow?'

'Ha-bloody-ha,' he said grimly. 'Oh, sorry. I forgot myself again. No, I meant incorrigible. In-corr-ig-ible.' He rolled the word around his mouth like a sweetie.

'Who says I'm teaching you to write?'

He slid down the bench, hooked one leg over the arm of it and rested his wavy locks on her shoulder, looking backwards up at her. 'You did. If I made good progress, you said. And I have, haven't I?'

She couldn't deny him that. 'Yes, you've worked hard. You're all arms and legs,' she observed, surveying him as he lay sprawled beside her. He was wearing his dark brown corduroy working trousers, an open-necked white shirt and his red neckerchief knotted round his throat. Combined with his current posture, the ensemble gave him a rather rakish air. 'You look like a gypsy.'

'Apart from the hair.' His face turned up towards the heat of the sun, his eyelids fluttered shut.

'Mmm,' she agreed. 'It's getting fairer, have you noticed?'

'Och, it aye does that in the summer.'

Carrie didn't really think about what she did next. She lifted one of the tresses in question. The strands of hair felt as smooth and silky as her own. Without opening his eyes, Ewen stretched a hand back, lifted her arm and placed it around his neck, imprisoning it there.

'You're no' resisting,' he murmured.

'It's too hot to resist.'

She saw his lips curve. A minute passed. Two. His warm fingers were curled around her forearm. She flexed her hand, her fingertips feeling the solid thump of his heartbeat. There was a constant hum of noise from the railway, but it seemed quite far away, the area immediately around them very quiet and still. Even the bees had moved on, off to collect pollen from some other flowers.

'This is nice,' he said.

She muttered something non-committal. He opened his eyes, swivelled his head round on her shoulder and spoke softly into her face. 'Would I be pushing ma luck if I tried

107

anything else?' The pale blue eyes dropped to her mouth, leaving her in little doubt as to what that anything else might be.

'What do you think?'

She'd intended the words to come out briskly, friendly but dismissive. Instead, her voice sounded husky, and oddly breathless.

'What dae I think?' His voice was as warm and lazy as the summer day which shimmered around them. 'What I think is that you'll have tae sound an awful lot more convincing than that, Miss Burgess. If you really don't want me to try anything else.'

Their faces only inches apart, their concentration on each other intense, neither of them heard the sound of the back door opening.

'For the umpteenth time, Mother, Ewen is not my new boyfriend!'

'Does he know that?' muttered Esther darkly. 'The way yon laddie smiles when he sees you. Are you telling me you don't notice the look in his eyes?'

The two women were squaring up to each other in the living room, Ewen having hurriedly made his excuses and left. Before Ma could physically throw him out, thought Carrie wryly. Never mind the look in his eyes when he saw Carrie, there had been something approaching holy terror in those blue-grey pools when he had glanced up to find Esther standing there glaring down at them – hands on hips and more or less breathing fire.

She was adopting the same posture now, using the few minutes before her husband was due home for his tea to express her pent-up feelings.

'He practically had his head in your lap!' she yelled. 'A

month ago you were crying your eyes out over Matthew Campbell. I didn't think you were that sort of a lassie, Carrie!'

In the silence which followed this accusation she heard with relief the sound of the back door being pushed open. Pity her hearing hadn't been so acute ten minutes ago. Esther had heard it too. 'That's your father.' She turned to walk through to the kitchen to greet him, throwing a softly spoken threat back over her shoulder. 'Don't think we're finished with this, miss.'

Waiting for sleep to come that night, Carrie reached out a hand to the small bookcase which stood between her bed and the door. The books on the top shelf were adorned with half a dozen soft toys. Like so much of what made her room cosy and pleasant – the plump quilt under which she lay, the embroidered Duchess mats on her dressing-table – they were all her mother's creations.

Gertie the giraffe had always been Carrie's favourite. Made of dark brown felt, her long legs stiffened so she could stand up if necessary, she was covered with small fawn patches to mimic a real giraffe's coat. Each one of the footery wee pieces had been painstakingly cut out and stitched on by Esther.

Carrie stretched out her arms and held Gertie above her head. 'So tell me,' she asked, 'what am I going to do about all this?'

The giraffe regarded her impassively. Apparently she didn't feel capable of expressing an opinion on the subject.

'I don't blame you,' Carrie said softly. 'I'm finding the whole thing quite difficult myself. It's horrible when you know you're making one of the people you love most in the whole world unhappy. How can I convince her there's nothing to worry about? That I think of Ewen as a friend? Like the brother I've never had?'

Now she could have sworn that Gertie's two glassy eyes held a tell-that-to-the-marines-my-girl expression. She put the light out and tucked the toy in beside her, underneath the covers.

Did your brother rest his head on your shoulder while you coiled your arm about his neck? Did the feel of his heartbeat under your fingers give you an odd, fluttery little feeling in your chest and throat?

Yet her feelings for Matt hadn't gone away either. She remembered those passionate kisses and embraces, and how they had made her feel . . .

She allowed the memories to wash over her for a few minutes, blushing in the darkness as she felt her body begin to stir into response. All at once uncomfortably warm, she pushed the covers down and rolled on to her side, blowing out a long exasperated breath. There was no point in thinking like that if Matt didn't want her any more.

Could she be sure of that, though? She knew he'd had equally as strong feelings for her. She couldn't believe he was the kind of man to slough them off with scarcely a backward glance. She had seen him two or three times since the break-up, but only at the station where there were always other people around. Hardly the ideal place for a private chat.

The railway bush telegraph was working well enough as it was. Esther had been entirely right in her prediction. The tongues were wagging about the stationmaster's daughter and the Permanent Way lad. Outside the Burgess family, only Martin Sharkey knew about the reading and writing lessons. Ewen had confided in the older man. Since he had also sworn him to secrecy, everyone else was busily drawing the obvious conclusion.

There was even a joke going the rounds. *Caroline Burgess is seeing someone beneath her station*. She had prised that out of an embarrassed Mary, who in turn had got it from her fiancé Douglas. Carrie turned once more on to her back, remembering to move Gertie so she wouldn't squash her.

None of this made it easy for Matt to approach her. Perhaps she ought to take matters into her own hands. She thought about it for a minute or two, eyes wide open and staring at the dark ceiling.

'Got it,' she whispered. Thinking about Mary and Douglas had given her an idea. She wrapped her arms around Gertie. Within five minutes she was sound asleep.

Chapter 11

'Hello, Carrie.'

Deep in apparent contemplation of an Egyptian mummy in a glass case, she turned immediately at the sound of his voice.

'Hello, Matt,' she responded. Well, her ploy had worked, and there was nobody else in this section of the Art Galleries, although she could have done without spotting Janice Muirhead a few minutes ago. There were lots of people she knew here today. There always were, particularly in the summer. She had come with Mary and Douglas. The former, in on the plot, had agreed they would fade discreetly into the background if they saw Matthew approaching.

The first floor of the building, reached by a couple of impressively sweeping stone staircases, housed a fine collection of paintings; the ground floor a wide variety of museum exhibits. Universally, however, the whole place was always referred to simply as the Art Galleries or Kelvingrove, the latter being the park in which the ornate and beautiful red sandstone building stood.

Some girls professed to find the mummies spooky, shrieking a horrified refusal if a boy suggested visiting the small side gallery which they occupied. Carrie had always heartily despised that attitude. Why some members of her own sex thought they had to behave like empty-headed little pieces of fluff when there were men about was beyond her.

However, this Sunday afternoon she was glad of it. It meant she and Matt were alone together, however briefly. She wouldn't have put it past Janice to be lurking somewhere not very far away, but since this looked like being her best chance of getting him on his own, Carrie plunged in.

'How are you?' she asked.

'How do you think I am?' His voice was low and impassioned. 'Without you in my life?'

'How am I supposed to know how you feel when you haven't tried to see me to tell me?' she responded, striving to keep her voice light, although her heart had leaped into her throat at his words. He still wanted her. *He still wanted her!*

'How could I? You're always with someone when I see you.'

'I'm not with anyone at the moment,' she pointed out. 'And neither are you.' She gestured towards the glass cases. 'I doubt the mummies will clype on us.'

They were standing in a bay formed by two display cases which jutted out into the middle of the room. The mummies within them lay with their heads to the wall and their feet towards the long windows which framed the main building of Glasgow University up on the other side of the Kelvin.

Matt's face showed no response to her joke. Her timing had always been bad when it came to trying to get him to see the funny side of things. He was, as ever, immaculately dressed, but he looked miserable – pale, and thinner than he had been before. He found himself a spare patch of wall between the two exhibits and leaned one shoulder against it, folding his arms across his chest as he did so.

'Where's your little boyfriend today, then?' he asked bitterly. The jealousy in his voice was unmistakable. It was also undeniably exciting. 'Not much point in him coming here, I suppose. He wouldn't be able to read the captions.' Matt extracted one hand from his folded arms and flicked his elegant fingers towards the printed card giving all the known facts about the mummy. A narrow band of spotless white cuff showed beneath the dark material of his jacket.

The gesture he had made was so dismissive, cold and heartless. Yet Carrie could remember only too well what else those long fingers could do . . . Those had been warm and loving things. Thrilling things.

'I suppose he could go upstairs and look at the pictures. That would be about his level.'

Carrie took a deep breath. 'He's not my boyfriend.'

'No?' Matthew pushed himself off the wall and came towards her, peering down into her face. 'You do know that everyone's gossiping about the two of you, don't you?' he sneered. 'I'm surprised your father's letting you see Livingstone, I really am.'

'Let them gossip.' Carrie tilted her chin. She was wearing the same outfit she'd worn to Oban, and the pheasant's feather on her Tyrolean hat bounced with the angry movement of her head. The thought of her father letting – or not letting – her do anything was a fairly mind-boggling concept. That wasn't how things worked in the Burgess family.

She'd been on the point of explaining the situation, making it clear all she was doing was helping someone learn to read and write, but that implied criticism of her father had put her off her stroke. And however hurt Matt was, she couldn't let him get away with those sarcastic comments about Ewen.

'Do you really want to know how I am, Carrie?'

'Why do you think I came here today?'

That stopped him in his tracks, and she saw a spark of hope in his eyes. When he spoke, his words winged their way to her like a simple plea from his heart. 'Come back to me, Carrie. Please.'

'Och, Matt . . .' She took a step towards him. She was almost in his arms.

'You'll have to dump *him*, of course.'

'Matthew, it's not a question of dumping anybody.' She put as much reassurance as she could into her smile. First they would kiss and then she would tell him the whole story, make it crystal clear that while Ewen was her friend, it was Matthew who was her lover. Lover. What a beautiful word that was.

Her smile became dreamy, but he had taken a step away from her. 'If we get back together again, you'll have to promise never to see him again.'

'I'll do no such thing!'

Her defence of her right to see Ewen had been instinctive. It sent Matt right back on to his high horse. 'I can't believe you prefer him to me. An illiterate navvy!' He was sneering now. 'Do you know anything at all about his background, Carrie?'

'That again,' she said contemptuously. Honestly, she might expect it of her parents' generation, but she was bitterly disappointed that Matt didn't appear to have a more modern attitude.

His eyes narrowed. 'He's told you about his mother?' He sounded disbelieving, almost incredulous.

'Of course he has,' she said. 'I know it all. Goodbye, Matt.'

She could feel his eyes boring into her back as she turned and walked away.

'I'm not asking you to put on the pan loaf!' Carrie exclaimed, completely exasperated with her pupil. Both of them seemed to be on a short fuse this warm Monday afternoon.

'It's the way I speak,' Ewen said belligerently. 'It's the way most people I know speak. What's wrong wi' it? I'm no' gonnae speak with marbles in ma mouth for anybody.'

'I'm only saying you might try to be a wee bit more precise when you're talking to certain people. It'll help you get on.'

'What d'ye mean, help me get on?'

'Well, are you planning to stay a P-way man all your life?'

'Something wrong wi' that?' he growled.

'Nothing,' she said carefully. 'It's an important job.' She was feeling a bit fragile, unsettled after her meeting with Matt the day before. Ewen's unusually bad temper wasn't helping at all. 'I just think you could do better for yourself. Maybe consider applying for a clerkship,' she suggested. 'Once you've had a bit more practice at reading and writing.'

'Away and boil yer heid, Carrie,' he said irritably. 'I'm no' brainy enough for that kind o' a job. Look at this,' he said dismissively, gesturing to the words he had painstakingly copied out in the jotter which lay on the gate-leg table. 'It's hopeless.' He sounded disgusted with himself. 'I'm never gonnae be able to write wee enough to get it between the lines.'

'Of course you will,' she said, her voice gentling. 'You're doing really well.'

'Och, Carrie, let's stop kidding ourselves!' He dropped the pencil and thrust out his hands towards her. 'Look at them! They're fine for wielding a pick-axe or a thirty-two-pound hammer, but they're no good for this sort of thing. Far too big and clumsy.'

She shook her head. 'Big,' she agreed, 'but not clumsy.'

She'd seen him using the heavy hammer. There had been a curious grace about it. Stripped to the waist, the muscles in his back and shoulders rippling like wave patterns on a sandy beach under the outgoing tide, he'd swung it with what had looked to her like effortless ease, bringing it down through the air in a smooth arc.

'You had to learn how to use the hammer, didn't you? The

pick-axe too. Then you had to practise with them. It's exactly the same with a pencil and paper. They're tools too, that anybody can learn to use. Practice makes perfect, whatever it is you're doing.'

He looked doubtfully at her. Since he wasn't actually biting her head off, she took her courage in both hands and dared to go on. 'You could easily pass a clerkship exam. I've seen the papers. I know you could do it. If you stick in at your reading and writing.'

Her words had penetrated his black mood. 'D'ye really think so, Carrie?'

'I know so,' she said firmly.

Sometimes, when he let his guard down, she got a searing glimpse of exactly how low an opinion he had of himself and his capabilities. Very few people had encouraged him to think otherwise, she supposed: maybe only ever his mother – until he'd been brave enough to seek Carrie's help.

'Come on,' she wheedled, 'try it a few more times.'

He started off well enough, but ran out of space before he was halfway through his surname. 'Och, damn and bloody blast!'

He rose angrily to his feet, snapped the pencil in two and flung it on to the table. 'It's no use. I'll never be able to do it. We might as well admit that and agree to call it a day. Your ma cannae stand me anyway, can she? Hates having me around the place.'

'What had my poor wee pencil done to you?' Carrie asked mildly, ignoring those last observations.

'I'll give you the money for a dozen bloody pencils!' The words came out jerkily and she guessed he'd had to hold himself back from peppering the statement with a few more expletives. 'I'm away,' he said abruptly. 'I'll see you the morn. Or maybe I'll not.'

He edged out from behind the table, but she got up too and came quickly round the other side of it. She laid a light hand on his arm, checking his headlong flight towards the corner of the house.

'Ewen, what's the matter with you today?' She could feel how tense he was. Under her fingers, the muscles of his forearm were as rigid as a washboard. 'Come and sit down again,' she said gently.

He shook his head. 'No. I cannae.'

'Let's walk up to the end of the garden, then,' she suggested, recognising that he was too restless to sit still.

He struck off across the drying green towards the clump of silver birch trees which stood in the farthest corner of the garden, overlooking the goods yard. That was as good a place as any. At least they'd have some privacy over there.

Gazing up at the cloudless blue sky earlier that morning Esther had decreed it to be a rare drying day and highly suitable for what her husband laughingly designated the ceremonial annual wash of the bedclothes. There were two blankets on each side of the square formed by the four clothes poles which defined the business end of the drying green. Carrie had stretched an additional length of rope diagonally between two of the poles for the covers which she personally had trampled in the bath, her soft cotton summer skirt tucked up into her knickers to keep it dry.

Having, perforce, to stop when he came up against the barrier of the fence, Ewen grasped the tops of two of the palings in both hands. She caught up with him and came to stand beside him. Glancing at his hands, she saw that his knuckles were white. He must be holding on very hard indeed.

'Will you tell me what's the matter?'

He stopped pretending to be fascinated by the activities of the sturdy, if unprepossessing, little engine shunting coal

119

trucks about in the goods yards and turned to look at her, releasing his grip on the fence.

'You went to the Art Galleries yesterday. You met Matthew Campbell there.'

It was an accusation, and a demand for her to explain herself. She wasn't sure he had the right to expect a response to either of those, but she answered him anyway.

'I needed to talk to Matthew privately,' she said quietly. 'That was the only place I could be sure of getting him on his own.'

'And you were just talking to him? That's no' the way I heard it.'

You didn't have to be Sherlock Holmes to work out who his informant had been. Carrie's determination not to lose her temper wavered. This was the second time that young lady had stuck her oar in.

'Oh?' she enquired haughtily, taking a step away from him along the fence. 'Tell me, Ewen. What *exactly* did Janice Muirhead say to you?'

He didn't flinch. 'She said you and him were in a wee side room by yourselves for ages. She said she thought you were kissing.'

'Well, she was wrong,' snapped Carrie. 'We most definitely were not kissing.'

'Do you tell me that, Carrie?'

She glared at him, infuriated by his refusal to believe her emphatic denial. Who the hell did he think he was? The thought that he'd take Janice Muirhead's word over her own made her blood boil. She was reminded suddenly of Matt. Hadn't she had a very similar conversation with him – although perhaps interrogation would be a better word – over her afternoon in Oban with Ewen? Her temper cranked up a few notches. She didn't have red hair for nothing.

'Yes!' she yelled. 'I do bloody tell you that! And you'd better bloody believe me! Because it's the truth!'

He folded his arms across his broad chest. 'I've tellt you before about swearing,' he said sternly. 'It doesnae become a lady like you. Don't do it again.'

'Oh!' She clenched her fists in frustration. 'Stop bossing me about! I won't have it!'

'You'd take it from Matthew Campbell!'

'I would not! That's why I split up with him! Remember?'

'So why did you go to the Art Galleries yesterday?'

'Maybe I wanted to sort out how I felt about him! Maybe I'm confused! Maybe I don't know how I feel about *you*!'

Ewen flushed. 'I didnae know you felt anything about me,' he said quietly. In the goods yard, the little locomotive chuntered. Carrie glanced over at it, then returned her eyes to Ewen's face.

'Why do you think I'm helping you to read and write?'

'I've nae bloody idea,' he flung back. Apparently it was all right for him to swear. 'Just why are you doing the Lady Bountiful act?'

She was struck dumb for a full five seconds. Then she let rip. 'How dare you, Ewen Livingstone? Of all the ungrateful . . .' She shook her coppery head. If she hadn't felt the need to speak up for Ewen yesterday, she and Matt might be back together again now.

'You're the main reason I fell out with Matt in the first place!' she yelled. Too angry to watch her words, she stormed furiously on. 'You're quite right, by the way. My mother does hate having you here. I'm having fights with her almost every day over you. And I never fight with my mother!'

His earlier flush had faded. He was pale now, and tight-lipped. 'So why bother? I wouldnae have thought I was worth it.'

121

'Has the thought ever penetrated your thick skull that I might be helping you because I quite like you?'

He swayed towards her, chin jutting out, his face inches from her own. 'Quite like me?' he howled. 'QUITE LIKE ME? Is that supposed to make me delirious wi' joy, Miss Burgess?'

Delirious. It was his word of the week. The phrase was one she had used to illustrate the different ways it might be used. Fatally, they both realised that at precisely the same moment. For a frozen moment they continued to glare at each other. Then Carrie's lips twitched.

'Well, I do feel quite *affectionate* towards you. Is that better?'

'There's no need to be *supercilious* about it.'

He'd caught on immediately. He waited patiently for her to trot out another former word of the week, and for his own chance to lob one neatly back to her.

'Do you feel I'm *patronising* you, then?'

'Do you think I'm completely *incorrigible*?'

They both burst out laughing. Carrie bent over, hugging her middle. She straightened up, saw he was still in fits and had to lift a hand to his broad shoulder for support.

'Oh, Ewen . . . I haven't laughed so much in ages!'

'Are you really not going back to Matthew Campbell?' he asked a minute or two later, the amusement fading slowly from his face.

'Mind your own business, Livingstone,' she said cheerfully. She had enjoyed the laughter. She didn't want this conversation to get serious again.

He had other ideas. 'Maybe it is my business.'

'You think so?'

'I think it could be. If you would permit it.' He smiled faintly. *Permit* had been another of his words.

She wasn't sure what to say to him. She didn't want to raise any false hopes. Above their heads, the branches of the silver birches creaked as the summer breeze freshened and became brisker. Behind her, she heard sharp thwacks as the blankets on the washing line shook themselves out, reacting to the wind. Ewen lifted his hand to her face.

Big. Definitely not clumsy. His fingers felt like thistledown against her smooth cheek. Or a dandelion clock, perhaps. That was an odd metaphor to pop into her head at a moment when time seemed to have taken it into its head to stand still. The shy fingers on her face became infinitesimally more confident. He bent his head forward.

'No,' she whispered. Then she added two more words. Perhaps to soften the blow. Perhaps because they were what came to mind. 'Not yet,' she said.

Ewen hesitated. 'Is it because you're still confused about how ye feel about him? Or how ye feel about me?'

'Something like that.'

He dropped his hand and took a step back from her. 'And you want me to keep ma distance,' he said in matter-of-fact tones. 'At least for the time being.'

'That's about it,' she agreed.

He took a deep breath, lifted his shoulders and considered. Then he exhaled a long breath. 'I can do that, Carrie. Nae bother at all. But I can keep coming for my lessons?' His fair eyebrows drew together in anxious enquiry.

'Of course you can!' On impulse, grateful for his under-standing, she stepped forward, stretched up and kissed him swiftly on the cheek. When she pulled back she saw that he was pointing to the other side of his face.

'This one too. Otherwise I'll be lopsided. Might fall into Dumbarton Road on the way home and get run over by a tram. You wouldnae want that on your conscience, would you?'

'Chancer,' she muttered, but she gave him what he had asked for.

The next day he brought her an apple. 'Because I was so grumpy yesterday,' he said, giving her the sunniest of smiles. Removing the apple from a somewhat crumpled brown paper bag, he extended it to her with a surprisingly elegant flourish of the hand, like an experienced waiter balancing a tray on his fingertips.

'The reddest and shiniest one in the shop. Selected especially for you. That old cow in the greengrocer's round the corner from me –'

She narrowed her eyes at him, but he carried on, unrepentant. 'She is an old cow, Carrie, always trying to palm folk off wi' tatties with black bits in them and suchlike. She didnae want to give me a bag either – because I was only buying the one piece of fruit – but I insisted,' he added proudly. 'I couldnae have your apple jostling around among my tools all day.'

'I'm pleased to hear you stood up for yourself,' Carrie told him gravely. 'And thank you for the apple. Can I save it and eat it later? I'll have it after my tea.'

'But no' too long after your tea,' he admonished. 'Ye shouldnae eat an apple just before you go to bed. You'll no' digest it properly.'

She grinned. 'My mother always says that.'

He had no comment to make on that. She regarded him thoughtfully, and wondered if he thought her mother was an old cow too.

'Here,' he was saying, 'put it back in the poke if ye're no' going to eat it now.' He handed her the bag and explained further. 'I meant it to be an apple for the teacher, like.'

'I could have worked that one out,' Carrie replied in a

passable imitation of the way he had growled at her yesterday. 'Right,' she said briskly. 'I want you to start off by writing your name out properly. Six times.'

He sketched her a salute. 'Yes, miss. No, miss. Three bags full, miss.'

She administered a swipe to the back of his head. His hair was so thick he would hardly feel it. 'Less of your impertinence, boy. Now, sit down and let's get on with it.'

She watched him as he wrote. Bent over the jotter, his whole attention was directed towards the task which had defeated him yesterday. His autographs weren't exactly neat, but his handwriting was smaller and more controlled and so far he hadn't run out of space. His lips were slightly parted and she guessed he was completely unaware that his tongue was sticking out a little to one side in concentration. Like a wee laddie at school, she thought fondly.

Chapter 12

Carrie's brolly was fighting a losing battle with the elements.

'Sure, you'd hardly believe it was August, would you now? I'm thinking we should both be making a dash for it, Miss Burgess. Mind and give my regards to your mother, now.'

'I think you're right, Mrs Sharkey,' said Carrie politely. 'And I hope your husband will be better soon,' she added, for she'd been listening to a blow-by-blow account of the ganger's current attack of bronchitis.

She regarded the bent spokes of her umbrella in disgust. It might be summer according to the calendar, but it was blowing a force-eight gale on Dumbarton Road. The accompanying squally showers had been alternating with brief spells of dazzling sunshine all day. What a country!

Bidding farewell to Martin Sharkey's wife, whom she'd bumped into as she came out of the baker's, she folded her now useless protection against the rain, pulled her mother's message bag in closer to her body in an attempt to keep both it and its contents dry and sped towards the covered stairs which led up to the station. It was an obvious shortcut back to the house, especially on a day like this.

Ewen would be coming off duty soon. It was too wet to have their lesson today, but they could have a quick word with each other, protected from the rain by the canopy which projected out from the roof of the station buildings. Coming down the last few steps of the bridge, where the wooden treads came way to stone steps, she saw that her father was already standing under there. She pushed a strand of sodden hair out of her eyes and smiled at him. She hadn't wanted to get any of her hats wet. So now her hair was soaking. Very logical.

'I'm waiting to catch Ewen and his mates when they come off-duty,' said Archie. 'I need to have a word with them about the general manager's visit.'

That exalted being – high heid yin for the entire Scottish region of the LNER – was scheduled to spend most of the following Wednesday afternoon at Partick. A letter from his office at Waverley Station in Edinburgh had communicated his desire to meet the stationmaster's family and, of course, to see as much as possible of the work of the station. He was particularly keen to talk to younger employees, both salaried staff and those in the waged or conciliation grades.

'Is this about the protective clothing dispute, Daddy?'

Archie nodded. That old favourite had reared its head again recently. It had caused a substantial amount of friction when the surfacemen discovered that several of the clerks had blithely indented for new railway-issue waterproof jackets for themselves – and received them.

The Permanent Way staff, whose stock of oilskins kept in the bothy was now so old as to be more or less useless at keeping the rain out, were up in arms about it. They spent a hell of a lot more time out of doors than some clerk who did most of his work sitting in a warm and dry office.

Archie had tried to get them new waterproofs only to be told by the railway offices in Glasgow that the clothing budget for this year was spent. They would have to wait till next spring. Sharkey and his men, facing the approaching autumn and winter without adequate protection against wind and driving rain, had expressed themselves rather frankly on the subject. Sharkey now being off sick with bronchitis had only added force to their argument.

Heavy footsteps were crunching down the wet platform. Archie stuck his head out from under the protection of the canopy. 'Ah, here they come. Like a platoon of soldiers. How are you today, boys?' he asked in a louder voice.

'Wet,' said one man, coming in under the shelter and throwing an uncompromising look at his boss. Under cover of the discussion which ensued, Ewen edged his way round the backs of his workmates. Like the rest of them, he was extremely wet. The sleeves of his heavy jacket were sticking to his arms and his hair, plastered to his head, was beginning to go into curls.

'You look like a drowned rat.'

'So do you.' He reached out a hand and tugged her hair. 'Yee-uch! You'll need to put yourself through the mangle.' He made great play of wiping his fingers on his jacket, grinning at her all the while.

Everyone else was grinning too, something the two of them unfortunately didn't realise until Archie Burgess spoke Ewen's name for the second time. Embarrassed, Carrie did her best to blend into the background as her father and the other P-way men put a proposal to him. Since the general manager wanted to have a formal meeting with as many of the younger members of staff as could be crammed into the booking office, why didn't Ewen take that opportunity to put their complaints to him on the question of waterproof jackets?

'Oh, I couldnae! I wouldnae know where to start!'

Carrie came forward. 'If I helped you, Ewen?'

He turned eagerly to her. 'Would you, Carrie?'

'We'll leave you to convince him then, Miss Burgess,' said the man who'd earlier given the succinct answer to Archie's enquiry after their health. 'Use your womanly wiles on him.'

He gave her an outrageous wink. 'Come on, lads. See you later, Ewen.'

There were a few sly glances as they left, plus a parting shot from another of the surfacemen, an older man. 'I cannae imagine he'll be able to resist ye, pet.'

The three of them stood and watched the men head home, trudging through the rain with their heads down.

'I don't think I like the implications of that last statement,' Carrie muttered, but she was talking to herself. Her father was busy trying to convince a panic-stricken Ewen that he was perfectly capable of carrying out the task his mates had saddled him with.

'You'd be helping all your mates,' Archie was saying. 'And yourself too. It never hurts a young man who wants to get on in the railway to seize an opportunity to shine in front of senior management.'

'I doubt I'll shine very brightly, Mr Burgess. I'll more than likely make a pig's ear out o' it.'

'No, you'll not,' insisted Carrie. 'You'll manage it fine. I think,' she went on, 'that you should write down the points you want to make on a wee index card. That'll make you look really businesslike and well-prepared. I've got some of those.'

'Write them down? And then read them out? Carrie, I cannae!'

'Of course you can,' she said robustly. 'If you like, I'll do the writing bit. I'll print the words out in block capitals, and quite large. We'll practise reading them out loud between now and next week. I'll try to stand near you so I can prompt you if necessary.'

He was looking at her very doubtfully. Behind his head, the rain was driving against the glass panels of the screen which supported the roof canopy at both ends of the station buildings. Archie Burgess laughed and clapped them both on the shoulder, joining them together through him.

'I'd give in now, son. You know she'll persuade you in the end.'

On the following Wednesday they all packed into the booking office. Waiting for everyone to assemble, Carrie spoke out of the corner of her mouth.

'It all seems to be going well.'

'It's like the swan,' murmured one of the senior clerks in reply. 'Gliding smoothly on the surface, paddling like hell underneath. Excuse my French, Miss Burgess.'

Accompanied by Archie, and followed by three or four other railway officials, the general manager swept in. He was a tall and elegant man, wearing a well-cut grey suit. He told a couple of surprisingly funny jokes, made a little speech, assured them he was on their side and asked if they had any comments to make.

'Don't be shy, now,' he said encouragingly. 'If you have any complaints, I want to hear them.'

There was some shuffling of feet. One or two minor points were raised. They were either answered there and then, or a promise was made to look into them. Carrie, who hadn't managed to get anywhere near Ewen, chanced a look at where he stood, over by the arched booking-office ticket window. He was looking a little green about the gills, and he was standing next to Matt. That wasn't going to help his confidence.

'Nobody else then?' asked the general manager, looking around the room. He was very pleasant, but both his official position and his commanding presence made him just a wee bit daunting . . . One of the officials glanced up at the clock on the wall.

Carrie caught Ewen's eye. *Go on*, she mouthed. She heard him clear his throat nervously and saw him bring the small white card she'd prepared out of his pocket. If she hadn't been so concerned with willing him through the next few minutes, Matt's double take as he began to read out from it would have been hilarious.

Ewen stumbled over a word and stopped dead for what seemed like ages, but could only have been a second or two. It was a bit stilted at first, but when he had finished reading and looked up, he became more fluent.

'It's not only a matter of fairness,' he said with considerable dignity. 'It's also one of practicality. No' having the right gear leads to people getting soaked and catching a chill, and then they're off work. That's hardly an efficient way of going about things.'

Despite his previous resistance to putting on the pan loaf, he was speaking a good deal more precisely than he normally did. He could do it when he wanted to, the wee toerag.

'You spoke about respect just now,' he went on, warming to his theme. 'You said we young people ought to have respect for the passengers, the company and our colleagues.' He had used the exact words which the general manager had used in his pep talk. 'Well,' he said, lifting a mutinous-looking chin, 'I think respect has to be earned.'

There was an audible intake of breath from one of the officials. Carrie looked anxiously at his boss. Was he going to bawl Ewen out? Sack him on the spot? To her amazement she saw the general manager nod slowly in agreement.

'I also think respect has to be mutual.' Ewen gave Carrie the ghost of a smile, acknowledging his use of a word of the week. 'Some folk – including some of our own colleagues – seem to think Permanent Way men are the lowest of the low.' He couldn't quite prevent his gaze sliding briefly to his left, where Matt was standing. 'But the trains couldnae run without us. And we're out there in all weathers. If the company really had respect for us and the job we do, they'd issue us with the equipment we need.'

He finished, and for a few seconds you could have heard the proverbial pin drop. Then the general manager spoke. 'What's your name, lad?'

'L-Livingstone, s-sir.' So confident a minute or two before, now he was nervous again. Carrie saw Matt's lip curl.

'First name?'

'Ewen.' He looked surprised to have been asked.

'Ewen Livingstone.' The general manager broke off. 'Forebears from Appin, eh?'

'Th-that's right, s-sir.'

'Well, young man, you've made your case very well, and I'm pleased to see someone who's so concerned for the well-being of his workmates. You and your squad will have new oilskins or waterproof jackets by the middle of next week. If they haven't arrived by Wednesday, ask Mr Burgess to get in touch with me immediately.' He walked across to where Ewen stood and stuck out his hand. 'Good day, Mr Livingstone.'

He and his entourage swept out as swiftly as they had swept in. A few mouths had dropped open, including Ewen's. There was a look of astonished delight on his face. He'd succeeded in solving the problem and the general manager of the Scottish region of the LNER had shaken a humble P-way man by the hand and called him 'Mr Livingstone'.

'Well said, Ewen.' That was Douglas, Mary's fiancé, perched up on the counter at the back of the booking office. A glower from one of the senior clerks sent him sliding sheepishly off it on to his feet.

'Aye, congratulations . . . *Mr Livingstone*,' put in another of the young signalmen.

'Gather round, *colleagues*,' chipped in a lad porter.

There was general laughter, the younger members of the

conciliation grades obviously feeling Ewen had struck some sort of a blow for them too. Several of the clerks were generous-spirited enough to clap him on the back or shake him by the hand as they piled out of the over-crowded office.

Carrie stood back, as pleased as punch. This must be how the teachers of clever pupils feel at prize-giving, she thought. Laughing at someone's parting shot, Ewen spun round as she came up behind him. 'Did I do all right?'

'You know you did,' she said warmly. 'You were great.'

'Aye. Well done,' came a cool voice. 'I'd never have believed you had it in you. Shouldn't you be running along now, though? The company doesn't pay any of us to stand around doing nothing, you know.' Matt gave a cold little laugh. 'Although P-way men do seem to spend an awful lot of time leaning on their shovels.'

Everyone else had disappeared. There were only the three of them in the booking office. Beside her, Carrie felt Ewen stiffen. She sent out a silent but heartfelt message. *Don't rise to it. Please don't rise to it.*

'As a matter of fact,' she heard him saying, 'I'm on my own time at the moment. I've got a rest day today and tomorrow. So no, I don't need to be running along now.'

He had said that last sentence perfectly, each word carefully and precisely enunciated.

'Well, in that case, get out of my booking office.' Matt's voice sank to a low growl. 'Or do I have to throw you out?'

Carrie put herself physically between them. They could both lose their jobs if anything developed here.

'Matt,' she pleaded, looking up into his dark eyes, 'please don't be so horrible. Can't we all be friends?'

'Friends?' he asked bleakly. 'You expect me to be friends with someone who was born in the gutter and who's never going to climb out of it? He'll drag you down there with him,

134

Carrie. Don't you know that going out with him is already beginning to damage your reputation?'

'Right, that's it. *That is it!*'

'Ewen! No!'

But he wasn't listening to her. It all happened so fast. First Ewen thrust her out of the way, then she was watching, horrified, as he grabbed Matt by the throat and slammed him up against the wall. He drew his hand back and made a fist . . . This can't be happening, she thought. Please God, let this not be happening.

'Told-her-about-your-mother-yet?' panted Matt, clawing at the fingers splayed across his throat. Ewen froze.

Carrie darted forward. She had to get him out of here very soon, before anyone else came back in. He seemed dazed, but he had released his grip on Matthew's throat and he was allowing her to pull him away.

'I told you that day at the Art Galleries, Matt,' she said quietly. 'I know all about him being illegitimate.'

Unexpectedly, Matthew laughed. But it was Ewen his gaze was fixed on, not her. 'Didn't have the guts to tell her, Livingstone? Like me to do it for you?'

'Tell me what?'

Neither of them answered her. Matt was smiling: a horrid, knowing, thin-lipped little smile. Ewen stood slumped against the door. He'd been the aggressor, ready and willing to smash his fist into Matthew's face, but right now he looked like a man who'd taken a blow.

'Tell me what?' she asked again.

Ewen straightened up. 'No' here,' he said. 'Not in front of him.' He turned on his heel and wrenched open the door.

They were in Kelvingrove Park, standing in front of one of the statues.

'That's Lord Kelvin.'

'And what's he famous for?' Carrie asked gently. The three words were the first Ewen had uttered since she'd followed him out of the station. They'd taken the tram along Dumbarton Road in complete silence.

'He was a great scientist and inventor. Starting studying at the Uni when he was only eleven years old. Later on he came up with a different temperature scale. Different from Fahrenheit and Centigrade, I mean. They call it degrees Kelvin, after him.'

And what, she wondered, as they walked slowly through the park towards the Art Galleries, are you about to come up with? The trees which lined the path gave way to grass, allowing Glasgow University to come into view. High up on Gilmorehill, its ornate neo-Gothic tower reached into an azure sky, unmarred by the smallest patch of white.

'I've always wanted to climb up there,' said Ewen suddenly. 'I used to imagine jumping off it. Only I wouldnae plummet to the ground like a stone, I'd turn into a bird and fly away. Leave my life behind, become a different person altogether . . .'

His voice trailed off. Thoroughly alarmed by this queer little speech, Carrie tugged on his sleeve.

'Ewen, why don't we go and have afternoon tea somewhere? There's that nice Italian café in Byres Road. My treat. What d'you say?'

He stopped dead under an old beech tree which stood in solitary splendour by the side of the path and looked at her. 'You mean you don't want to know what the great mystery is?'

'Is it such a mystery?'

'There's times when I think the whole world knows. Apart from you. Somehow it hasnae come to your ears. No' for the lack o' some folk trying,' he added, his voice filled with bitterness. He set his back against the trunk of the tree. 'I

136

suppose I always knew it was too much to hope for that you wouldnae find out.'

'You don't have to tell me,' she said firmly. 'Only if you want to.'

The grim expression on his face relaxed. 'You're so sweet, Caroline Burgess,' he said softly. His eyes flickered briefly shut, then opened again. He regarded her thoughtfully. 'My mother was a streetwalker, hen. That's how she made her living.'

'Oh,' breathed Carrie. Only she thought she had spoken, but nothing seemed to have come out.

Chapter 13

'Did you hear what I said, Carrie? My mother went with men for money. She was a prostitute. What folk hereabouts call a *hure.*'

Ewen was still pronouncing his words carefully. He'd uttered that most dreadful of all the insults which could be flung at a woman with an almost delicate precision. Carrie had always thought the Scottish version sounded a great deal worse than its standard English equivalent.

'That makes me the son of a *hure*, of course.'

'I heard you,' she whispered, wincing at this apparently calm description of himself.

'She hated it, you know,' he said conversationally. 'It made her feel dirty. She was always washing herself. Down there. Between her legs.'

Carrie's face burst into flame. His head tilted back against the tree, Ewen didn't notice the effect his brutally frank words were having on her. He was too busy remembering.

'She was aye cleaning the house, too. Trying to wash them away. All those respectable men who came to her behind their wives' backs. All those respectable men who go to church every Sunday.'

'She brought them home? Her –'

Carrie broke off. She didn't have the vocabulary for this. What was the correct word? Customers? Clients? Ewen gave her another alternative.

'I made her bring them home. She used to go up to Blythswood Square. That was her pitch. One night she came back from work in a hell of a state. One o' the punters had beaten her up, refused to pay for her services.'

Back from work. Her services. It sounded so matter-of-fact.

'So after that I followed her a couple of times, kept out of sight, but within earshot in case she met wi' that kind o' trouble again.'

He turned his head to look at her, a sad little smile playing about his wide mouth. 'Pathetic, eh? What could I have done, skinny wee runt that I was? I didnae have the muscles then that I do now. I could only have been about twelve.'

He looked away again, towards the spire of the university. Carrie wondered what he was really seeing. In his mind's eye.

'She found me out, of course. One of her pals spotted me. Ma hit the roof. *Christ!* My ears rang for a week wi' the tongue-lashing she gave me that night.'

The momentary spurt of amusement faded from his face. 'Then it happened again. Someone else who didnae want to pay for his pleasure.' His voice hardened. 'Or who found some o' that pleasure in hitting a defenceless woman. You get men like that. There's a woman up my close who's married to one o' them. He lays into her every Saturday night when he comes home from the pub. He's no' the only one. No' by a long chalk.'

Carrie shook her head. She knew nothing of this world. For the first time, with a strange mixture of shame and humility and pity for Ewen, she realised how protected and safe her own life had been. 'And you insisted your mother brought them home after that? Did the neighbours not object?

Somehow the shrewd wryness of his glance summed up the huge gulf between them. They'd been brought up in the same small place, but the distance between the way their lives had

140

been led was as great as the millions of miles which separated the earth from the moon.

'Do you think she was the only working girl in Partick, hen?'

That was another phrase Carrie had learned, then. A working girl. And no, it had never really occurred to her that things like that were going on a few hundred yards from her own front door. Lots of things had never occurred to her.

They had to her mother, she realised now. The revelation came with a jolt, like the feeling Carrie sometimes got as she lay in bed, that sense of missing a step: an odd little flutter of blind and unreasoning panic. Life was precarious. Respectability was even more so. One false step and you would plunge into the abyss, falling down a fissure so deep you'd never be able to claw your way back up to the surface.

'She'd take them into the house,' Ewen said, 'and I'd sit outside on the stairs until they had finished.'

She could see him: a skinny wee runt, hunched miserably on a cold tenement landing, his knees drawn up and his tousled head sunk forward on them. Until his mother and the man she'd brought home with her had finished. A business transaction. Something bought and something sold.

She studied his face, watching the shadows cast on it by the sun-dappled leaves above his head as the branches of the old beech tree bobbed gently to and fro.

'She met this man . . . thought he was going to help her get out of it. He was nice to me. At first.' Ewen gave a mirthless laugh. 'That soon changed. He wanted to live off her, you see. There are men like that, too,' he said drily. 'He thought knocking me about a bit would persuade her to go out more. She'd been doing the bare minimum when she met him, enough to pay the rent and keep us going.' Ewen's tone of voice became reflective. 'I think him having a go at me was the final straw.'

'What happened?' whispered Carrie, her heart aching for him. With an upbringing like that, she supposed it was inevitable that he himself would turn to violence when he was roused. The thought of his fist pounding into Matt's face made her sick to her stomach.

'On the night after my sixteenth birthday she couldnae stand it any more,' the quiet voice continued. 'She cooked me a meal – toad-in-the-hole, my favourite. I couldnae figure out why I was getting a treat two days in row. She'd baked me a cake the night before, you see.'

Carrie did see. It must have brought it all back when she'd done the same for his nineteenth birthday.

'She lifted one of the floorboards and showed me where there was some money hidden. Forty pounds that she'd saved. From her work,' he added carefully. 'She kissed me and told me she loved me, said I was the best thing that had ever happened to her.' The deceptively calm voice grew husky. 'I was never to forget that. Then she said she was going out for a walk. I asked if I would come with her, but she just smiled and told me to enjoy my tea. She needed to clear her head.' He paused. 'I'll never know if she managed that. I hope she did.'

He paused again. Carrie's heart was thumping, dreading whatever was coming next.

'What I do know is that she didnae walk very far,' he said at last. 'Only as far as the Clyde. They fished her body out at the Dalmuir Bend a week later.'

Carrie's eyes flooded with tears. She wanted to say something, attempt to offer him some comfort, but she couldn't speak. She moved closer to him and laid her hands on his arms. 'Och, I've made you sad,' he said softly. 'I didnae mean to do that.'

She could only shake her head, and for a few minutes they stood together in silence under the beech tree. 'How did you manage?' she asked at last. 'You were still only a boy.'

'I grew up quickly,' he said drily. 'My ma's pal helped. The money under the floorboards paid the rent for a good long while. Then your father gave me a job. I'll aye be grateful to him for that.' He was studying her face. 'Come on,' he said abruptly. 'I'll walk you home.'

'I'll get the tram.'

'I'll see you to the tram stop then.'

They walked round the outside of the Art Galleries building, not through it as they could have done. It would be full of high-spirited children, dispatched there by harassed mothers wondering if the school holidays were ever going to be over. Some of the wee Partick scruffs would be sticking their tongues out at the middle-class children from Hyndland and Hillhead and Park Circus trailing around dutifully after their mothers or nursemaids.

Rich or poor, well-dressed or in hand-me-downs, most of those children would have loving mothers. Your mother loved you. That was a given fact. Despite his terrible childhood, it was obvious that Ewen's mother had cared very deeply for him. As he walked beside her towards the main road, silent now that his terrible story was told, Carrie hoped with all her heart that he found consolation in that.

She sat on the side seat of the tram, and made the mistake of looking back. He was walking slowly away from the Kelvin Hall, shoulders hunched and head bowed. Her tram gathered speed, clanked over the Kelvin and swung round, heading for Partick Cross. Ewen was lost to view.

Carrie was in her mother's arms, sobbing her heart out. 'Oh, Ma, I didn't know! I never realised what you were talking about all this time! You should have told me!'

Standing beside his entwined womenfolk, her father patted

143

her on the shoulder. 'There, there, lass. Your mother couldn't tell you. You had to hear it for yourself. I'm glad young Ewen found the courage to tell you.'

Carrie lifted her head from her mother's shoulder and wiped her eyes with her hands. Esther's grip on her daughter's waist slackened. 'Come and sit down, pet.' She guided her into one of the big red armchairs, pulled up a footstool and started rubbing her daughter's hands, as she had when Carrie was a child and had gone to play outside on a winter's day forgetting to put her mittens on.

'She's awful cold, Archie. Maybe we should light the fire.'

Once, when she was about ten years old, the three of them had gone on a railway outing to St Andrew's. The *haar* had been down, the East Coast fog. Carrie felt now as she had that day, that there was something important out there, hidden within the folds of the all-enveloping mist, but she couldn't seem to reach it.

A sound came back to her: the deep note of a lighthouse's foghorn, tolling like a muffled bell somewhere in the distance. Her mother's voice, too, seemed to be coming from a long way off. Carrie fought her way up out of the mist, slid one hand out of Esther's grasp, wiped her eyes again and sniffed.

'Don't be daft, Ma, we don't need the fire lit. It's not even the end of August yet.'

Her father was hovering over both of them. She needed to lift those anxious lines from his forehead. 'Maybe I'll just go to bed early with a piggy. That'll keep me warm.'

Esther jumped to her feet. 'Aye, that's the best thing. I'll bring you some soup on a tray and sit with you for a wee while.'

'You take the lassie through to her bedroom, Esther. I'll boil the kettle for the hot water bottle and put the soup on to heat.'

She turned at the door of the living room. Her father was on his way to the kitchen and her mother was at her elbow.

'I'll be all right,' she said, directing the comment at both of them. 'Don't worry about me.'

'You'll be fine,' agreed Esther. 'A good night's sleep and you'll be right as rain. We know that. Don't we, Archie?'

'Aye, of course we do,' he said stoutly.

Her father was watching her. It was the evening of the following day and Carrie was helping him in the garden.

'What next, Daddy?' she asked cheerfully.

She knew she hadn't fooled him, but he smiled and asked her to fetch him the graip. He needed to level out the areas in the potato patch from which they'd already lifted tatties. There would be some still lying there, fallen back below the surface when Carrie or Esther had shaken the shaw free of earth.

'There's maybe enough to do the next couple o' days,' he said. 'Then we can leave the rest to grow a wee bit more.' He scowled at the summer sky. 'If we get some rain to allow them to swell up, that is.'

She fetched the big fork from the garden shed. While the central part of this remarkable structure had been purchased, it had been added to over the years, acquiring what Carrie irreverently referred to as the west wing and the east wing. To her father's considerable amusement, a few school lessons on architecture had supplied her with another description: the semi-Gothic shed.

He raised his tomato plants in the lean-to greenhouse which adjoined it, carefully explaining to his daughter that, contrary to popular opinion, tomatoes were a fruit, not a vegetable. Like an apple or an orange, they carried their seeds on the inside.

He had taught her a lot about gardening. She knew that

potatoes were an excellent plant for cleansing the soil, that you should have your early varieties in no later than St Patrick's Day – 17 March – and that you should practise rotation of crops if at all possible.

Apart from five neat rows of raspberry bushes, which needed sturdy and permanent support and consequently had to stay where they were from year to year, Archie religiously followed his own advice. The ground became tired if you continually planted the same thing in it. It wasn't easy soil to work, being heavy and full of clay. Both he and Carrie were firmly of the opinion that you could probably make very good pots out of it.

He fed and lightened it regularly with bone meal. Sprinkling a little of it along the drills before the seed potatoes were planted had always been one of Carrie's jobs. She couldn't help him much with the heavier jobs, but the lighter tasks were fine.

'Thanks, hen,' he said, taking the graip from her. She'd remembered to bring the old tin basin too, the one in which they usually gathered the tatties. 'You're a big help.'

Her bottom lip wobbled.

'Och, lassie,' he said gently. 'It'll all come out in the wash, you know.'

She raised the back of her hand to her mouth, forced the tears back. 'I keep thinking about Ewen. Wondering how he's feeling.'

'You're fond of the laddie.' It was a statement, not a question, but she gave him a quick nod of agreement anyway. Archie's eyes narrowed consideringly. 'But you're fond of Matthew Campbell too?'

She nodded again. Impossible to tell her father that while fond might be exactly the right word to describe her emotions towards Ewen, it didn't begin to cover the feelings Matt aroused in her. It was the difference between affection and passion, she supposed. Yet that affection had grown very deep over the past couple of months, had begun to seem something very real and solid . . .

'I'm all mixed-up, Daddy,' she confessed. 'I don't know what I feel and I don't know what I think.'

'Dangerous occupation, thinking. Probably why lots o' folk try to avoid it altogether. That's better,' he said, seeing her smile. He put his hand on her shoulder and gave it a quick squeeze. 'Will you take some advice from your ancient father?'

'Any time he cares to offer it.'

'Sleep on it, lass. Things aye look clearer in the morning.'

'You think so?' He released her shoulder and started sifting through the earth for the lost potatoes.

'I know so.'

He was right, of course he was. And she would see Ewen tomorrow when he came back to work, and would assure him that what he had told her about his mother would make absolutely no difference to their friendship. She knew he'd be worrying about that.

'I'll go and help Ma get the supper,' she said. 'Would you be wanting some Welsh rarebit?'

'That'll do me fine.' Archie had unearthed three decent-sized potatoes. He stooped, and tossed them gently into the basin.

'You're not scared the cheese will make you dream of your granny?'

That was another of Esther's admonitions, one she'd given up on some time ago. Archie was very fond of toasted cheese before he went to bed at night. He straightened up, winced, and put a hand to his back. Then he started wielding the graip again.

'I wouldnae mind if I did,' he confided. 'My granny was a

nice old soul. On ye go now. I'll be in as soon as I've done this.'

'I wish I'd been a boy,' Carrie said suddenly. 'I could have helped you more in the garden.'

He stopped swinging the fork and regarded her with loving eyes. 'I wouldnae want you any different, lass. I'm gey proud of you, you know.' His voice softened as he surveyed her. 'Beauty and brains and a kind heart too. What more could any father want?'

Her lip started to wobble again. She wanted to tell him she was proud of him too, that she loved him with all her heart, put into words how grateful she was for the way he'd brought her up. He had never laid down the law to her as so many other fathers did to their children. Throughout her life he had always shown her that he valued and respected her opinions and wanted to hear them.

She wanted to tell him all of those things, but they were both Scots, with the national tendency to shy away from public protestations of affection, so she didn't. All the same, standing there on the grass and looking at him smiling back at her from the middle of his vegetable patch, she couldn't resist asking a question.

'Shall I give you a kiss?' She took a step towards him, but he laughed and waved a jokingly dismissive hand in the direction of the back door.

'Don't be daft! Away ye go now. Tell your mother I'll be along in a wee minute.'

'What can your father be doing?' said Esther in exasperation fifteen minutes later. Six pieces of bread lay neatly on the rack of the grill pan, already toasted on their undersides. She'd placed slices of cheese on top of all of them, preparatory to sliding the pan back under the heat. She peered out of the window. 'And it'll be getting dark soon. The nights are fair drawing in, you know. Go and give him a shout, lass.'

Hiding a smile, Carrie went to the open back door. *The nights are fair drawing in.* It was an expression lots of people used at this time of year. It stated the obvious, and she didn't think she could be the only person who found it unintentionally hilarious. Summer in Scotland meant long days and light evenings, winter the opposite. There obviously had to be a transitional period, but each year this fact of life took some folk by surprise. There were those who seemed to regard it as a personal affront when the days began to shorten at the end of August.

She went to the open back door. Funny. She couldn't see him. Could he be tidying some tools away in the semi-Gothic shed, or perhaps working out of sight behind it? Maybe he was at the fence, speaking to someone he knew on the platform.

She stepped out into the garden and made her way along the back of the house. She looked in the shed. He wasn't there. She walked the few steps necessary to bring her round the other side of it and stopped dead. Through the tattie shaws she had caught a glimpse of something which shouldn't be there. Something black.

She went closer, and stumbled. She looked down stupidly at the graip. What on earth was it doing there? Never in a million years would her father have tossed it aside so carelessly. He was careful about things like that.

She lifted her eyes again to that unexplained splash of black. It was cloth, a heavy material. Trousers. Her father's black trousers. Lying flat on the ground.

'Ma!' she shouted, her voice thin and high-pitched. 'Ma!'

Carrie did what came naturally. She ran to the station for help. She found Matt. He hardly needed to listen to what she said.

One look at her face was enough to send him striding over to the porters' room. He was back in ten seconds flat, throwing out an instruction to the concerned-looking man who was following him into the booking-office.

'Hold the fort till I get back.'

'Is your father all right, pet?' asked the porter anxiously.

Carrie could only shake her head.

'That's what we're going to find out,' said Matt decisively. He reached for her hand. 'Come on, you, let's run.'

Esther was kneeling beside her husband, clutching his limp hand against her breast. Carrie went round and stood behind her, leaving space on the other side of the big body which lay so still and quiet among the potatoes. Matt would be able to do something. Like a great many railwaymen, he was a regular attender at first-aid classes run by the St Andrew's Ambulance Association.

He felt for a pulse: at the wrist and at the throat. He put his finger under Archie's nose. He bent his dark head and listened. Then he looked up at the two women. Carrie saw the compassion in his eyes, and waited while he tried to find a kind way to say it.

She had known anyway. From the moment she had stumbled on the graip. Archie Burgess was beyond first-aid. Her beloved father was beyond any kind of aid.

Chapter 14

There was a huge turnout for Archie's funeral. It brought Partick to a standstill, men doffing their bunnets as the cortège passed and women on the route it took to the church and the cemetery closing their curtains and lowering their window blinds as a mark of respect. The general manager of the LNER, so recently a visitor to the station, came back through from Edinburgh to witness the interment of a loyal and long-standing servant of the company. He even read the lesson at the funeral service.

That meant a lot to Esther, but Carrie found herself more touched by the sincerity of the expressions of sympathy made to them by many less exalted folk. Martin and Rita Sharkey, uncomfortable and uncertain of their welcome in a Protestant church, but nevertheless determined to pay their respects, were among them. With her mother's blessing, Carrie asked Sharkey to be one of the pall-bearers. He accepted with tears in his eyes.

Matthew was another of those carrying a cord as her father was laid to rest. That had been her mother's idea, but Carrie had concurred whole-heartedly with it. She had seen a different side of him since that dreadful moment in the garden – a considerate and sensitive aspect to his nature.

She stood with her mother and watched Martin Sharkey and Matthew and the others – old friends and colleagues all –

lay her father to rest. She did so with a mounting sense of unreality, understanding for the first time what people meant when they said they couldn't accept that someone was dead. She couldn't accept that she was never going to see her father again. Absurdly, as they sat at the funeral tea, she kept expecting him to walk through the door. It was like being at a party where the guest of honour was unaccountably absent.

In the days after the funeral there was a steady stream of callers to the station house. Some came to offer practical advice, others simply to express their condolences. Ewen was one of them, part of a small deputation of Permanent Way men, shunters and signalmen, all led by Sharkey. The ganger sat awkwardly opposite her mother in the living room, perched on the edge of one of the red armchairs. Ewen and the other men who'd come with him stood, even more awkwardly, behind it.

Sharkey fished something out of his pocket. It was a red neckerchief, done up as a bundle. Carrie heard the clink of coins as the Irishman leaned forward and held it out to her mother.

'We had a wee whip-round.' He coughed. 'We would be honoured if you and Miss Burgess would accept this small token of the esteem in which we held your husband.'

She saw her mother's eyebrows go up. Please God, she prayed silently, let her accept it in the spirit in which it's being offered. Esther didn't let her down, putting her hand out for the none-too-clean handkerchief, grubby after its sojourn in the deep pocket of the foreman's working jacket.

'Thank you, Martin,' she said gravely. 'And please thank all the other men most sincerely on behalf of Caroline and myself.'

Carrie saw the little group to the door, deliberately taking them through the front porch and round the side of the house to the platform gate. It had been a formal visit. It seemed to require a formal seeing out. They went out on to the platform one by one, solemnly shaking her hand as they did so. Sharkey and Ewen were the last to leave.

'Did you get your waterproof clothing?' she asked, suddenly remembering.

'Thank you, Miss B, we did indeed. They came the day we buried your poor father, God rest his soul.' He crossed himself – hurriedly, as though he were afraid the action might offend her Protestant sensibilities. 'That was something else he did for us.'

'Well,' she said lightly, hoping her voice wasn't going to break, 'Ewen helped quite a bit, did he not?'

She half-turned. He was standing behind her, deliberately hanging back. She had caught a glimpse of him at the funeral, white-faced and sombre at the back of the crowd gathered round the grave, but they hadn't spoken to each other since that day at Kelvingrove when he had made his great revelation. Only a week ago, she realised. It seemed a lot longer.

'Well, I'll be for home,' announced Sharkey. They barely noticed him go.

'How are you?'

She tucked a strand of hair behind her ear and managed a smile. 'Och, I'm fine. Well, not exactly fine, but we'll manage. Everyone's being so kind.'

Ewen's pale eyes were fixed on her face. 'If there's anything I can do, Carrie . . . For you or your ma . . . Well, you know you only have tae ask.'

'Thank you,' she said gravely. 'I appreciate that.'

'I mean it,' he said. 'Anything at all.' His gaze shifted, focusing on what lay behind her. 'Yer faither loved his garden, didn't he?'

'Yes,' she managed. 'He did.'

'It would be a shame for all his good work to go to waste over the autumn. I'd be glad to keep lending a hand. Whatever needs doin' before the winter comes.'

'Thanks, Ewen, but we're going to be out of here long before the winter arrives.'

That had been one of the official visits she and Esther had received. The man from the railway company's headquarters in Glasgow had been very kind too, but Partick was a busy station. It needed a firm hand at the helm. They already had a most suitable candidate in mind. Mrs and Miss Burgess were of course entitled to the statutory period of notice, but it had been tactfully suggested that if they could manage to move out sooner, it would be better for everyone.

Ewen turned surprised eyes on her. 'But that's terrible! Could they no' give you some more time?'

Carrie shrugged. 'There's no real point in delaying. Mrs Sharkey knows of a flat in White Street that might be suitable for us. We're going to look at it tomorrow.'

'White Street's nice,' he offered.

'Is it?' she asked indifferently. 'That's good. Ma would probably prefer somewhere up Crow Road or Hyndland, but we can't afford that.'

'Are ye no' left very well off?'

'You could put it that way,' she said drily. 'There's a pension, but it's not great.'

That had been last night's nasty surprise. Sifting through the family papers while her mother sat listlessly in front of the empty grate, Carrie had discovered that her father's pension amounted to the princely sum of ten shillings a week. Her parents had some savings, but after she'd done the arithmetic and calculated how many weeks or months that would keep them going for, she had realised how quickly the money could evaporate if they didn't have a regular wage coming in.

'I'm going to have to become a wage slave, Ewen,' she told him, striving for lightness. 'I'll not be doing my teacher training now.' That had been a bitter pill to swallow. Her exam results had dropped on to the doormat this morning. She had passed with flying colours.

He frowned. 'Is there no' a bursary ye could get or something?'

'I've written to Jordanhill to ask, but I'm not very hopeful. And I can't imagine that any bursary would pay enough to support two people, can you?'

Carrie gave him a brittle little smile.

She'd anticipated an argument when she told Esther she wouldn't be going to college. She didn't get one. That worried her, as did the fact that her mother was so calm. Frighteningly calm.

On the night of Archie's death the two Burgess women had clung to each other, weeping. The next day they'd had to compose themselves to deal with the hundred and one things a sudden death, or indeed any death, throws up: the funeral arrangements, informing officialdom, receiving all the visitors and telling the story of Archie's last moments over and over again, working out the state of their finances and exactly how they were going to adjust to their new circumstances.

Finding a new home was the first priority. The harassed and bad-tempered little man at the factor's office gave Carrie the key to the flat in White Street and told her he needed a decision that day. He had other people interested in taking over the tenancy.

She could believe it. It was a sought-after area, and the two apartment-room and kitchen was spick and span, if a little poky. Properties on the ground floor usually were, the entrance close to a building cutting into the available space. However small they were, whichever floor they were on, tenement homes in Glasgow were always referred to as houses, never flats.

'Well, Ma, what d'you think?' Carrie asked as they walked through the tiny lobby from the front room – which didn't really seem large enough to merit that title – into the equally small kitchen. It was like a hundred others she had seen: box bed against one wall, huge old range on the other, sink under the window and built-in cupboards occupying the fourth wall of the room. Carrie surveyed the remaining floor space. They'd be hard pressed to fit their dining table and chairs into it.

'It's a bit dark,' said Esther. She was standing staring at the range. Was she thinking of how much she was going to miss her smart and efficient little Baby Belling? There were lots of things they weren't going to be able to bring with them from the station house. Suppressing a pang, Carrie walked over to the window to look out at the back court.

Her mother was right. The house was dark. Hemmed in by tenements front and back, that was inevitable. Her eyes lit on an earth border running alongside the wall which divided their back court from the neighbouring one. There were a few straggly flowers in it.

'Looks like someone does a bit of gardening,' she said brightly.

'That's nice,' said Esther, but she didn't move from her position in front of the range.

Carrie turned, and indicated the built-in cupboards. 'You know,' she said, 'if we stripped those down and painted them a lighter colour that would make a big difference.'

'I suppose it would.' Esther had turned obediently to look, but her face was expressionless, her eyes empty and vacant.

'So shall we take it?' Carrie asked. They didn't really have much choice. Time was of the essence, and the rent was affordable.

'Do as you think best, pet,' said Esther.

It was a phrase Carrie was to hear more and more over the days and weeks which followed. Her mother pretended to listen to discussions about the future, but at the end of them she always left any decisions to be made to her daughter.

It was an awesome responsibility for a seventeen-year-old girl, but Carrie gritted her teeth and got on with it. There was no alternative – although she knew very well that Matthew Campbell wanted to offer her one. He was once again a frequent caller at the station house. As her mother grew more withdrawn, and the day of their removal to White Street drew ever nearer, Carrie was often glad of his company.

He had changed. He seemed softer, more humble somehow. He was also willing to let her hold him at arm's length – as she was doing at the moment. There was still the matter of how awful he had been to Ewen.

'Jealousy,' he told her, as he helped her sort out her father's clothes, a task she'd been dreading. Mary and Douglas were through in the living room, gently encouraging Esther to select which pieces of furniture and ornaments were to make the journey to their new home.

'Somebody could maybe get the use out of this suit.' He refolded a pair of trousers and slipped them neatly on to a hanger, replacing the waistcoat and jacket over them.

'He hardly wore it. That's what he called his funeral suit.' Her breath caught in her throat. 'Only he went to his own before he could wear it to anybody else's!'

'Och, Carrie. Come here.' Matt held out his arms, but she shook her head.

'I'm all right.' She took a deep breath and squared her

157

shoulders. 'You were explaining to me why you were so nasty to poor Ewen.'

Matt dropped his arms. 'I was jealous,' he repeated. 'Plain and simple. I'm not proud of myself, but the green-eyed monster had me in its grip.' When his comments evoked no response, his face grew more serious. 'I love you, you know,' he said quietly.

She did know. Matthew had always known what he wanted, never left her in any doubt about his feelings, but if she'd been too young to marry him before she was still too young to marry him now. What she needed was a job.

She might have her Higher Leaving Certificate, but she wasn't trained for anything. She enquired about doing a course in shorthand and typing, but even the short ones seemed to cost quite a lot of money. Nor was there any guarantee she would get a position at the end of it. There were so many people looking for work these days.

She wondered about applying to a shop, perhaps one of the high-class ones which required well-spoken and intelligent assistants to deal with their wealthy clientele. She tried several. They all told her the same thing: she was too young, she had no training or experience, come back when she had done something else for a year or two. It was all very dispiriting.

'Are you sure you'll be all right, Carrie?'

'I'll be fine, Mary.' She gave the Baby Belling one last wipe. 'Is that Douglas come for you now?'

Her friend nodded. She'd been helping with the final cleaning of the house, preparatory to Mr and Mrs Gibson, the new stationmaster and his wife, moving in the next day. 'Let's see now,' she said. 'All the floors are done, aren't they? So that means we can take the galvanised bucket and the mop. I've got the sweeping brushes, the stiff one and the softer one. What does that leave you to carry?'

'Just the shovel, the wee brush and the clouts and things. Matthew's calling past when he finishes his shift. He said he'd walk me along to White Street, so he can help me with those.'

Douglas strolled into the kitchen. 'It's gey sad to see it so empty –' he began, and then broke off, yowling in pain and turning accusing eyes on his beloved. 'What did you kick me for, Mary?'

'Men,' she said, rolling her own eyes heavenwards. 'Not the most tactful o' creatures, are they?'

Carrie smiled. 'It's all right,' she said. 'I'll forgive you, Douglas.'

'We could stay with you till Matthew comes,' said Mary. 'It's no bother.'

Carrie shook her head. 'You've done enough already, Mary. Both of you,' she said, including a still rather perplexed-looking Douglas in her thanks. He'd helped with the removal two days before. 'I'm really grateful. My mother just couldn't face coming back today. You know?'

'Aye. I know,' said Mary, her brown eyes soft with sympathy. 'Well, if you're sure, Carrie . . .'

'I'm sure. I'd kind of like a wee while here on my own, anyway.'

'Aye,' repeated Mary. Then she grew brisk, indicating the heavy bucket in the corner of the kitchen. 'Douglas, if you would be so kind.'

After they had left, Carrie walked slowly through the echoing rooms, quickly giving up any pretence she was checking to see that everything had been done. She was saying her goodbyes.

The grate of the living room fire was empty. The vase of dried flowers had made it along the road, but they had no room for the big red armchairs. The beds were staying too. Carrie had negotiated a price for everything they were leaving with the Gibsons. The extra money would come in handy.

She went in and out of her parents' bedroom quickly. That was altogether too painful. Oh, Daddy, she thought, we're going to miss you so very much!

Fighting back tears, she stood in the middle of her own bedroom. This was where she had grown up, dreamed her girl's dreams. She remembered winter days playing in here, evenings spent studying, Sunday afternoons laughingly trying to stand still while Esther pinned up the hem on a skirt, or fitted a new dress on her.

She could see her father carefully carrying through a shovel full of hot coals from the living room to start off her own fire so that she wouldn't be cold. She'd been so well loved and cared for. Now it was up to her to return that love and care, to hold together what was left of the Burgess family.

About to leave the room, she checked herself. She'd almost forgotten Gertie the giraffe, standing up on her stiffened legs in the middle of the bare mattress of Carrie's bed. Holding the stuffed toy to her as though it were a baby, she went out into the garden.

Matthew found her there twenty minutes later, standing with her back to the semi-Gothic shed and clutching Gertie tightly to her bosom.

'Carrie?'

It came out like a dam bursting. 'I can't bear to leave this house! I was so happy here! We were all so happy here!'

He pulled her to him, giraffe and all. 'Life's never going to be the same again,' she said brokenly, her cheek pressed against his shoulder.

His hand was at the back of her head, gently rubbing her hair. 'No,' he agreed, 'but life will be good again, I promise you.'

She began to sob. 'I've always belonged here. I was

the stationmaster's daughter. Now I'm not going to belong anywhere.'

His arms felt solid and warm and heavy. Possessive too, but there was something comforting in that now she was adrift in a cold, hard world.

'You could belong with me. You only have to say the word.'

She turned her face up to him, and he bent his dark head and kissed her brow, the gentlest she had ever known him. 'One day I'll be the stationmaster here, Carrie. I could bring you back home.'

Her tear-filled eyes were wide and sad and trusting. 'Could you, Matt? Could you?'

'Say yes,' he urged. 'Please, Carrie, say yes!'

She laid her head once more against his shoulder. Her voice came out muffled by the fine wool of his jacket. 'Not now, Matt. Not now. Will you . . . will you ask me again another time? When I'm not so upset?'

His arms tightened around her. 'You can count on it.'

A few days later Carrie had a brainwave. The railway! Although she'd never actually heard of any female clerks – it was regarded as a man's job – she didn't think there was any formal rule about not employing women. She was sure she could pass the exam and that she would be perfectly capable of doing the job.

The pay for a junior clerk wasn't great, but it wasn't awful either. With her father's pension, and if they were really careful, they might just manage to make ends meet. It was also a job she would enjoy and it would keep their connection with the railway.

She composed a careful letter to the general manager in Edinburgh – nothing like going straight to the top – and waited eagerly for his reply. When it arrived, her heart soared. He had arranged an interview for her at the company's offices in central Glasgow.

She told Esther there was some paperwork to be sorted out about her father's pension, put on her forest green costume and her Tyrolean hat, and set off with a spring in her step. With a bit of luck, she might be coming home with news which would really cheer her mother up.

Her optimism was to be short-lived. The man who saw her was very mannerly. He gave her tea out of a china cup and saucer. He sympathised with her in her great loss and told her what an asset men like Archie Burgess were to the railway company. He also made it absolutely clear he had no job to give to Archie's daughter.

'You see, Miss Burgess,' he explained, brushing some biscuit crumbs off his pin-stripe suit, 'whilst you would very probably make an excellent clerk . . .' he smiled benignly at her '. . . or in your case, *clerkess* – we really can't give a man's job to a woman, particularly not with the state the country's in at the moment. A man has a family to support, after all.'

'But I've got my mother to support,' Carrie said in exasperation. 'We're out of the station house and have rent to pay.'

He placed his own cup and saucer on a silver tray on the beautiful mahogany desk between Carrie and himself and stood up. The interview was over. She found herself being ushered politely to the door, biting her lip in disappointment.

'There, there, my dear,' he said soothingly, 'a pretty girl like you will be married soon, I've no doubt. Then you can give all your problems to your husband to sort out.'

She was still smouldering with rage and frustration when she got back to White Street.

'It's only me,' she called as she took her key out of the lock, but there was no reply. She found Esther in the kitchen, sitting on the edge of the box bed with her head bowed. Carrie knelt down in front of her, expecting to see tears, but her mother's face bore the calm expression she was beginning to find just a wee bit unnerving.

Her mother spoke without preamble. 'I've been to the Western Infirmary this afternoon. While you were up in Glasgow.'

Alarmed, Carrie wrapped her fingers round Esther's wrist. 'What's wrong, Ma? Did you have an accident while I was out?'

She looked her mother over in puzzlement. She seemed fine, blooming with health and curiously peaceful. Esther extended her free hand and touched her daughter's face. 'That hat really suits you. You're such a bonnie girl.'

'Ma, tell me what's happened. Are you all right?'

Esther took her hand from Carrie's face and laid it against her own chest.

'I've got a growth,' she said. She placed her hand underneath the curve of her breast, sliding her fingers round towards the armpit. 'Right about here. There's nothing they can do.'

Carrie rose to her feet and sat down heavily on the bed. 'What do you mean, there's nothing they can do? Doctors can work miracles these days. If they catch things in time.'

'I've had it for nearly a year, lass. Seemingly it's spread right through me. That's what the doctor at the Infirmary said, anyway.' She smiled. 'He was very kind.'

'A year! Oh, Ma, why didn't you go to the doctor when you first noticed it?'

'I was more concerned about your father's health. I thought this wee thing I had couldn't matter very much compared to that.' Esther's smile faltered. 'I thought it might go away.'

'Oh, Ma,' Carrie said again, and her eyes filled with tears. In an instant, comforting arms were placed around her, pulling her into the warmth of her mother's body.

'Don't cry for me, pet,' said the quiet voice above her head. 'It means I'll be going to join your father a wee bit sooner than I had thought, that's all.'

'I can't lose the two of you! God couldn't be so cruel!'

'Hush, now. Sit up a wee minute. There now.' Esther had removed her daughter's jaunty little hat. Turning, she placed it carefully on the narrow shelf which ran between the box bed and the cooking range. Then she patted her lap.

'Lay your head down, lass, and I'll stroke your hair.'

Like a little child, Carrie did as her mother bid, curling her legs up on to the bed. When she had been a wee girl, this had been her special treat, a reward for submitting to having her hair brushed and combed and held back with clasps, tied up in rags at night to make ringlets or scraped back from her forehead during the day to make a neat ponytail.

'How long?' she asked, some time later. It might have been five minutes. It might have been fifteen.

The loving hand which was smoothing her hair didn't falter. 'A matter of months. Maybe six.'

She was lying facing the window. The sky was beginning to darken, the days shortening as the autumn approached. Esther must have felt the slight movement of her head, realised what she was looking at.

'The nights are fair drawing in.'

'Aye, Ma,' Carrie said softly. 'That they are.'

Someone had called her name. Lost in thought, she couldn't at first make out where the words had come from.

'Up here,' came the voice again. She lifted her gaze and saw Ewen, sitting atop a wall, a half-munched apple in his hand. He must be on one of his rest days.

'How's it going?' he asked easily.

'Not very well,' she confessed, looking up at him. He wore

164

no jacket or waistcoat, and his blue shirt was collarless and open at the neck. He needed a shave, she noticed. Probably he didn't always bother on the days he wasn't at work.

'Are you not cold?' she enquired. 'It's a bit nippy today.' It was approaching the end of October and there had been a businesslike frost the night before. She had left the buttons of her brown wool jacket open, but she was glad of its warmth and length, skimming down over her hips.

He contradicted her cheerfully. 'It's a beautiful day. Golden, ye might say.' He took two healthy bites from the apple and lobbed it over his shoulder.

She snorted. 'It might be golden for you, but it's been black and sooty for me. I've spent all morning trying to get the blasted range lit.'

She turned away from him, responding to a greeting called out from the other side of the road. There was a thud and she whirled around, startled. Ewen was standing right in front of her. 'Want me to come round and give it a go?'

'No, thanks, I think it's burning all right now.'

Her rejection of his offer had been too swift. His face clouded. 'And your mammy wouldnae give me houseroom anyway?' The coldness in his voice was the last straw. Tears welled up in her eyes. Sometimes she wondered where they all came from. Surely you had to run out of them eventually.

'Och, Carrie,' he said. 'I'm sorry, hen. I didnae meant to upset ye.'

'I don't want to disgrace myself in the middle of the street,' she told him in an anguished whisper. She remembered Oban and managed a strangled laugh. 'Isn't this where we came in?'

'Maybe, but I know a way out. Up ye come.'

Before she had time to think about it, he had interlaced the fingers of his hands to make a step and helped her shin up the wall on which he'd been sitting. Then he was there beside her.

'It's not as far to go on this side. Jump down.' He suited the action to the words and looked up at her in laughing invitation. The surprise had dried her tears. She blinked and swung her legs over. The wall enclosed a small grassy area, overgrown with grass and a few wild flowers. She reviewed the situation. Ewen had done it easily. Then again, he was used to leaping on and off railway platforms.

'Go on,' he urged. 'I double dare you. And I'll catch you anyway.'

He not only caught her, he also held on to her. Carrie looked him straight in the eye and issued a silent dare of her own: for him to go any further. He dared.

He might have looked rough and ready, but he smelled of fresh air and soapy skin and newly washed shirt. She laid her two hands flat on his chest, but she wasn't pushing him away. His mouth was cool and firm on her own and the feel of the bristles on his jaw and upper lip was a new, but not unpleasant, sensation.

When it was over, he pulled back and said a few simple words. 'I've wanted to do that for such a long time.'

A golden day, he'd said. His hair looked golden, sticking out from his head as usual and lit like a halo by the autumn sunlight. She peered over his shoulder and felt his grasp on her waist slacken slightly.

'What is this place?'

'The Quaker graveyard.'

'I don't see any gravestones. Do Quakers not approve of them?'

'I don't know. Can I kiss you again?'

She dropped the contrived fascination with their surroundings and looked sadly at him. 'I don't think that would be a very good idea.'

'Why not?'

'Because I'm going to marry Matthew Campbell. I decided this morning.'

It had been while she'd been struggling to get the range lit, as a matter of fact, sitting on a cold floor surrounded by crumpled up newspaper and half-charred bits of kindling and trying to choose between bursting into tears or swearing her head off at the antiquated piece of machinery, but Ewen didn't need to know that.

His hands slid off her waist. 'Why are you going to marry Matthew Campbell?' he asked, pale to his very lips.

'Because I love him,' Carrie replied, wondering why that was so hard to say. 'Because my mother wants to see me settled.' She shrugged her shoulders. 'Because I've got to marry someone.'

She realised too late that her attempt at flippancy had given an immediate hostage to fortune.

'You've got to marry someone? What's wrong with me, then?'

'You've never asked me,' she whispered.

'Well, I'm asking you now.' Ewen's breath was coming fast and shallow. 'Don't marry him, Carrie. Marry me instead.'

Chapter 15

The words came tumbling out, falling over each other in his urgency to convince her of his case.

'I know I'm no' on your level, but I could pull myself up. I know I could, Carrie. With you helping me with my reading and writing, I could go after a better job, make you proud of me. And we wouldnae need to have children straightaway if ye didnae want to. I could wear a French letter when we went to bed together.'

'Ewen Livingstone!' Her face was burning.

'Think about it, Carrie,' he urged. 'We could have fun together, you and me.'

'Fun?' She said it as though she had no idea what the word meant.

'With you coaching me maybe I could go in for a clerkship. Perhaps even become a stationmaster one day – take you and your ma back to the station house.'

It was the thought of Ewen and her mother living under the same roof that did it. Fatally, she laughed at him – and saw the eager light in his pale eyes fade.

'Ye think I'm no' capable of it?'

She shook her head in denial of that, but it was only her words which penetrated his brain. 'I'm going to marry Matt.'

'Ye cannae marry him, Carrie, ye cannae!'

All she could see was his angry face. He seized her arms

above the elbows and pushed her back against the wall of the little graveyard. He looked wild and despairing and it occurred to her to wonder if anyone would hear her if she screamed.

'So you love Matthew Campbell, do ye?'

Several things went through her head then. Before she could express any of them, Ewen spoke again. 'Are you sure ye don't love the fact that he lives up the hill, that his family's well off, that marrying him's going to save you from having to go out and work for a living like normal people? You and your precious mother, you're a right couple o' snobs!'

Carrie squirmed, trying vainly to release herself, the stone wall hard and rough against her back. 'How dare you say that about me?' She was shouting at him now. 'How dare you be rude about my mother!'

'How dare I? This is how I dare!'

He tightened his hold on her arms and jerked her towards him. His mouth was hard and passionate and demanding . . . and despite her anger, she felt herself respond to it. She was kissing him back.

The punishing fingers relaxed their grip. His lips grew gentle and coaxing. She relaxed into his body, her arms snaking up around his neck. He made a funny little noise somewhere way back in his throat and slid his hand inside her jacket.

She started violently, but he lifted his mouth off her own long enough to murmur a quick little reassurance. 'It's all right, lassie, it's all right.'

His fingers travelled up over the cream-coloured lacy jumper she wore, found the curve of her breast, began slowly to stroke it. Carrie wondered how it was possible that such a strong hand could be so gentle . . .

He was wrong. This wasn't all right. She began to struggle in earnest. He let go of her.

'What's wrong?' he asked thickly.

'I want you to stop. Right now.'

Carrie eyed him warily. You weren't supposed to lead a man on. That got them to a point where they weren't willing to stop, where they were no longer able to stop. If a girl did that she only had herself to blame. Ewen was staring at her, breathing heavily. Had he reached that point?

'Gonnae tell me you werenae enjoying that? Still gonnae tell me it's Matthew Campbell you love?'

He looked very menacing, bigger somehow, with his hands bunched into fists at his sides. Carrie panicked. 'If you don't let me out of here, I'm going to scream!'

In her whole life, nobody had ever looked at her in such a contemptuous way. 'What d'ye take me for? You really think I'm that kind o' a man? There's a gate over there.' He raised his arm and pointed. 'You'll find it easier to get out that way. We wouldnae want you doing anything that's beneath your dignity, would we now? Like being seen wi' me, for instance.' He hoisted himself up on to the wall.

'So long, Miss Burgess,' he said, his voice laden with sarcasm. 'I would say that it's been nice knowing ye, but ma mammy didnae bring me up to tell lies. Funny that, eh, a woman like her?' He gave her one last, unforgiving look before he dropped out of sight.

Carrie stood staring stupidly at the wall. Then, very slowly, she turned and headed for the gate out on to the street. It was behind two or three poor-looking trees. A golden day, he'd said. None of it felt very golden to her.

She pushed open the heavy wrought-iron gate and walked out into Keith Street. Ewen was nowhere to be seen, although presumably one of the closes she was walking past led to his house. Some children were playing in the middle of the road. A few of them were barefoot.

171

Three men stood round a close mouth on the other side of the narrow street. One of them said something and his two friends looked across at her and laughed. She quickened her step, heading for the main road with the sense of escaping from something. Nonetheless, she couldn't help throwing a swift glance back to the wall surrounding the old graveyard just before she turned the corner.

She'd gone in there like a child, clambering up the old stones and jumping down the other side. She'd left like a grown-up, walking sedately through the gate. She was a woman now, not a girl. That part of her life was over.

Chapter 16

'Show of presents?'

Her mother hadn't noticed the note of disapproval in Shona Campbell's voice. The three women were taking afternoon tea together in Byres Road, discussing arrangements for the wedding. Carrie heard the disdain loud and clear, saw also the little wrinkle of the nose which accompanied it. Her future mother-in-law obviously found the custom too working-class for her taste. Esther, she knew, had been fishing for an invitation, anxious to show off the towels and tablecloths and half tea sets her daughter had received up the hill rather than at White Street.

Carrie had privately determined that wild horses wouldn't drag her and her gifts to the Campbell family home any sooner than was strictly necessary. She wasn't going to have Matthew's mother looking down her elegant nose at good friends like Mary and Douglas and Rita Sharkey and her daughters.

'Yes,' she put in, 'we're having it the weekend before, on the Friday night and the Saturday afternoon. You'd be very welcome to come along, Mrs Campbell.'

She'd be Mrs Campbell herself soon. The knot was to be tied on the first Saturday in December. She supposed it was natural to feel a flutter of nerves. Getting married was a big step.

Matt was doing his best to reassure her she'd made the right decision. He was so happy: promising he'd look after her forever, promising her the earth. She'd told him about Esther's diagnosis and he'd simply wrapped his arms about her and held her close for a long, long time. When she finished crying he started planting little kisses all over her face.

'You've got me now,' he said. 'You don't have to cope with it all by yourself. I'll look after you. I'll look after everything.'

After that, his kisses became more passionate . . . Everything became more passionate. Carrie blushed to think of it, but she knew she would have let him go on, had even mumbled as much to him . . . but he had pushed her away.

'Not till we're married,' he'd said hoarsely. 'Then I'll show you how I really feel about you.'

She didn't doubt it. She had to take another drink of coffee. She could really have done with some iced water.

'Anything else I can do for you, ladies?'

It was the café owner's son, a boy Carrie knew to say hello to. Young as he was, he'd obviously inherited not only his father's dark good looks but also his continental charm. He'd been flirting outrageously with her since they'd come in here, and she'd been flirting right back.

Carrie felt a little spurt of childish pleasure when she sensed Shona Campbell's disapproval of the banter being tossed backwards and forwards between the young man and herself. She was going to be living in the same house as this woman very soon, not a prospect she relished – to put it mildly.

Matt said it was the sensible thing to do. They didn't have enough money put by yet to get a decent place of their own. Living with his parents for a few months would allow them to save towards that. She wondered if he was thinking that a few months' delay might see the house in White Street becoming available. She'd chosen not to put that thought into words.

Esther, insisting that all the usual traditions and customs

were observed, was throwing herself into the preparations for the wedding with an enthusiasm which some folk were surprised to see in a recently widowed woman. Carrie, the only person able to see the frantic edge underlying the happy bustle of activity, was finding some things almost unbearably poignant.

Stroking one set of particularly good quality towels, Esther had come out with a pleased, 'These will last you a lifetime,' seemingly unaware of the pathos of the statement.

This morning, Carrie had stood back and watched her in animated discussion with the people at the City Bakeries about the wedding cake, and the little favours which were going to adorn it. Esther was determined to give her daughter as good a wedding as she could afford. At the same time, in a display of down-to-earth practicality which took the breath away, she was calculating how much money needed to be left to pay for another up-coming event: one which wouldn't include little silver slippers and bells and lucky horseshoes.

He deserved a treat. These were his last few days as a bachelor. He'd had his stag night, of course, but although a fair amount of drink had been consumed and a great many off-colour stories recounted and dirty jokes told, that had been a relatively sedate celebration. The presence of his father and various other older male relatives had seen to that.

The slope of the street flattened out. Matthew continued to walk purposefully towards Dumbarton Road. It was much better to look confident, not slink along in the shadow of the buildings like a thief. It was early yet. Most people would still be finishing their tea. All the same, he was glad of the darkness of the evening, the inadequacy of the street lights and the wisps of November fog. He would hate to bump into Carrie or any of her friends tonight.

He felt the usual stirrings at the thought of his bride-to-be. She was so young and lovely, so fresh and untouched – so unlike the young women he was planning on spending the next hour or so with, tarts and strumpets all.

Mind you, they knew their trade. Over the years women like them had taught him a lot. Once they saw the colour of your money they were all over you. Quite literally. He crossed over the main road, his lips curving in anticipation. Tonight was a special occasion. Could he justify the expense of having two girls at once? The thought quickened his blood and his step.

Carrie would be shocked to the core if she knew his plans for the evening. Not that she would ever find out about any of this. Once they were married he wouldn't need the outlet. He was looking forward to doing some teaching himself . . .

That might give her a few shocks too, but it was only to be expected. She was a nice girl, after all, but at the same time she'd be anxious to please him. He turned into the side street. He was definitely going to have two of the strumpets tonight.

Carrie was wearing a grass skirt. Mary had fashioned it out of green crêpe paper, graciously decreeing that she might be allowed to wear her tennis skirt underneath, thus preserving some degree of maidenly modesty. At the moment, however, one of the other girls was kneeling at her feet, shortening the hems of the divided skirt with safety pins.

'They'll give you more money if they get a good flash o' leg. And you've got nice legs, Carrie. What's wrong wi' showing them off a wee bit?'

'It's November,' she muttered, doing her best to scowl at the image looking back at her from the long mirror on the front of the wardrobe. 'I'll freeze.'

'No, you'll not,' said Mary, coming into the front room

carrying assorted bits and pieces over her arm. 'You might be a South Sea maiden, but we are letting you keep your jumper on,' she pointed out, looping three shell necklaces over Carrie's head.

'The alternative being?'

'Something your intended wouldn't care for one little bit,' said Mary, grinning wickedly. 'Here, take this.'

'My intended wouldn't care for any of this, I don't think,' she replied, trying to make sense of the piece of white cotton Mary had handed her. It had two straps and a large broderie anglaise frill. An apron?

'They don't go in for this sort of thing up the hill?'

'What d'you think? Mary, what on earth . . .'

Her friend took the material from her, shook it out and swung it up and on to Carrie's head, tying the straps in a large bow under her chin. It was an outsize baby's bonnet.

'There. What do you think?'

'The phrase "dog's breakfast" springs to mind.'

Esther, sitting on the edge of the bed and watching with great interest, chuckled. Carrie caught her eye in the mirror, and heaved a mournful sigh. 'I suppose I'll have to go along with it, Ma.'

'I think you will, pet,' responded Esther, her eyes twinkling.

The girls led Carrie along Dumbarton Road, making as much noise as possible. One of them had a tambourine, two of the others home-made drums: empty biscuit tins and wooden spoons. Mary was in charge of collecting donations for the happy couple – in a chamber pot, as tradition dictated.

'Chuck your change in the chanty!' she yelled happily.

'And I always thought you were such a nice refined girl,' said one man with a roguish wink as he emerged from one of the many pubs on their route. 'You too, Miss Burgess,' he said, taking in her costume.

Carrie winked back. She was beginning to enjoy herself. The noise had brought other drinkers outside, even some she recognised as men who, given half a chance, could drink for Scotland. They cheered her on, tossing jokes into the air and change into the chamber pot. It was the same all the way along the street.

At one hostelry it was suggested the girls ought to sing for their supper. Nothing daunted, Mary launched into *Sweet Sixteen And Never Been Kissed*, which had been a big hit round the dance halls a year or so before. She couldn't hold a tune, and the title prompted hoots of good-natured derision – which made it all the funnier.

When she had finished, one of the men watching came back with *Button Up Your Overcoat*. Everyone joined in. Considering the time of year, it was a good selection, although Carrie had to admit she wasn't feeling the cold. She'd even pushed up the sleeves of her jumper.

Despite the many voices, some of them rather tuneful, Mary's off-key notes were still managing to make themselves heard. Wondering if she was ever going to recover from the fit of the giggles she was having, Carrie swung round towards the pub, aware of a couple of people standing there. She hoped they were enjoying themselves too.

She found she was able to stop laughing rather more easily than she had anticipated. Hands behind his back, one leg bent up so that the sole of his boot rested flat against the wood panelling of the pub frontage, Ewen Livingstone was standing watching her. He didn't look as if he was enjoying himself.

'Hello,' said Carrie. 'How's it going?' Her heart sank when she realised who was standing next to him: Janice Muirhead, gazing at her out of sullen eyes.

'I'm perfectly fine, Miss Burgess,' he said. 'It's real kind o' you to ask.'

Janice giggled, but Ewen didn't crack a smile. He was giving Carrie the top-to-toe treatment, eyes lingering on her bare legs, visible through the paper strips of the grass skirt. He spoke again, his voice too loud. She was glad the impromptu choir had gone on to perform another number.

'No need to ask how it's going wi' you. You're obviously delir . . . delir . . .' He took a run at it. 'Obviously deliriously happy.'

It still hadn't come out quite right. Carrie took a couple of steps towards him. 'Have you been drinking?' Hit by the smell of alcohol on his breath, she reeled back in disgust, but his hand shot out.

'Is it any o' your business if I want to buy myself a wee drink?'

'A wee drink?' she asked contemptuously. 'More like a great big drink.'

His hand tightened, and she remembered how he had held her in the Quaker graveyard. If she hadn't put a stop to it, how far would he have gone that day? *You really think I'm that kind o' a man?* No, she hadn't thought so, but then he'd never struck her as the kind to take strong drink either. She was disappointed in him.

Even in drink he was still strong. His fingers were digging into the soft skin of her forearm like Chinese bracelets, the tests of stoicism they used to do at school.

'You're hurting my arm.'

The words of his reply were perfectly clear but softly spoken, intended for her ears alone:

'You're hurting my heart.'

For a frozen moment, they lost themselves in each other's eyes. Then Janice came sauntering forward.

'Come on, Ewen, this is boring. I thought you and me were going for a walk.' She laid a hand on his shoulder and smiled insolently at Carrie. 'Somewhere nice and quiet.'

She reached between the two of them, placing her free hand on the back of Ewen's head, pulling him round to face her. 'Give us a kiss, handsome.'

Carrie made an exclamation of disgust, and would have turned away, but he was still holding on to her. Janice, lips parted in readiness, stretched up and kissed him. She took her time about it. Ewen responded in kind, but his eyes kept flickering to Carrie, making sure she was watching. She had very little choice.

When Janice finally came up for air, he ignored her, his attention all on Carrie.

'Let go of me,' she said quietly.

'Oh, look, Carrie,' shrieked a voice from behind her. One of the girls had broken off in mid-song. 'It's your *fee-on-say*!'

Her arm was dropped. Janice pulled Ewen away. Carrie turned and saw Matt.

'What exactly do you think you're doing, Carrie?'

She laughed nervously. 'Hello, Matt. Where did you spring from?'

He brushed the question aside. 'Never mind that. What's all this?'

Somehow she had known he would disapprove. Which was, she supposed, why she had accidentally-on-purpose forgotten to mention to him that she was going out with the girls this evening.

'It's only a bit of fun, Matt.'

'Fun? Getting dressed up and begging for money in the street?'

'It's not begging,' she protested. 'It's a way for people to wish us good luck. Everyone does it.'

'You're not everyone,' he said sternly. 'You're the station-master's daughter.'

She laid a conciliatory hand on his dark sleeve. 'Och, Matt, my father would have loved all this.'

'Well, I don't, and in a few days' time I'll be your husband. So I'm taking you home right now so you can get out of that silly rig-out. Look at the state of you! And showing your legs off to every Tom, Dick and Harry too.'

He shook her hand off and stood there, waiting. Over his shoulder she could see Ewen and Janet, watching to see how things were going to develop. Mary, despite being out of earshot, must also have sensed that all was not well. Carrie was aware of her friend's anxious eyes on her.

In a few days' time I'll be your husband. I haven't promised to obey you yet, she thought mutinously. His brows were down, straight and angry lines over stormy eyes. He was so angry with her he hadn't even noticed that Ewen was standing a few yards away.

Mary appeared at her shoulder. 'Hello, Matthew,' she said politely. 'Everything all right, Carrie?' An undercurrent of anxiety ran through the simple question.

'I'm taking Caroline home, Mary.'

'Oh?' Mary's eyebrows flew up. 'Are you wanting to go home now, Carrie?'

No, she wasn't. However, this situation was only going to be resolved if one of them was prepared to back down. It wasn't going to be Matthew. That much was obvious. She really didn't want to have a major falling-out with him a matter of days before their wedding. It would upset her mother, for one thing.

Added to which, if she went meekly with him now, and Janice Muirhead used the brains she undoubtedly had to haul Ewen off somewhere, there would be no need for another, potentially rather more dangerous, confrontation to erupt.

'Let's call it a day, Mary. You were only going to tie me up to a lamp-post anyway, weren't you? I think I can live without that.'

Carrie tried to smile. She felt like bursting into tears.

On the day Caroline Burgess married Matthew Campbell, Ewen Livingstone went out with the express intention of getting himself blind drunk. He did it so quietly, sitting in a corner of the pub with some of the other surfacemen, that it was well on into the evening before Martin Sharkey noticed how far gone he was, and put a fatherly hand on his shoulder.

'Is it not about time you were heading for home, lad? I think you've had enough for one day.'

Talkative at last, Ewen began arguing with his foreman. Ignoring the half-coherent protests that another pint of heavy and maybe a wee whisky wouldn't do him any harm, Martin tipped the wink to another man who, like himself, had only had a couple of drinks. One on either side, they picked the boy up and frog-marched him to the half-glazed double doors of the pub.

Ewen gulped and swallowed hard as a fresh blast of December air hit him. The two men supporting him looked at each other. Before they could debate which of them was going to take him home and put him to bed, a girl who'd been leaning against a lamp-post came forward. She looked cold, as though she'd been waiting there for a while. A few flecks of snow swirled about her dark head.

'I'll make sure he gets home safe, Mr Sharkey.' She put her arm around Ewen's waist and he leaned against her, smiling stupidly.

'Janice! I knew ye wouldnae desert me, hen.'

Martin Sharkey knew the girl by sight – and reputation. It wasn't a good one. He looked at Ewen, one floppy arm draped heavily over Janice's shoulders.

'Promise me ye'll no' talk about Caroline Bloody Burgess's wedding dress,' he was saying, his words slurred with the drink. 'Or where she's goin' for her effin' honeymoon.'

'Not a word.'

'Good girl! That's all – that's all every other – every other lassie in Partick's been talking about a' day.' He scowled ferociously. The concentration involved in trying to get the words out was considerable. 'A wee bit boring, d'ye no' think, Janice?'

'Boring as hell,' the girl agreed, and Ewen beamed at her.

Jesus, Mary and Saint Joseph, thought Martin, why hadn't he spotted earlier on that the lad was set on drinking himself into oblivion today? It should have occurred to him. Over the last few weeks his young workmate had been as unhappy as he'd ever seen him. The boy needed some comforting, right enough. If this young lady was hell-bent on providing that, who was he to stop her?

Hell-bent was probably the right word. Good Catholic that he was, he watched their unsteady progress along the street and consoled himself by concluding that in his present state Ewen probably wasn't going to be capable of very much. A quick fumble up the nearest close would be the most Janice could hope for. Martin held out his hand, checking on how much snow was falling. Hopefully that and the snell breeze which was blowing would send the two of them scurrying indoors as well.

A few minutes later Janice was dragging Ewen through to the back court behind her own home. She pulled him out of the way of the cold air whistling through the close and leaned back against the wall. Taking his hand, she guided it up under her threadbare coat and skirt.

'French knickers,' he mumbled, as his fingers found warm female flesh.

'Easy feelers, Ewen. Help yourself. I don't mind.' She opened her mouth to his kiss, and pulled his other hand to her breasts.

He was very rough, but Janice giggled and undid the buttons of her blouse, allowing him even greater access. She seemed to like it.

He'd been this far before with a lassie. A little further, in fact, although never all the way. Meeting Caroline Burgess had arrested his sexual development. He'd had some half-baked idea of keeping himself pure for her. Pathetic. Stupid. Humiliating. Through the alcoholic haze, it came to him that it was only because of her he knew what the last word meant.

Janice's fingers were at the solid brass buckle of his belt. 'D'ye want to, Ewen?' she whispered. 'I'd let you, you know. I know what all you lads are after, and I'm willing to give it. Not like that stuck-up cow Carrie Burgess.'

The hand between her legs tightened convulsively. Janice yelped in pain. 'Ewen! That hurts.'

'Sorry,' he mumbled. He moved both of his hands and placed them carefully on either side of her head, his sweaty palms flat against the cold and damp stone of the building.

'Go on,' Janice said in a wheedling tone, 'it'll be quite safe. I've got some johnnies with me. Do you know how to put them on?' She giggled again. 'I can help you. I've had a lot of practice.'

He was a child again. About eight years old. He'd found these funny balloon things in the drawer under the box bed, had taken them out and started playing with them. His mother, coming back into the house after hanging some washing out in the back court, had smacked him hard.

'I need all of those!' she'd cried.

Then she had burst into tears and hugged him to her, rocking him backwards and forwards in her arms. That's when she had told him what she did for a living.

And right now he was no better than any of those men he had learned to hate so much. He was just another drunk pressing some girl up against a cold hard wall, seeking release without caring at all about the person who was providing it. Squalid. That was another big word that he knew thanks to Caroline Bloody Burgess.

He took his hands from the wall and straightened up. 'Ye shouldnae sell yourself so cheap, Janice. You're worth more than this. Good-night, hen.'

Perplexed, she stood and watched him go, placing one foot precisely in front of the other in the over-careful walk of the drunk.

He made it to his own street before he was sick, the vomit rising in his throat so fast he barely had time to make it to the gutter. When the spasm had passed, he could think of only one place he wanted to go.

His first try at vaulting the wall of the old graveyard got him nowhere. He lay sprawled on the ground, winded. He succeeded at the third attempt, but he scraped his side on the way down the wall, his shirt and jacket riding up and exposing sensitive skin to the rough stone. That was going to hurt like buggery in the morning, but at the moment he was feeling no pain. No physical pain, at any rate.

He sat down cross-legged in a corner, bowed his head and wrapped his arms about himself. Like a cowering child, he was trying to make himself as small as possible. This place had always been his bolt-hole. When the nameless ache inside him became too much to cope with, when the knowledge of where the money came from to feed and clothe him overwhelmed him, he had always come here. The old Quakers didn't judge him, or his mother.

He hated everybody, himself most of all. He hated Janice.

He hated Matthew Campbell. He hated Caroline Bloody Burgess. No, he didn't. Everyone else, aye, but not her.

She'd be Mrs Matthew Campbell by now. That swine was probably making love to her right this minute. That wouldn't be a sordid fumble up against a close wall. Ewen knew exactly where she was spending her wedding night. Since Esther had been showing off about it for weeks, overwhelmed by Charles Campbell's generosity in paying for the honeymoon, everybody in Partick did.

He could visualise them in their de-luxe suite in their luxurious hotel on the Ayrshire coast. He'd never been in such an establishment, but he'd seen plenty like it at the pictures. The room would be enormous and there would be vases of flowers everywhere. The bed would be huge too and she'd be lying in it waiting for her new husband, her bonnie hair a startling splash of colour against a snowy white pillow.

Matthew Campbell was climbing in beside her. She was turning to him, lips parted, arms open and welcoming ... With a sob, Ewen swung round and smashed his fist against the graveyard wall. Shite! That had hurt enough to penetrate the fog in his brain.

Welcoming the pain, he did it again. He punched the wall a third time before some sort of sense began to prevail. If he hurt his hand real bad, he wouldn't be able to work. If he didn't work, he wouldn't get paid. He had to live, although he wasn't quite sure why that mattered any more.

He put his grazed and bloody knuckles to his mouth. Christ, they'd probably hurt for days, maybe even weeks. Good. That would remind him of her every moment of the day, whenever he curled his fingers round the shaft of his hammer, or lifted a shovel.

He wouldn't be able to write for a while, but why should he ever want to write again anyway? He'd been practising his

186

skills before she'd gone back to Matthew Campbell, making several attempts at writing a letter to her. He'd even thought about trying to write a wee poem. She liked poems.

His knuckles were stinging now, but it wasn't the pain which was making the tears roll down his face. It was the thought of what he had lost. She had never been his in the first place, but there had been moments, during the happiest summer of his life, when he had dared to hope.

It was winter now. The wind had died down, but the flecks of snow had became large flakes, floating gently down on to the scrubby grass in front of him. In here, they would probably lie for a while. He turned the collar of his reefer jacket up in automatic response, but he wasn't really paying any attention to the weather.

He slid down the wall and rolled over on to his side, drawing his knees up so that he lay like a baby. Eventually, cradled by the bones and dust of the old Quakers, he slept. The soft snow settled on him like a lacy blanket.

All the cosier because of the snow dashing against the long windows, Carrie snuggled deeper under the covers. Matt, propped up on his elbow beside her, was looking amused.

'Liked it then, did you?'

'You could say that,' she murmured. 'Can we do it again?'

He laughed and tapped her nose with one long finger. 'Not going to wait to be asked, my little hussy?'

'We're married,' she told him happily. 'We're allowed to do it whenever we like.'

'So we are.'

He pushed the covers down, exposing her breasts to his hungry gaze. 'It doesn't embarrass you if I look at you like this?'

She shook her shining head, her smile widening when he

leaned over to plant a kiss on each breast. She laid a hand on the thick dark waves of his hair.

'You know what is going to embarrass me? Us going to bed so early tonight. I'm a bit worried about facing our fellow guests at breakfast tomorrow.'

He looked up at her, his eyes darkening. There was no amusement left in his face now, only passion.

'Who says we're going to make breakfast?' he asked, and bent his head once more to his work.

Chapter 17

It was several weeks after the wedding and Carrie had invited her mother to North Gardner Street, deliberately picking an afternoon when she knew both of her parents-in-law would be out. Esther had visited several times already, of course, but Shona Campbell's frigidly polite formality had made it impossible to suggest showing her round the flat, something Carrie knew she would love. She was in her element today, entranced by the spacious rooms, the high ceilings and the elegant furnishings. The huge kitchen sent her off into paroxysms of delight.

'Do they have a cook?' she asked, looking longingly at the modern gas cooker. 'Or a maid?'

Carrie laughed. Gazing now at an impressive row of copper pans neatly placed in order of size on a high shelf, Esther had lowered her voice to a reverential whisper, as though she were in a church – or maybe even a cathedral.

'Not living in. There's a woman comes each day to cook and clean. She makes us lunch and leaves something for our evening meal. They call it a cold collation.'

Esther turned surprised eyes on to her daughter. 'Not every night, surely? Matthew would need something hot when he comes in from his work on a cold day. Does Mrs Campbell not like to cook?'

Carrie shook her head. How could she tell her mother, a

woman whose life had been devoted to making a comfortable home for her family, that Shona Campbell considered any form of domestic work beneath her dignity?

'Och, well,' said Esther, clearly finding the arrangement almost impossible to understand, 'she'll be glad you're such a good cook then, Carrie.'

'Eh . . . yes . . . Do you want to see our bedroom now, Ma? Then we can come back here and have our tea.'

Seeing her mother-in-law's evident distaste for even heating up a pot of soup, Carrie had enthusiastically offered to help with the cooking for the meal she was learning to refer to as dinner. She had thought it might be a way for her to fit in to the household, find a role for herself within the Campbell family. The well-intentioned suggestion had been dismissed out of hand. Apparently doing your own cooking was as bad as working for a living.

Carrie led her mother across the wood-panelled lobby. Large enough to be considered a room in itself, it could easily have held a dining table and chairs. Thankfully, Esther was too busy commenting on this fact to go back to the previous topic of conversation. Then she got her first good look at the newly-weds' bedroom.

'My goodness, Carrie, it's about twice the size of the rooms at White Street put together! Was this always Matthew's room?'

'No, he was in a smaller one at the back of the house.'

'These curtains are lovely,' said Esther, walking across to the bay window and fingering the heavily draped material with a needlewoman's appreciation.

Carrie sat down in a low antique chair covered in the same colourful chintz as the curtains and sighed happily. Her mother was looking well, although she'd already lost a lot of weight. Her trim curves were becoming angular. Despite that, there were days when it was possible to hope against hope that the doctors had got it wrong.

Esther indicated a door in the corner of the room. 'Is this a press?'

'No, it's a wee dressing room. Have a look.' She rose to her feet, walked across the room and opened the door, ushering her mother in.

'Some dressing room,' said Esther admiringly. 'It's even got a window.' She looked about her. 'You know,' she said, 'this would make an ideal nursery.'

Carrie folded her arms and leaned against the door jamb. 'You think so?' she asked innocently.

Esther spun round. 'You don't mean . . .?'

'Well,' she replied, completely incapable of halting the grin which was spreading out all over her face, 'I've just missed a second period, and I'm beginning to feel a wee bit queasy in the mornings. What do you think it could be?'

'Oh, Carrie, it must have happened on your honeymoon!'

'Mother!' she protested, but her momentary embarrassment was swiftly submerged, both by the arms which were flung about her neck and by the joy the news had clearly brought her mother.

She returned the hug, holding the too-thin body to her. One of us waxing and one of us waning, she thought sadly. The sorrow of that pierced her happiness like a lance. Head on Esther's shoulder, she squeezed her eyes tight shut to contain the tears, and felt the familiar comfort being offered. Her mother had lifted a hand to smooth her hair.

When Carrie eventually raised her head, she spoke in a fierce whisper. 'I want my baby to have two grandmothers!'

The sad and loving eyes held the wisdom of the ages. 'I'll do my best, lass,' Esther said gently. 'I'll do my best.'

* * *

191

She did a lot more than that, baffling the doctors by holding out several months longer than they had predicted. She spent the last two of those months up the hill, despite Shona Campbell's clear reluctance to have a dying woman in her house. In any other family, there might have been an almighty row about it, but that wasn't the way things were done in North Gardner Street.

In a tone of sweet reason, Matthew's mother had asked if it wouldn't be better all round for Mrs Burgess to go into the Infirmary. Easier for everybody, surely. Charles Campbell, as was usual when anything serious was being discussed, was nowhere to be seen.

'Especially you, Caroline,' Shona said, surveying her heavily pregnant daughter-in-law with cool and critical eyes. 'You really shouldn't be going out and about so much in your condition.'

Tired and emotional and exhausted from toiling up and down to White Street to sit with her mother all day and every day, Carrie looked at Matt, a mute appeal in her eyes. Part of her could see very well how difficult it was for him, caught between his mother and his wife like this, but she desperately needed him to support her. He walked over to her, gently touched her face.

'You're very pale,' he said. 'You need to rest more.' His smile was wry. 'If your mother goes into the Western you'll just struggle along there every day, won't you?' Without waiting for an answer, he turned and spoke to his mother. 'Mrs Burgess can have my old room.' He lowered his voice, said something Carrie wasn't supposed to hear, 'It'll not be for long.'

But it was for longer than they all thought – except Carrie herself. She knew exactly how long her mother would hold out. And so it was that as new life began to make its way into the world in one room, across the hall another was slowly ebbing away. Esther lived long enough to hold the baby, although her frail grip had to be supported by her daughter's loving arms.

A few hours after the birth Matt carried his wife through to her mother, laying her gently on the bed beside her. Then he came back with a shawl-wrapped bundle.

'A wee boy,' he said, leaning over and placing his son in Esther's embrace. She was propped up on a heap of pillows, Carrie's arm about the painfully thin and sharp shoulders.

'Och . . . he's so bonnie . . .' Esther's eyes flickered. Her strength was fading fast.

'Aye, Ma,' whispered Carrie, wondering how much emotion a heart could take before it split in two. Joy for her son, aching grief for her mother. She glanced up at Matt, and he gave her a little nod. They'd discussed this before he'd brought her through. 'We're going to call him Archie,' she said gently.

The bony face lit up. 'That's . . . a . . . grand . . . name . . .' Esther smiled down at her grandson. 'Archie . . .' she repeated.

She said that name one more time before the end. It came later that night. Carrie was by her side, holding the baby. Matt stood sentinel behind her chair, one hand resting lightly on her shoulder. He'd given up his attempts to persuade her to go back to their room and lie down several hours ago. She felt his fingers tighten and her head snapped up. Something was happening.

Esther had been motionless for hours, her face impassive. Suddenly her eyes opened wide and a smile of great sweetness suffused her face. She raised her arms, as though she were greeting someone.

'Archie . . .' she said, her voice clear and strong.

There was a quick little breath. Then the room fell silent.

PART II
1937

Chapter 18

Carrie checked the time by the beautiful old grandfather clock which had spent much of its life in the mansion a few hundred yards away on Partickhill Road which had been her father-in-law's childhood home. *A piece of flotsam salvaged from the wreckage of the family fortunes after the fall of the house of Campbell.*

One mocking eyebrow raised, a self-deprecating smile on his handsome face, that was how Charles Campbell always referred to the family's losses in the stock market crash. He had a way with words. He earned some sort of an income at it, writing the occasional article for newspapers and magazines.

Given the erratic nature of that income, the comfort of her surroundings and the fact that he had paid for her honeymoon, Carrie assumed that the fall of the house of Campbell hadn't been total. Presumably there had been some investments left which enabled Matt's parents to live in reasonable style without either of them appearing to exert themselves very much.

Both Charles and Shona Campbell spent most of their time socialising. She played bridge, attended luncheon parties and had friends round for afternoon tea. He played a lot of golf. In the evenings there were cocktail parties and visits to the theatre. With that example before him, Carrie regarded it as all the more commendable that Matt had chosen to follow a career.

She suspected there had been some quixotic gallantry in his deciding to go out and work for a living, a desire to do something concrete about the economic disaster which had befallen his family. That seemed entirely honourable, and for his sake, it distressed her that his mother didn't see it that way. Shona Campbell was less than impressed with the social status of her son's occupation.

Carrie was quite sure she was even less impressed with her daughter-in-law's social standing. That had come as a bit of a shock. The Burgess family had enjoyed a certain position in their own community, a respect earned through Archie's job and the way he'd carried it out. As far as Shona Campbell and many of her friends up the hill here were concerned, you only seemed to be worthy of their attention if you didn't work for a living. Carrie found that attitude hard to understand and even harder to stomach.

The gilded Roman numerals on the clock face were showing twenty-past four. There was no need to worry about Matt just yet. Shoes kicked off, sitting on the hearthrug with her back against an armchair for support, Carrie stretched her legs out in front of the cosy but well-guarded fire burning in the elegant fireplace. The meeting at Partick Burgh Hall wasn't due to finish until half-past.

She glanced at her son, playing with his building blocks on the rug beside her. At least she could keep him safe. Her eyes lingered fondly on the dark waves of Archie's hair, so like his father's. She wondered if the new baby would have the same colouring or take after herself. Maybe she'd have a girl this time. That would be nice, although another boy would be fine too, especially if he turned out to be as happy a baby as Archie.

He looked so adorable in the wee yellow romper-suit with farmyard animals embroidered on the front and the collar. All her own work. She had very little else to do with her time in this house. She'd be a lot busier when the new baby arrived. That great event was still over four months away, well into the new year.

The new baby's soon-to-be big brother was concentrating ferociously at the moment, his normally smooth forehead furrowed and his small pink tongue sticking out of the corner of his mouth. He was trying to build a tower out of his blocks. He could get it two-high, but the addition of a third brick always made it wobble and fall over. Carrie had tried to demonstrate the proper technique to him, but now she was quite literally sitting on her hands. Observing his frustration each time the tower fell, she was desperate to help him, but knew he was determined to perform the task unaided.

'By myself, Mammy!' he had told her ten minutes ago, firmly pushing her helping hands away with his own chubby little fingers. Stubborn and independent. She couldn't imagine where he got that from.

She lifted her head to the large bay window overlooking the tiny but neat front garden and street. Above the beautiful leaded-glass screens which covered the bottom of the panes she could see that the dreich December day was shaping up into a foul night, the rain beginning to lash against the glass. That was good.

Matt had assured her stewards would prevent what he called troublemakers from actually attending the rally, but Carrie knew Partick. Matt's troublemakers – socialists, communists, trade unionists and other opponents of Sir Oswald Mosley's fascist message – were incensed that his Blackshirt supporters were even being permitted to hold a meeting in the Burgh Hall this Saturday afternoon.

They would be waiting outside for them, probably conducting their own impromptu meeting at Partick's traditional speakers' corner on Peel Street. Both sides had some great orators. That could get folk awful riled up. Look what had happened in the East End of London last year when Mosley himself had addressed the crowd. There had been a riot and people had got hurt.

A miserable day would hopefully make it more likely that a lot of people would slope off home before anything nasty could develop between the opposing factions. The whole thing, and especially Matthew's involvement with it, dismayed Carrie terribly.

Disillusioned with the Labour Party, his own socialism was a thing of the past, as was his membership of the National Union of Railwaymen. At first she had remonstrated with him. Didn't he know what was going on in Germany and Italy? How could he support such an anti-democratic group as the Blackshirts?

He had retaliated by asking her if she really thought democracy was working. Was it doing anything to end the misery of the Depression? Uncertain of the answer to that, she had held her tongue and hoped that, in the fullness of time, he would see the error of his ways. Hating herself for the disloyal thought, she had reflected that his support for left-wing views had also been short-lived.

His parents voted Conservative in the same way as they got up in the morning, went to church each Sunday and knew exactly which were the correct knives and forks to use. It was an article of faith, and quite preposterous that anyone in their social circle should think of holding different views. Sometimes Carrie wondered if Matt's socialism had simply been a method of rebelling against them. Sometimes she wondered if his choice of her as a wife had also been an act of rebellion . . .

Her gaze landed on her mother-in-law, sitting at her writing bureau attending to her correspondence: giving and receiving invitations to the social events which were so important to her. There might be a terrible civil war raging in Spain, fascists, communists and socialists fighting each other in the streets of Britain and the pessimists insisting that a war with Germany was simply a matter of time, but Shona Campbell's chief worry still seemed to be finding the ideal cocktail dress.

Archie was tugging at Carrie's skirt, beaming with pride. He had built his tower at last.

'Clever boy!' she cried. 'Three blocks high! Well done, wee man.' She leaned forward and dropped a kiss on his smooth hair.

Should she call on Shona to witness this great event, the possible first signs of Archie's future as the foremost engineer of his generation? As she was contemplating it, he swiped his hand against the bricks and knocked his achievement down.

'Och, Archie!'

'Build it again,' he announced happily and set to doing exactly that.

It was probably just as well. Shona's interest in her grandson was pretty limited. Fishing for information, Carrie had found out that Matthew had been brought up by a succession of nursemaids. The picture which emerged was of a young boy always taking second place to his parents' social life. She had learned not to attempt to discuss the topic with him. He wouldn't hear a word of criticism against his family.

People called his mother beautiful, but Carrie thought Shona Campbell too often looked as if a piece of fish was slowly decomposing under her nose. Like now, when she twisted round in her chair and looked disapprovingly at her daughter-in-law sitting on the floor. Too bad. As her pregnancy advanced, Carrie found it one of the most comfortable postures to adopt. Shona seemed to find most things to do with the getting or rearing of children distasteful, so Carrie was

201

surprised to hear her posing a direct question about one aspect of it.

'Use baby milk? Oh, no, I'm going to breast-feed again. I've already decided.'

Matt's mother closed her discreetly made-up eyes for a second, looking pained. *Breast* obviously counted as a vulgar word in her vocabulary. 'Bottle-feeding is so much more up-to-date and convenient, Caroline.'

Carrie shook her vibrant head. Past the morning sickness stage, she was beginning to bloom, skin and hair shining again.

'I disagree,' she said pleasantly. 'Breast-feeding is a lot more convenient.' Maybe if she kept using the word, Shona would let the subject go. Some hopes. All three members of the Campbell family were like terriers when they got their teeth into something. A somewhat unfortunate metaphor to use when discussing breast-feeding.

'It's unhygienic.' The invisible decomposing fish was firmly in position.

'It's the most hygienic thing there is.' Despite her best efforts, Carrie's voice had sharpened. She was fed-up having to justify everything she did to this cold woman.

Shona wrinkled her elegant nose in obvious distaste. 'Don't you think that nursing the baby yourself is rather . . . lower-class?'

'No, I don't. I think it's natural. You'd have to admit that Archie thrived on it.'

Sensing his mother's gaze, Archie, still in training for his future as a great engineer, looked up briefly and gave her his characteristic wrinkled-nose smile. It was horribly reminiscent of the gesture his grandmother had just made. I'll not hold that against you, son, thought Carrie with the grim and private humour which had saved her sanity several times over the past two years.

Shona stood up in one graceful movement. 'Don't you think Matthew would prefer you to bottle-feed?'

'No, I don't.'

'Have you discussed it with him?'

Mind your own business was the phrase which came to mind, but there was no point in causing trouble unnecessarily. 'Of course.'

'You're terribly stubborn, Caroline. I can't think why your parents brought you up to be so defiant.' Shona gathered up her letters and swept out of the room.

Carrie put her arms under Archie's shoulders and lifted him on to her lap. 'Well, young man, I think I've just been paid a compliment.'

'Compliment,' he repeated.

'Clever boy,' she said automatically, but didn't try to stop him when he squirmed out of her arms and went back to his blocks. Carrie rose slowly to her feet.

'Where Mammy going?'

She laid a reassuring hand on his head. 'Only over to the window, my wee sugar dumpling. I'm going to watch for your daddy coming home.'

She stood in the wood-panelled bay, one eye on the outside world, one eye checking that Archie stayed where he was. At fifteen months, he was becoming alarmingly mobile. She had to watch him like a hawk. The spacious and roomy flat had too many interesting corners ripe for exploration by an inquisitive small boy who was beginning to find his feet.

Spacious and roomy it might be, but it wasn't big enough for Shona Campbell. Like her husband, she'd been used to better things. When it was just the family, she referred to where Carrie and Archie were at the moment as the morning room. When there were guests for dinner it metamorphosed into the drawing room. Brought up in a simpler home, Carrie often found her tongue tripping over the two designations for the one room, a mistake which always put her on the receiving end of a look of withering scorn from her mother-in-law.

She put her hands behind her and leaned back, gazing out at the increasingly wild night. Her twentieth birthday was still a few months away, but here she was, the mother of a toddler and expecting a second child. She'd have preferred a longer gap between the two, but Matt had been horrified when she had mumbled an embarrassed suggestion in the days following Archie's birth that they should practise some form of birth control once they resumed marital relations.

She hadn't known exactly how to put it, and had blurted out something about French letters. He'd gone on at some length about her using such a coarse expression, had expressed some surprise, and considerable disapproval, that she should even know what it meant.

Carrie sighed. Then she straightened up. The man in question was coming along the road. As far as she could tell from here he looked unscathed.

'Here comes your daddy,' she said. 'Hopefully he's kept himself out of trouble. Let's get to him first before your grandma manages to cause any either.'

'Daddy trouble,' said Archie. 'Grandma trouble.'

Carrie scooped him up and carried him towards the front door. She'd have to give this up soon. He was getting too heavy.

'You know,' she told him, 'it's all very well you being such a good speaker, but I may have to stop confiding in you if you're going to become such a blabbermouth. And your grandma is a sweet and wonderful woman.'

Well, the other one was, she thought, absolving herself from having told her son a fib.

Archie chortled, and started playing with her hair.

'Mother says you told her you're not going to bottle-feed the next baby, that you want to feed him yourself.'

'Him?' asked Carrie, sitting on their bed taking off her stockings. 'It might be a girl, you know.'

'You do realise she found it quite distasteful the last time,' said Matt, ignoring her attempt to divert the conversation.

'*She* wasn't actually doing it. *I* was.'

'Don't be dim, Carrie, you know what I mean. There was the occasion when you sat and fed Archie while Mother's friends were here.'

She stood up and shrugged into her nightie. 'I was dog-tired, Matt. They were all women. I was sitting by the fire and they were at the wee table in the corner playing cards. I had a twin set on and I pushed the jumper up a bit and the cardigan hid most of the rest. There was practically nothing to be seen.'

'That's not what Mother says. She was deeply embarrassed by the whole thing.'

Struggling to hold on to her temper, Carrie folded back the covers and got into bed. 'I'm not really sure it's any of your mother's business, Matt.'

He began unbuttoning his shirt. 'I should have thought you would have appreciated her taking an interest, what with your own mother no longer being with us.'

Carrie slid down on to her side, turning her back to him. Mention of her parents never failed to bring a tear to her eye. Lately she'd been feeling the pain of their loss acutely, with an added dimension which gave it the sharpest of edges. Her mother could have helped and advised her with Archie, shared the pleasure of all the little milestones as he grew and developed. Nor did it take much effort of imagination to visualise a slightly older version of her son helping his grandfather in the garden of the station house.

'I find it a bit distasteful myself, Carrie.' Matt had come round her side of the bed, was pulling the tail of his shirt out from his trousers. Lost in memories and a longing for what now could never be, she looked up blankly.

'Distasteful?'

'When you were feeding Archie, you didn't want me to touch you. Here, I mean.' He trailed his fingertips across her breasts. 'You fed him for nine months. That's a long time for a man to be deprived.'

'It's the best start in life, Matt. Surely that's what you want for our children?'

He tossed his shirt into a corner. 'You're so stubborn, Carrie.'

'That's what your mother said.'

'And? Shift over a wee bit,' he said, sitting down on the edge of the bed to finish removing his trousers.

'And nothing. Matt,' she continued, 'what happened about us getting a place of our own?'

'How many times do I have to say this, Carrie?' he asked irritably. 'Not till we can afford somewhere really nice.'

'The house in White Street was nice enough.'

'No, it wasn't, and you hated that old range, so take that butter-wouldn't-melt-in-my-mouth look off your face, Mrs Campbell Junior. I was thinking of something more like those new flats they're building along at Anniesland.'

'Kelvin Court? You've got delusions of grandeur, Mr Campbell Junior.'

He grinned. It transformed him back into the man she'd fallen in love with. 'Are you coming in this side?' she asked.

'Only if you're going to make it worth my while.'

He stood up to place his trousers over the back of a chair, divested himself of socks and underwear and sent them in the same direction as his shirt. Then he put out the light and got in beside her.

'That's your answer to everything, isn't it?' she asked, but she had rolled over to face him and her hand was already resting on his bare shoulder.

'I don't normally hear you complaining,' he murmured. His own hand was busily seeking, pushing up her nightdress, roaming warm and intimate over her smooth skin.

'Matt ... I'm not sure if we should ... what about the baby?'

'I'll be gentle,' he promised, 'and I thought the later on in pregnancy you are, the safer it is anyway.'

'I knew I shouldn't have let you read those books the lady doctor loaned me.'

He chuckled, and smothered her protests with kisses.

Afterwards, he fell asleep quickly but Carrie lay awake for a while. Sometimes, despite the spaciousness and the high-ceilinged rooms, she felt stifled here. In the summer she sat out as much as possible. There was a good-sized back garden, with a lawn and flowers kept neat and tidy by a gardener paid for by all the residents of the building.

It was pretty, but a little too regimented for Carrie's taste. She didn't believe flowers were meant to stand in neat rows, like soldiers on parade. She missed the clumps of lupins and marguerites and red hot pokers which had adorned the garden of the station house like splashes of colour on an artist's palette. She missed her father's vegetable patch. She missed the trains.

She had told Matt once, half joking, but part of her completely serious, that she found it difficult to live in a house which didn't shake from time to time. He had looked at her as if she were mad and read her a lecture on how grateful they should be for living in such a nice house well away from the noise and dirt caused by trains and coal trucks.

She listened to him snoring quietly by her side. That was

the trouble, of course, he was too comfortable here. She had become a wife and mother, her life changed immeasurably from how it had been before, but Matt had continued to be the son of the household in which he'd grown up. His life had gone on much as it had been before. He had no real responsibilities to cope with.

She would have to use her powers of persuasion on him. A luxury flat was a pipe-dream, not something she really fancied anyway. She'd rather move down the hill, be among people she knew. There were lots of good houses, nice closes and respectable streets. It was simply a matter of finding the right one. Maybe she could get somewhere near the railway. That would be her ideal, much better than any luxury flat.

Up here on the hill it was only at night, when everything else had fallen silent, that she heard the occasional train in the distance. She could hear one now. The sound was absurdly comforting in spite of the memories it brought with it.

On the day she married Matthew she had made a conscious decision not to think about him, but there were unguarded moments, especially at times like this, when Ewen Livingstone stole back into her head like a thief in the night.

He had left Partick. That much she knew. In the middle of his first week back at work after their honeymoon, Matt had come home with an announcement. 'Your wee friend's slung his hook. Gone off to seek his fortune elsewhere, apparently.'

Thinking it more diplomatic to evince little interest in the information, she hadn't asked for any details. She had also told herself sternly that she didn't need them. Later on, when her curiosity got the better of her, she had spoken discreetly to Mary. Could Douglas maybe find out where Ewen was? She'd like to write to him, make sure he was all right. Mary gave her an old-fashioned look and asked if she thought that was wise. Carrie hadn't pressed the point.

It was too late to do it now. Douglas and Mary had married in the summer – Carrie had been matron of honour – and gone to live near Fort William. Douglas was in charge of the signal box at a small highland station and they'd been allocated a railway house. Mary's letters were a joy to read, full of tales of her new neighbours and the beauty of their surroundings and how she and Douglas were knocking their garden into shape. They were really looking forward to eating their own vege-tables next summer. Carrie would have to visit. Wee Archie would love it. Matthew was welcome to come too, of course.

Carrie rolled from her back on to her side, and stretched an arm across her sleeping husband. She'd been disappointed by Ewen's behaviour that night before her wedding, but what stuck in her memory wasn't the sheer awfulness of being forced to watch him kissing Janice Muirhead or seeing him the worse for drink.

What she remembered was a handful of softly spoken words. *You're hurting my heart.* She could hear him saying them, see the bleakness in his wintry eyes. He must have been so unhappy . . .

She hoped he'd got over her. She hoped he was keeping up his reading and writing. She hoped he'd met a nice girl. As long as she wasn't called Janice Muirhead. To the best of her knowledge, however, Janice was still swanning about Partick.

Carrie yawned and snuggled into Matt's warm body. She imagined that some men might be put off by their wives being pregnant, but it didn't seem to bother him at all. Quite the reverse. He was a wonderful lover, more passionate than ever. Some of the things he liked to do and tried to coax her into doing . . . well. She suspected they might make even Janice Muirhead blush.

Chapter 19

'Aye, only the one son. I think she tried it the once and didnae like it! Mind you, he's got a wean already and there's another on the way, so maybe he takes after his faither . . . the old goat!'

Carrie, approaching the kitchen door, unannounced and unheard, turned smartly about – or as smartly as a woman in the sixth month of pregnancy could – and headed back to the morning room. She could make herself a cup of tea later.

What she had overheard the daily say to whoever was in the kitchen with her hadn't come as much of a surprise. She had long since put her father-in-law down as having a roving eye. As for Shona trying it once and not liking it – well, Carrie knew exactly what the woman meant.

She put it out of her mind, having other fish to fry today – more or less literally. Heartily sick of eating cold evening meals, she'd decided there was going to be something really tasty for tea tonight, cooked by her own fair hand. The daily was having the afternoon off, which would give Carrie the kitchen to herself, and she was planning a wee foray out to Byres Road to buy the ingredients. The January day was crisp but sunny. The frost on the pavements would soon melt and Archie would enjoy the expedition as much as she would, wrapped up snugly in his pushchair.

There were also guests coming round this Friday evening:

Matthew's Uncle Roddy, a journalist on a Glasgow news-paper, and his colleague – according to Matt also his ladyfriend – Josephine Shaw. Carrie liked them both. They were friendly and open and always great company. She was sure they would appreciate a good hot meal on a chilly winter's night.

Shona Campbell's welcome to her much younger brother would no doubt be as cold as one of her collations. She disapproved of his relationship with his colleague – whatever it actually was – and made her feelings all too clear. Carrie found the frigid politeness her mother-in-law displayed towards the poised young woman quite embarrassing. Picking up on the silent messages flashing between Roderick Cunningham and Josephine Shaw last time they'd visited, she suspected they laughed it off once they were alone together. However, once or twice she felt sure she had seen real hurt in Miss Shaw's clear grey eyes.

Her greatest sin seemed to be not speaking with the right accent. Although she never mentioned her family, it was obvious she came from a humble background. It was equally obvious that Roderick was immensely proud of her and her achievements. He was always telling them about some great article she'd written, or some story she'd uncovered – usually to the accompaniment of Miss Shaw herself telling him to shut up.

Shona remained unimpressed. Her brother was letting the side down. Socially, Josephine Shaw was beneath him. Which is probably why she and I get on so well, thought Carrie ruefully.

Roderick also committed the unforgivable sin of having a career which he took seriously. That didn't stop him joking about it and almost everything else in his life. Carrie hadn't known him for very long before she recognised his flippant manner for what it was: a smokescreen he threw up to hide his true feelings.

After lunch, feeling a bit like Christopher Columbus going off in search of America, she betook herself to the fishmonger's in Byres Road which her mother had always declared to be the best in Glasgow. Its marble slab presented Carrie with a cornucopia of fruits of the sea. She chose some luscious-looking haddock and then headed for the greengrocers to buy vegetables and cooking apples. She took her time about it, enjoying the bustling atmosphere of the busy street and the feeling of being out in the world again.

When they got back to North Gardner Street – she could never really bring herself to call it home – she put Archie down for his nap and set to work. The menu was fish in white sauce followed by apple crumble and custard. She made the dessert first, then prepared as much of the main course as could be done in advance.

Carrie laid the fish in the bottom of a large enamel ashet and poured the freshly prepared white sauce over it. She peeled the potatoes, cut them into slices and parboiled them. She would fry them just before serving up the meal. At this time of year the peas had to come out of a tin, but she scraped and chopped carrots and left them to steep in a pan on top of the stove. Once everything was completed to her satisfaction she went through to check on Archie.

He was still sound asleep. That gave her time to have a quick wash and change her clothes. Taking clean underwear out of a drawer, she came upon the canteen of cutlery which held her mother's fish knives and forks. They would provide the perfect finishing touch.

She was in the kitchen washing them when she heard the front door of the flat open. At precisely the same moment, the child inside her began to move. The sensation always made her laugh with delight. She looked up expectantly. It was unlikely that Matt had been let off early, but you never knew. It was his father who put his head round the kitchen door.

'Something smells good,' he said appreciatively.

Carrie beamed at him. 'The baby's kicking me,' she said, wanting to share the pleasure with somebody.

Charles Campbell was beside her in an instant. Before she had quite realised what he intended, his hands were on her stomach. She tried not to recoil. He was the baby's grandfather after all.

'Why, so he is!'

She smiled nervously, wondering when he was going to take his hands away. He looked closely into her face. 'You're looking forward to the new baby coming?'

'Oh, aye. Of course.'

'You're a good little mother to your boy,' he said. 'I'm sure it's hard work sometimes.'

Carrie shrugged. 'I enjoy being with Archie. It's a pleasure.'

Her father-in-law was standing awfully close to her. 'I hope the getting of him gave you as much pleasure. This one, too,' he added, beginning gently to stroke her abdomen.

She swallowed. She hoped he didn't mean what she thought he meant. She also really wished he would take his hands off her. He lifted one of them, but it only travelled as far as her face.

'I hope my son's being good to you, Caroline.'

'M-Matt's very good to me,' she managed. Maybe he'd leave her alone if she pretended to misunderstand what he was on about.

'I'm very glad to hear it,' he murmured. 'I'd like to think the ability to keep a woman happy runs in the family.'

The door bell rang. She felt dizzy with relief.

'What a pity. Just when you and I were getting to know

214

each other better.' He gave her cheek two soft little slaps. 'Another time, my dear.'

Carrie stood staring after him. Surely she had misunderstood. He was calling something from the hall. 'Our guests have arrived.'

She put a smile on her face and went out to meet them.

'My favourite niece-in-law!' cried Roderick.

'Your only niece-in-law, I think.'

'Not the point, dear girl. Keeping well, I trust?'

He kissed her warmly on the cheek and gave her a hug. She'd been taken aback when he had first greeted her that way, but his exuberance had never made her feel uncomfortable. It was the way he was. Her family and their friends had never gone in much for kisses and hugs, but posh people were different, she knew. Maybe she was over-reacting to what had happened in the kitchen.

'Can I get you a drink?' she asked, turning to include Miss Shaw in the conversation. She was standing back, looking wryly amused.

'Those are the most beautiful words I've heard all day,' said Roderick. 'You're an absolute angel, young Mrs Campbell. I should have brought you some flowers.' He paused for dramatic effect, lifted her hand and bestowed a delicate kiss upon it. 'Only no bloom could hope to match your own glow.'

'Stop hamming it up, Roddy,' said Josephine Shaw. She came forward to say hello to Carrie. 'You've been cooking?'

'Yes.' She frowned. 'I hope you both like fish.'

'We love it. There's a new restaurant specialising in it not far from our office. Mr Cunningham would be there every evening if I didn't occasionally remind him he's now a wage slave and no longer has a limitless private income.'

Roderick adopted an air of immense and wounded dignity.

215

'I'll have you know that I'm proud to call myself a member of the working classes.'

Josephine Shaw put her hands on her hips. 'Away and boil your head and make soup with it, Roddy. Come the revolution you'll be one of the first up against the wall.'

He grinned at her. Carrie laughed. She loved the way this pair were with each other. She had often privately wondered if they *were* more than just good friends. Despite his theatrical manner, there was nothing unmanly about Roderick's broad shoulders and handsome face. Once, watching him as he glanced at Miss Shaw and thought himself unobserved, Carrie had seen a look in his eyes which was not only all-male, but also full of a kind of wistful longing.

'Anything we can do to help?' he asked. 'Set the table or something?'

'Most of it's done, but you could put the cutlery out for me, if you like.'

'Nae bother,' said Miss Shaw, turning at the sound of a key in the lock.

'Ah,' said Charles, 'it's my son and heir. Now we're only waiting for Shona to complete the party.'

Out of sight of his brother-in-law, Roderick rolled his eyes at Carrie. She wondered, not for the first time, how the same parents could have produced a brother and sister who were so different from each other.

'You cooked this yourself?'

'Isn't she clever, Shona?' asked Roderick. He lifted a crystal goblet to his lips and took a healthy swig of the white wine Charles had poured out for everybody except Carrie and Archie. The baby was sitting between his parents, laughing at the faces his great-uncle was pulling at him from the opposite side of the table. Carrie was aware that Matt was very quiet.

He seemed to have something on his mind.

Having checked three times that the piece of fish she'd chosen for Archie had absolutely no bones in it, she placed it in his porringer which was lying beside her own plate. The small dish already contained some chopped up peas and carrots. She cut a couple of slices of potato, added them to the fish and placed the porringer on the tray of the high chair, between Archie's own knife, fork and spoon. He was beginning to manage them quite well.

'What?' She had missed the question. Her mother-in-law repeated it, pronouncing each word as though she were talking to a person of limited intelligence.

'Where did the fish come from?'

'The sea?' suggested Roderick. 'Ow!' He turned and glared at Josephine Shaw. That reminded Carrie of Mary and Douglas. Oh, how she wished she was sitting round a table with them!

'The fishmonger's in Byres Road,' she said in response to Shona's question.

'You went out shopping, when you're so obviously *expecting*?'

'I didn't realise it was something I was supposed to be ashamed of,' Carrie said evenly, although her temper was flaring. 'Matthew and I are married, you know.'

Shona drew her breath in sharply. Her son's head snapped up. Charles Campbell, public face firmly in place, looked pained. Roderick and Josephine gazed sympathetically at Carrie.

'What on earth are these?' Shona had picked up one of Esther's fish knives. She turned it over in her hand, examining it as if it were a laboratory specimen.

'They were m-my m-mother's,' stuttered Carrie, realising too late that she must have committed some social gaffe. 'I thought they'd help make the meal special.'

'Don't you know anything?' The cultured voice was as icy as the January night, held at bay by the heavy curtains drawn across the windows of the dining room. 'No one with any breeding eats fish other than with two forks. They're not even silver. For heaven's sake, take them away.'

She dropped the knife on to the tablecloth and made an elaborate gesture of distaste which reminded Carrie of Matt. Both mother and son had a tendency to overdo the dramatics on occasions like these. She was trying to stay angry. It seemed preferable to bursting into tears. Her mother had been so proud of her fish knives and forks . . .

She wished somebody would say something. Somebody did. It was Roderick, his voice unusually hard-edged.

'Caroline has cooked us what smells and looks like a delicious meal, and I think we should all do her the compliment of tucking in and enjoying it.' He picked up his cutlery. '*Bon appétit*, everyone.'

Everyone followed suit, even Shona. No doubt she didn't want to make a scene.

'Delicious,' pronounced Roderick a few moments later. 'Moist . . . juicy. . .' He turned to Miss Shaw. 'Help me out here, Jo. What's the word?'

'Succulent,' she suggested, throwing a smile across the table to Carrie. 'And beautifully cooked.'

She knew what they were doing. She was grateful, touched too, but she was bitterly disappointed that Matt had uttered not one word in her defence.

'For God's sake,' he said irritably as they were getting ready for bed. 'You're making a big fuss over nothing. Apologise to Mother tomorrow and everything will be smoothed over.'

Carrie stared at him, incredulous. 'You want *me* to apologise to *her*? You don't think it should be the other way around?'

'Whatever,' he said absently. The realisation that he wasn't even listening properly made her desperate. She knew she hadn't picked his father up wrong. Charles Campbell really had made those horribly suggestive remarks to her earlier this evening.

'Matt, we've got to move out. I can't stand this any longer. Please, Matt!'

She'd been doing her best not to cry, but she was six months pregnant and worn out by the stresses of the day. She sank down on to the bed.

'Carrie, you're overtired. Walking to Byres Road and back was obviously too much for you, and now you're getting yourself all het up over nothing.'

'It's not nothing,' she sobbed, pressing her fingers to her hot and sweaty forehead. Last time she'd got upset like this she'd ended up being sick. That wasn't good for the baby. She took a deep breath and looked up at him, forcing herself to speak calmly. 'I want a place of our own.'

'And how are we going to afford that when I've had to take a pay cut?'

'A pay cut?' she repeated. 'For everybody?' It was a bit of a blow, but it didn't surprise her. The country might be slowly beginning to pull itself out of the Depression, but there was a long way to go yet. Workers in more than one industry had been obliged to accept a reduction in wages.

Matthew shook his head. 'Not everyone. Only Pascal Sharkey and me.'

'I don't understand.'

He had the oddest of looks on his face. 'We had a slight difference of opinion. Over politics.'

She still didn't understand. Lots of people argued the toss over politics. They were living in interesting times.

'If you must know,' said Matt reluctantly, 'it got a bit heated.

219

He's a socialist, Carrie!' He spat the word out as if it explained everything. 'I ended up taking a swing at him. He retaliated, of course. What else can you expect from a bloody Paddy?'

That statement, and the sneer which accompanied it, defeated her. It was all right for Matthew to lash out, but not for Pascal to defend himself? Like his father Martin, the young man confounded the stereotype of the fighting Irish. She knew him as the most peaceable of lads.

People could, of course, be provoked beyond endurance. That made her think of another occasion in the station booking office when violence had been narrowly avoided. She had seen Ewen Livingstone as the aggressor then. Now she looked at her husband . . . and wondered. She had a dreadful sinking feeling in the pit of her stomach.

'Oh, Matthew,' she breathed, 'whatever possessed you? You might have lost your job.'

'You think I don't know that?' It came out petulantly. 'I was tired and fed up, and he was being all smart and clever, demolishing my argument, making a fool of me in front of other people.'

'So you hit him?' Her voice rose in mingled outrage and disbelief.

He scowled at her. 'You think this unpleasantness between you and my mother doesn't affect me, Carrie? You could make more of an effort to get on with her, you know.'

That took her breath away. By one of those tortuous swings of logic Matthew seemed to specialise in, it was now she who was in the wrong. She stood up and went to stand in front of him.

'Make more of an effort?' she demanded with an angry toss of the head. 'I do nothing *but* make an effort with your bloody mother. Perhaps it might help if Lady Muck would condescend to do the same!'

He had gone very still. 'What did you call my mother?'

'Lady Muck,' she muttered, already ashamed of the impulse which had led her to use the name.

She saw it coming. It was in the darkening of his eyes. She just didn't believe it, that was all. Not when his hand came up. Not when she saw it swing towards her face. Not until she heard the noise it made and felt her cheek sting as he hit her.

He looked as shocked as she felt, and it was she who spoke first. 'I'm going to sleep in Archie's room.' She sounded dazed. She *was* dazed, unable to believe what he had done. Unwilling to believe it.

'No, you're not.'

She started to shake her head, but he grabbed her by the upper arms and spoke softly into her face. 'Would you like another slap, Carrie?'

They went to bed in silence. She lay on her side, facing away from him, and couldn't believe it when she felt his hand snake round her waist.

'I'm tired,' she said, her voice dull.

His hand slid up to her breasts. She pushed it away, but it returned, more demanding this time. 'I'm not in the mood.'

'Maybe not,' he said into the darkness, 'but I am.' His fingers tightened. 'Turn around, Carrie.'

She thought of Archie, lying sleeping on the other side of the dressing room door. She thought of the baby she was carrying. She turned around.

'Shall we take Archie out for a walk? It seems a nice enough day.'

Matt, off duty for the whole weekend, turned from his inspection of the weather and smiled warmly at his young wife. It was shortly after breakfast on Saturday morning, and everyone had gathered in the morning room.

'It's too cold.'

He strode across the room, swung a chair round from the small table in the corner and pulled it up beside her where she sat by the fire, opposite his mother. He sat back to front on the upright chair, straddling it. Laying his hands along the back of it he turned his mouth down, mock mournful.

'Oh, go on,' he said. 'A bit of fresh air will do him good. And you,' he added, 'you're looking a bit peelie-wally.' She had to steel herself not to jump when he stretched out one long finger and touched her lightly on the cheek.

Charles folded the newspaper he'd been reading and threw a glance at the outside world. 'Brrr! I think Caroline's right. I'm out later on this morning, but I'm planning to sit here and toast my toes for the next hour or so. Perhaps your mother would go with you and the young fellow, Matthew.'

'I'm afraid not,' said Shona, arching her beautifully plucked eyebrows. 'I'm meeting a friend for lunch in town, and I want to do some shopping beforehand.'

Matthew stood up and replaced the chair. 'Well, my boy and I are going, aren't we, son?'

Archie, playing happily on the rug at his mother's feet, gave his father a wrinkled-nose smile. 'Walk?' he asked.

'A walk,' Matt confirmed, lifting the little boy into his arms. He splayed his hand out over the small chest, holding Archie strong and secure.

'Mammy come too?'

'Maybe if we ask her nicely.' Father and son turned as one. 'Please come,' Matt said softly.

She went. It might have been because she didn't relish the prospect of being left alone with her father-in-law, or because she didn't want to disappoint Archie. Or perhaps it was because Matthew had asked her nicely.

She walked beside him like a silent ghost. He was being

determinedly cheerful, pointing things out to Archie and not showing any irritation at her own lack of conversation. However, when the little boy nodded off on the journey home, Matthew also grew quiet. The air between them began to fizz with tension.

The house was empty when they got back. Matt, who'd lifted the pushchair up the front steps whilst Carrie held the door open, stood in the echoing hallway and looked down at his sleeping son.

'Should we wake him up for his lunch?' he whispered.

She shook her head and pointed to their bedroom. He lifted Archie out of the pushchair. The shawl wrapped around him tangled on a metal bar. Carrie hastened to free it, Matt waiting patiently while she did so. He stood back to let her go ahead of him into their bedroom and through to the dressing room. She pulled back the cot blankets and he laid the baby down. Together, they laid the covers over him and tiptoed out of the small room.

Laying his palm flat on the finger-plate Matthew pushed the door gently closed and walked a few steps away from it. Carrie was standing by their bed. He folded his arms and indicated the dressing room with an inclination of his head. 'You know, whatever the two of us do with our lives, he'll always be our greatest achievement.' His eyes went to her body. 'The one that's coming as well, of course.'

Carrie made no comment.

'Well,' he said, 'shall I make us some lunch?'

She couldn't help smiling at that. 'You wouldn't know where to start.'

'Maybe I'm trying to make a peace offering,' he said. 'Maybe I'm trying to say sorry.' He raised his eyebrows and uncrossed his arms. 'I've never found it an easy thing to do.'

'You hit me,' she said. 'You –' She broke off, sat down on

the bed and put the heel of her hand to her mouth. She couldn't bring herself to say that word.

'Carrie . . .' He came towards her, but she put an arm out, trying to fend him off.

'I felt invaded. Used.' She wasn't crying, but Matt was. He slid to his knees in front of her, seized her hands and pressed them to his brow, his head bent over her lap.

'I'm sorry,' he said brokenly. 'I apologise. I don't know what came over me. It'll never happen again, I promise.'

He raised his head and she caught her breath at the sight of those glittering eyes. 'But I love you so much, and I want you so much. You've been busy with Archie lately and concerned about the new baby too, and I understand that, I really do, but I need your time and attention as well.'

'Oh, Matt,' she said sorrowfully.

'Tell me you forgive me, Carrie. Tell me you still love me.'

She was no match for that plea. 'Of course I still love you,' she said, not understanding how he could doubt her, 'but we need a new start, Matt. Away from here.'

He threw his arms about her waist, placed his heavy head against her stomach. 'Anything,' he said. 'Anything you want, my little wife.'

Chapter 20

Knowing Matt would inevitably find their new home small, Carrie was careful to look for the nicest place they could comfortably afford. For starters, it was in a red sandstone block whose entrance passageway and stairs were decorated with beautiful dark green china tiles. A wally close was always a mark of superiority.

Their own two-apartment house had a lovely bay window in the front room and was also on the first floor. One up was the best position, away from the noise and dirt of the street, but not necessitating a strenuous climb carrying washing, messages or babies to the top of the building. As in most tenements in Glasgow, this was indicated on the outside of the building.

The first-floor windows were surmounted by a projecting piece of decorative stonework which followed the lines of the bay. The second-floor ones also had their crowns, although as usual the adornment was a little simpler than on the floor below. The third floor, which had no bay windows, was completely plain. This was common practice. However, Carrie considered her block vastly superior to many others she had seen because there were some architectural frills and furbelows between the third storey and the top floor. The building was undeniably handsome.

Best of all as far as she was concerned was that it was very central: round the corner from the steamie, along from the library and not too far from the station. If she looked out of the side panel of the bay window she could see the trains on the bridge which carried the railway across Dumbarton Road.

There were one or two flies in the ointment. Although most of her new neighbours were friendly, the woman across the landing was anything but. A bleached blonde in her mid-thirties with a cigarette dangling permanently from her lips, she greeted Carrie's friendly overtures with thinly veiled hostility. Baffled, she mentioned it to Matt, who advised her blithely to forget it.

'She's probably jealous of you. She lives with that old wifie, doesn't she? Her mother?'

'Mother-in-law, I think,' said Carrie, ladling him out a plate of Scotch broth. They were close enough to the station now for him to come home for his midday meal. She hadn't pointed out this advantage in so many words, but she was planning on cooking him something really tasty each day. 'They're both Mrs Cooke.'

'Where's Mr Cooke?' he asked idly. 'Away working somewhere? At sea? Gone to his reward?' He lifted his eyebrows and his spoon. 'Maybe she murdered him and buried him in the back court.'

'I dunno.' Carrie filled her own plate, sat down and buttered a slice of bread for him. 'I'm not likely to find out either. She seems to find it hard enough to say good morning to me.' She gave Archie his bowl of soup, which had been cooling down on the table, out of his reach. 'Why would she be jealous?'

'Because she lives on her own with the old bat, whereas you have a handsome husband and son.' He smiled across the table at Archie, who beamed in response. Unfortunately, the little boy's mouth was full of Scotch broth at the time. Carrie tutted and stood up to remedy the situation.

'It's all over your hands, you wee toerag!'

Matt laughed. 'You've got your work cut out with him, haven't you?' He applied himself to his own soup. 'And,' he said, several spoonfuls later, 'you're rather nice-looking yourself, Mrs Campbell.'

'Why, thank you, kind sir.' She gave the tray of Archie's high chair one last wipe and slipped back into her chair. If she didn't get to her own soup soon, it would be luke-warm. She reached for her spoon, but Matthew's hand took hers.

'I bet a lot of men are jealous of me,' he said softly.

'Because your wife's a dab hand at making soup?'

'That,' he agreed, his eyes roaming over her face, 'and the rest. Give us a kiss, gorgeous.'

Her broth was growing colder by the second, but she did as he had asked. He was on his best behaviour at the moment. The least she could do was meet him halfway.

The attitude of her nearest neighbour continued to bother Carrie. She found it all the more inexplicable because 'the old bat', as Matthew so charmingly called her, was friendly, and made a great fuss of Archie.

She refused to let it spoil her pleasure in being mistress of her own home at last. Not even the fact that her kitchen was dominated by an old black range identical to the one at White Street could do that. On her first morning in the house, a frosty February day, Carrie decided it wasn't going to beat her, and got busy getting to know her way around it. Within a week she was beginning to appreciate its good points, not least how quickly it dried clothes on the pulley suspended above it.

Unlike White Street, her new home didn't have its own wash-house in the back court. A visit to the steamie in Purdon

Street beckoned. Carrie took Archie by the hand, hoisted a wicker basket of washing on to her hip, and set off.

When she got there she stood awkwardly in the doorway, not quite sure of the procedure. The place seemed huge, and very noisy. There were pipes everywhere and clouds of steam condensing on the white-tiled walls. Women stood at deep sinks in individual stalls separated from each other by low and narrow wooden partitions. Some were bent over washboards, other were laughing and calling to each other as they worked. It was all a bit daunting.

The woman in the first stall, attacking a grimy shirt collar with a big bar of Sunlight soap, looked up. 'Is this your first time, hen?'

Someone laughed raucously. 'Look at the wee lad, Rena, no' to mention her belly. It cannae be her first time.'

Carrie's heart sank when the woman who had made the coarse remark stepped forward. It was her unfriendly neighbour, Mrs Cooke. Hair done up in curlers with a scarf over them, a flowery pinny wrapped round her skinny frame, she jabbed a finger at Archie. 'This is no place for a wean. It's dangerous wi' all this hot water aboot.'

'I've n-nowhere to l-leave him.'

The potential dangers of the steamie had occurred to Carrie, but she'd had no choice other than to bring Archie with her. She could hardly have taken him up the hill to her mother-in-law. Relations were a little strained at the moment, Shona being incapable of understanding Carrie's need to be mistress of her own home. She might have left him with Rita Sharkey but after Matthew's contretemps with her eldest son, Carrie would have been embarrassed to ask such a favour. The woman called Rena spoke.

'Stop going on at the lassie, Isa. We'll find something to amuse the wee laddie and keep him out of harm's way while

228

his ma's doing the washing.' She turned to Carrie. 'Miss Burgess as was, isn't it?'

'Yes,' she said gratefully.

'Come on then. I'll show ye the ropes.'

They knew who she was. She'd been accepted into the fold.

Carrie couldn't believe how lucky she was. She'd had another healthy child, a little girl this time.

'A redhead like her mother,' observed Matt, cupping the tiny head gently in his palm and walking slowly up and down in front of the bay window.

Propped up against two pillows watching him, Carrie was feeling rather pleased with herself. Confounding the predictions of all the women around her, her labour had lasted a few hours longer than with Archie, but the memories were already beginning to fade. Mother Nature's gift to mothers: selective amnesia.

She was wearing a pretty white lacy bed jacket which Josephine Shaw had presented her with yesterday when she and Roderick had called past to see the baby. She'd been touched and a little surprised by the evident emotion with which Josephine had held the wee one.

Matt holding his daughter also made a lovely picture. Whatever difficulties they'd had in the first two and a half years of their marriage, Carrie couldn't fault his love for his children. His dark eyes were soft as he surveyed the baby girl. He'd chosen her name: April, for the month of her birth.

'You're not disappointed because we haven't had another boy?'

'Disappointed? Of course not. We've got a gentleman's family now. A boy and a girl. Mind you,' he murmured, coming over and bending forward to carefully lay the shawl-wrapped bundle in the crook of her arm, 'I'm hoping we'll have some more.'

'Not for a while though, Matt.'

Her response had been too quick, and too anxious. The features of the dark face above her own stiffened.

'You don't need to remind me that my tap's stopped for the next few weeks, Carrie.'

More than a few, she hoped. That was the last thing on her mind at the moment. He straightened up and looked down at them both.

'I suppose you're determined to nurse her yourself?'

She laid her forefinger along April's downy cheek. 'Of course I am. You enjoy a feed from your mammy, don't you, wee lassie? And Mammy likes feeding you.'

'Carrie, honestly.' Matt looked faintly disgusted. 'Do you have to be quite so graphic?'

Determined the children shouldn't be deprived of contact with their grandparents on her account, Carrie made the effort to visit North Gardner Street from time to time. She'd spent an hour there this afternoon, a short enough period for Charles Campbell to be able to maintain an interest. He'd made faces at three-month-old April and got Archie thoroughly over-excited by some rumbustious play.

Shona had been her usual cool and aloof self. Taking the long way round to avoid having to push the big pram and attached baby seat down the steep slope of Gardner Street – the thought of what could happen if her hands slipped gave her the heebie-jeebies – Carrie was thinking about that as she made her way home.

Matt adored his mother and looked up to his father, but he'd never received the attention he craved from either of them. She guessed that was why he was often so demanding of her. There were times when she thought she had three children, not two.

He was always looking for something he couldn't seem to find, a niche where he would be appreciated and valued. He was good at his job, but that fight with Pascal Sharkey hadn't helped his chances of promotion. He'd blotted his copybook, and there had to be a period of penance before his superiors would trust him again. Most galling of all, Matt's support for Sir Oswald Mosley's political philosophy – the very thing which had caused the fight in the first place – had waned sharply. If only he could find something which would hold his interest and give him some real satisfaction!

April started to grizzle, needing her mother's breast. They were running a bit late today, but feeding her before they had left North Gardner Street hadn't been an option. Shona would have had a fit of the vapours. April's grandfather, on the other hand, would probably have been only too keen on the idea.

As Carrie approached her own close, a young girl who lived on the top floor of the building came running up and asked shyly if she'd like to come and watch the concert she and her friends were about to put on in the back court.

'Oh, I'm sorry, pet,' she said. 'I'd love to, but April's needing fed.'

The child's face fell, and Carrie hesitated. So far these summer holidays the children hadn't had much chance to put on any of their wee shows. The weather had been extremely wet. She was very fond of the girl, who loved to be allowed to help with Archie and April. Her mother was a really nice person too. When Carrie had been convalescing after the birth, she'd sent her daughter down with a large pot of soup and other bits and pieces to keep them going until she was up and about again.

Old Mrs Cooke was coming through the close. Despite her

younger namesake's continuing hostility, she'd been a great help in the months since April's birth. She and Archie had taken a real shine to each other. When she'd first offered to mind him for a wee while so his mother could put her feet up for an hour in the afternoon while the baby slept, Carrie had been grateful, but absolutely convinced that her son wouldn't go anywhere without her. She'd ended up muttering 'traitor' to his small retreating back as he toddled off happily hand in hand with the woman he now knew as Auntie Florence.

'There's people out here want to know when the entertainment's starting, young lady. Hello there, Carrie. Are you coming through to watch the bairns?'

She explained her predicament. Florence looked puzzled. 'Feed her outside. Naebody'll mind.'

The older woman led the way to the back court, where an assortment of chairs had been assembled. Most of them were already occupied, mainly by mothers and grannies. There were one or two men present, either on shift work or unemployed. Florence's daughter-in-law Isa was also there, turning to look at the newcomers with cool eyes.

'Sit doon here,' said Florence to Carrie. 'This seat's fine and low.'

A man came over to help unfasten Archie from the baby seat and lift him off. Before he set him down he raised him up into the air a couple of times, causing the little boy to laugh with delight. Carrie took her daughter out of the pram, sat down on the low chair and began unbuttoning her blouse. Dipping into the bundle of covers at the foot of the pram which had been discarded on such a warm day, Florence fished out a shawl. She draped it over Carrie's shoulders.

'There you are, pet,' she said. 'Discretion guaranteed.'

Carrie found herself enjoying the simple entertainment. The children had rehearsed their show well. There were

232

traditional songs and popular songs and a funny sketch involving Hitler and Mussolini. The boy playing the Italian dictator was particularly good. She transferred April from one side to the other and, with the rest of the audience, joined the young performers in a spirited rendition of *Roaming in the Gloaming*.

There was a harsh screeching sound as a sash window above their heads was thrown up. 'In the name o' God, how's a man on night shift supposed to get any sleep with this bloody racket going on?'

The protest was somewhat diluted by the grin on the man's face as he looked down at all the faces looking back up at him. His wife poked her head out of the window beside him. 'Pay him no mind, children. He was getting up for his tea anyway. And I think your singing's lovely.'

The couple lived directly above Carrie. She tilted her head back and gave them both a cheerful wave. Nuzzled against her breast, April had fallen asleep. She adjusted her arms around the sleeping baby and sat back comfortably in the chair, warm and relaxed. She became aware that someone was standing behind her and turned to see who it was.

'Oh, hello, Matt,' she said. 'You're a wee bit early.'

He waited till they'd had their tea and the children were safely asleep. Sometimes he helped get them ready for bed, but tonight he sat and watched in silence as she washed April and Archie in turn in the small round bath in front of the range. Normally, he disposed of the dirty water and put away its receptacle. He made no move to do so tonight.

She dried the children, got them into their nightclothes and put them to bed. Then she settled them down to sleep with a kiss on each small brow and went back through to the kitchen. She went forward to remove the tin bath.

233

'Leave it,' he said, his voice cracking like a whip. Then he started. What sort of trollop was she to be exposing herself to half of Partick, men as well as women? How did it make him look, that his wife conducted herself in such a common manner?

At first she tried to defend herself, but within five minutes she had fallen silent, no match for the verbal onslaught. He went on and on, his language growing ever coarser. Some of the words he used made her wince. By the time his fury was eventually spent Carrie was pale and trembling.

She stood at the open door of the flat, uncertain of her next move. It was the afternoon of the following day and she felt the need to get out of the house. She was only planning on going downstairs for a few minutes but wasn't sure about leaving the children. No, that was daft. They were both having their afternoon naps, tucked up securely in cot and pram respectively, and with the door left ajar she'd hardly be out of earshot.

She hesitated, hovering on the doorstep. She wasn't feeling very decisive today. The door of the flat opposite opened and Isa Cooke came out with a duster and a can of brass polish in her hands. Head bowed, she appeared lost in thought. She looked up, saw Carrie, and jumped.

'In the name o' the wee man! Have you nothing better to do than lurk about trying to give folk heart attacks?' Her hand went to her bosom, presumably to quell the frantic beating of the organ in question.

In a more cynical mood, Carrie would have recognised that her neighbour was rather making a meal of it. In her present state of mind, she could only stutter out an apology. Her voice trembled as she said the words. Isa Cooke took two steps forward and peered into Carrie's face.

'What the hell's wrang wi' ye?'

'Nothing.' She turned, blindly, to go back in, not wanting to disgrace herself in front of this woman who seemed to dislike her so much. She heard a sigh, felt her arm being taken, and the next thing she knew she was being pushed into one of the chairs set round the table in her neighbour's kitchen.

'Are the weans asleep?'

Carrie nodded.

'You'll be glad to get a wee rest yourself.'

That had been suspiciously close to a friendly comment. Carrie must really have given her a fright. Isa put her can of polish and duster on one shelf and lifted down a packet of cigarettes, a box of matches and an ashtray from another.

'Jimmy and me never had any children,' she said. She lit up, narrowing her eyes against the smoke. 'Then the stupid bugger went and got himself killed in the yard, so that was the end o' that.'

'I'm sorry.'

Isa shrugged, and took a pull on the cigarette. 'Why should you be sorry? It wisnae your fault. He went to work blootered, that was the long and the short o' it. Missed his footing, and down he went. Leaving me wi' his black-hearted bitch of a mother.'

'Who's not home at the moment, I presume,' said Carrie, beginning to recover. She knew it wouldn't have made much difference if the older woman had been there. The two Mrs Cookes seemed positively to enjoy hurling abuse at each other.

'Never mind that.' Isa laid the ashtray on the table and fixed her guest with a penetrating stare. 'You got yourself into trouble with your man yesterday. Am I right?'

Carrie pressed her eyes tightly shut for a few seconds. That was a mistake. It brought back the memory of Matt ranting and raving at her, looking at her out of cold and

235

unforgiving eyes, calling her horrible names.

'The walls here are no' as thick as you might think, hen.'

Carrie put her elbows on the table and sank her head into her hands. She hadn't the heart to deny it. Matt had knocked the heart out of her last night . . . Through the curtain of her hair, she was aware of the cigarette being stubbed out.

'Here,' came Isa's voice a minute or two later, 'you're a nursing mother. You need to keep your strength up.'

A plate with a piece of gingerbread on it was pushed under her nose. It was followed by a cup of milk. The unexpected kindness undid Carrie completely. Tears slid unchecked down her smooth cheeks. Isa said nothing, but she sat down at the table opposite her and waited.

Carrie wiped her eyes with her hands and sniffed. 'Sorry. It's just that this isn't how I expected my life to turn out.'

'You chose him.' If the rough voice had softened before, it became harder again now. 'You didnae have to. You had another choice.'

You had another choice. Carrie's head snapped up. It was as if Ewen had come into the room. She could see him: hair all over the place, open-necked shirt flapping in the breeze, rakish red kerchief knotted at his throat. He was chuckling at her – for being so stupid, probably.

A mother and daughter-in-law living together but arguing with each other all the time . . . A husband and son who'd died in a shipyard accident . . . Ewen laughing himself silly at the thought of the two women consoling each other in their hour of need. Now she could hear him as well as see him. '*I think black-hearted bitch is ma personal favourite.*'

'You're his mother's friend,' she breathed.

'Throw the girl a peanut,' said Isa sourly. 'She's managed to work it out at last.'

Chapter 21

Tears forgotten, Carrie began asking questions. 'Do you know where he is? How he's getting on?'

Isa pretended to study her fingernails. 'Do you care?'

'Of course I do!' Stung, she blurted out the words. 'Ewen was my friend.'

'Funny way to treat a friend.'

'What do you mean?'

The other woman made her wait, lighting another cigarette before she let Carrie have it. It was a bit like standing in the dock knowing you were about to be mercilessly harangued by the lawyer leading the case for the prosecution. Only instead of a neat legal wig, this attacker had a head of tight peroxide curls.

'You know exactly what I mean. You broke Ewen Livingstone's heart. You picked Matthew Campbell over him because you thought you'd have an easier life that way. Up the hill in your main door flat,' she spat out.

'It wasn't like that . . .'

Her impassioned protest was ignored.

'He told you about his mother – who, by the way, was one o' the nicest women I've ever met in my entire life – and you threw it back in his face.' Isa tossed her head. 'D'you think it was easy for him to tell you that story?' She stopped finally for breath and looked accusingly at Carrie.

'No,' she responded sadly. 'I don't think it was easy for him. I don't think anything was ever easy for him.'

'You are dead right there, hen,' said Isa fiercely. She took a couple of angry puffs and then the second cigarette joined the first, stubbed out in the ashtray barely smoked. 'He's done very well for himself. No thanks to you.'

Carrie waited. She could see there was a battle going on. Pride in Ewen was warring with condemnation of herself. Pride won.

'He's working in Edinburgh. Shameful thing for a Glasgow man, eh? He's a clerk at the Waverley. Went in for the exam a year and a half ago. Passed wi' flying colours.'

'He finally made it? I'm so pleased for him!' Carrie sat up in her chair. 'Do you hear from him regularly?'

She was getting an odd look. 'He writes to us once a month. Without fail.'

'He writes? Och, that's just great!'

Carrie was still on the receiving end of that appraising gaze. Then Isa looked pointedly at the plate and cup she'd placed in front of her.

'Drink your milk,' she said. 'And eat your gingerbread. I didnae put out good food for you to let it go to waste.'

She ought to be getting back, but she'd not been brought up to waste food either. 'Lovely gingerbread,' she said a minute or two later, lifting the last crumbs off the plate with a dampened finger.

'Aye,' said Isa grudgingly, 'the old yin's no' bad at the baking.'

Carrie finished the milk. 'Thank you. I'd better be getting back now.' She pushed her chair away and stood up. 'Isa when you next write to Ewen, would you let him know I was asking for him? And that I congratulate him – most warmly – on making clerk.'

Isa gave her a look but said nothing, simply got to her feet and saw her out. Four days later, however, she knocked on Carrie's front door, about half an hour after Matthew had gone to work.

'This came for you.' She turned on her heel and disappeared into her own house. When Carrie looked at the envelope she saw there was one word written on it: her own name.

It took her some time to summon up the courage to open it. Since her conversation with Isa, she'd been prey to an enormous sense of guilt about Ewen. She'd hurt him so badly, ridden roughshod over his feelings. How could she expect him to forgive her? Yet why would he have bothered to write to her if that was how he felt? Maybe he wanted to give her a piece of his mind, but he had written that simple *Carrie* on the envelope. If the letter contained a lambasting, surely he'd have been more formal.

She got on with her chores, settled Archie at the kitchen table with his toy farm, fed April and put her down for her morning nap. Only then did she take a knife out of the cutlery drawer, slide it under the flap and open the envelope.

Dear Carrie, she read as she put the knife back and walked slowly over to stand in front of the range. *Bet you never expected to get a letter from me!* It was as though he was there with her – smiling and friendly, his usual sunny self. She turned the page over to see how he had signed himself. *Your affectionate friend, Ewen Livingstone*. Her eyes misted over. He'd forgiven her. He still called himself her friend.

'Why Mammy crying?'

Archie, engaged in giving a sheep a bareback ride on a cow, had chosen that very moment to look up. Engrossed in Ewen's letter, Carrie answered him rather absently. 'Because I've just had a letter from an old friend, my wee petal.'

Well, now you know who your neighbours are, as it were!

239

I'm glad of the chance that gives me to say how sorry I was when I heard that your mother had passed away. That must have been very difficult for you coming so soon after Mr Burgess's death.

Isa tells me you have a fine wee boy and a beautiful baby daughter. They must be a great consolation to you. I'm sure they keep you busy!

He went on, briefly, to tell her he was doing well, beginning to move up the grades and enjoying the work. *A lot better than being out in all weathers, like I used to have to do. And I know who I have to thank for it all.*

That brought a lump to her throat. She read the whole thing again, right through to *Your affectionate friend, Ewen Livingstone.*

Affectionate. It had been one of their words of the week. That would be why he had chosen that adjective. They'd had a lot of fun over all that, she remembered, thinking back to those sunlit days in the garden of the station house.

She folded the single sheet of paper and slipped it back into the envelope. Stretching up, she tucked the letter in behind the big willow pattern platter which stood in pride of place on the shelf above the range, fitting in neatly under the gas mantle and flanked by two smaller plates in the same design. They had all belonged to her grandmother, Esther's mother. She often kept Mary's latest missive there for a few days, taking it down from time to time to re-read it.

Then she thought about it. However innocent the contents of the letter she had just received, Matt wasn't going to be very happy when he found out that Ewen had written to her. It might be better to get rid of it straightaway. Her fingers were on the envelope, ready to pull it back out and consign it to the flames of the fire – but that seemed a terrible thing to do.

I know who I have to thank for it all. It was sweet of him to

240

say so, but judging by the neat handwriting and excellent spelling, Ewen had put in an awful lot of hard work himself. Her thoughts drifted back once more to that summer three years ago. She was remembering the occasion when he had brought her an apple for the teacher. She could see him in her mind's eye, delving in his tool bag, then presenting it to her with a flourish.

She smiled. She'd keep his letter for a wee while, read it again in a couple of days. Then she would burn it. She pushed it back in behind the plate so that it was completely out of sight. No point in allowing it to cause trouble between her and Matt.

'How was work?'

'Don't ask,' he said gloomily, but he seemed to be in a good enough mood as he took off his jacket and loosened his collar and tie. He'd had a long day today, working over his midday break to cover for a colleague attending a funeral.

'Never mind,' said Carrie as he went to the sink to wash his hands. 'I've made something special for tea tonight.' She grabbed a cloth to protect her hands and crouched in front of the range to take an enamel ashet out of the oven. Turning, she placed the steep-sided dish carefully on a cork mat lying on top of the checked seersucker tablecloth. Archie, who liked his food, regarded his prospective tea with interest. His father peered at it suspiciously.

'Macaroni *au gratin*,' said Carrie proudly.

'That means with cheese sauce, doesn't it?' Matt looked doubtful. 'There's no meat in it, then?'

'I'm afraid not. But I think you'll find it tasty all the same. Give it a try.'

She spooned him out a small portion. After a few mouthfuls he declared it to be excellent and asked for more. Smiling with satisfaction, his young wife obliged.

'Where did you get the recipe?'

'They were demonstrating it at the Empire Exhibition when I went with Josephine Shaw last month.'

'She seems to like being with our two, doesn't she? Strange thing for a career woman like her.'

Carrie answered non-committally, 'She likes children.'

'Can't imagine why. They're all horrible wee monsters.' He leaned over and tickled Archie on the stomach.

'Matthew! Not while he's eating, please.'

'Women,' tutted Matt. 'What would you do with them?'

Evidently in total agreement with his father, Archie gave a shrug of his small shoulders and screwed up his face in a gesture of exasperation. Matthew grinned at him and turned to share the moment with Carrie. She smiled back, and the grin transformed itself into a long, slow smile.

'Dessert,' she said brightly, and leaped up to fetch it.

'Well, young man,' said Matthew, 'what have you been doing today?'

'I played with my farm.'

'With your sheep? Or your cows?'

'With my sheep *and* my cows.'

The smile was still on Carrie's face as she listened to them. Archie was a very good speaker, but then he'd always had lots of encouragement. She talked to him all the time as she went through her day, and Matt always took an interest when he came home from work. As he was taking an interest now.

'And what did Mammy do today?'

'She got a letter,' said the clear childish voice. 'From an old friend. It made her cry.'

Carrie set a bowl of blancmange on the table. Matt glanced up at her.

'A letter that made you cry? Who was that from?'

'A friend in Edinburgh,' she said brightly.

'I didn't know you had any friends through there.' Matt looked quizzical. 'Anybody I know?'

'No,' she said quickly, 'I don't think so.'

'So what's she called? It is a *she*, is it?'

She hesitated for the merest second. It was long enough. She saw what she had hoped never to see again. Something was happening behind Matt's eyes.

'Isn't that funny, Archie?' He was still speaking in that pleasant tone of voice, but it was sending shivers up and down Carrie's spine. 'Mammy doesn't seem to know the name of her friend. The one she got a letter from today. Isn't that odd? Maybe Mammy's friend can't write very well. That would explain it, wouldn't it?'

Carrie's blood ran cold in her veins. Archie was looking up at his father, not understanding what was going on.

'Don't bring him into it,' she said. 'Please.'

Matt's dark eyes flickered, but he lifted the little boy off his seat and hunkered down in front of him. 'I want you to go through to the front room, Archie, and make sure your sister's all right.'

'Take April some pudding?'

Matt shook his head. 'No, she's too wee for that. You can take your own though.' He spoke without turning around. 'Put some out for him.' In contrast to the way he was speaking to their son, it was a curt order.

Her hands trembling, Carrie obeyed and passed a bowl and spoon over to him. He took it and handed it to Archie. 'Now then,' he said, 'you've not to come back till Daddy comes for you. Understand?'

'Is it a game?'

'Sort of.'

Closing the heavy door behind the boy, Matt put his back

243

to it and surveyed her in silence. She stood between the table and the range, still holding the serving spoon with which she had dished out Archie's blancmange.

She noticed that the weight of her husband's tall and powerful body was pulling on the coats which hung on the back of the door. If he stayed there for much longer, the hanging loops would snap. Even as the thought flitted across her mind, he pushed himself off and took a few steps towards her.

'Where is it?' he asked. The game had begun.

Chapter 22

'Archie come back through now?'

The door creaked open. Carrie was lying where Matt had left her, on the floor with her back against the wooden cupboards under the box bed. She had her arms curled protectively about her head, still unconsciously trying to shield herself from the slaps and punches he had rained down on her. She hadn't managed to keep many of them out. He'd split her lip, and her left eye felt gritty and swollen.

Archie came round the door and into the room, his eyes as big as saucers. She tried to scramble to her feet, but one leg gave way. She winced as pain stabbed through her thigh. That must have happened when Matt had hurled her against a chair, demanding to know where Ewen's letter was: the letter whose hiding place the movement of her eyes had betrayed.

'I fell, Archie,' she said. 'Your silly mammy fell. Come here and give me a cuddle and that'll maybe help me get up.'

He trotted obediently to her and coiled his arms about her neck. 'Daddy gone back to work?' he asked, his voice muffled as he pressed his small face against her neck.

She pulled him more tightly to her. 'Yes, Daddy's gone back to work.' He was accepting it all, she thought gratefully. He was used to Matt working shifts, coming home and going back out again, and he was too young to question the oddness of his father having left his mother lying hurt on the floor.

He didn't need to know what had really happened here. Nor, even if he had heard anything, would he have understood any of the vile things Matt had said. He had read the letter out loud before crumpling it up and flinging it on the fire. He had seized on that *your affectionate friend* before he did so, demanding to know why Ewen had used that particular word. Carrie had tried to explain it was a simple word game, one they had played while she'd been teaching him to read and write.

'What other games did you and he play?' Matt demanded. He had her pinned down, his fingers handcuffing her wrists to the arms of the big chair in front of the range. To her horror, he accused her of having let Ewen make love to her. She protested in vain that Matt knew better than anybody that she had been a virgin on their wedding night.

'A virgin who knew what French letters were,' he spat into her face. 'That's the sort of thing only whores know about. Or sons of whores.'

He kept using that dreadful word, right up until he finally stopped hitting her, his breathing coming fast and ragged. Arms up, she was waiting for the next onslaught when she heard the front door bang with a force which must have echoed down to the close and up to the top floor of the building.

'Go get Auntie Florence and Auntie Isa?'

Dazed, she wondered when Archie had decided to confer that title not only on the old lady, but also on her sharp-tongued daughter-in-law.

'No!'

She had frightened him. He pulled himself out of her arms, and his wee face crumpled. It was hard to smile with a cut lip. It was hard to smile when your heart was breaking. Somehow Carrie managed it.

'Mammy'll be fine.' She made it to her feet. 'See? I'm all

246

right now. I'm fine,' she repeated. She found her way to the chair, extending an arm to bring him with her. That hurt. She settled herself gingerly into the seat. That hurt too. Her eyes went to a stain on the floor, the sticky trail left by the serving spoon she'd been using for the blancmange. It had flown out of her hand when Matthew had struck the first blow, skidding across the floor and ending up in front of the sink. Somebody knocked at the front door.

'Archie, go and say your mammy's a bit busy at the moment.'

'Can't reach the door.' He was standing in front of her, one finger in his mouth. He looked so worried.

'No,' she said gently. 'Of course you can't.'

It took her ages to get there, Archie hovering at her side, the knocking now continuous. 'I'm coming, I'm coming!'

From the front room she heard April start up. Should she go and see to the baby before she opened the door? She couldn't decide. Her head was swimming. In the end, she decided she had to make the knocking stop.

'In the name o' God, we thought he'd killed you all!'

'Shush,' she muttered, falling back against the open door. 'Archie's here . . .'

'Mammy fell,' he piped up.

'Did she, son?' exclaimed Florence. 'Och, that's a shame. Look,' she said, exchanging a swift glance with her daughter-in-law, 'why don't you come across to our hoose while your Auntie Isa helps your mammy? I'm needin' a hand to make some biscuits.'

'Aye.' Isa nodded her head in approval. 'That's a good idea. You run along, wee man.'

Carrie had her head tilted back against the solid wood of the door, but it was still spinning. 'April needs seeing to.'

Her voice seemed to be coming from a long way off, as did

the rough one which answered her. 'Well, I can change her, but you'll have to do the ten minutes each side!' She felt her arm being taken and Isa beginning to lead her through to the kitchen.

'April,' she protested. 'Need to feed April.'

'I'll get her for you in a wee minute, but first I'm going to see you into your chair. I hope you werenae planning on going to the dancing the night. You're no' in a very good state to be attempting the foxtrot.'

Isa settled her in front of the range, took a pillow off the bed and tucked it in behind her, and then fetched the baby. With unabashed practicality, she helped Carrie undo her blouse.

'Now,' she said briskly, 'while you're doing that, let's have a look at you. Will you and me be paying a wee visit to the Western Infirmary this evening, d'ye think? We'll have to lash out on a taxi if we do. You're no' fit to walk there and no' fit to be seen either, so the tram's out o' the question.'

'I'm not going to the hospital.' Carrie's voice was a little stronger.

'I'll be the judge o' that, young lady. Let's get you cleaned up and see what the damage is.'

Ten minutes later, Isa grudgingly allowed that hospital treatment wasn't going to be necessary. 'Mind you,' she said, 'you're gonnae have a right keeker the morn. That eye's swelling up nicely. Walloped you good and proper, didn't he? Made a bloody good job of it.'

Carrie almost laughed. Isa was looking her over like an artist surveying a work in progress. 'A wee cup of tea, hen?'

Carrie raised an exploratory finger to her mouth, drawing her breath in on a hiss when it made contact with the cut. 'Make some for yourself if you like. I don't think I can drink anything with this lip.'

'That's where fags come in handy,' said Isa sagely. 'Even if the bugger's planted a few on your mouth, ye can usually find a wee corner to stick your Woodbine.'

'Your Jimmy hit you?' Normally Carrie wouldn't have dreamed of asking such a question, but this wasn't exactly a normal evening.

'Once or twice,' said Isa drily. 'When he had a drink in him. Which was quite a lot o' the time, in actual fact. Not that the old bitch would ever admit her wee boy was capable o' anything like that.'

She dipped into her apron pocket and brought out her cigarettes. 'I thumped him back, mind,' she said thoughtfully. 'He didnae like that. Happy to dish it out, no' so happy to take it. His sort never are.' She lit up and sat down opposite Carrie. 'You're not the type to hit back though, are you?'

'I'm leaving him,' Carrie said calmly. 'I'm taking the children and I'm going.' Her voice shook.

'Of course you are, pet.' Isa blew out some smoke rings. Carrie had seen her do it before, but it was still a good trick. 'I'm no' very sure what you're going to do for money, mind. Or a place to stay.'

Carrie wasn't too sure about that either. Everyone she knew needed all the space they had. Apart from her parents-in-law, that was. Moving back in with them didn't seem a very realistic option . . .

'The three of you can stay with us tonight,' said Isa, 'but it's going to be a wee touch cramped. You'll have to sort something out with your man pretty damn' quick, especially if you don't want the laddie to twig that there's anything up. But none o' us are wanting a repeat performance of tonight's wee episode, are we now?'

Carrie stared at her, panic rising in her throat. 'You think he might do it again?'

'They usually do, hen.' Isa's voice was as dry as sandpaper.

'I could threaten to go to the police.'

Her neighbour looked at her pityingly. 'Don't make me laugh. The police'll no' help you. That would be intervening between husband and wife.' She said the phrase with considerable derision. 'They'll intervene if he murders you like, but no' before.' She stood up and looked down at her. 'You're on your own, kiddo. Except that you've got some friends.'

'I'm very grateful for them,' Carrie said tremulously. 'You and Florence have really come to my rescue tonight. Thank you.'

'Aye, well.' Isa tossed what was left of her cigarette on to the fire. 'Have you finished feeding the wean? Give her here, and I'll change her nappy.'

Matt came home at ten o'clock. He'd been drinking, but he wasn't drunk. He came into the room warily, like a man uncertain of what he was going to find. His eyes ranged over Carrie. She thought he seemed relieved at what he saw. Isa, who'd risen to her feet as soon as they heard the sound of his key in the lock, stood beside her chair like a personal bodyguard. Carrie was glad she was there. Her heart was thumping violently.

'I'd like to speak to my wife.'

'Would you now?'

Carrie waited for Matt to explode. He didn't. He transferred his gaze from Isa back to her. 'Are you all right?' he asked quietly.

'I'm as you see me,' she said levelly. *As you left me*. She considered a nonchalant shrug, but it would undoubtedly make her shoulders hurt more than they already did. Not knowing why he deserved to be given the slightest reassurance, she added something, forcing herself to use the same light tone of voice. 'There doesn't seem to be anything broken.'

'Thank God.' He ran a hand wildly through his hair. 'Oh, thank God.' He pulled a chair out and dropped into it like an apple falling off a tree. Putting an elbow on the table he leaned forward and shaded his eyes with his hand. Carrie glanced up at Isa. Her mouth was set in a cynical curve.

'Where are the children?' he asked.

Her heart rate had slowed. It was becoming easier to speak. 'With old Mrs Cooke. They're staying there tonight. So am I.'

Matt lifted his head and looked at her. 'I suppose I deserve that.'

Isa laughed. 'You deserve a lot more than that, pal. And I know a few good men who'd be more than happy to make sure you get it when they find out what you did to this lassie.'

Carrie saw panic flash across his face. *Happy to dish it out, no' so happy to take it*. Oh, Matt, she thought sadly, how have we come to this?

'Are you going to tell these few good men about . . . about what I did?' He was finding it hard to meet Isa's implacable gaze. His eyes were shifting all over the place.

'For some reason, your wife doesnae want me to. But I might still do it, a' the same. Let's just say the possibility is always there.' She let that sink in for a minute. 'Do we understand each other?' When he didn't answer her, she repeated the question.

'Yes,' he said, meeting Isa's eyes at last, 'we understand each other.'

Despite her pain and unhappiness, Carrie felt an odd little spurt of amusement. She was damned glad the redoubtable Mrs Cooke was on her side. What was the phrase – a better friend than an enemy?

Isa helped her up out of the chair, issuing instructions to

Matt. He could maybe speak to his wife tomorrow. If Carrie felt up to it.

'Ow! Sorry,' she said apologetically to Isa as she made her slow and tortuous way to the door. 'I think everything's stiffened up.'

'Can I help?' Matt was beside her, holding out his hand. She flinched back, and for a few seconds the three of them froze. Unsurprisingly, Isa was the first to recover her composure.

'Bit of a comedian, your husband,' she observed. 'You can open the doors,' she told him roughly. 'That's all.'

Carrie woke early the next morning, aching all over. She gazed at the outside world, visible through the curtains Florence had drawn back last night after she'd put them all to bed. Archie was on a camp bed under the bay window and April was in her pram at Carrie's feet. The day was overcast, and it was drizzling.

Isa and Florence had doubled up in the kitchen, the former threatening the latter with dire consequences if her snoring kept her awake. A panful of cold water was mentioned. Carrie was, however, beginning to see cracks in the apparent mutual hostility. The two women had made a highly effective team yesterday.

Florence had tucked her in like a child, bringing her warm milk and a straw to drink it through. All that was missing was Gertie the giraffe. She lived in Archie's bed now, through the wall from where the three of them lay. Carrie hoped she hadn't been lonely during the night . . .

She closed her eyes and the events of the previous evening started replaying themselves in her mind's eye. The pictures and sensations were so vivid they had her snapping her eyes wide open again and sitting bolt upright to check the children were safe.

Satisfied that they were sleeping peacefully, she subsided slowly on to the pillows. Now she had other pictures in her head. They were all of a very different Matt to the cold-eyed man who had beaten her last night.

She could see him pushing Archie in a swing, kicking a ball around with him in the park, tenderly cupping April's head in his palm, looking up and smiling directly into her own eyes. She flung herself on to her side and had to stifle a cry as the pain in her hip made itself felt.

Oh, God. Oh, God. Oh, God. What was she going to do?

He was full of contrition, unable to apologise enough. It was six o'clock that evening, and they were in their own front room. Isa and Florence were in the kitchen with the children. As far as Archie was concerned, his two aunties were simply paying a neighbourly visit. In reality, Isa had refused to allow Matt to speak to his wife under any other circumstances.

'We'll not be far away,' she'd said meaningly, ostentatiously making sure Carrie was comfortably ensconced in the low nursing seat. She pointed to the upright chair she had carried through and set in the bay window and gave Matt his orders. 'You're too tall. Sit doon.'

He obeyed her without a whimper, but as soon as she left the room, carefully leaving the door half open, he bent forward, hands on knees.

'Don't get up!'

Carrie hadn't realised till that moment how panicky she was at the thought of being left alone with him. He could move much faster than she could, especially at the moment. He hesitated, and settled back into his chair.

'You're scared of me,' he said bleakly.

'Do you blame me? Look at the state I'm in.' She gestured towards her black eye and bruised face. 'I'm in pain, Matthew.

Because of what you did. I don't understand how you could do that to me.'

He bit his lip and turned his head to look out of the narrow pane of glass at the end of the bay window. 'I don't understand it either, Carrie. I got so angry . . . it was like a rage . . . a red rage. I knew I was hurting you, but I couldn't seem to stop myself.'

He didn't need to tell her that. He'd been out of control. That was what had been so frightening about it. 'I suppose I was jealous,' he said. 'Because you'd had that letter from Ewen Livingstone.'

'Matt . . . you have absolutely no reason to be jealous of him. I haven't seen him for years. I got his letter via Isa.'

He stopped looking out of the window. 'So why did you hide it behind the plate? You weren't going to tell me about it, were you?'

'No,' she agreed slowly.

He pressed his advantage. 'Wives shouldn't have secrets from their husbands.'

'It wasn't a case of keeping something secret. You and Ewen always hated each other. I knew you'd be angry if you found out that he'd written to me.'

'How does Isa Cooke know him, anyway?'

'She was a friend of his mother.'

'Oh.' There was a wealth of meaning in that little word. Matt's eyes narrowed. 'Did you know that when we moved in here?' She met the suspicious look head on.

'No, of course not. I only found out a few days ago.'

'Were you planning on writing back to him?'

'He and I were good friends once,' Carrie said carefully.

'I don't want you to write back to him. And I don't like him talking about the children either. The three of you belong to me, not him.'

'Of course we do,' she said, although she didn't much care for the way he had put it.

'You do still want to belong to me?' He sounded so humble.

'Och, Matt . . .'

Before she had time to realise what was happening, he was on his feet and striding across the room. She looked up in alarm, but he knelt in front of her, an impassioned torrent of words pouring out of his mouth.

'Please forgive me, Carrie. I'll never do it again, I promise. It'll never happen again. Please, Carrie. Please.'

He said the words over and over, pleading with her. He began to weep.

'Och, Matt . . .' she said again. This was how it had ended before, with him on his knees in front of her. She didn't have the strength left to resist him. It would have been like refusing comfort to Archie or April when they needed her.

Wincing as she walked, Carrie made her way through to the kitchen. Florence was sitting with Archie on her lap. One of his picture books lay open in front of them.

'All right, pet?' she asked, glancing up.

'Fine. Isa, can I have a quick word?'

They went across the landing. Isa reached for her cigarettes and matches. 'Don't tell me,' she said, 'let me guess. He's been on his hands and knees to you. Crawled across the floor to beg your forgiveness. Swears he'll never do it again.'

Carrie said nothing. That picture was too accurate by half.

'They're all like that the first time, hen.' She tossed the spent match into the fire. 'They'll promise you the earth if you'll only take them back. But once they discover that hitting you is a hell of a good way of getting you to shut up, they'll not stop at just the once.'

Carrie shook her head. 'No, you're wrong. He's really upset.

255

Isa, he's in there sobbing,' she breathed, incredibly moved by the emotion Matt had shown. 'He hates himself for what he did.'

Isa's face remained set in cynical lines. 'I thought you were an educated woman. Have you never heard o' crocodile tears?'

'No,' Carrie said vehemently. 'It's not like that.'

Isa stared at her for a long moment. Then she sighed. 'Fine. I wish you all the best, hen.'

'Can we still be friends?'

'Aye, sure. Why not?'

'Will you thank Ewen for his letter the next time you write back to him?'

'You're no' going to reply to him yourself?'

'I don't think that would be a very good idea.' She hesitated. 'You'll not tell him anything about all this, I presume.'

'And why would you presume that, Mrs Campbell?'

'Because I'm asking you not to. Please.'

That got her a grunt, presumably of assent. 'Have I to say anything else to Ewen?'

'Tell him I wish him well for the future.'

Isa looked unimpressed. 'That's it?'

'That's it,' Carrie said firmly. 'And I do wish him well, Isa. I wish him all the luck in the world.'

Matt was her husband and the father of her children. He loved them all deeply. He was a passionate man, and a jealous one. She had known that from the outset. Now, however unfounded his suspicions, they had resulted in her getting hurt and him tearing himself to pieces over what he had done to her.

Carrie's way was clear. From now on she would have to make absolutely sure she gave him nothing to be jealous about. Not the slightest thing. It was up to her.

PART III
1942

Chapter 23

'Is Archie still liking the school, Carrie?' called the woman in the next stall. 'Now that the novelty's worn off?'

'He loves it. Can't wait to get there every morning.'

'Does your lassie miss him during the day?'

'A bit,' she said, looking with satisfaction at one of April's dresses from which she'd just managed to remove a stain. 'They've always been good pals, my two.'

'You'll need to be giving her a wee brother or sister to keep her company,' shouted another woman. 'Unless you and your man have forgotten how to go about it!'

'Give me a break,' Carrie said cheerfully. 'April's not four yet, you know.'

'Well,' said Rita Sharkey, 'I've borne my Martin eight children and I wouldn't be without a single one of them.'

'Aye, but you're a Catholic. Carrie's a Proddy.'

'And do Catholics and Proddies do it differently?' asked another interested voice.

Carrie grinned, and reached for a grimy shirt. Despite the hard work involved in doing the weekly wash, she felt able to relax here, be herself in a way which no longer seemed possible at home, at least when Matt was around. The public wash-house was a woman's world, a place to let off steam in more ways than one. Some of the discussions she had listened to over the scrubbing boards and sinks would have made a sailor blush.

'Keep it clean,' she suggested now.

'Oh, my,' came a very creditable attempt at a refined Kelvinside accent, 'is our young Mrs Campbell not awfy polite?'

'Born to be a lady,' said Carrie in a superior tone, 'but never required. Although,' she added, 'Isa's new gentleman friend makes us all feel like royalty. I've never met anyone so well-mannered. Stands up when you come into the room and kisses your hand when he says hello.'

She was bombarded with questions. Isa's romance with a Polish soldier had been the talk of the steamie for the past few weeks.

'Is he good-looking, Carrie? What's his name?'

'Where did she meet him? Do you think he might have any friends going spare?'

'Aye, but none o' them are that desperate!'

Carrie grinned again. 'He's called Leon, he's very handsome and she met him at that club for foreign servicemen at St George's Cross. I expect there's a few lonely lads from Warsaw there.'

Like most British cities, particularly the great ports, Glasgow had become quite a cosmopolitan place since the outbreak of war three years before.

'What does old Mrs Cooke think about it?' asked Rita Sharkey. 'Is she worried Isa'll up sticks and leave her on her own?'

'I suppose she might be.' Carrie rested briefly from her labours and considered the point. 'I don't really know.'

She tucked a strand of her red-gold locks under her headscarf. Knotted at the front, it kept her hair neatly and safely off her face and the back of her neck. With so many women working or contributing to the war effort in some way, fashion was being led by practicality these days.

Shortly before the hostilities started, Carrie and the children had been evacuated to the safety of the countryside, but when the air raids everyone feared so much failed to materialise, many of the mothers and children who'd come with them began to drift back home. Matt had written letter after letter pleading with Carrie to return too. Eventually he simply came and fetched his family. She hadn't argued with him. She'd learned the hard way that wasn't a good idea.

She'd learned a lot of things the hard way over the past few years. Unfortunately, how to spot one of Matt's outbursts coming wasn't one of them. Sometimes she would be convinced the ceiling was about to fall in and he'd be as nice as ninepence, wanting to know what on earth was the matter with her. Couldn't she be a bit more cheerful?

At other times it came completely out of the blue. It was almost a relief when it did. The guilt he experienced afterwards guaranteed a few months' respite to follow. The pattern was always the same. Once the fury of the storm was spent he'd come home and throw himself at her feet, making abject apologies and tearful promises never to hurt her again. She had grown so tired of it all, but his need for her forgiveness was overwhelming. Like a broken tree branch borne away on a flooded stream she found herself being swept along with it.

As far as she could she kept it hidden from Archie and April. She didn't want them thinking badly of their daddy. She kept it from Isa and Florence too, not so much because she was fearful of the former carrying out her threat of getting someone to administer a beating to him, but more out of a stubborn pride. She knew they had their suspicions, but Matt had learned some things too: to keep his voice down and to hit her where it wouldn't show. He was careful now only ever to slap her face, not punch it.

He was desperate to join up, but as a railwayman he was in

a reserved occupation, permission to resign his post to be granted only under the most exceptional of circumstances. Somehow Carrie got the blame for that. If he had been a single man with no ties the army would surely have welcomed him with open arms.

Offended by his lack of logic, she had answered him back on that one. Her temerity brought down a torrent of verbal abuse on her head. It left Archie and April, sitting at the tea table with them, wide-eyed and pale as their father stormed out of the house. An hour later he came back with ice-creams all round. The smiles returned to the children's faces, but Carrie recognised the pattern: unforgivable behaviour followed by an apology you had no choice but to accept.

In bed later that night, Matt had joked about how quiet she was and tried to coax her into responding to his questing hands and mouth. When she failed to co-operate, he did what he wanted to anyway. That was something else she had grown very tired of.

And yet he had been wonderful during those terrifying nights when the bombs had finally dropped, making sure everyone in the building took shelter and that the necessary supplies and equipment were at hand. She remembered how strong he had been when both her father and her mother had died. He was good in a crisis, needed something like that in his life – a challenge he could rise to. If only he could get an exemption from his job!

Archie gave his mother and sister a nonchalant wave and ran over to join the queue of children waiting to go in at the infants' entrance. Before Carrie could yell at him to avoid the icy puddle in the middle of the playground he glided smoothly over it, the gas-mask case he wore bandolier-style over his coat swinging out in a graceful arc. Just as well, she supposed.

He might have more than a term to go before he completed primary one, but he hated his little friends to see his mother babying him.

'Right then, young lady. Out you come.'

Although her daughter would be four years old in less than a month and liked to walk everywhere, Carrie still used the pushchair when she was in a hurry or didn't want to take too long to get somewhere, like on this cold March morning. However, it was milder than she'd thought today. They could take their time going home.

They might have visited April's grandparents – they weren't too far from North Gardner Street – only Charles and Shona Campbell were no longer there. Within a month of war having been declared in September 1939, they'd taken themselves off to a hotel on the coast which offered very modest rates for long-term residents.

She brought the pushchair to a halt. April had stopped to pat a dog out for a walk with its elderly master. She was very fond of animals, as was her brother, currently trying to persuade his mother to allow him to have a white mouse as a pet. Carrie had offered him a choice.

'You can have a white mouse, or you can have me.' Fortunately, Archie had made the wise decision.

They said goodbye to the elderly man and made their way home. April was chattering away, seeming not to notice that her mother was unusually absent-minded today. Carrie was steeling herself for a confrontation with Matthew.

Almost everybody she knew was doing something towards the war effort. Florence was knitting comforts for the troops. Isa, a part-time shop assistant before the war and now doing a far more physical job in a local factory, made fun of the socks, gloves and scarves in front of her mother-in-law and told everyone else how beautifully made they were.

There was a new resolve in the air. This war was only going to be won if everyone pulled together. It had started as a matter of principle, a refusal to let an evil dictator rewrite the map of Europe and deprive millions of innocent people of their rights and their freedom. Carrie read the newspapers and listened to the wireless. She knew what was going on in Germany and the occupied countries.

Trouble was, that knowledge could made you feel so helpless. Did the people who were suffering know you were thinking about them and sympathising with their plight? She hoped so. She wanted to do an awful lot more than think about it.

As the mother of young children, she was exempt from any obligation to do war work, but some pretty strong encouragement was being offered. Government-run crèches had been established. There was one locally. Without telling Matthew, she had made a tour of inspection last week. It was bright and airy and full of toys and staffed by pleasant nursery nurses – and they could offer April a place for four hours a day, five days a week.

Carrie was sure her daughter would love it. She did miss her brother when he was at school. That night, however, wondering if she was doing the right thing, she had confided her plans to Florence and Isa. 'What if she doesn't settle at the nursery? What if I have to work more than four hours a day, or do odd shifts?'

'Then I'll take her,' said Florence stoutly. 'You know I'd love to, pet. And I'd easy take Archie to and from the school, and keep him afterwards. Nae bother at all.'

So that was all settled. Now all she had to do was get Matt to agree to it. *All she had to do.* That was a laugh. He was going to hit the roof. She knew that for a fact.

The shortage of manpower in the forces had caused a major

rethink about railway work remaining a reserved occupation. While amateurs couldn't do the work of drivers and other technical staff, many exemptions had been granted to men in the clerical grades, their posts taken over by women.

Despite being so keen to get an exemption himself, and infuriated when Pascal Sharkey was allowed to go, Matt had heaped scorn on the idea of extensive female labour being used to keep the railways running. Take signal boxes, for example. What woman would have the strength to pull the long and heavy levers which operated the gantries by the track outside? Carrie, who'd tried her hand at the task whilst visiting Mary and Douglas the previous summer, had found it hard to bite her tongue. She told him she was quite sure she'd be capable of it and what's more, she'd like to try.

Matt told her coldly that he'd never heard such a piece of nonsense in his life. And who was she proposing would look after the children if she wasn't here – that old witch across the landing? When she tentatively mentioned the crèche, he declared that no child of his was going to be looked after by strangers for half the week. Carrie's place was at home, looking after him and the children.

'If we're lucky, you'll maybe have a new baby to look after soon,' he had added, giving her a significant look. He had made it painfully clear on a previous occasion that he suspected her of having done something to prevent that. She hadn't, but she'd been given some advice on how she might have done so, and from someone she would previously have considered an unlikely source of such information.

Leon the Polish soldier was long gone. He had been superseded by another impeccably mannered fellow country-man who in turn had been followed by a Free Frenchman. Carrie didn't think Florence needed to worry about losing the companionship of her daughter-in-law but she did worry that

Isa was in danger of getting herself a reputation. When she remonstrated with her friend, she was astounded by the response she got.

'We might all be dead tomorrow. I'm having a bit of fun before I'm too old for it. I'm no' the only one, no' by a long chalk.'

'You're not too old to get yourself into trouble,' Carrie had tossed back. 'What would you do then?'

'I'll not get myself into trouble,' came the calm reply. 'If Pierre doesnae do something beforehand, I do it afterwards – if you catch my drift.' She went on to give Carrie the details.

'And that works, does it?'

'I bloody hope so. I'm a bit past the motherhood stage.'

'Oh, Isa!'

Her friend laid a hand on her shoulder. 'I know you mean well, hen, but folk gossip whatever you do. I might as well give them something to talk about.'

Carrie put her key in the lock and ushered April into the house. She was still quiet, silently rehearsing the arguments she was going to put to Matt as to why she should go out to work. She had to persuade him to listen to her without flying off the handle. Or worse. The very thought gave her the usual symptoms: a churning stomach and clammy hands.

She wanted to do her bit, make her contribution to the struggle the whole country was engaged in, but it had occurred to her that going out to work could be important for another reason too. Maybe when Matt saw that she could cope with a part-time job and running the house and caring for the children he'd see her in a different light. She'd long ago lost the status she'd enjoyed while he'd been courting her. She had been the stationmaster's daughter then, and he had liked that. He didn't seem to have any respect for her now.

Carrie knew one thing. They couldn't go on like this. She was dying slowly inside. Another few years of being browbeaten by him and there would be very little left of the girl who used to be Caroline Burgess. Their marriage would be a hollow sham. For both their sakes she had to do something about it.

She filled the kettle and set it on top of the range. Settling April at the table, she gave her a biscuit and a cup of milk. Then she took a sketch pad and pencils from a drawer and laid them beside her.

'After you've finished your piece,' she said.

The little girl beamed at her with a mouth full of biscuit. She was such a cute wee thing, and so loveable. 'Going to draw Bobby,' she announced. Donald Nicholson's faithful canine companion was one of her special friends.

Carrie watched the masterpiece take shape as she sipped her tea. *Obviously going to be a vet when she grows up. Maybe an artist, of course. That would be fine too.*

A doting mama, that was her all right. She could laugh at herself, but she knew that whatever her children's dreams and ambitions might be, it was her job to support them in their endeavours. She would rejoice with them when they succeeded and offer comfort when they met with reverses and disappointments. They needed her strong and happy. She needed herself strong and happy. So did Matt.

For all our sakes then, she thought, for all our sakes.

He was due home in a few minutes. Everything was ready: house and children spotless, a nice meal – or as nice as rationing would allow – prepared. She would tell him before she served the pudding, reminding him that the children were present. She would also casually drop into the conversation that Isa was coming across later, the excuse being that she wanted help with trying out a new hairstyle.

Isa and Matt lived in a state of armed neutrality, speaking to each other only when absolutely necessary, but Carrie knew he had a healthy respect for their sharp-tongued neighbour. She'd cooked up the plot with her this afternoon. Isa had strict instructions as to exactly what time she was to chap at the door.

'Don't you worry, hen,' she'd said grimly. 'I'll no' go away without seeing you and making sure you're all right.'

Carrie had been forced to tell her the truth about Matt's sporadic but continuing violence over the past couple of years. Isa had reacted angrily, demanding to know why Carrie had kept it to herself for so long, and extracted a solemn promise that she would let her know when it happened again.

'But, Isa,' she protested, 'I'm hoping there won't be a next time. Things are going to be different from now on. As long as I can get him to agree to this.'

'There's one born every minute, Carrie, and you're it,' retorted Isa in exasperation. She gave her a pitying look. 'Does your mammy know you're oot? The leopard doesnae change his spots, you know.'

Carrie shook her head. Hair freshly washed, she intended to leave it loose for the rest of the day. 'No,' she insisted. 'People can change. I know they can.'

She wasn't sure if she was quite so confident about that when she heard Matt come in that evening. She did her best to look natural, head tilted expectantly towards the door. Some hopes. She didn't have butterflies in her stomach, it was more like Hurricanes and Spitfires screaming around in there.

She knew as soon as he entered the room that something had happened. His face was glowing. She walked over to greet him, unable to resist his obvious excitement. He seized her hands.

'They've granted the exemption! I can join up!'

Chapter 24

They talked solidly for the next hour, all through their meal. To be more accurate, Matthew talked and Carrie listened. He was full of it: which service he might be directed towards – army, navy or air force; whether or not he would get a choice about that; how he himself would prefer the army. The Argyll and Sutherland Highlanders would be his first choice of regiment, the most appropriate for a Campbell, didn't she think? They'd been in the Mediterranean since before the outbreak of war. He'd probably end up in North Africa.

His father had served with the Argylls during the Great War. That reminded him, he'd better write to his parents tonight, share the good news with them. He could be whisked away to start basic training within the next two weeks, you know. They'd have to get themselves organised for his departure.

When he stopped to draw breath, Carrie took a deep breath of her own and plunged in. This was the best chance she would ever have to persuade him that she ought to be doing her bit too.

Matt looked faintly startled, but then he shrugged. 'Why not?' He grinned. 'They might even give you my job.'

'I'll only be working part-time,' she pointed out, and started to explain the arrangements which would ensure the children were cared for every minute of the day. Matthew brushed that aside, and went back to talking about his own plans.

Carrie sat back in her chair, wondering whether she ought to be laughing or crying – hysterically, in both cases. She'd been building up to this for weeks, had spent most of today bracing herself for a battle royal. Now the solid wall of his opposition was crumbling away before her eyes. It was a funny old world. She felt giddy with shock and relief.

When Isa came round as arranged shortly after tea, Matthew couldn't resist telling her his news. She listened without comment.

'Could you not have shown a wee bit more enthusiasm?' muttered Carrie as she took her friend by the elbow and steered her through to the front room. 'For my sake, if not for his?' Isa waited until the door was safely shut behind them.

'So he's the blue-eyed boy now, is he? Have you forgotten why you asked me to knock on your door tonight? What you were scared he might do to you?'

'I know, Isa, but I really think him joining up is going to make a big difference. He could come home a changed man. He's always been searching for something. Maybe this could be it. Don't you remember how good he was during the Blitz?'

'How many chances are you going to give him, hen? Personally, I think he's had a few too many.'

Isa plonked herself down at the dressing-table and handed over the hairbrush she'd brought with her. Standing behind her, Carrie began smoothing her hair, but her subject's attention wasn't on her coiffure. She was studying their combined reflections in the mirror.

'I'm happy for you,' she said finally. 'You'll get a bit o' bloody peace at last. Men,' she said in disgust, 'who needs them?'

Carrie snorted. 'I thought you quite liked them as a species, Mrs Cooke.'

'They're only good for one thing,' said Isa darkly, 'plus they come in handy when you need a piano shifted. Otherwise I wouldnae give them houseroom.'

Matt was still smiling as they got ready for bed that night.

'I'm happy for you,' Carrie said, unconsciously repeating the words Isa had used to her earlier in the evening. She darted a little glance at him as he took off his shirt. 'I think . . . perhaps . . . that you've needed something like this.'

He paused in his undressing. 'Carrie . . . it hasn't always been as it should have been. Maybe this could be a new start for us.'

She lifted her chin. 'Do you want it to be?'

'Yes. Oh, yes!'

He was beside her, wrapping his arms around her, kissing her eyelids, her cheeks, her lips. 'I love you,' he said, 'I really love you.'

'I know you do,' she said sadly, placing a hand on his chest and looking up at him, 'but things have got to change.'

'They will. I promise.'

Her eyes scoured his face. 'Can I believe you this time?'

'You can,' he said, and bent his head to her lips. His kiss was light, and rather formal. He had kissed her like that on their wedding day, after the minister had pronounced them man and wife. A promise given, and a promise received. A promise which had been broken so many times. 'You'll wait for me?'

'Of course I will. I'm your wife.'

'So I don't need to worry about you getting up to anything while I'm away?' he asked lightly.

She chose to take that as a joke. 'As long as I don't either. No consorting with pretty servicewomen after working hours.'

'There won't be any as pretty as you.' He put his hand to

271

the back of her head, buried his fingers in her smooth hair. 'Kiss me again,' he said. His voice had grown husky with desire. 'Properly, this time.'

It had never occurred to Carrie that she would work anywhere else than on the railway and it came as something of a shock to find she couldn't simply walk up the stairs to the station and start. While they were sure there would be a place for her, she would have to go through the official channels and apply via the women's section of the labour exchange.

With typical tact, Isa told her she'd better smarten herself up a wee bit. Since Matt had taken most of the spare cash with him when he went off to training camp, it was a case of make do and mend. Carrie had a square-shouldered navy costume she'd bought a couple of years ago which wasn't bad, but the cheap hat she'd bought to go with it was looking a bit sorry for itself.

'It's too plain,' pronounced the fashion expert, eyeing it suspiciously. Florence triumphantly produced a box of trimmings.

'What would she be wanting wi' those old things?' said Isa in disgust. 'We're looking for something up-to-date and modern.' She picked up an ornate hat-pin and threw it back into the box with an expression of disgust.

'You hold your tongue, Isabella Cooke!' The old woman winked at Carrie. 'I know exactly what we're going to find in here.' With a cry of satisfaction, she fished out a little sprig of fabric daisies and held them against the navy felt hat.

'What d'ye think, hen? I'll stitch them on for you. It would all fit nicely together if you wore your white blouse with the scalloped collar.'

'That would be ideal,' Carrie agreed. She was perfectly capable of sewing them on by herself, but she knew Florence wanted to perform the small task for her. 'Don't you think so, Isa?'

She was trying not to laugh at the way the younger Mrs Cooke's fashion sense was warring with her accustomed reluctance to admit that her mother-in-law might be right about anything. Putting the hat on, Carrie tried the daisies in one position and then another as she studied her head and shoulders in the mirror. The little white flowers lifted the dark hat, but they weren't too fussy, and if she did her hair nicely . . . well, there would be no stopping her. Suddenly light-hearted, she whirled round, an impish smile on her face.

'You're that bonnie, Carrie,' said Florence. 'I was bonnie like you once.'

'When was that?' asked Isa with a magnificent curl of the lip. 'When the old queen was on the throne? And I'm no' talking about Mary – unless it was Mary, Queen of Scots.' She looked up at Carrie. 'She is bonnie and the hat looks good, but only because the lassie sets it off properly wi' her lovely hair. Nothing to do wi' yon daft wee trimmings o' yours.'

'So should Florence *not* sew them on then?' asked Carrie innocently.

'I suppose there's no harm in having them. It'll keep the auld yin out o' mischief for ten minutes. You know what they say – the devil makes work for idle hands.'

Carrie and Florence exchanged serene smiles.

The young woman sitting behind the small pine desk couldn't have been much older than Carrie herself, but she oozed confidence. Her suit might have been cut in approved Utility style, obeying all the wartime restrictions designed to avoid wasteful use of cloth, but you could tell by looking at it that the fabric was of a much better quality than Carrie's costume. She also had a lovely hat, which she had removed and laid in front of her. It was like a small plate, designed to be worn at a forward tilt, and adorned with two different colours of net and a large artificial lily.

'Railway work, you say.' She paused. 'And why would you think you were suitable for that, Mrs . . .' her eyes dropped to the pad of paper in front of her '. . . Campbell? It is Mrs?'

Carrie nodded. She'd felt confident when she had left the house, ready to take on the world. Florence and Isa had admired her and told her how smart she looked and both Archie and April had given her a kiss for luck. Now she was beginning to feel nervous. Why did she think she was suitable for railway work? Because she was a stationmaster's daughter? She swallowed. Answer the simple question first.

'Yes,' she said, 'I'm married. My husband's currently serving with the Argyll and Sutherland Highlanders. He's anticipating embarking for North Africa before the end of the year.' Maybe that piece of information would impress her interviewer. However, the girl didn't react to it, only asked if she had any children.

'Two. A boy of six and a girl of four.'

'But that would give you an exemption from war work. You do understand that, Mrs Campbell?' Her brow creased in obvious perplexity at Carrie's obtuseness.

'I understand that perfectly,' she said steadily, 'but I want to do my bit like everyone else.'

She'd changed her mind about the girl's hat. It was a ridiculous object, too fussy for words. Her own was far more chic.

The young woman looked doubtful. 'It could be very demanding on you, you know, especially if you've been merely a housewife for the past few years, and not working at all.'

Merely a housewife. Not working at all. Carrie toyed briefly with the idea of asking little Miss Snooty which window she wished to leave by. No, she'd go for the supercilious air herself. She'd been able to do it very well once upon a time.

'Perhaps in the circles in which you mix that's the case, but I can assure you that housewives in Partick work extremely hard, Miss . . .' Carrie stopped. 'I'm sorry,' she said sweetly, 'I don't know your name. You didn't introduce yourself, did you?'

Miss Snooty blinked twice. She looked like a startled haddock. Any minute now bubbles would float out of her mouth and drift slowly up to the ceiling.

'Simpson,' she said hurriedly. 'Rachel Simpson.'

'Well, Miss Simpson, I can assure you I'm no stranger to hard work and I also have a reasonably good brain. It still functions quite efficiently. Now, will you kindly tell me how I go about applying to work on the railway?'

Although she'd had a notion of working in the signal box – partially to prove to Matt that she could do it – Carrie was very happy when she was directed into the booking office. It felt like coming home. She knew quite a few of the staff members, too old for the call-up, from her father's time. One of the clerks kept calling her Miss Burgess. She liked that. It made her feel like a girl again.

A lot of the drivers remembered her, as did many of the regular business travellers. Several people from both groups shared their memories of Archie with her. She liked that too. She was part of the railway family again, in a way she never had been with Matt. He hadn't cared for her and the children visiting him at work. He'd considered it unprofessional.

It was hard work: learning the job, making sure she gave the children enough of her time, keeping the household running smoothly. She had no trouble sleeping at night, but the shift work she hadn't much fancied delivered an unexpected bonus. Every so often she found herself with the oddest of commodities: time to herself.

Normally she filled a free morning with housework, getting twice as much done without the children under her feet. Once or twice, feeling deliciously guilty, she'd given herself a home-made face mask or sat down and read a book. She'd started going to the library again. It was a long while since she'd had the time or the inclination to do that.

Carrie pondered the illogicality of the situation. Here she was, working harder than ever, effectively doing two jobs. She ought to be feeling harassed, but she was more relaxed than she'd been for ages. She wasn't too happy when the obvious deduction presented itself. Matt wasn't at home.

Apart from a brief leave in August, he'd been away now for over seven months, but she was uncomfortably aware of not missing him very much. The bed was certainly cold at night when she climbed in, but that was counteracted by other things. The most important of those was the pleasure of settling down for a comfortable evening by the fire and knowing the peace and quiet wasn't going to be shattered by one of Matt's outbursts.

He was an erratic correspondent, but he seemed to be enjoying himself. From time to time she found herself wondering if he might be enjoying himself a bit too much. His letters were full of names. Mention of male comrades was fine and she was glad he was meeting new people, but she was uneasy about the occasional passing reference to the service-women, nurses and female civilian staff connected with the training camp. Perhaps it was what she suspected he was leaving out. Matthew was a handsome man, and this war did seem to be having rather an adverse effect on people's morals . . .

Carrie could understand it to a certain extent. The poster

beside the booking-office window might ask people if their journey was really necessary, but sometimes it seemed as if the whole world was on the move. There were so many lonely folk far from home.

There were the servicemen and women from all corners of Britain and the Empire, the Poles, the Free French, and now that the United States had entered the war, the Americans. The latter had an appeal all of their own, with their music, their stylish uniforms and their film-star accents. Overpaid, over-sexed and over here, as a well-spoken young English airman she met at the servicemen's club had put it acerbically to Carrie.

Isa had more or less dragged her along there, insisting that she needed a night out. According to her, the young man definitely had his eye on Carrie.

'He just needs a wee bit of encouragement,' she said when the two of them paid a trip to the ladies' room in the middle of the evening. 'Put your hand on his knee or something.'

'I'll do no such thing,' she said indignantly. 'I'm a married woman.'

Isa gave her a look. 'And do you think your dear husband is remembering that he's a married man? I hae ma doots.'

Carrie had her doubts too, especially when Matthew wrote to say he was going to spend a seventy-two-hour leave visiting London with a group of the chaps, rather than coming home. Rumour had it that their departure for the Med was going to be postponed until the beginning of 1943, and Glasgow was a long way to come for such a short time. She knew what the delays were like on the railway these days, what with the blackout, air-raid alerts and all the rest! He knew she'd understand.

Matt wasn't the only man who found it hard to believe that women were physically capable of operating signals. Despite

277

all the evidence to the contrary, there was interminable discussion about it. While the signalwomen themselves insisted there was no problem, they had other complaints about their working conditions. A major one was the absence of toilet facilities in or near the box. If you were covering a shift on your own, walking back to the station to use the ladies' room meant leaving your post unstaffed for a potentially dangerous length of time.

'What did the men do?' asked one new recruit, as the female staff sat in the booking office mulling over the problem.

'Use your loaf,' said Carrie drily. She turned to Anne-Marie, the girl who'd raised the issue. She was Pascal Sharkey's fiancée. 'What about installing a chemical toilet at the box itself?'

Anne-Marie nodded her head enthusiastically. 'Aye. But this is a problem all along the line, Carrie. And there's a few other things we're concerned about. Like getting to and from work late at night or early in the morning. We're wondering if it might be possible to give more consideration to pairing women up when the rosters are prepared. Say you were on a late shift and I was too. We'd both be happier about walking home if we had company.'

'Yes,' she replied, thinking about it. 'That's a good idea.' She'd had a few nervous moments going home in the blackout, especially at this time of year. They were into November, with its attendant fogs. 'Why not put it all in a letter to Mr Gibson? You know how everything has to go through official channels. That gives him something to send to Queen Street – or Edinburgh. You could get up a petition, too. Collect as many signatures as you can to go along with it.'

'I can do that bit, but would you compose the letter, Carrie? I'm a rotten speller and you're good at that sort of thing. You'll know how to put it.'

'Gladly,' she said. 'Leave it with me.'

'Well,' said George Gibson jovially, 'you ladies have started something, and no mistake.'

Carrie looked up from her ledger. It was two weeks later, and her boss had come into the booking office with a piece of paper in his hand.

'We have?'

He nodded. 'They've decided to do a survey of all female employees. Make sure working conditions are . . .' he read out from the letter he held '. . . "comfortable, suitable and appropriate to their needs". Someone's coming through from Edinburgh to interview you all.'

'Oh, good. Are they sending a man or a woman?'

He checked the letter again. 'They don't give a name, but he or she will arrive next Monday afternoon and base themselves with us for two or three weeks, travelling up and down the line to do inspections and interviews. They wonder if it would be possible to collate and type up the information here.' He looked around 'We'd better clear that table in the corner. Can you get on to that sometime before Monday, Mrs Campbell?'

'Nae bother,' said Carrie, and went back to her columns, pleased that the petition and her letter had produced such a positive result.

She was doing a sort of half back shift, working from one o'clock till six. It meant a late tea for the children, but Florence always gave them something to tide them over. In the winter she insisted Archie needed something hot as soon as he came in from school. Glancing at the clock, Carrie knew that he and April would be sitting down right now to a plate of Florence's home-made soup. Her Scotch broth was legendary, so thick with vegetables and pearl barley you could almost stick the spoon up in it. It was a feat both Archie and April had been known to attempt. She smiled. It was good to know they were being so well looked after.

When she got home that evening, she saw that the door 'to the flat' on the other side of the landing was open a crack. Isa emerged from it, pulling the door shut behind her. 'Your hoose. Now.' She hustled a bemused Carrie into her own kitchen.

'Fine,' she said, 'but why all the cloak and dagger stuff?'

'Because we cannae discuss this in front o' the children,' said Isa. 'Sit doon.' She pulled a chair out from the table. Carrie remained standing.

'Isa,' she said in exasperation, 'what are you on about?'

'This railway official who's coming through from Edinburgh next week.'

'What about him? Or her?' she added. 'We don't know yet whether we're getting a man or a woman. How do you know about it?' she asked curiously. 'I only found out a couple of hours ago.'

'Oh, it's a man you're getting, all right,' said Isa grimly.

Carrie sat down. She no longer needed an answer to the question she'd posed. Not now she knew who the inspector was.

Chapter 25

'Ewen's still with the railway, then?' She'd wondered about that. 'Do you ever see him?'

Isa took her cigarettes out of the pocket of her apron. 'Now and again. He gave us a great day out in Edinburgh last summer, showed us all the sights and treated us to a slap-up meal. He was celebrating his engagement. To a lovely lassie called Moira. We met her too.'

'Oh,' Carrie said. 'That's nice.' She stood up, undid her coat and walked across to hang it up on the back of the door. She turned. Isa was lighting up. 'Is he staying with you and Florence while he's on his tour of inspection here?'

'That's what I need to speak to you about. Your man's no' due home on leave soon, is he?'

The quick stab of anxiety was like a fist clenching inside Carrie's stomach. 'You think the sparks might fly if he and Ewen were ever to meet up again?'

Isa picked a piece of tobacco off her tongue. 'I think it would be like Guy Fawkes night. Or probably mair like the Blitz. The ARP would have to evacuate the surrounding area to prevent innocent bystanders getting caught in the crossfire. Or cut by the flying glass. Is he coming home soon?'

'Not as far as I know. He's got some leave, but he's going to spend it in London.'

'All right for some, eh?'

'What does that mean?'

'Oh, nothing,' said Isa airily, 'maybe I'm thinking that what's sauce for the gander ought to be sauce for the goose.'

'I'm a married woman, Isa,' said Carrie levelly.

'Aye,' came the reply. 'So you are, pet.'

Ewen was ushered into the booking office by the stationmaster at half-past three on the following Monday afternoon.

'And here we have –'

'No need for introductions. Mrs Campbell and I are old friends.'

The voice was deeper than she remembered, but then he was a lot older now. She'd done the sums over the weekend. If she was twenty-four, he had to be twenty-six.

Old friends? Maybe. She had known the boy. It was the man who was standing there smiling at her. She was having some difficulty in recognising him. Oh, he had the same physical characteristics as Ewen Livingstone, although the neatly cut fair hair was attractively windswept rather than tousled, but he had an air of sophistication about him which the rough and ready lad she had known could never have aspired to.

He came forward, and she took in the well-cut dark suit and casually unbuttoned overcoat. Beneath his waistcoat he wore a white shirt and a discreetly striped tie. He looked more than smart: the overall impression was stylish. She wondered if he'd effected the transformation himself or if his fiancée was responsible for it.

He switched the briefcase he carried to his left hand and held out the right one. 'How are you?' he asked.

'Ewen,' she said, and felt strong fingers wrap themselves firmly around her own. Out of the corner of her eye, she saw that her boss was a little taken aback by her familiarity with this representative of head office. 'You're looking well.'

'I'm all the better for seeing you,' he told her warmly. There was still something very youthful there, a sense of boundless vigour and energy. No doubt she looked to him exactly what she was, a tired mother-of-two.

'Well,' said Mr Gibson. 'Mrs Campbell has prepared this table for you to work at. And you'll render every assistance to Mr Livingstone, won't you, Mrs Campbell?' He seemed determined to keep things on a formal footing.

Ewen coughed, put a hand to his mouth and turned his head to one side. Carrie knew immediately he was covering up a laugh.

'Well,' she said, when the other man had finally left the office, 'where would you like to start, *Mr Livingstone*?'

His eyes gleamed and he gestured with his thumb in the direction of the door. 'Doesn't remember me, does he? I've been with him for the past half hour and it's been Mr Livingstone this and Mr Livingstone that. I must say, *Mrs Campbell*, I'm mightily amused by all this deference.'

His accent had undergone quite a shift. He still had a warm west of Scotland burr, but there were touches of Edinburgh in there – polite Edinburgh at that.

'That's why you were laughing,' she said, suddenly realising. 'I'd forgotten you and he had coincided for a few months.'

'I obviously made such an impact he doesn't recall he was once my boss,' said Ewen wryly, laying his briefcase on the table he'd been allocated. 'He hasn't even made the connection as to how you and I know each other.' He shrugged off his coat.

Carrie took it from him and hung it up on the coat-stand to the right of the coal fire which was burning sluggishly in the back wall. The action seemed to take him by surprise, although he murmured his thanks as she smoothed down the soft dark blue woollen folds and returned to her stool in front of the ticket window.

'It has been seven years,' she pointed out. 'You've changed a lot.'

He perched himself on the edge of the table, one leg straight, one crooked over the corner of it. 'Have I?'

'I would say so.' She waved her hand in a gesture designed to encompass his appearance, his position in the company and the respect which the stationmaster had just shown him. 'And you're obviously an important person these days.'

'I don't know about that,' he said, looking faintly embarrassed.

'But you're in a special department?' she persisted. 'Doing some kind of war work?'

'Sort of. I suppose you'd call it strategic planning.'

'How did that come about?'

'Well,' he said, 'it occurred to me a couple of years before the war broke out that the railways were going to be crucially important – in lots of ways – but especially if Hitler attempted an invasion. We had to get ourselves ready for that, I thought, have contingency plans, and not only for the obvious places like the big cities and ports.' He adjusted his position, relaxing into his subject.

'I thought German parachutists were more likely to land somewhere quiet and remote – like the Highlands, for instance. Somewhere they would stand a better chance of landing undetected.'

Carrie nodded, taking his point. 'But they would plan to be close to a railway station?' she suggested. 'Or several railway stations? The smaller ones?'

He waited while she thought it out.

'Either to use the train to get to where they needed to go,' she said slowly, 'in small groups less likely to cause suspicion.'

She thought about it some more. Ewen remained silent. He'd have made a good teacher. 'Or perhaps . . . to take over a station as a base . . . maybe even a whole line. Control supplies and information – people too – coming into and going out of that particular area.'

'All of those and more,' he said approvingly. Now he even looked like a teacher, pleased but unsurprised that a bright pupil had come up with the right answer. 'I started looking into it in my own time – working out what might happen, how we ought to react to it, how we could train people to be prepared for every eventuality. Hopefully.' The face-splitting smile was exactly the same, at any rate. 'I wrote up a report, made a set of recommendations. That's when I decided to learn how to type.'

'You thought it would look more impressive?'

'Aye. I was a bit embarrassed to ask any of the lassies at Waverley to do it for me, but I got one of them to teach me the rudiments of typewriting. We had a good laugh over it,' he said. 'Me and my big hands.' He stretched them out in front of him, still smiling broadly. 'Anyway,' he went on, 'I typed it up and submitted it to the general manager.'

'He was impressed, I take it.'

He made a face, self-deprecating. 'Well, I think a lot of other people were coming to the same conclusions as me, but it all kind of came together. And the general manager's always taken an interest in me,' he glanced round at their surroundings, 'ever since that day in here, when you coached me to make that wee speech about the waterproof clothing. This is where it all started. If I've made anything of my life, it's all thanks to you, Carrie.'

'It's nice of you to say so, but you're giving me far too much credit.' She stood up. 'Right then, I suppose you'll want to get started as soon as possible. You've a lot of ground to cover. Would you like to go straight down to our signal box now?'

'Is the bummer from Edinburgh here yet? Oh!'

The young clerkess who had just looked into the room had gone scarlet, but Ewen was laughing. 'Please introduce me to your colleague, Mrs Campbell.'

'I'm the parcels clerkess,' said the girl, letting go of the heavy booking-office door and holding out her hand. 'And foot-in-mouth specialist. Maybe you'd like to interview me first?'

'It would be a pleasure,' he said expansively. 'Take a seat.' He indicated the table. 'Oh, damn. I've left my portable typewriter through in the stationmaster's office.'

'I'll get it,' offered the girl. Carrie laid a hand on her shoulder, preventing her from rising from the table. 'No. Let me.'

Twenty minutes later Mr Gibson popped his head round the door.

'Got everything you need, Mr Livingstone?'

Ewen looked up. 'Aye, I'm fine. We've just completed the first interview of the project.' He smiled at the foot-in-mouth specialist. 'I think I'll go and see the local signalwomen now.'

'Will one of these ladies go along to show you the way? Mrs Campbell,' the stationmaster said, 'you might appreciate the fresh air, you're looking a wee touch pale today. I'll cover for you.'

'No need for that,' said Ewen smoothly. He rose to his feet, put some plain sheets of paper in a buff folder, lifted a pen and slipped it into the inside pocket of his jacket. 'I'm sure I can manage.'

'Do you have a good torch?' Carrie asked. 'It'll be dark soon. Certainly by the time you're coming back.'

The railway and all other modes of transport were as subject to the blackout regulations as everywhere else – much to the disgust of the men and women trying to operate them. However, there had been a spate of accidents during the first two winters of the war, mainly trains going into the back of other trains because the drivers simply couldn't see each other. Some railway workers moving about stations and marshalling yards had also been hurt. The government had been forced to make some concessions about lighting.

Carrie pointed to four small but sturdy paraffin lamps sitting in a neat row to one side of the booking-office window. 'Borrow one of those if you like. Your clothes are dark. A lamp will make you a lot more visible.'

'It's nice to know she cares,' said the parcels clerkess teasingly. 'Isn't it, Mr Livingstone?'

'It certainly is,' he said. He turned to Carrie. 'Will you still be here when I get back?'

'I go off duty at six.'

'Good. I'll be back well before then.'

The office seemed very empty after he had gone, although there were people coming in and out all the time: staff members on various errands and passengers at the ticket window. She thought of him out in the cold December afternoon on his way to the signal box. He must have done that walk hundreds of times. At least he was warmly clad this time, and he was wielding a fountain pen, not a pick-axe. Funny how much his life had changed. Funny how much her own had.

Her eyes lit on the fire in the back wall. It wasn't exactly a cheerful blaze. She'd better do something about that. Anyone coming in from the outside world would appreciate the warmth. Slipping off her stool, she walked across the room and lifted the poker from its hook. She gave the coals in the nest a vigorous rake, pulled out the ash pan, opened up the air vent and replenished the fire from the brass scuttle which stood beside it. Samuel the lad porter came in at that moment and she asked him to empty the ashes for her and refill the coal scuttle.

'Nae bother,' he said cheerily. 'It's a right cold day, eh, Mrs Campbell?'

'Aye,' she agreed, 'and it always gets chillier when the daylight goes.'

The late afternoon was usually something of a nightmare for Carrie. People keen to get home after their day's work were inclined to thrust their tickets at her from all directions, occasionally prompting her to issue a gentle reminder: 'I'm not an octopus, you know.' The special trains bringing the workers home from the Singer sewing machine factory at Clydebank, now given over to munitions, were the worst. A sea of impatient humanity piled off them.

At twenty to six, when the peak of the passenger traffic had passed, she took time off to warm her hands by the booking-office fire. You couldn't wear gloves when you were collecting tickets. She glanced up at the clock. Ewen was taking an awfully long time.

He came in ten minutes later, bubbling with vitality, filling the room with his presence. 'I met Martin Sharkey on the way back,' he announced. 'We were talking for a while.'

'He'd have been delighted to see you,' she said, touched by his obvious pleasure in meeting his old foreman.

'Aye,' he agreed, placing the now extinguished lamp back with its fellows. 'He greeted me like a long-lost son.' Ewen's voice had grown husky. 'Seemed quite proud of me, in fact.'

'Did he take you into the bothy?'

'Och, no.' He laughed. 'Although we stood outside it for nearly half an hour.'

Carrie tutted. 'In this cold? You must be frozen. Come here and get a warm.'

He laid his folder on the table, took off his coat and threw it over a chair before joining her by the fire. He turned and looked at her, mischief sparking in his eyes. 'Aye, Mammy,' he said, his accent pure Partick.

'Well,' she said mildly, 'I am a mammy.'

'And your bairns are a credit to you.' He stretched his hands out to the flames. She straightened up and watched the pale skin of his face reflect their flickering pink glow.

'When did you meet my children?'

'Earlier on today,' he said easily, concentrating on warming his hands. 'I dropped my bags off at Isa's before I came here. We all had our dinner together. After Isa had scolded me for something or other and Florence had made me try on the jumper she's knitted for me, of course. You know what they're like. It makes me think of the Gestapo in the war pictures.' He put on a German accent. 'Resistance is useless. Your daughter's a wee chatterbox, eh? And Archie's a fine lad, Carrie. That was nice that you named him for your father. We had a long conversation about how cruel his mother is to him.'

'Cruel?' She was busy assimilating what he'd just said. Her daughter, normally shy with strangers, had apparently taken to this one. Archie had also seemed to like him and Ewen had referred to both of them as though he knew them well.

Of course, someone might well have kept him informed of their progress. She was going to kill Isabella Cooke. Then she wondered what other information might have been given, not about the children, but about Matt and her.

'Cruel?' Carrie repeated, moving away from the fire. She couldn't bear it if he knew about the violence. She thought of it as something shameful, and that shame belonged as much

289

to her as to Matthew. Somehow she ought to have been able to prevent it from happening.

'You won't let him have a white mouse,' Ewen teased.

'Oh, that,' she said vaguely.

He turned away from the fire and looked at her. 'Are you all right, Carrie?'

'I'm fine.' She looked pointedly at the clock. 'My relief will be here any minute. Are you going along the road now too?'

He moved over to the table and started tidying up his papers. 'Aye, if that's all right with you. It's been a long day. There was a big forward planning meeting at Waverley this morning and . . .' He broke off and looked directly at her. 'And I've had quite an emotional afternoon, what with one thing and another.'

'Emotional?' The word surprised her, jolting her out of her self-absorption.

'I didn't find coming back here too easy, to tell you the truth,' he confessed. 'I can't forget how I started off in life, and I'm sure there's a lot of folk out there who'd be only too glad to remind me,' he said grimly.

'Perhaps,' she conceded, thinking about it, 'but there are lots of others who'll admire you for how far you've got. Like Martin Sharkey. And Isa and Florence. Me too,' she added, 'if that's any consolation. And I'd appreciate your company on the way home. It's nice to have someone with you in the blackout.'

'That was one of the points you raised in your letter, wasn't it?'

'You saw my letter?'

'Why else do you think I'm here?'

'But they had to twist your arm to get you to come back to Partick?'

'No,' he said sweetly. 'I was a volunteer.' He tilted his head towards the door. 'Ah, those sound like purposeful footsteps outside. Must be whoever's taking over from you.'

Coming indoors after the darkness of the blacked-out streets always made Carrie blink until her eyes grew accustomed to the light, but she was blinking for another reason at the moment: disbelief, tinged with an edge of anxiety she hadn't felt since Matt had left. April came running forward, gave her mother a cursory greeting and turned immediately to the young man by her side. Archie was shyer, hanging back a little, but like his sister, his face was glowing as he looked up at Ewen. When he crouched down to talk to them, April immediately put her arm around his neck and Archie came forward, thrusting out his hand. It had a large marble in it.

'This is my best one, Uncle Ewen,' he said. 'You said at dinner time you'd like to see it, so Auntie Florence let me into our house when I came home from school and I got it to show you.'

'That's a corker,' said Ewen admiringly, taking it and examining it from every possible angle. 'Thank you for letting me see it, Archie.'

'You can keep it for a while if you like,' said the little boy gravely.

'Thank you. I will.' Closing his fingers over the glass sphere, he slid it into the pocket of his jacket. 'Shall I give it back to you at the weekend?'

Carrie found her voice. 'Uncle Ewen?' she croaked.

He smiled up at her. 'You don't mind, do you? We got on to first-name terms at dinner time, and there've been too many people calling me Mr Livingstone today.'

'Och,' said Isa in disgust, 'the weans couldnae call him that, could they?'

'I suppose not,' said Carrie faintly. It didn't seem to have occurred to anyone but herself how Matt would react if he came home and found his children chattering about their Uncle Ewen. Her stomach churned at the very thought.

Chapter 26

'Hello there,' said Ewen brightly as Carrie came into the booking office the following afternoon to start her shift. He was standing at the table in the corner sifting through some sheets of paper.

She returned his greeting and walked across the room, undoing the buttons of her coat as she went. 'You look as though you've been busy this morning,' she said, indicating the papers which lay in front of him. 'More interviews?'

'Aye. Most of the female staff here.' He glanced down at them. 'How do you spell Egypt?'

She told him, and saw him run his index finger underneath one typewritten word. He looked up again, giving her a relieved smile. 'I'd got it right. The husband of one of your colleagues is serving there, but I couldn't find it in my trusty dictionary.' He tapped his fingers on a small book lying on the table.

'Is that the one I gave you?' Carrie couldn't resist picking it up. 'It's been in the wars,' she observed.

'Oh, it's been well-used,' he said, still smiling at her.

She replaced the book on the table, moved away from him and began taking off her coat.

'Can I help you with that?' he asked politely.

'I'm fine, thanks. When would you like to interview me?'

'When it's convenient.'

'Maybe not this week. We're a bit short-staffed.' She hung up her coat, took her place at the ticket window and removed the cardboard placard which communicated that fact to the travelling public. 'More short-staffed than usual, that is,' she said ruefully. 'People down with the flu. I'm starting two weeks on full back shift this Saturday though, so I'll have a bit more time next week. I won't be trying to cram everything into five hours.'

'I'll start the other stations this afternoon, then,' he said. 'I'll just make some phone calls, let them know I'm on my way.

'That's me off,' he announced some ten minutes later, half in and half out of the door. 'Will I maybe see you tonight?'

'Probably,' she said, glancing over at him. 'We see quite a bit of Isa and Florence as it is and you seem to be an added attraction as far as Archie and April are concerned.'

'I like them too,' he said. 'They're nice children. See you later, then.'

He gave her a wave as he passed the ticket window on his way through the booking hall. He had to bend down to do it. That was funny. She didn't remember him as having been that tall. Then she recalled the defensiveness which had once cloaked him from head to toe, born of sensitivity about his mother, his illegitimacy and his lack of education. That seemed to have evaporated completely. Coupled with the aura of quiet confidence, maybe that was what gave the impression of a few extra inches of height. Or perhaps he simply stood up straighter these days.

Carrie sat for a moment or two staring into space. Then she turned and looked at the table where he'd been working. The little dictionary wasn't there. He must have taken it with him. She'd chosen it to be handy to carry, after all.

She could remember buying it. She had selected it with

great care, as she had the paper and ribbon with which she had wrapped it. She had wanted it to be special: a treat for someone who didn't get many treats. He'd been so appreciative too, despite the fact that she had unwittingly upset him that day, making him think about his mother's death. She could see still the way he had bowed his head . . .

'Miss?'

With a professional smile, she turned and dealt with the customer who had just tapped impatiently on the window.

She did see Ewen that night – and Wednesday and Thursday nights too. As she'd predicted, the children were keener than usual to spend time at their aunties'. That didn't surprise Carrie. Both of them had been missing the presence of a man in their lives. Ewen played with them as Matt did – robustly and energetically – communicating with them in an entirely different way from herself.

Watching the horseplay which developed over the next few evenings she could see there was more of the boy in Ewen than she had first thought. He could almost have been their big brother. He had a way of getting on to their level which wasn't in the least patronising, and seemed to be enjoying himself as much as they were. Perhaps he was making up for lost time. She couldn't imagine that his own childhood had included much of the carefree rough and tumble he indulged in with Archie and April.

She could see that Florence was relishing it all. It was obvious she adored Ewen as much as she doted on Carrie's children, and was taking enormous pleasure in having all three of them together under her roof. Even Isa, who normally regarded the world cynically through a plume of cigarette smoke, looked on with an indulgent eye.

Everyone was having a wonderful time – except for Carrie

herself. All too uncomfortably aware that she was the main reason why Isa and Florence had seen so little of Ewen over the past few years, she tried to suppress her growing feeling of unease. She would just have to hope that by the time Matt got his next leave, the memory of Ewen Livingstone and his visit would be long gone.

Coming home from the steamie midway through Friday morning, she was lugging a basket of clean clothes up the stairs when she met Ewen coming down.

'You should have called me,' he reproached her. 'I'd have helped you with that. Don't tell me,' he said, reading the expression on her face. 'You've managed fine without me up till now.'

She took pity on him, allowing him to take the laundry from her. 'Something like that. I thought you'd be at work anyway.'

He ran nimbly back up the stairs and placed the basket on the mat outside her front door. 'Lunch and a meeting at Queen Street today. With some of the high heid yins.' He grimaced. 'I seem to spend half my life going to meetings. I've got a big one at Waverley next Sunday.'

'Sunday?'

'That's the only day we can get everybody together,' he said gloomily, rejoining her on the half-landing. Today's meeting explained the extra attention to his appearance. He looked particularly smart, and she said as much.

He grimaced again. 'I think I'd look a lot smarter in a uniform.'

'You're in a reserved occupation,' she pointed out, 'and you're doing an important job.'

'Maybe.' He sounded unconvinced.

'Well,' she said again, 'you do look very smart.'

'And you look very beautiful.'

She turned, and smiled at him. He had turned too, and stood now looking up at her. She was wearing her headscarf, knotted at the front as usual. She could feel a few tendrils of hair, still damp from the steamie, against her face.

Her clothes consisted of a pair of Matt's trousers she'd altered to fit herself, an ancient creamy-coloured lacy jumper and a jacket which had done sterling service as a blanket before being pressed into the war effort. It saved the good checked woollen coat she wore to work or on the rare occasions when she went out for the evening.

She'd dyed the old blanket dark green, cut a big square collar for it and put a fringe round that made out of a spare ball of Aran wool Florence had given her. Isa called the whole ensemble her Rosie the Riveter outfit.

'I don't look at all beautiful,' she said, 'but it's kind of you to say so.'

'There's nothing kind about it.'

Carrie shrugged, a little embarrassed. He was being gallant, no doubt. She moved away from him and put her foot on the first step of the stairs. 'We'll see you on Monday, then?'

'Monday?' He looked up at her in apparent perplexity.

'Aren't you going back through to Edinburgh for the weekend?'

'No. I'm staying here. In fact, I was wondering if you'd let me take the children to the pantomime tomorrow. I'm going to see if I can get seats today. It only started last week, so they might not be fully booked up for the Saturday matinées yet.'

The unease clawed at her again. The pantomime. Archie and April would talk about that for months . . .

'Isa and Florence are coming,' he said, obviously thinking she needed some persuading. 'It's a pity you're on duty or you could have come too.'

It seemed churlish to refuse. Especially as he appeared to

be giving up a weekend with his girlfriend in favour of her children. And she knew the two of them would love it. 'I'll give you the money for their tickets, then. If you manage to get them.'

'No you will not,' he said. 'It's my treat.'

He did get tickets and Carrie spent Saturday morning coping with two children high as kites with the excitement of it. She felt a little forlorn at work that afternoon and evening, knowing everyone else was out enjoying themselves. She loved the pantomime, and apart from that one visit to the foreign servicemen's club with Isa and an occasional trip to the pictures with the children, it was an awful long time since she'd had a night out.

The children were full of it the following morning, chattering away as she took them to Sunday school. She heard all about it: the man dressed up as a woman, the woman dressed up as a man, the evil sorcerer. According to April, he'd been really scary. Archie pooh-poohed that idea. *He* hadn't been feart at all.

He was more interested in telling his mother how Uncle Ewen had bought them sweeties and then taken them for high tea afterwards. They had even, the little boy confided breathlessly to his mother, come home in a taxi!

Carrie handed them over to their Sunday school teacher at the entrance to the church and debated whether she was going in to hear the service herself. She decided against it. She wasn't exactly feeling full of the milk of human kindness this morning. When she got back home Florence was waiting for her on the landing.

'Come in for a wee minute, Carrie,' she said, 'we want to tell you all about our trip yesterday!'

Ewen was sitting in front of a roaring fire, relaxed in his shirt sleeves, laughing at something Isa was saying to him. He stood up when Carrie came into the room. She was perversely irritated by that. Where had he acquired those kind of manners?

'Good morning,' he said cheerfully.

'What's good about it?' she muttered. 'It's freezing out there.' Out of the corner of her eye, she saw Isa raise her eyebrows at him.

Florence had gone to fetch the theatre programme. She came back through with it, her face bright and animated. She told Carrie exactly what the children had, apparently as excited as they had been by the show, the sweeties, the meal out and the taxi. All paid for by Mr Ewen Livingstone. All guaranteed to give Archie and April an afternoon out they would remember for a very long time.

Unless Carrie made liars out of her children – as impossible as it was unthinkable – Matt was inevitably going to hear all about this from their innocent lips. It would be she herself who would bear the brunt of his reaction. Her unease ballooned suddenly into full-scale anxiety, tinged with a sharp edge of resentment.

She supposed she couldn't blame Ewen – although he must remember how jealous Matthew had always been of him – but Isa and Florence were a different matter. Isa had been concerned enough to check with her before Ewen had arrived that Matt wasn't due home at the same time. She seemed to have forgotten all about that now. Carrie hadn't realised how fragile her control was until it broke.

'For goodness' sake, Florence,' she snapped, 'you're as bad as Archie and April! It can't have been that exciting.'

She had never seen anybody's face fall in quite the same way as Florence's did at that moment.

Carrie looked up with a start when the booking-office door was pushed open at nine o'clock that evening. George Gibson, as regular on his evening rounds as her father had been, wasn't due for another half hour, and by this time on a Sunday evening things were usually pretty quiet. She was taken aback when she saw who her unexpected visitor was. Surprise – and embarrassment stemming from the circumstances of their meeting earlier in the day – lent an edge to her voice.

'What are you doing here?'

'I was out for a walk,' Ewen said, 'and found myself in Crow Road, so I thought I'd come and see you home.'

'I've still got an hour to go,' she pointed out, indicating the clock on the wall.

'I'll go through some of my interviews. Start analysing the information.' Despite his words, he made no move to take off his coat, just stood there looking at her, arms folded across his broad chest. She knew she wasn't imagining the reproach. It was evident in every line of his stance.

She shrugged. 'Please yourself, but I don't need anyone to see me home.'

'I thought that was one of the points I'm supposed to be investigating.' His tone of voice was deceptively mild. 'That it's not very pleasant for a woman to have to walk home alone on a dark winter's night.' He backed up towards his table, stood leaning against it.

'I'm used to it,' she said shortly. 'I can manage. There's really no need for you to hang on.'

'Oh, you can manage everything, can't you?' His eyes had darkened, gone the wintry blue colour she remembered as a sign that he was angry about something.

'What's that supposed to mean?' she demanded, her own temper ready to flare up. All it needed was the tiniest spark.

'You know exactly what it means,' he said grimly. 'Don't you think you owe Florence an apology for the way you spoke to her this morning?'

Carrie didn't think it. She knew it. She got up and went to stand in front of the fire, turning her back on him. His condemnation couldn't make her feel any worse than she already did. She'd been miserable all afternoon and evening, hating herself for taking it out on the woman who cared for her and her children so much, who even now was looking after them so that she was free to go to work.

'I don't want to believe this,' came the harsh voice from behind her, 'but are you put out because we were enjoying ourselves while you were stuck here?'

Did he think her so shallow she was capable of being jealous of her own children, then? She ached to defend herself, but how could she possibly tell him the truth? He would look at her with pity in his eyes . . . and she knew she couldn't bear that. She took a deep breath.

'Maybe that's it,' she agreed, allowing her head to fall forward as she put a hand out to the narrow mantelpiece to steady herself.

His tone of voice was no longer mild. It was contemptuous. 'Then I think you should grow up, Carrie. Don't you?'

Her fingers gripped hard on the warm cast iron. 'You think I should grow up?' she repeated. She sounded remarkably calm, but when she turned to look at him her eyes were glowing as brightly as the coals in the fire behind her. Looking suddenly alert, Ewen straightened up and opened his mouth to say something.

She didn't give him the chance, her apparent calmness disappearing into a series of angry questions and statements. 'How dare you say that to me, Ewen Livingstone? I've *had* to bloody well grow up! What do you think it was like for me, losing my parents within a year of each other? Archie was born the day my mother died. The very day. That was all she held on for. What d'you think it felt like to nurse my baby

301

with my mother lying dead in a room across the hall? I was only eighteen years old, for God's sake!' Her voice quavered.

'Carrie,' he began, rising to his feet. 'I'm sorry. I didn't know that –'

She got control of herself, swallowed hard. 'I've had to do a hell of a lot of growing up since we last knew each other,' she said bitterly. 'Dealing with all that, living with my horrible in-laws, bringing up my children, holding down a job, coping with a husband who . . .'

She stopped dead. Ewen came towards her and peered into her face. 'A husband who what?' he asked.

She narrowed her eyes at him. 'What has Isa told you?'

'Not a thing,' he said, his voice grim. 'But you just have.'

Her chin flew up. 'I've told you nothing,' she said. 'Absolutely nothing.'

'Carrie . . .' He put his hand on her arm, but she side-stepped him and walked back to the ticket window. When she got there she lifted a pencil and bent her head over the bundles of tickets she'd been checking when he came in.

'I've got to get on with my work. I think you should go now.'

'I came to walk you home,' came the quiet voice from behind her. 'And that's what I'm going to do.'

She stopped pretending to check the tickets. 'Please go away. Please.'

'Is that what you really want?'

'Yes,' she said. Her voice was flat and lifeless. 'That's what I really want.'

Carrie had never felt quite so lonely as she did on her walk home that night.

'You look tired, lass,' said Florence, looking up as she walked into the kitchen. 'Shall I make you a wee cup of tea?'

302

'Oh, Florence, I'm so sorry! Please forgive me!' She went forward, down on to her knees beside the older woman's chair.

'Least said, soonest mended, pet,' Florence said calmly. 'Lay your head down in my lap and have a wee greet. You look like that's what you're needing.'

Carrie did as she was bid.

Chapter 27

Carrie sat down opposite Ewen on the following Wednesday afternoon and watched him feed a sheet of foolscap paper into the portable typewriter. She was on duty with another girl today and they had chosen the mid-afternoon lull for the interview so they could conduct it without any interruptions. She could hear her colleague behind her at the ticket window, dealing with a passenger who had a complicated travel enquiry.

'I'll type your answers directly on to my proformas,' Ewen said, somewhat unnecessarily. She could see what he was doing.

'Now then . . .' He was muttering to himself. 'Name, address, date of birth, maiden name . . . I know all of those. Your grade and how long you've worked here I don't.'

She told him and he typed it in without looking up. 'Your opinion of your working conditions,' he said.

'I'm very satisfied with them. Only I agree with the idea of trying to pair women up when they're working late. Like I put in the letter.'

He typed that in too. His fingers were surprisingly nimble on the keyboard. The girl at Waverley with whom he'd had such a good laugh must have taught him well.

'Your domestic circumstances. I need to ask you about them.'

'You know them too,' she said, doing her best to shrug

305

nonchalantly. 'Married with two children, both cared for by friends when my hours don't fit in with school and crèche times.'

'I have to ask you about your husband,' he said carefully.

A train pulled in, and the other clerkess went out to collect the tickets. Behind Ewen, there was a crackle from the open fire. They both turned and looked at it. A little mound of coals had collapsed in on itself.

'I should put more on,' she said, half-rising from her chair, bracing herself with one hand on the table.

Ewen swung back round to face her. 'It'll keep for five minutes.'

She subsided. 'My husband's serving with the army,' she said. 'The Argyll and Sutherland Highlanders. What more do you need to know?'

He lifted one of his hands from the typewriter and laid it over hers. Her fingers contracted beneath his, but his grip was firm. He looked her straight in the eye. 'I need to know how best I can help you.'

'Take your hand away,' she said.

He remembered. She could see it in his eyes. He had said exactly the same thing to her once. She bit her lip, summoned up her last reserves of strength. 'Take your hand away, please.' She looked at him, a silent plea in her green eyes.

He took his hand away.

Carrie tilted the horseshoe purse so that its entire contents slid forward and were visible, staring at the silver and copper coins as though she could conjure up the ten shillings she was sure she'd neatly folded and put in there before she'd left the house this Saturday morning. It didn't work. The note simply wasn't there.

She tugged off one glove – it was nearly as cold inside the shop on this wintry day as it was outside – and flicked her index finger over the money she did have, adding it up in her head. She was three and tenpence short for the messages which sat in front of her. She deposited the entire contents of her purse beside them and said as much. The face on the other side of the dark wood counter looked less than sympathetic.

'I'm s-sorry,' she said, stuttering in embarrassment. 'I've miscalculated somewhere. I'll need to put something back.'

'Well, what then?' snapped the shop assistant. She wasn't known for her friendly nature.

A dark-coated arm came over Carrie's shoulder. The hand which belonged to it set two florins down next to the small pile of groceries. 'She's not putting anything back. And we'll have two o' those penny caramels as well.' He lifted the paper-wrapped toffees out of a cardboard box which sat on the counter. 'Here's the sweetie coupons.'

Archie and April were looking up at Ewen with broad smiles. He handed them a sweet each. 'The dentist will love me,' he told them brightly. He gestured towards the groceries lying on the counter. 'Shouldn't you pack them away?'

When the four of them were back out on the pavement he reached for the message bag. 'I'll take that.'

Carrie swung it out of his reach. 'Haven't you some shopping of your own to do? Did Florence send you for something?'

'I can get it later,' he said easily. 'I was really out for a walk. Revisiting my old haunts. Like Keith Street and the Quaker graveyard.'

'I know where that is,' piped up Archie. 'It's a spooky place.'

His Uncle Ewen took his eyes off Carrie's face long enough

to smilingly contradict him. 'Oh, no it's not. It's a special place. A magical place.'

He looked so relaxed, his woollen coat slung casually over the intricately patterned Aran sweater Florence had knitted for him. Flecks of snow swirling down from a heavy sky were beginning to settle on his shoulders. He hadn't shaved today. There was a faint shadowing of bristles on his jaw.

Carrie was in her Rosie the Riveter outfit. Now that she thought about it, she realised the wool Florence had given her to make the jacket's fringe must have come from the leftovers of that same Aran sweater, the raw material painstakingly unpicked from two smaller jumble sale finds.

'What are you doing here anyway?' she demanded. 'Don't you have a meeting in Edinburgh tomorrow?'

'Yes, but it doesn't start till late morning. I'll go through first thing.'

'Won't your fiancée be missing you?'

He looked nonplussed. 'Moira? I shouldn't think so. She joined the WAAF six months ago. Decided she wanted to see a bit of the world before she settled down.'

'She broke off your engagement?'

'No,' he said. 'I did.'

Archie was growing impatient with this grown-up conversation. 'Can we eat the sweeties now, Mammy?' he asked, already unwrapping his penny caramel.

'No,' she replied, unusually short with him. 'You know you're not allowed to eat in the street.' She turned to Ewen. 'Thank you for lending me the money,' she said stiffly. 'If you come back with me to the house, I'll reimburse you straightaway.'

'Don't be daft, Carrie. I'm not going to miss four bob.'

'I'm not short of money,' she snapped. 'My pay packet's lying unopened on the kitchen table. I forgot to put the money in my purse, that's all.'

'Take the money as a gift.' He looked down at April, tugging on her mother's blanket jacket and pleading to be allowed to eat her caramel. 'What's wrong with the bairns eating the sweeties now?'

April was still tugging. 'Stop it!' cried Carrie. Leaning down, she administered a smack to her daughter's bottom. Neither April nor Archie was accustomed to being physically chastised. It wasn't the way their mother normally went about things. A small shocked face looked up at her. Then the tears came.

'I'm sorry,' she said desperately. 'I'm sorry, pet.' But before she could get down to take her daughter into her arms, Ewen had swept the little girl up into his.

'Now, what's all this nonsense?' he said, tickling her under the chin. He had her smiling again in seconds, especially when he lifted her up to ride on his shoulders.

'Can you manage your mammy's messages, Archie son? Right then, let's get back to the house.'

Carrie gritted her teeth. 'There's absolutely no need for you to see us home.'

Ewen gave her a bland smile. 'Yes, there is. You owe me three and tenpence.'

When they got back home he set April down and took the shopping bag from Archie. Then he unlocked the door to Isa and Florence's and shooed the children in, one large hand gently but firmly on each small back.

'Tell your aunties your mother and I will be along in a wee minute.' He closed the door on any protest. 'Open up, Carrie,' he said grimly.

She started to argue with him. He fixed her with a determined look, and she thought better of it. Her hand was shaking as she took the key out of the pocket of her jacket. She couldn't

309

seem to get it lined up with the lock. Ewen's fingers closed over hers. 'I'll do it.'

When they got in she headed for the kitchen, knowing he was right behind her. She pulled off her jacket and threw it over a chair, not noticing when it slid to the floor. The damned pay packet, as she'd remembered too late, was lying in the middle of the table. Picking it up, she ripped it open and tipped out the contents.

'Four shillings,' she said, snapping the coins down on the hard wood of the table. She slid them towards him.

'That's tuppence too much,' Ewen said. 'The sweets are a present from me to the bairns. A wee treat.'

'They don't need treats.'

'Everyone needs treats, Carrie,' he said evenly. 'Children especially.'

'I don't have any change. Take the money.'

'No, I don't want it. Any of it.' He put her shopping bag on the table and laid the door key beside it. He stooped, lifted her jacket and placed it carefully over the back of a chair. Then he stood and looked at her, and the grim expression on his face relaxed.

'You look dead cute in that rig-out, you know. Especially the breeks. I hate that stupid-looking headscarf, though. It hides your lovely hair.'

'Take-the-bloody-money!'

'There's no need to swear,' he said mildly. 'It's not necessary if one has an adequate vocabulary.'

She ignored the implicit invitation to share that particular memory. 'There's every need to swear!'

'And was there every need to smack the wee lassie when what you really wanted to do was hit me? It's me you're angry with, isn't it? Because I've found out something you'd rather I didn't know.'

She moved quickly to stand in front of the range, putting the table between them. Then she turned, folding her arms across her chest. 'So you're a student of psychology among all your other talents, are you? Psychologist, child-care expert, strategic planning expert, esteemed servant of the railway company, dispenser of sweeties to the children of Partick?'

He raised one eyebrow. She hadn't known he could do that. 'My, my, Mrs Campbell, shall I fetch you a saucer of milk? That sounded a wee touch catty.'

Her precarious control shattered. 'Well, what do you expect?' she demanded, waving one arm wildly in the air. 'You come breezing back into my life, you charm my children, you charm my friends, you charm everybody. And you're all clever and debonair and attractive . . .'

He was coming round the table, heading straight for her. She hastily resumed her defensive posture.

'Clever?' he repeated, a quizzical expression on his face. '*Debonair?*' He paused, and pretended to consider. 'I think that's my favourite, Carrie. Shall we make it the word of the week? Although I like *attractive* too. In fact,' he said, sauntering forward to stand right in front of her, 'I like all of them. Especially when they fall from your lips.' His eyes dropped to the lips in question, and she took a step back – and almost burned herself on the range.

'Careful.' He coiled his fingers around her wrist and pulled her away from the heat. Into a different kind of warmth.

Chapter 28

She was a girl again, standing in the Quaker graveyard with the October sun warm on her back, the stubble on his chin pleasantly rough on the smooth skin of her face.

'Tell me you didn't want me to do that,' Ewen murmured against her mouth. He sounded calm, but his breathing was fast and shallow.

'I didn't want you to do that,' said Carrie, and heard for herself how dazed she sounded. 'Do it again,' she whispered.

His arms came about her waist, tightening around her body, pressing the lacy patterns of her jumper into her skin. Hadn't she been wearing it that day too, the last time he had kissed her? She lifted her hands and placed them flat against his chest. Through the softness of the Aran sweater she felt the rhythm of his heart: a rapid but solid thump.

Then it came to her what they were doing. This wasn't a boy kissing a girl in a corner of an old graveyard. The heat she could feel on her back wasn't the autumn sunshine of seven years ago, it was the glow of her own hearth. That hearth which belonged to Matt too.

What sort of a wife was she to be acting like this with his children mere yards away? What sort of a mother? She began to struggle, pushed Ewen violently away. For a few seconds they simply stared at each other. Then he spoke.

'Tell me one thing, Carrie. Tell me you still love your

husband.' He took a quick little breath. 'Tell me that and I'll go away and leave you in peace.'

Her eyes found the willow pattern platter on the high mantelpiece above the range. It had been a similar gesture on her part which had betrayed it as the location of Ewen's letter that fateful day four years ago.

Afterwards, even while she'd been enduring what its discovery had provoked, she'd been aware that the base of the platter had been pulled out of place by Matt's furious and searching hand, forward of the thin strip of wood which kept it secure and upright. She'd been terrified that her grandmother's treasure might slide off the mantelpiece and be smashed to pieces on the range or the hard floor. But it had survived, and so had she. After a fashion. She turned her head again, met Ewen's intense gaze.

'I'm his wife,' she said.

'That doesn't answer my question.'

Carrie knew it didn't, but she didn't know what else to say. She didn't know how she felt about Matt any more. All that came to her when she considered the question was a numbness, an inability to feel very much at all. But he was her husband. And the father of her children.

'I made a commitment to him. Took vows in the church.'

Ewen's expression grew cynical. 'And do you think he takes that commitment as seriously as you obviously do?'

She took a breath, squared her shoulders. 'You can't know that he doesn't.'

'Yes, I can,' he said. 'Some sons take after their fathers. And he does hit you, doesn't he?'

'What do you want from me, Ewen?' she asked desperately.

'Och, Carrie,' he said, his face softening. 'Only to help. In whatever way I can.'

'That's why you kissed me just now then, is it?'

'No,' he said slowly. 'There was another reason for that.'

Matthew Campbell was in a state of some indecision. The pretty ATS officer had just asked him which destination she should make his rail warrant out for. He had planned to go up to London again. He loved the city, and the opportunities it afforded: especially to a handsome Scotsman in kilted battle dress. But, he thought, peering through the window behind the young woman's head at a sky filled with ominous blue-grey clouds, he was missing his family.

He thought of Archie and April's innocent smiles and how pleased they would be to see him. He thought of Carrie. She had an innocence about her too, unlike most of the girls he'd had while he'd been down here. He felt vaguely guilty about that, but what she didn't know wouldn't hurt her, would it?

'Make up your mind, soldier,' said the girl pertly.

He couldn't help sizing her up. Was she one of those who would or one of those who wouldn't? Making that judgement about every good-looking woman he met had become second nature – and there were quite a lot who would . . .

Lately, in low moments, he'd begun thinking it was all a bit sordid. During his last encounter he hadn't even bothered finding out the girl's name. She hadn't asked for his either. He'd found himself longing for Carrie: her honesty and freshness, that passion which had only ever been given to him.

He glanced once more at the outside world. The journey north was going to be hellish. The forecast was for heavy snow all over the British Isles. Was it worth going so far for such a short stay? He thought about it.

Carrie was in his mind's eye, lying underneath him in the box bed, her vibrant hair splashed over the pillow. Dammit, he was going home.

'Glasgow,' he said firmly. 'Make it out for Glasgow.'

Carrie had to stop him saying the words. It seemed important. So she asked a question, and succeeded only in landing them both in more trouble.

'Why did you break off your engagement with Moira? Isa said she was a lovely girl.'

'She was,' agreed Ewen. 'We had some great times together. She was pretty and funny. Passionate too,' he added, a gleam of mischief lurking in the corner of his eye.

Carrie stiffened. 'So what exactly was wrong with this paragon?'

The mischievous look vanished. 'She wasn't you,' he said simply.

Despite the weather – the scenery whizzing past outside looked like something off a Christmas card – the train was making good enough progress. Crewe. Preston. Lancaster. Then the light faded and they drew the blackout curtains across the windows – not that there was a great deal of light inside the carriage anyway. The low level of illumination permitted by the wartime restrictions was barely enough to read by or to play cards, although the other men in Matthew's compartment were attempting the latter.

He'd declined an invitation to join in, preferring to think about his reunion with his family. He peered at his watch. Six o'clock. Would they make Glasgow by ten? No, that was over-optimistic. They had two notorious summits to negotiate: Shap and Beattock. They'd be hard going in conditions like these. Midnight would be more like it. The children would be sound asleep by then. He wouldn't disturb them, but he could surprise their mother, creep in beside her . . .

Train heating was subject to wartime restrictions too. Although they'd been promised it would come on again in an hour's time, it was bloody freezing at the moment. Matt had been one of the most vociferous complainants about that earlier on, but he wasn't noticing the cold at the moment. There was a warm glow creeping up his body. He adjusted his position, closed his eyes and enjoyed it. It was nothing compared to the pleasure he'd be feeling after midnight . . .

Then, brakes screeching like chalk being drawn across a blackboard, the train ground to a halt. The card-players cursed as the upended suitcase which formed their impromptu table jerked and fell over, throwing the completed hands to the dusty floor.

Matt curled his slim fingers round the curtain which covered the window, pulled it back a crack and looked out. Through the driving snow, he could just make out station buildings. There were no signs to identify the place, of course, a measure designed to confuse German spies. It also confused a lot of weary travellers.

'Where are we?' asked one of the card-players.

'How the hell should I know?' he responded irritably.

'Well,' said the man reasonably, 'you did tell us you were a railwayman in civvy street.'

'I think it might be Penrith,' he said grudgingly. And, he thought glumly, there's probably too much snow on Shap Fell and we're going to sit here for hours. He should have gone to London, after all. By this time he could have been sitting opposite a pretty girl in a nice warm bar having a drink, anticipating further delights to come – especially if she had a room of her own not too far away.

'Cover that light up!' bellowed a voice from the platform.

'One of Hitler's long-lost brothers, d'ye think?'

Matt dropped the curtain and forced a smile. He was going to be stuck with these men for several hours. He was annoyed with himself for having made the wrong decision. Nothing he could do about that now. Carrie had better be grateful for what he'd gone through for the sake of what was now rapidly diminishing into little more than a few hours with her. That was all. She'd better be extremely grateful indeed.

She had told him not to, but Carrie wasn't surprised when Ewen came into the booking office at ten o'clock that night, observing as he did so that there was quite a bit of the white stuff falling this evening.

'So I see,' she said. 'You look like you've just returned from the Russian front.'

He squinted down at his coat. The dark material was covered in lacy cobwebs of snow. 'I should have given myself a shake before I came in. Like Bobby the dog does after a swim.' He looked back up at her with a grin.

You're all sparkly, she thought, with your flashing smile and the snowflakes glistening on your coat. Even your eyes look silvery-blue tonight. You're like Jack Frost. Only he stretches out a bony finger and freezes everything solid, whereas your fingers have begun to melt something in me. But I can't allow that to happen . . .

Ewen did the one eyebrow-raising trick. 'What are you thinking about?'

'Oh . . . nothing really. I'll get my coat.' She lifted it down from the stand in the corner, buttoned it up and then reached for her scarf. It was a home-made effort, in multi-coloured stripes. She'd knitted three altogether, for herself and the children, out of leftover bits of wool. She pulled on matching mittens and crocheted tammy, looked up and caught an amused look.

'What's so funny?'

'Well, as you would say . . . nothing really. You look like Nanook of the North, that's all. Should we no' cross the scarf over your front and fasten it round the back with a couple of safety pins?'

'Ha, ha. At least I'm dressed for the weather. You haven't even got a hat or gloves on.'

'Gloves are for cissies,' he said grandly. 'No' manly types like myself.'

The snow was beginning to lie. You could see it. Despite the blackout, the deserted pavements were glowing like dull ribbons. Even Dumbarton Road, normally kept clear by the continual toing and froing of trams and other traffic, was beginning to acquire a ghostly white coating. Everything seemed eerily quiet.

'How did you spend your day?' The snow wasn't falling too heavily at the moment. There was no need to make a mad dash for home.

'I took Archie and April to the pictures. You don't mind, do you?'

'Why should I mind?'

'After last weekend,' he enquired wryly, 'when I thought I was going to get my head in my hands to play with for taking them to the panto?'

'There was a reason for that.'

She heard him take a deep breath. 'Yes,' he said. 'I'm sorry. I didn't think. None o' us did.'

'Aye, well,' she said wryly. 'I suppose the damage is done now. What did you see tonight?'

'*The Wizard of Oz.*'

'They'd have enjoyed that.'

'They did. It didn't seem to bother them that they'd seen it before.'

'It never does. April had great fun being terrified of the Wicked Witch of the West last time.'

'This time too,' he said. 'She hid her face in my coat

319

whenever the witch cackled. I think Archie was a bit frightened too, but he was very brave about it. They were both real excited. Could hardly keep their eyes open after we got back from the cinema. More or less fell asleep into their supper. Their aunties got them undressed and into their night clothes and I carried them across to their beds. Florence is sitting with them till you get home.'

A little flurry of snow blew into Carrie's face, and she bent her head to let her hat take the brunt of it. That made her wonder why he had come out without any headgear. She asked him. It had seemed a simple enough question, but he took his time about answering it.

'I wanted to feel the snow on me,' he said at last. 'To help me relive a memory.' He stopped dead beside her. They were almost home.

'Would you come somewhere with me? It's not much further.'

'It was the day of your wedding,' said the deep voice in the soft darkness. They were in the Quaker graveyard, the snow-covered grass beneath their feet springy as a newly stitched quilt. 'I went out and got myself drunk. I thought it might deaden the pain.' He paused briefly. 'It didnae.'

She was listening carefully. Since he had been back in Partick he'd begun to re-acquire aspects of his original accent.

'At some point during the evening – I've no idea exactly when, I was well away with it by that time – Martin Sharkey noticed what I was up to and told me I'd had enough. He got this other surfaceman to help him get me to the door. I think they'd have taken me right home, only Janice was waiting outside, and she volunteered.'

'Janice Muirhead?'

'Aye.' Eyes grown accustomed to the dark, she saw him

raise his head. 'Where is she, by the way? I haven't seen her around since I've been back.'

'Nobody knows. She went off somewhere. Not long after the war broke out.'

Carrie didn't think she'd intended to sound disapproving, but Ewen must have heard something in her voice. 'You shouldn't blame her for what happened the night of your hen party. That was my fault. I behaved very badly.'

'I had hurt you very badly.' Carrie hesitated. 'Did you and Janice ever . . .' She stopped short of completing the question, but he answered it anyway.

'No. Well . . . nothing to speak of.'

She wondered what that meant. Exactly.

'We might have that night,' he went on, 'but we didn't. I'd like to think it was because I came to my senses but it was probably because I was too blootered,' he said with brutal honesty. 'I was sick into the gutter, Carrie. Out there on Keith Street.' The self-disgust was evident in his voice. 'Then I came here. It was snowing then too, but it was a bit sheltered in that corner over behind where you're standing now. That's where I curled up.'

'You spent the night here?'

'Aye,' came the calm voice. 'Martin discovered me at six o'clock the next morning. He'd been worried about me. When he didn't find me at home, something made him look in here.'

She remembered very well that it had been snowing that night. While she'd been taking her ease with Matt in a warm and luxurious hotel, Ewen had been alone in the freezing darkness. Huddled in a corner like an animal which had skulked off somewhere to lick its wounds.

'You'd fallen asleep?' She was trying to emulate his own level tones, but she was aware of a turbulent mixture of emotions within her breast: guilt for the part she had played in his unhappiness at the time; pity for the boy he had been; admiration for the man he had become. No, it was a lot more than admiration . . .

'I fell asleep eventually. I spent some time thinking first.'

She whispered a question into the blue blackness. 'What did you think about?'

His answer came back at her like an arrow hitting its target. 'I thought about you. I thought about Matthew Campbell making love to you.' She heard him take a deep breath. 'And it made me so angry that I smashed my fist into the wall. Three times.'

She moved forward. 'Oh, Ewen,' she breathed. 'That must have hurt so much.'

'I wanted it to hurt.' A faint colouring of humour crept into his voice. 'My wish was granted. It was sore for weeks.'

She took another step towards him and slipped her gloved fingers into his. 'Was it this hand?'

'Aye. My right hand. My working hand.'

'It's cold,' she said, automatically beginning to rub the frozen digits to restore circulation to them.

'Always the little mother,' he said lightly.

'Don't be so bloody cheeky,' Carrie murmured, 'and don't tell me not to swear either. Does this not feel nice?'

'It would feel a whole lot nicer if you took your wee mitten off. Your skin against my skin.'

Her fingers stopped moving. Her whole body stiffened. He didn't speak for a second or two, but when he did his voice was slow and gentle. 'I know. You're not ready for that yet.'

Her next words came out on a great rush of breath: a plume of white in the darkness between them. 'Ewen, I'm not ready for any of this!'

'I know that too,' he said calmly. 'But there's something I

have to tell you all the same.' He paused briefly. 'Something I need to tell you.'

She waited, knowing she couldn't stop it this time. Not knowing if she wanted to . . .

'I love you,' he said. 'I've never stopped loving you.'

'Ewen . . .'

'Wheesht. It's all right. You don't have to say anything. I understand.'

Florence was sitting by the fire knitting, but stopped as soon as they came into the kitchen. Thrusting her needles into the ball of wool, she rose to her feet and started gathering together her bits and pieces. 'I looked in on the weans a wee minute ago, Carrie. They're both sound asleep.'

'Thanks, Florence,' she said softly, divesting herself of her scarf and tammy before removing her coat and draping it over the back of a chair. 'Would you be wanting a cup of tea before you go?'

'No, I'm fine, pet.' She glanced at Ewen. He hadn't taken his coat off but had gone to stand against the wall beside the range, hands behind his back. 'Will I leave the two of you to say goodnight?' she asked doubtfully.

The young eyes and the old ones met. 'Leave the door on the latch, Florence,' said Ewen in his deep voice. 'I'll not be long.'

'Aye.' Her lined face softened as she looked at him. 'You're a good lad,' she said.

Carrie saw her out, did a quick check of her own on Archie and April and walked back through to the kitchen. Ewen was still standing with his back to the wall.

'At least Florence approves of me. Though at this precise moment I can't say I'm finding that much of a comfort.'

The realisation of what he meant threw Carrie into

stammering confusion. 'You mean you want to – You would have wanted to –'

'Of course,' he said calmly, pushing himself off the wall. 'If the lassie was ready and willing. But she's not, is she? And I've always made that a golden rule.'

'Oh,' she said faintly. 'Did you and Moira –'

She stopped, horrified that she'd been about to ask him such an intimate question – and for the second time that evening – but Ewen's face was alive with mischief as he walked towards her.

'A wee bit of curiosity? That's a good sign. Not only with Moira,' he murmured, 'although a gentleman should never discuss such things, of course. Suffice it to say that I'm no longer the innocent lad you once knew. Haven't been for quite some time, in fact.'

'Oh,' Carrie said again, and he laughed softly.

'Any chance of a goodnight kiss as a consolation prize?'

'Ewen . . . I can't. You know I can't.'

He lifted his hand, touched her cheek with his fingertips. 'I know that you let me kiss you in this very room this morning. I know that you kissed me back. I know that you asked me to kiss you again. That's what I know, Caroline Burgess.'

'I'm not Caroline Burgess any more,' she said sadly. 'That's the whole problem, isn't it?'

He dropped his hand. 'It doesn't have to be,' he said quietly. 'Not in this day and age.'

She could only shake her head at that.

'It's too late to talk about this now,' he said briskly. 'We'll leave it till tomorrow night when I get back from Edinburgh. And shall I come and have breakfast with you and the bairns in the morning before I go, take them to Sunday school for you on my way to the station?'

She shook her head again. 'I can't fight you any more. I haven't the strength left.'

'You don't need to fight me. We're on the same side, you and me. We always have been. Since we were a boy and girl together that day in Oban. Remember?'

'That was a hundred years ago,' Carrie said sadly. 'We're different people now.'

'No,' he insisted. He made a fist of his hand, tapped it lightly against his chest. 'Not in here. Not in the part which makes us what we really are.' He smiled at her, his eyes full of tenderness. 'I think it's called the heart.'

Another bloody delay. Matt lowered the window and poked his head cautiously out of it. The snow which blew in provoked a profane but sleepy protest from one of the card-players. The rest of them were out for the count, slumped in their seats snoring and wheezing. He called to an older man in railway uniform standing further up the platform. 'Where are we?'

'Carstairs Junction,' came the reply, the words almost whipped away by the snell breeze whistling along the side of the train.

'Any idea how long we're going to be held up here?'

'Your guess is as good as mine, pal. We're waiting for the snow plough to clear the track ahead o' ye.'

Matt slammed the window shut and sat down. He supposed it could be worse. Carstairs wasn't that far from Glasgow. He glanced at his watch. Half-past five. Maybe he'd make it home in time for breakfast.

'People don't come for breakfast!' cried April, gleeful that she had caught the grown-ups out. Ewen had knocked but then, using Isa and Florence's key, let himself in to Carrie's house. 'People come for their tea, or dinner on a Sunday.'

'Well, I've come for breakfast,' Ewen told her, 'and what's more I've also come bearing gifts. One of your Auntie Florence's home-made loaves and this.' He laid the loaf on the table, put a hand to the inside pocket of his coat and, with the air of a conjurer producing a rabbit out of a top hat, set down a jar of jam. His hosts regarded it with some awe.

'Rita Sharkey,' he said as Carrie took his coat from him and hung it up on the back of the door. 'She gave it to me last week.'

'Where on earth did she get the sugar?' Carrie asked, making the tea and bringing it to the table.

Ewen tapped his nose significantly as he sat down opposite her. 'I thought it best not to enquire. Let us simply enjoy it. Come closer, you two. You're about to smell the summer.'

Obediently, Archie and April leaned forward. Ewen twisted open the lid of the jar.

Archie took a deep breath. 'Raspberries,' he said. 'My favourite!'

'My favourite too!' cried April.

Wide mouth curving in a slow smile, Ewen looked across the table at Carrie. 'Shall I pour out their milk?'

It was all so natural and relaxed. Afterwards, he insisted on doing the fire for her, giving it a thorough raking and taking the ashes down to the midden before adding fresh coal. 'To save you having to go out in the snow till you fetch this pair,' he said. 'Will I help you with the dishes before we go?'

She declined, although she was amused by the offer of help. 'No, I think you'd better watch your time. You don't want to be late for your meeting.'

She saw them out, reminding the children to be quiet as they went down the stairs. There were still people asleep at this time on a Sunday morning. She stood at the open door after the three of them had gone out of sight, smiling as she listened to the stage whispers floating back up to her. Then she heard Ewen's voice, a little louder than the children.

'Hold on, bairns, I've forgotten something.'

He was taking the stairs two at a time, his unbuttoned coat flying out behind him.

'What did you forget?' she asked.

'This,' he said, and planted a kiss on her mouth before taking off again. He paused briefly on the half landing, grinning up at her. 'If you won't give them to me, I'll just have to steal them.'

'*Ewen Livingstone!*' she hissed, but she couldn't help smiling at him.

'The word you are looking for,' he pronounced, 'is *incorrigible*.' He waved his hand and disappeared down the stairs.

Carrie went back into the kitchen and looked without enthusiasm at the breakfast dishes. Nothing could come of it, of course. He must know that as well as she did. Only he didn't seem to. She glanced over at the fire. It was burning merrily. She'd do the dishes in a minute. She'd have a wee sit down first.

Half an hour later she heard the scrape of a key in the lock.

'All right,' she called, 'what did you forget this time?' Despite herself, she sat up eagerly, looking towards the door with a smile on her face.

A soldier in battledress and Glengarry bonnet walked into the room. 'What did who forget, Carrie?' he asked. His gaze went to the table: four plates, the two chunky tumblers she used for the children's milk, her own tea cup, the extra one opposite. He lifted the tea cosy, felt the pot with his hand. 'Still warm,' he said. Quietly, as though he were talking to himself. Then he looked at her. 'Odd time of day to be entertaining,' he observed.

As he walked towards her Carrie saw the shutters come down on his beautiful dark eyes.

Chapter 29

She had to stop shaking. There were things she had to do: important things. Before she could do any of them she had to get up off the floor, and before she could attempt that feat she had to stop shaking.

He had started on her while she was still in the chair, using both hands to administer stinging little slaps to her face. First the right cheek, then the left. She lost count of how many times. Then he threaded one hand through her hair and hauled her to her feet, his long fingers digging painfully into her scalp. 'Who is he?' he hissed into her face. 'I want his name.'

'Matt,' she sobbed. 'Please let me go. You've got it all wrong. Please, Matt!'

He pushed her towards the wall, banged her head against it. 'I want his name!' he repeated. 'Tell me, you little whore! Tell me!' He spat the words out. It was like a machine gun firing, each word punctuated by him banging her head once more against the wall. 'I-want-his-name!' Every impact sent a jagged ache and waves of nausea searing through her.

Tears streaming down her face, reeling with pain and dizziness, Carrie begged him to stop, kept telling him nothing had happened, but he showed no sign of hearing her pleas. Yet, despite the blank look in his eyes, he wasn't shouting and although he was hurting her, he was controlling it too – enough to cause pain, not enough to knock her out. He had a question to which he wanted an answer.

She mustn't tell him. She wouldn't tell him. But her refusal to supply that answer told him what he needed to know. The punishing hand slipped out of her hair, and she was dimly aware of him taking a step back from her, leaving her slumped against the wall.

'It's Ewen Livingstone,' he said. 'He's come back, hasn't he?'

She had waited for him to start hitting her again, but this time he had attacked her with words. Horrible words. Terrifying words.

She had to stop shaking. She started with her hands, convulsively clutching at the material of her skirt. With all her might, she willed them to become still.

'In the name o' God, lassie! What's happened to you?'

Florence, in tartan dressing-gown and slippers and with her grey hair done up in a fat plait down the side of her neck, pulled Carrie into the flat.

'For pity's sake,' came a querulous voice from the kitchen, 'would youse both put a sock in it? It's bad enough folk coming in here shaving themselves at the crack of dawn. Has everybody forgotten that today's Sunday?'

Florence hustled Carrie out of the lobby and into the kitchen, carefully shutting the door behind them. 'It's you that's making all the row, Isabella Cooke,' she hissed. 'Now, get out o' your bed and give me a hand wi' Carrie.' Her voice softened. 'Come on now, pet. You sit doon here by the fire and we'll see what's what.'

Isa, a vision of loveliness in nightie and hairnet, swung her legs over the side of the bed. 'What's wrang wi' her?'

By the time she made it to Carrie's side, it was clear that irritation had been replaced by other emotions. First there was

330

concern and curiosity. Then, as realisation dawned, came anger. Without taking her eyes off the red mark on the side of Carrie's face, she stretched out a hand to the mantelpiece for her cigarettes.

'I take it your man's home,' she said drily. 'Would I be correct in thinking that he dropped in unexpectedly?' She opened the packet she held in her hand, then looked up abruptly. 'My God, hen, he and Ewen didnae meet up, did they?'

'Ewen took the children off to Sunday school about half an hour before Matt arrived.' She could still speak. That was something. Then a thought struck her. How long would it have taken Ewen to walk the children to church and deposit them with their Sunday school teacher? Ten minutes? Quarter of an hour? Then he would have needed another five to ten minutes to get to the station, perhaps slightly longer on pavements still covered in snow.

'They must have just missed each other,' she whispered. She closed her eyes, visualising it: Matt's train coming in on the westbound platform as Ewen climbed up the stairs to the eastbound one. There could only have been a minute or two in it. She bent forward, burying her face in her hands. 'Thank God. *Thank God!*'

There was a silence punctuated only by the noise of Isa taking a few hasty puffs. 'Where's your ever-loving husband now, then?'

'I don't know,' Carrie said helplessly, her voice muffled by her hands. 'I don't know.'

Florence put an arm about her shoulders. 'Sit up, pet,' she coaxed.

She tried not to wince as delicate fingers went to her hair, smoothing it back to assess the damage. 'A cold compress,' pronounced Florence. 'That's what we're needing here.' She swung round to the sink to prepare the remedy.

'Will that stop it from coming up in a bruise? I don't want to look a sight at work this afternoon.'

Isa sat on the arm of the chair opposite Carrie and drew some more nicotine into her lungs. 'You're planning on going in the day, are ye?'

The message was clear. If that *was* her intention, she'd have to climb over Isa's dead body to accomplish it.

'I have to,' she said. 'I can't let Ewen come back here tonight. I can phone Waverley from work, pretend I need to speak to him on railway business. He's going to some big meeting. I might not get him the first time I call, I'll probably have to try a few times. That'll be much easier if I can do it from the booking office. Then, when I get him, I can tell him he's got to stay through there for a couple of days. At least until Matt's leave is over.'

That earned her a pitying look. 'And you really think he will? When he finds out what that bloody bugger's done to ye?'

'He's not going to find out. I'll think of some reason why he shouldn't come back tonight.'

'Ye might have your work cut out on that one, hen.'

'Do you think I don't know that?' Carrie's voice faltered, and a solitary tear slid slowly down her cheek. Approaching with a pad of lint, Florence blotted it with her finger and applied the compress to the side of Carrie's head.

Isa grunted. Florence swung round to her. 'Could you no' be making us all a cup o' tea, instead o' standing there puffing on yon horrible thing?'

'I'm thinking,' said Isa, with dignity. 'If Ewen had gone by the time he got there, how did Mr Campbell know it was him you were having breakfast with?' She narrowed her eyes accusingly. 'Ye werenae stupid enough to tell him, were ye?'

332

'Of course she didnae tell him,' snapped Florence. 'He guessed. Any fool would have known that with Carrie it could only have been Ewen. Not that the two o' them did anything last night. I heard him coming in, five minutes after me. The lassie's no' a trollop, jumping from one man to the next like a demented rabbit.' She lifted the damp lint and examined the skin underneath. 'Unlike some folk I could mention.'

Isa straightened up. 'Don't you talk to me like that, you old bitch!'

'Truth hurts, does it, Isabella Cooke?'

'Oh, stop it!'

Carrie pushed Florence and the cold compress away and half-rose out of the chair. 'Stop it!' she said again. 'I don't want the two of you fighting because of me. And according to Matt, I *am* a trollop! And a lot worse than that besides!'

She subsided again. The shaking had come back. She looked up at both of them through a shimmering curtain of tears. 'He said awful things to me. Called me dreadful names. He wouldn't believe Ewen and I hadn't spent last night together, said no one else would believe it either. He said he could divorce me for something like that and the judge would say I was . . . I was . . . a loose woman. Sleeping with another man while my husband was away serving his country.' Her voice rose on a note of anguish. 'They'd call me an unfit mother and take the children away from me! He said he'd make sure I never saw Archie and April again!'

She was finding it hard to catch her breath. She put a hand to her chest and broke into a storm of weeping. Florence's arms came round her immediately and Isa stepped forward to kneel at her feet, reaching for her other hand.

'Listen to me,' said Isa urgently. 'Your weans have got the best mother in the world.' She squeezed Carrie's hand. 'And you know the both o' us would stand up in court and say that.'

333

'Aye,' said Florence stoutly, 'and lots o' other folk in Partick besides.'

'That's right,' said Isa, glancing up at her mother-in-law. The two of them began listing names, batting them backwards and forwards like tennis balls over a net.

'But Matt could bring out all his well-connected relatives!' Carrie said when they finally stopped.

'They wouldnae all be on his side,' said Florence. 'There's that nice Mr Cunningham, for a start.'

'Aye,' said Isa, nodding approvingly. 'The weans' Uncle Roddy. He'd speak up for you, hen. Defin-ately. Come on now. Dry your tears. You've not got your troubles to seek, but you've got friends to help you.' She squeezed Carrie's hand again. 'And you've got Ewen. D'you know what it means to have a man who loves you like that? There's lots o' folk would envy you, you know.'

Carrie lifted her head and looked into wistful eyes. 'Isa?' she said uncertainly.

Her friend gave her the most rueful of smiles, dropped her hand and rose to her feet. 'I suppose I'd better make us all some tea.' She transferred her gaze to Florence. 'Will that shut you up, ye old bisom?'

'Less of the old, ye wee flibbertigibbet,' said Florence. 'There's a lot of years left in me yet. I'll maybe even see you out.'

'Huh!' said Isa.

'Mr Livingstone, please.'

It was four o'clock that afternoon and this was the fourth time Carrie had phoned. She kept getting the same tele-phonist, and being put through to the same secretary. It was a Sunday, of course, there would only be a skeleton staff working. The two voices were beginning to sound familiar.

The secretary was beginning to sound irritable.

'Is this Partick station again?'

'Yes. It's really quite important that we get hold of Mr Livingstone.' Carrie gripped the heavy black receiver hard.

'Well, as I told you half an hour ago, he's still in the meeting. These are not the sort of people you interrupt lightly. It's a very high-level affair, you know.'

'I understand that,' said Carrie, gritting her teeth at the patronising tone of voice, 'but as I told *you* half an hour ago, my business with him is rather urgent.'

'But you won't tell me what it concerns so that I could pass a note in to him?'

'No, I'm afraid that's not possible.'

The voice at the other end of the line grew suspicious. 'Is this a personal matter?'

Carrie denied that and reluctantly ended the conversation. She could get Ewen into trouble if she kept phoning. She could get him into trouble if she didn't.

She walked across to the window to pull down the blinds. The weather was atrocious. While no further snow had fallen that morning, it had started again as she was on her way to work. Isa had insisted on accompanying her, fearful that Matthew might be waiting for her at the station.

Carrie would have preferred her to stay with Florence and the children, but both Mrs Cookes had insisted she needed an escort. There were enough able-bodied men within earshot on a Sunday afternoon if Matt decided he was going to come home and cause trouble. And despite the act she was putting on, Florence had said sternly, they could both see fine that Carrie was still feeling gey wobbly.

They were right about that. Her head ached – inside and out – and she was ready to jump at her own shadow. Anxious that Isa should get back home quickly, Carrie had confidently assured her that there were always plenty of people around at the station. She peered out of the window at the platform. That was normally the case, but on a snowy Sunday afternoon in the depths of winter there weren't many passengers, and like Waverley, Partick too was operating with the bare minimum of staff today. Everyone in the goods yard had gone home early. There was little point in trying to shunt wagons in conditions like these.

Samuel the young porter was still working. Carrie kept putting her head round the door of the porters' room across the hall, making excuses to chat to him for a few minutes. He probably thought she was checking up on him, but she simply wanted the reassurance and comfort of knowing there was someone else around and not too far away.

The stationmaster had gone home early for his tea. He'd be back on his rounds about half-past nine, he'd told Carrie. She'd been unable to think of any reason to detain him.

The snow had brought a chilly wind with it. Meeting Donald Nicholson and Bobby on their walk along Dumbarton Road, he had opined that it must be blowing in from Siberia, it was so cold.

The train driver she'd spoken to twenty minutes ago had been complaining bitterly about lack of visibility. With the blackout restrictions, it was poor enough on a December afternoon, but the snow was turning his job into a nightmare. 'It'll soon be blizzard conditions, Mrs Campbell! You mark my words. And yet folks still expect the trains to run on time! Whatever the weather.'

She lowered the blinds on the hostile white darkness. If this did escalate into a blizzard, trains would surely have to be cancelled. Oh, please God, let the trains from Edinburgh to Glasgow be cancelled!

* * *

He came off the 8.22 to Helensburgh, the only passenger to alight from the train. Expecting there to be nobody at all – the night had grown even wilder – Carrie was waiting outside the booking-office door just in case there were any tickets to be collected.

'You're not going to believe this but I left Waverley on the five o'clock. It's taken me hours to get back here!'

Ewen followed her as she backed into the booking office. As the door swung shut behind them his voice became low and intimate. 'Oh, I've been thinking about you all day!'

She went to him then, laid her head on his shoulder. The pressure on her sore face hurt, but she didn't care. She was glad she hadn't been able to reach him on the phone. She was glad the trains from Edinburgh to Glasgow hadn't been cancelled. She was glad he was here.

She could feel his surprise at her action, but instead of the joking comment she expected, two surprisingly hesitant arms settled gently about her. For a minute or two they stood together in silence. Then he pulled back, lifted his hands to her head.

'I've always loved your hair,' he said dreamily, letting the red-gold strands trail through his fingers. 'Such a bonnie colour, and as smooth as silk. You're wearing it loose tonight. Is that for me?' The caressing hands stopped abruptly. 'What's this mark on the side of your face?'

He touched it, and she started back, drawing her breath in on a hiss of pain. He frowned. 'Carrie, what's happened? Did you fall in the snow or something? You should have phoned me. I'd have come back earlier.'

'I've been trying to phone you all day,' she said sorrowfully. 'To tell you to stay in Edinburgh.'

'Stay in Edinburgh?' he repeated. 'But why?' His frown deepened. Then she saw the same emotions chase themselves across his face as she had seen on Isa's that morning: slowly dawning realisation, followed by quick and furious anger. But his fingers were exquisitely gentle as he raised them once more to her wounded face. 'How did he do this to you?'

She told him, her voice breaking as she described the assault.

'I'll kill him,' Ewen said softly. Behind him, someone pushed open the door.

'Not if I kill you first.'

Tall and handsome in his uniform, Matt walked into the room. Ewen turned to face him, pushing Carrie behind him. The protective gesture wasn't lost on her husband.

'It's you I'm interested in at the moment, Livingstone. I've been waiting for you to arrive. I'll deal with my whore of a wife later.'

'I thought you'd already dealt with her.' Ewen sounded calm, but Carrie knew he was fizzing with anger. 'Like hitting women, do you?'

'She's my wife,' Matt said coolly. 'I'm entitled.' His gaze flickered briefly to her. 'Even with that nasty bruise she still looks lovely, don't you think? I'll have to do something about that. Prevent any more like you fancying a quick dip between her thighs.'

'She hasn't been unfaithful to you, you know.'

'You expect me to believe that?'

'No,' Ewen said evenly, 'I suppose it's too much to expect that you'd be capable of believing that.'

The irony seemed to be lost on Matthew. 'I always thought she was different, but it turns out she's just like the rest of them. Comes of being friendly with that slut Isabella Cooke, I daresay. Definitely not the kind of person children should be exposed to. Don't you think so, Livingstone?'

Matt folded his arms and tilted his head to one side, as

338

though this were a dinner party conversation Ewen and he were having. 'You would have different views on that, of course. I suppose you naturally gravitate to strumpets and tarts – being the bastard son of a whore yourself.'

Every word was deliberate. Designed to wound. Calculated to provoke.

Carrie gripped Ewen's arms above the elbows, pressing as hard as she could through the heavy material of his coat. 'Ewen, please don't. Think of your job.'

Matt snorted. 'He's not even in uniform, Carrie. What sort of a man does that make him?'

She lifted her chin and looked him in the eye. 'A better man than you,' she said steadily.

Matt's face darkened. 'His mother was a whore, Carrie. Can you not understand that? Christ knows who his father was. Any one of a hundred drunken sailors with a few pounds in their pockets.' His voice dripped contempt. 'More likely a few coins. That's all it took to buy Annie Livingstone for half an hour.'

She waited for Ewen to stride forward and smash his fist into Matt's face, but he didn't move. Instead, he struck back with words. Stunning, heart-stopping words.

'I know exactly who my father is,' he said quietly. 'I also know very well who my brother is. Half-brother, at any rate.'

And the last piece of the jigsaw fell into place.

Chapter 30

'My brother? A guttersnipe like you? Don't make me laugh.' Matt tossed his dark head. 'Bred in the sewer,' he sneered. 'And however high you climb, you'll always slide back down there. Where you belong. Where your whore of a mother belonged.'

Carrie waited for Ewen to explode into violence, but instead he turned and looked at her.

'Do you know how my mother ended up on the streets, Carrie? I don't think I ever told you that part of the story, did I?'

'No,' she said. 'You didn't.' He sounded calm enough. Maybe, just maybe, if she kept him talking, things could stay that way.

'She came to Glasgow to go into service.' He raised an arm. Ramrod-stiff, it pointed accusingly at Matt. 'Up the hill in his grandfather's house. She was seventeen years old, fresh from the Highlands. She didn't stand a chance against a man like your father-in-law.'

'He took advantage of her?' Carrie whispered.

Matt snorted, but Ewen ignored him. 'Yes. Told her he loved her, of course, promised he'd look after her. But he wasn't there when they flung her out into the snow. Pregnant and friendless and with nowhere to go.'

It fitted all too well with what she knew of Charles

Campbell's character. And she recalled the acerbic comment Ewen had made yesterday morning. *Some sons take after their fathers.* Now she understood the ambiguity of the way the observation had been worded. He'd been exempting himself from that character assessment.

'How very affecting,' said Matt. 'Did she get that from some music-hall melodrama? A nice fairy story which meant she didn't have to tell you the truth. A slut like your mother wouldn't have the faintest idea who had fathered her bastard. How could she when she spent her life opening her legs for one man after the other?'

Ewen took a step forward, his hands bunching into fists. Carrie followed him, slipped her own hands over those fists. She felt him react to her touch, but knew also that every word was eating away like acid at his self-esteem and his self-control.

She recognised the strategy. That was exactly what Matt wanted. She listened, horrified, as he continued to deploy it. There had to be some way she could stop this.

'I know what women like that are like.' He laughed suddenly. 'I should do, I've had plenty of them over the years. Professional and amateur. More of the latter than the former recently.'

Carrie's eyes opened wide. Her fingers fell off Ewen's hands. He turned to look at her pale and shocked face, then swung back round to her husband.

'No, she didn't know that,' Matthew said casually. 'I've always been a gentleman, spared her the knowledge. I won't need to from now on, will I? I'll be able to do as I damn' well please.' His voice slithered like silk. 'Considering I now hold all the cards.'

'What the hell do you mean by that?'

Matt folded his arms across his chest, apparently relaxed.

'It appears you have a brain. Try using it. Think how this will look. While I'm off serving King and Country, you're screwing my wife. Who then flaunts you in front of our innocent children.' He unfolded his arms, put one hand to his chest. 'Then, when I – the broken-hearted husband – come home and confront my faithless wife and her lover, you lay me out cold while she stands by and watches. Think any court in the country would let her keep her children after they've listened to that story? Think you'd keep your position in the company? You'd be back swinging a hammer before you knew what had hit you.'

It was a variation on what he'd said to Carrie that morning, but Ewen was hearing it for the first time. He went white. 'You evil bastard,' he breathed.

Matt raised his eyebrows. 'Strange insult for you to use.'

'Ewen! No!' Carrie grabbed the arm he'd started to raise. His eyes were glittering like gunmetal.

'Let me at him, Carrie. We cannae let him get away wi' saying all those things about you – and ma mother. I'm goin' tae fuckin' kill him!' In the midst of her distress, she registered that he had reverted completely to his original accent. Matt's strategy had worked well, searing away the layers which made Ewen what he was today, unerringly finding the lost boy beneath.

'No, Ewen, no! He's right. Can't you see that? Think of your job,' she begged again. 'Think of how far you've come! Don't throw it all away now!'

She held on to him. It was hard work, but because he didn't want to hurt her, he was allowing her to do it – while Matt looked on and watched them both.

'Come outside with me,' she urged Ewen. 'For a minute. Till we all calm down. Then we can discuss this like rational adults.'

She forced herself to meet Matt's dark eyes. 'There's nothing to discuss, Carrie,' he said calmly. 'You and the children stay with me. End of story. Unless you want to lose them – and ruin your little friend's career. Not to mention his life. I'll hold the door open for you, shall I?' His voice hardened. 'You've got ten minutes. After that I'm coming out there to get you.'

They went on to the platform, sheltering from the snow under the canopy. When they got there, Ewen turned abruptly and made as if to go back in. Carrie raised her hands to his shoulders, trying to shove him against the wall of the building.

'No! That's what he wants you to do.'

His breathing was ragged, his voice raw. 'What about what I want to do, Carrie?' But he let her push him back.

She stood beside him, staring out at the blizzard. 'What do you want to do?'

The reply was immediate. 'I want to do to him what he did to you. I want to smash his face into a pulp. I want to break all his fingers because he used them to hurt you.'

'Ewen,' she said, chilled by his words, 'he's your brother.'

'He doesn't believe that,' he said bitterly. 'Why should you?'

'Because I know your mother didn't bring you up to tell lies. She was a good woman. An honest woman.'

He found her hand. 'We'll fight him for the bairns,' he said. 'Through the courts. What he told us about himself . . .' He threaded his fingers through hers. 'We can use that against him.'

'He'll deny it. We've got no proof. And,' she said sadly, 'he does love Archie and April. They are his children.' She gave an odd little laugh. 'You really are their Uncle Ewen.'

'Aye. I am.' He squeezed her hand, but even as he was doing it she was extracting her fingers from his grasp.

Something else had struck her. Something which didn't make her laugh. 'I'm your brother's wife.' She took a step back. 'You would never have told me. Would you?'

There was a train coming. Carrie turned mechanically as it pulled in to the platform and just as mechanically returned the smile and wave of a small girl sitting at the window of a third-class compartment. She and her mother were in the second last carriage and looked to be the only passengers on board. Nobody got off and the driver started up again.

The train swayed along the platform. 'They're not showing any rear lights,' said Ewen dully. 'You'd better get on the blower to Hyndland so the guard can do something about that before he leaves there.'

Carrie had also noticed the lack of illumination. The strong wind must have blown the lamps out. She swung open the booking-hall door and Ewen followed her in.

Matt was a railwayman too. He understood the urgency of the situation. When the clerkess at Hyndland phoned them back five minutes later with the news that the train still wasn't with them, he took the instrument out of Carrie's hand and tried to raise the signal box at Partick. They had all made the same deduction: that the train had halted at a red light somewhere on the brief stretch of track between the two stations.

'I'm not getting through to the box. The line's dead.'

'Maybe the wind's brought down the telephone cable,' suggested Ewen. 'The spur that goes to the box.' The three of them looked at each other. A few hundred yards along the line they had a standing train. In a blizzard. With no lights showing. Ewen asked the obvious question.

'When's the next westbound service due?'

'Nine-twelve to Dalmuir Park,' said Carrie. She took a deep breath to calm herself down.

'Then we've got less than twenty minutes,' said Matt, glancing at the clock. 'Any of the porters on?'

'Young Samuel.'

'Get him to run round for the stationmaster. You wait here and alert the driver of the nine-twelve, and the two of us will go down to the signal box. All right?' That final question, accompanied by a questioning lift of the head, was directed at Ewen. He got a cool look back, then a quick nod of agreement.

'All right,' Ewen replied. 'Let's get the hand lamps lit. Two each.'

Carrie picked up the phone. 'I'll inform Queen Street. Then they can get word through to everyone else.'

There was a rumble, the slowly building vibration which indicated the approach of another train.

'Eastbound, one trusts,' muttered Matt.

'No,' cried Carrie. 'It's not!' She thrust the telephone down and ran out on to the platform, but she was too late. The train had already rattled past. The two men were right behind her.

'If the next train's the nine-twelve, what the hell was that?' yelled Ewen, fighting against the noise made by the fast disappearing carriages and the wind.

'It looked like empty coaches, but the first Home James isn't due for another hour yet. Oh, God,' she wailed. 'Oh, God!'

They heard it thirty seconds later, the sound of the impact rising above the blizzard. An almighty bang, like the report of the biggest gun imaginable. Then a dreadful splintering sound and the screech of metal against metal. A long drawn-out banshee wail which seemed to go on for hours. Then there was silence.

The sleet was driving into their faces, so at first it was hard to make out what lay in front of them. It was Ewen who deciphered it first, memories of his days working the line helping him discern the lie of the land by the inadequate light of the hand lamps. Carrie and Samuel had followed him and Matt down, bringing four more with them. They had left the stationmaster phoning for help.

A group of men were sitting on the ground. Carrie went quickly to them and established that they were the drivers and firemen of both trains and the guard of the first one. They all had cuts and bruises but appeared otherwise to be largely uninjured.

'Ah didnae see it, hen!' said the driver of the second train. 'Ah just didnae see it! It loomed up out o' nowhere!'

'It had no rear lights,' she soothed him. 'You hadn't a hope of seeing it. Not on a night like this.' And, she thought, there was a curve in the line here. He wouldn't have seen the red signal either – especially with several carriages of a stationary train in front of it.

She did what she could to comfort him, relieved beyond words that he and his fireman and the guard of the first train were physically unhurt. They'd been at the centre of the impact. Hopefully that boded well for the mother and child she'd seen. The guard on their train, also unhurt and apparently with nerves of steel, was standing in a huddle with Matt and Ewen, all of them discussing what to do next. He had confirmed that the two had been his only passengers on arrival at Partick.

There were swaying lights approaching: staff from Hyndland also carrying hand lamps. Carrie left the shocked train crews in their care and walked over to where the three men stood. 'What about the woman and the little girl?'

'We're going to try and get them out,' Ewen told her, 'but there's a wee bit of a problem. The collision's made the standing train jackknife – the carriage they're in and the carriage in front of them. Can you see?'

She could barely make it out through the swirling snow. The two carriages, both half on and half off the tracks, now formed two sides of a triangle. Whilst the empty coach lay at a crazy angle, leaning away from them, the other coach had rolled completely. Its side was now its roof. The bogeys which held the wheels had broken off at either end and there was a large gap between them and the carriage.

It was going to be a bit of a scramble to get up there, with nothing solid remaining on the undercarriage which could be used as a stepping stone, but otherwise she couldn't see what the problem was. Braving the other coach would be hazardous – it was still tilting – but this one appeared to have fallen as far as it could go.

Surely all that was needed was for one or more of them to climb up on to the side, walk along it and get the woman and child out. Maybe someone could go for a ladder so they could give them a fireman's lift back down on to solid ground. Even if they weren't injured – and please God let that be the case – they'd be badly shocked and frightened. She couldn't hear any cries, but it was hard to hear anything in this wind. She expressed her thoughts aloud.

'If only it was that simple,' said Ewen. He lifted an arm to indicate. 'There's a sort of embankment over there, Carrie. Remember that subsidence there was a few years back? The engineers had to do a bit of earth-moving over there. They allowed the hole which had formed to exist and shored up the railway line above it. The ground slopes away steeply from the track.'

Everyone was listening carefully to him. 'The ends of both carriages are suspended over the drop. From about their middle points.' Samuel shifted nervously from one foot to the other. 'Exactly where you said the woman and wee lassie are.'

The implications were crystal clear. Any undue pressure and the coach could seesaw and fall. Not a slide down an embankment which might just protect the people inside, but a drop through fresh air with a heavy impact at the end of it.

Sombre faces were cast into relief by the paraffin lamps at their feet. If they did nothing, waited for further help to arrive, the tilting coach might fall further, taking itself and the other one with it. With the same outcome.

All at once Matt laughed. 'So it's a case of damned if we do and damned if we don't.' He squared his shoulders. 'Which one of us is the lightest?'

Carrie saw the Adam's apple in Samuel's throat bob. 'I am,' he offered gamely.

'Get away,' said Matthew. 'Your mammy would never forgive us if anything happened to you. And don't bother volunteering either, Carrie. I doubt you'd have the strength in your arms to pull them out.'

He glanced across the flickering lamplight at Ewen. 'I'm taller than you. I can inch along on my belly that bit further without tipping the balance. Hopefully,' he added, smiling wryly.

Ewen's brows knitted. 'You're sure? I'll easy do it.'

'I'm sure. I'll need someone strong enough to grab them and swing them away from the gap when I lower them down. You'll be right on the edge of it, mind. Give us a kiss for luck, Carrie,' he added casually.

He walked over to her and kissed her hard on the mouth, his arm coming briefly about her waist. 'I love you,' he said. Then he released her and headed for the tumbled carriage.

'Good luck,' called Ewen.

Matthew turned and looked at him. 'Aye,' he said. 'You too.'

* * *

'He'll have been trained how to do that, Mrs Campbell. In the army, like.'

'I suppose so, Samuel.'

The boy was chattering, giving a running commentary she didn't want or need on Matt's agonisingly slow progress along the carriage, but she wasn't going to tell him to keep quiet. Nerves took different people different ways.

In her own case, it was an inability to look away, however much she wanted to. He'd mounted the carriage fairly far back, where it still lay on solid ground. She was willing him on – and praying hard. Should she offer God a bargain in exchange for his safety? It came to her what that bargain would be, and she hesitated. There was a loud creak, and she ran forward to where Ewen and the guard stood, Samuel in hot pursuit.

'The other coach,' said Ewen. 'It's shifted a bit.' He laid a comforting hand on her shoulder. 'Don't worry. He seems to know what he's doing, and he's taking it real slow.'

She followed his gaze to where Matt was crawling along the upended side of the wooden carriage. The movement did look like something he'd learned in the army. She'd seen soldiers in newsreels doing something very similar.

'That one,' she called up through the snow. 'You've reached it.'

He stretched forward, curled his fingers around the door handle and tugged. 'It's stuck fast. I'll have to break the window.'

'It's not broken already?' asked the guard.

'Nope. Anybody got a hammer about their person, by any chance?' Matt sounded quite cheerful.

'I brought one!' shouted Samuel. 'I thought about that!' He gave it to Ewen who stretched up to hand it over, holding it by the head and extending the shaft to Matt, straining to get it as

350

close to his reaching fingers as possible.

'Thanks.' He edged a little further forward before using it. As the glass shattered, they heard screaming from inside the compartment. A child's voice. Carrie clutched Samuel in relief. Ewen was standing on the very edge of the embankment, getting ready to receive the girl and her mother as they were handed down. She didn't want to disturb his concentration.

Matthew was reaching down, hauling someone up by the armpits. It was the mother. Her body looked limp, but she was muttering. Carrie wondered if she was concussed. She might well have been, but she was no sooner surrendered to Ewen's waiting arms than she was fighting him, trying to get back into the wreckage.

'The girl's trapped,' Matthew called. 'Her foot's caught under something.'

Hysterical the mother might be, but she had heard that comment. She started howling, pounding her fists against Ewen's chest. Carrie moved quickly forward, pulling her away from him before her struggles could send them both over the edge. With a strength she didn't know she had, she dragged her back and shook her hard.

'Listen!' she said. 'They're doing their best to get your lassie out! Do you think you shouting and screaming is helping them any? For God's sake – for your daughter's sake – for my husband's sake – SHUT YOUR BLOODY MOUTH!'

Stunned, the woman stared into her face. Then she burst into tears. Carrie put her arms about her and held her tight. 'That's better,' she said. 'Have a wee greet. Only a wee one, mind. Your girl will need you looking cheerful when they bring her out.'

Ten minutes later they heard a shout of triumph. It was Matt's voice, carrying above the blizzard. 'Got her!'

Carrie was powerless to stop the woman from running back

to the wreckage, but this time she stood and waited as her daughter was passed carefully down to Ewen. The little bundle in his arms said one word: 'Mammy.' One word was enough. He handed her over to her mother with tears sliding down his face.

'Getting a wee bit emotional here,' he said a little shamefacedly.

Carrie touched his arm. 'That's all right,' she said. 'Now Matt's got to get himself off there.'

'Out of there,' Ewen corrected. 'He had to go inside the compartment to free the girl.'

As he said the words, a head appeared through the shattered window.

'D'you want to wait till we get a rope?' called the guard.

'I'm thinking there might not be time for that,' muttered Ewen, but Matthew had already got up on to the side of the carriage, and was shaking his head. 'Maybe I should jump.'

'Don't be so bloody stupid,' said Ewen sharply, 'you'll break your legs. Come back the way you got there.'

'Matthew,' Carrie called. 'Don't take any risks.'

Snowflakes dancing around him, he smiled down at her. 'Life's a risk, Carrie. Didn't you know?'

There was an ominous creak. She called out, and her hand went to her mouth. He put his hands on his hips and shook his head at her in mocking reproach. 'That was the other coach,' he said. 'For all we know this one's as solid as the Rock of Gibraltar.'

He was standing in the elegant pose she knew so well, one leg extended a little to the side. He looked as though he was about to do some Highland dancing. The only thing missing was the crossed swords at his feet. He tapped one foot on the wood on which he stood. Once. Twice. 'See? Nothing to worry about.'

'For Christ's sake,' said Ewen. 'Get on to your front and come back down here.'

There was another creak. Then the sound of wood splintering.

'That wasn't the other coach,' Ewen said grimly. 'You're going to have to bloody jump. Do it now!'

Matt was still smiling. Then, beneath his feet, the coach fell away. He went with it.

There was help now. Plenty of it. Nurses and ambulance men and people with ropes. A squad of them were down in the gully, searching for Matthew.

'Maybe we should have waited till we had ropes,' Ewen was saying. 'Then we'd have been able to hang on to him.'

'We couldn't have waited,' said the guard. 'We'd have lost the passengers.'

Someone had slung a blanket around Carrie's shoulders and pressed an enamel mug of hot sweet tea into her frozen hands. They'd done the same for Ewen and Samuel and the guard too. Her teeth were chattering. So were Samuel's.

'Drink your tea,' she told him automatically. She was beginning to get that distant feeling, the sense of watching it all happen, like being at the pictures. Only when you were at the cinema you could get all caught up in the story, but you knew you weren't really involved in it. Here, in the corner of her brain which was refusing to allow her to drift away from what was unfolding in front of her, she knew all too well that this was cold and bloody reality.

It got colder and bloodier still. They were pulling a stretcher up the embankment. The long body on it was wrapped in a dark blanket. Including the face.

Chapter 31

Matt's funeral was every bit the ordeal Carrie had expected it to be, with Archie and April confused and bewildered and asking all sorts of questions she found it hard to answer. How could the daddy they hadn't seen for months be lying in that box at the front of the church? And how could he be in there anyway when Auntie Florence had said he was in heaven now?

Florence had told them that the day before, comforting them in the best way she knew how. Mercifully, neither of them had appeared to register Isa's muttered: 'More likely the other place.'

Carrie sat in the front pew of the church, between the children. Her father-in-law had his arm around the shoulders of a somewhat bemused Archie. His wife wasn't with him.

'Shona felt she wouldn't be able to face it,' he'd told Carrie, tenderly embracing his daughter-in-law before she had a chance to resist.

Poor Matt, she thought sadly. Your mother put herself before you until the last.

The enquiry into the accident was postponed until the beginning of February 1943. The convenor began by expressing the deepest condolences of all those present to Mrs Campbell. He was most solicitous when Carrie gave her account of events, ensuring she was entirely comfortable and had a glass of water to hand.

She caught Ewen's eye, and he gave her a little smile of encouragement. At her request, he'd gone back to Edinburgh the day before Matt's funeral. She hadn't seen him since, although she knew he'd written to Isa several times. He gave his own evidence clearly and concisely. He didn't think they could have waited for help to arrive. It had been a matter of life or death and they had done as they thought appropriate in the circumstances.

'A course of action which unfortunately led to the death of Mr Matthew Campbell. Is it your opinion that Mr Campbell was foolhardy to attempt a rescue of the two passengers on board the derailed train?'

'No,' said Ewen vehemently. 'It is my opinion that Mr Campbell acted very bravely. He saved two lives. At the expense of his own.'

Beside Carrie, Charles Campbell bent his head and shaded his eyes. She hated herself for it, but she couldn't help noticing how elegantly the gesture was performed.

The conclusions drawn at the end of the day were what everyone had expected them to be. Whilst criticisms might be made against the guard of the first train for failing to ensure that the blizzard hadn't extinguished his rear lamps, he had been checking them frequently that night. He had, in fact, intended to do so again at Hyndland. A recommendation was made that in future such a check should be made at every stop.

Otherwise, it was decided that the accident had been just that, a tragic sequence of events sparked off by the atrocious weather conditions that night. It was because of the storm and train cancellations elsewhere that the empty carriages had gone through at an unexpected time. No blame attached itself to their driver. Nobody was to be blamed. It was an act of God. Sympathy was once again extended to Mrs Campbell and her children in their sad loss.

As the enquiry broke up, she stood up and made her way to the exit. Ewen had beaten her to it. He was in his dark coat and suit, hat held politely in his hand. 'Mrs Campbell, can you spare me half an hour of your time? Perhaps you would allow me to take you to tea.'

Her father-in-law was right behind her. 'Mr Livingstone, isn't it?' he said affably. He held out his hand, but Ewen didn't take it. Charles narrowed his eyes. 'Have we met before, young man?'

Ewen took his intense grey gaze off Carrie's face. 'I believe you may have known my mother,' he said levelly.

Charles lowered his hand and pondered. He was obviously doing a mental rundown of his female acquaintanceship, the sort who might have a son like Ewen. 'No,' he said, with a charmingly apologetic smile, 'I can't think I've ever had the pleasure of knowing a Mrs Livingstone.'

A girl with a notebook and pencil materialised at Carrie's elbow. 'Both you and your late husband worked on the railways, Mrs Campbell?'

She was joined by a colleague – a gentleman of the press this time. 'Do your children know their daddy died a hero, Mrs Campbell?' he asked. 'Would you give us the wee ones' names?'

'For God's sake,' said Ewen irritably, 'can you not leave her alone?'

'It's all right,' Carrie said, 'they're only doing their job.' Josephine Shaw had told her all about human interest stories. They made good copy. She would answer their questions and they would go away happy.

'And this gentleman?' the girl asked after she'd got the

357

information she wanted out of Carrie. 'Are you a relative of Mrs Campbell's, sir?'

'I'm the dear girl's father-in-law,' replied Charles. 'Matthew was my son.' There was a catch in his voice.

'And . . .' the reporter asked hesitantly '. . . would you mind answering a few questions about him? You wouldn't find it too painful?'

Charles smiled bravely. 'Perhaps we could go somewhere more congenial?'

They were in George Square. Carrie had declined to go for tea with Ewen, but had agreed to walk for a while. It wasn't cold – one of those bright and sunny February days which seem to carry the promise of spring not too far around the corner. They stopped in front of the cenotaph, by one of the two stone lions flanking the memorial.

'Do you think he'll work out who you are?'

'I don't know.' Ewen shrugged his broad shoulders. 'He probably hardly even knew my mother's surname. She would have been "Annie" to him. Just another parlour maid. To tell you the truth, I don't much care. I used to, but I've got other things on my mind at the moment.'

Carrie looked away. 'Ewen, please don't say what I think you're going to say.'

'Why not?'

She was studying the lion's huge paws. 'Can't you see how Matt's death has changed everything?'

'Yes, I can. It makes it much easier for us.'

She whirled round, gazed at him in horror. 'That's a brutal thing to say!'

'Carrie,' he said urgently. 'I'm sorry for the way he died. I suppose I'm sorry he *is* dead. I wouldn't wish that on anybody. Not even him. But if you're expecting me to act like a hypocrite, you're looking at the wrong man.'

'Ewen . . .'

'Just listen to me for a minute. Please? Will you hear me out?'

'All right,' she said reluctantly. 'Say what you have to say.'

'Come for tea?'

'No. Tell me here.'

He sighed. 'You're a hard woman.' He raised his eyes for a moment to the City Chambers, standing solidly behind the cenotaph. Then, as though he had marshalled his thoughts, he turned back to her and began. 'Here goes, then. They're planning on forming this railway regiment. More like a company really. Probably going to come under the Royal Engineers.'

'A railway regiment?' She was struggling with surprise. This wasn't at all what she'd expected him to say.

He nodded. 'The tide's beginning to turn, Carrie. We'll soon have Hitler on the run. Then we'll go after him, hit him where it really hurts.'

'The invasion of Europe?'

People were beginning to talk about it. For so long, Britain had been on the defensive, straining every sinew to keep the invader out. Now, with that battle at last won, it was time to start turning the tables.

Ewen nodded again. 'And wherever we go in – France or Italy or somewhere else where they least expect it – communications and lines of supply for men and materials are going to be crucial.'

'Roads, railways and bridges.'

'Aye,' he said grimly. 'We know it and they know it. They'll try to destroy it all as they retreat. So we'll need people who can throw it back down again as quickly as possible. And people who can study the maps before we go, work out where the crucial points are. So advance troops can maybe go on ahead to try to stop them from mining the bridges and railway lines.'

Carrie had been studying his face as he spoke. 'People like you,' she said. 'You've got the practical experience and the strategic planning experience.'

'Yes,' he agreed. 'People like me.'

'You want to go, don't you?'

'Aye,' he said slowly. 'I want to go. I think I probably need to go. But there's a large part of me wants to stay here too.'

He slid a hand inside his coat, brought out an official-looking buff envelope. He surprised her again, sent the conversation spinning off in another direction.

'I went to see a solicitor in Edinburgh a couple of weeks ago. Asked him about the brother's wife business. Not that it would really matter, of course. You and I aren't related in any way, and we're also the only people who know that he and I were half-brothers. Apart from Isa, and she's not going to tell anybody.' He smiled nervously at her. 'But I thought it might be something that would worry you, so I asked the lawyer what the position is. Apparently it used to be the case that a man couldn't marry his brother's widow, but the law was changed several years ago.' He extended the envelope to her. 'It's all in here, if you want to read it.'

She looked at the letter, but made no move to take it from him.

'Carrie, did you hear what I said?'

She raised her eyes to his face. 'You really think it's that simple?'

'No. I know it's not.' He swallowed. 'First I have to ask you to marry me and hope you'll say yes. Then I have to ask you to wait for me, and hope you'll say yes to that too.'

There was a couple walking past them – a young man in a

360

sailor's uniform carrying a kitbag and a girl clinging on to his arm. She was clutching a handkerchief and she'd obviously been crying. Carrie followed their progress across the square. They weren't going to Queen Street. They had headed off in the direction of Central Station. Probably he was going to join his ship at Gourock. Would the girl travel down with him, or would they say their farewells at the station?

'I know I'm asking you at a bad time,' Ewen said. 'Especially with this being the day of the enquiry. I'm sorry about that – but I don't have much time, Carrie. I'll probably be away within the month. I don't want to wait, but I'll understand if you think getting married before I go would be a bit too quick.'

The couple had disappeared from view, out of sight somewhere on St Vincent Place, heading for Buchanan Street and then Gordon Street.

'Say something, Carrie,' he said. 'So I'll know I haven't been talking to myself for the last five minutes.' He was wearing that nervous smile again.

'I can't say yes.'

'I've rushed you, haven't I? I should have given you a day or two to get over the enquiry.'

'Ewen, I can't ever say yes. Not now. Can't you see that? Don't look at me like that!'

For he had gone deathly pale and very still. 'I don't understand,' he said. 'I thought you loved me. Like I love you. And however it happened, you're free now.'

'Free?' She gave a harsh little laugh. 'I'll never be free. Every time I close my eyes, I go over his last moments, see it all happening again.'

'That's natural.' His voice softened. 'I've been doing that too, wondering if he might still be alive if we'd done something differently. It'll pass, I think.'

She shook her head. 'Not for me. I keep remembering that whole day, how he must have felt when he came home and found out about you . . .'

Ewen's voice was hard as tempered steel. 'When he came home and banged your head off the wall, you mean.'

'Ewen,' she said, 'you told Matt I hadn't been unfaithful to him – but I had. Don't you see that? Not physically maybe, but in my heart and in my head. I think he knew that. And I think it hurt him just as much.'

His eyes opened wide in disbelief. 'You're making excuses for him? How many times had he broken *his* wedding vows? He treated you like a dog, Carrie. Isa told me what happened after I sent you that first letter.' He slammed his fist violently into his other hand, startling her. '*Christ!* I'm so angry about that. And he didn't stop there, did he? She's told me the whole story.'

'No,' Carrie said passionately. 'Isa's told you her version of the story. There was more to Matt than that. A lot more. He loved Archie and April. He loved me.'

Ewen's hands shot out, gripped her by the upper arms. 'Carrie, for God's sake! Don't you remember the way he behaved that night? The things he said to you? How he told you about the other women he'd had? He threatened to take Archie and April away from you. Was any of that love?'

'He told me he loved me,' she insisted. 'Before he went up on the carriage. You were there. You must have heard him.'

'Oh, I heard him all right,' Ewen said grimly. 'He did it for my benefit. To remind me he was your husband and that I had no claim on you. He was so sure he was going to win.' He stopped, breathing heavily, and his hands fell from her arms. 'He has won, hasn't he?'

'He's dead,' she said harshly. 'You're still alive.' She was silent, remembering how she had thought of bargaining with

362

God in return for Matthew's safety. She remembered too how she had pulled back from that sacrifice. It was being demanded of her all the same. If she was to have the faintest hope of being able to live with herself. She dropped her eyes and bent her head, waited for him to go.

There was a pause. Then she heard him give a bitter little laugh. 'You never actually told me you loved me, did you? Maybe I got it all wrong anyway.'

She didn't raise her head.

'Goodbye, then Carrie,' he said at last. 'I'll always love you, you know.'

She waited till she could no longer hear his footsteps. When she looked up he was almost at the station. She watched him cross the road and disappear into it. This time she knew he was walking out of her life for ever.

PART IV
1946

Chapter 32

There was something different about Isa, but Carrie was having difficulty in pinpointing exactly what it was. She'd been talking to her for a good ten minutes before she worked it out. Not one cigarette had been smoked. She commented on this amazing development.

'Donald doesn't approve of smoking. I'm trying to give them up.'

'Donald?' Carrie wrinkled her brow in puzzlement. Of all Isa's gentlemen friends, past and present, she couldn't bring a Donald to mind. Pierre the Free Frenchman had lasted quite some time. Then there had been Eugene, a charming American. He had endeared himself greatly to Carrie by presenting her with an unaccustomed luxury: her very first nylon stockings – two pairs of them.

He'd gone off to help liberate Europe in June 1944 and had now returned to his home in New Jersey. Isa had received a Christmas card from him and his wife at the end of 1945. Although she refused to admit it, Carrie suspected that was the first she had known of the existence of the lady.

Eugene had been superseded by Harry. He'd been a Royal Navy man from Portsmouth but doing a shore job in Glasgow connected with the huge amount of activity the war had brought to the Clyde. He'd stayed on for six months after the end of the war in Europe, then he too had returned home.

'Donald,' she repeated thoughtfully. Then her mouth dropped open. 'You surely don't mean Donald Nicholson?'

'What other Donald would I be talking about?'

Carrie couldn't quite hide a smile. 'Well, you'd have to admit there have been quite a few men to choose from over the years.'

Isa gave her a hard stare, and reached into her pinny pocket. It was difficult not to laugh when the searching hand came back out empty.

'If Donald wants you to give up the fags,' Carrie said wickedly, 'you're not going to be able to sit there and blow smoke rings at me any more. You'll have to find another prop. Maybe you should take up knitting. Then you could jab a needle in my direction when you want to make a point.'

'Ha-bloody-ha,' snarled Isa.

Carrie responded with an impish look. 'So it's serious, is it?' she asked. 'With you and Donald?' She had always liked Bobby the dog's quiet master but the combination of him and Isa seemed an unlikely one. Now she came to think about it, he had always hovered around her a bit, but while Isa liked going out and enjoying herself, Donald's idea of a riotous time was taking his dog for a long walk or visiting the library.

'He's a good man, Carrie. Intelligent too. He's very well-read, you know. We have some great talks – about all sorts o' things.' That was another mind-boggling concept. Donald seemed to operate a kind of self-censorship, speaking only when it was strictly necessary. Nobody needed to tell him that careless talk cost lives or that loose lips sank ships.

Nonetheless, Carrie was touched by the note of tenderness in the smoke-roughened voice and by the way Isa's face had changed when she had spoken of him. She looked younger . . . softer somehow.

'You two have been getting to know each other, then?' she asked gently.

'He's asked me to marry him.' Now the expression on Isa's face was different again. She looked nervous, wanting reassurance. 'I've said yes, hen. Am I aff my heid?'

'Do you love each other?'

'Aye. I'm afraid so.' She put the back of her hand to her mouth. This was another first. The redoubtable Isabella Cooke succumbing to tears? 'He knows all about me, Carrie,' she said in a tremulous voice. 'That I've been a wee bit . . . well, what ye might call flighty . . . and he doesn't care. He says that's all in the past. It's our future together that matters to him.'

Touched, Carrie jumped to her feet and threw her arms around Isa's neck. 'If Donald said a lovely thing like that you're most definitely not aff yer heid. Congratulations. I hope you'll both be very happy. Can I interest you in a bridesmaid and pageboy for the wedding ceremony?'

So she attended Isa's wedding, and witnessed with maternal pride Archie and April's part in the proceedings. Her son, now a strapping lad a couple of months short of his tenth birthday, wore a kilt gifted by a friend whose own boy had grown out of it. The war might be over, but it was still a case of make do and mend. However, the kilt was in excellent condition and Archie looked fine and handsome in it. He had his father's dark hair and eyes, although Carrie could see a good bit of her own father in him too.

Between them, she and Florence had done their best to fulfil April's requirements. Not long turned eight, she was a mischievous red-haired tomboy, but had surprised her mother by requesting a 'fairy princess' dress for her role as bridesmaid. This was not, as she carefully explained, because she herself

369

cared for that sort of thing, but because she knew her Auntie Isa would like it.

Rita Sharkey had come up with the material, supplying a dark green taffeta party dress which had been worn by all of her daughters in turn and was now too small for any of them. A little worn in places, its pre-war style and full skirt had allowed for some nifty cutting to fashion a new creation for April.

Florence's collection of bits and bobs had supplied the trimmings: crocheted lace at the collar and cuffs, broad tartan ribbon to tie as a sash round the waist, stiff net underneath to make a sticky-out petticoat. The colours complemented each other beautifully and the contrast between the overall green and April's red-gold hair was very striking.

'I shouldnae say it, hen,' said Florence, 'but we made a good job o' yon frock, did we no'? April looks a treat in it.'

'She does,' Carrie agreed, her eyes on her daughter. She was dancing with Donald, giggling as he twirled her round the dance floor, April standing on his feet. It looked funny, her dainty little shoes on top of his heavy ones. Bobby, an honoured guest at the festivities, currently sitting on the floor next to Carrie, was watching them with great interest.

'Aye. She's a bonnie girl. Takes after her mother.'

Carrie smiled. 'What would I do without you, Florence?'

She put her hand to the small plate in front of her and picked at the crumbs of wedding cake – a masterpiece of creative shopping and cooking over the rationing which was still in force – found a decent-sized morsel and lowered her hand to give it to the dog. 'You'll be pleased that Donald's moving in. It'll be nice for you to have a man about the house.'

'Aye.' Florence nodded happily. 'He appreciates good cooking when he tastes it, and he's already done quite a few o'

370

the wee jobs that lazy lump Isabella Cooke never manages to get round to.'

Carrie bent solicitously over Bobby, the better to hide her amusement. She'd been worried at first that the newly-weds might set up home together elsewhere, leaving Florence to cope on her own after all these years. Then, with relief and a few covert chuckles, she had watched Isa's reluctance to admit that she didn't actually want to leave her former mother-in-law. All the excuses were trotted out.

Donald's single-end was too small for both of them, especially with the dog being there too. A bigger flat would certainly be nice, but bomb damage and proposed slum clearance were leading to a post-war housing shortage rapidly approaching crisis point. The waiting lists were as long as your arm and as a couple without children, Isa and Donald weren't going to be given priority.

It would surely make more sense for them to take over the front room – spacious enough and Isa's domain anyway – and save their pennies for something else. Donald, she had told Carrie excitedly, was talking about maybe getting a caravan on the coast. He had quite a lot of money put by already. It wouldn't be anything fancy, of course, but something cosy and comfortable, with a view of the sea. They could all use it for weekends and holidays. Carrie and the weans too, naturally. Wouldn't that be great?

All of this might very well be true, but as Carrie had worked out a long time ago, Isa and Florence were also extremely fond of each other, although brutal and prolonged torture wouldn't have dragged that admission out of either of them.

'Archie and April think it'll be great to have Bobby across the landing.' She patted him on the head. 'You'll have plenty of folk wanting to take you out for walks, son. Although you're getting on a bit now, aren't you? You must be about fourteen. What's that in doggie years – ninety-eight? My, my.' She gave him another pat. 'You're remarkably fit for your age, sir.'

Carrie straightened up and found Florence doing the folded arms and pursed lips act. 'What?' she asked.

'Would you not like a man about your own house, pet?'

A waitress carrying an outsize teapot was approaching. Carrie looked up with relief, but it was short-lived. As soon as the woman had filled their cups and moved on, Florence returned to the topic. She'd brought it up several times over the past year: since the war had ended and the men had begun to come home. Some of the men, that was. There were those who were never going to return. Others seemed to be choosing not to do so.

Pascal Sharkey and Anne-Marie waltzed past their table, and Carrie gave them a wave. Pascal was one of those who had come home safe, and three months ago she had danced at his and Anne-Marie's wedding. She was glad for them, as she was glad for all those who'd been reunited with their loved ones after the years of upheaval.

All the same, she'd been guiltily aware of a little pang of envy both at that celebration and at this one. The uncomfortable sensation had been swiftly followed by a resolution to count her blessings, as she did now.

'I'm quite happy as I am. I have my children, I have my friends and I have my work.' She hid a grimace. There was a wee bit of a problem brewing on that front. She hadn't mentioned it to Isa because she had been all caught up in the preparations for the wedding, and she hadn't told Florence because she didn't want her worrying.

With a bit of luck – and Pascal Sharkey's help – Carrie was sure she could get the problem solved. Back working on the railways after his demobilisation, he was now her official union representative.

A bony hand reached across the table. 'You don't need me to tell you what else you need. Who else you need.'

Carrie didn't reply, and Florence's thin fingers tightened around her wrist. 'Are you going to punish yourself forever for what happened to your man? It was an accident, you know.'

'I do know that, Florence,' Carrie said quietly. The waltz finished and the dancers began to leave the floor. 'For a long time I didn't, but I've sorted it out in my head now. What the enquiry found was right. It was a terrible accident. Nobody's fault.'

'I'm real glad to hear you say that, lass.' The worried look on her interrogator's face relaxed a little, but the questioning wasn't quite over. 'Do you not think you should let a certain person know that's how you feel now?'

'No,' she said firmly. 'We don't know where he is anyway. Do we?' Carrie was playing with the crumbs on her plate again. She raised her eyes. 'I suppose we would have heard if there had been bad news.'

There was a question in her voice. Florence answered it robustly. 'Of course we would. He put Isa and me down as his next-of-kin, after all.' She gave Carrie's hand a little shake. 'Of course we'd have heard.'

'But he hasn't written to either of you since he joined up, has he?'

'No,' came the reluctant reply. 'But that doesnae necessarily mean anything. At first he'd have been too busy. Then he'd have been on the continent . . .'

'Florence, the war's been over for more than a year. I've got to face facts. If he'd wanted to get in touch, he'd have done it by now. I'm sorry for your sake. And Isa's.'

The older woman dismissed that. 'You could try and find

out where he is now. The army must have records of him. Or the railway. He's more than likely come back to work for the LNER.'

Carrie shook her head. 'I sent him away, Florence. I've got absolutely no right to expect him to come back and try again. Even if I wanted him to,' she added. She turned away, unwilling to continue meeting that surprisingly penetrating gaze. 'Can we talk about something else now? Please?'

She heard Florence sigh. Then her voice changed. 'Here's Pascal coming to ask you to dance, anyway.'

Carrie stood up with him with alacrity. 'So,' she asked as he steered her round the dance floor, 'what do you think of the detailed proposals for the railways?'

He gave her an enthusiastic and comprehensive response. Sweeping to power on a tidal wave of popular support the year before, the Labour Party had announced its intention of giving the returning servicemen and women who had voted for it exactly what they wanted. Evoking the spirit of Dunkirk and of the Blitz, they had declared that this time the land fit for heroes would be delivered.

There was to be a guarantee that the hardship endured during the Hungry Thirties would never be allowed to happen again. Declaring itself to be socialist and proud of it, the new government had a clear vision of how that could be achieved. Control of all aspects of life – industry, the press, the banks, the coal mines – had to pass from those they referred to as the 'hard-faced men' to the ordinary people of the country. Nationalisation of the railways, the backbone of Britain, was a major plank of this policy.

Like Pascal, Carrie was all in favour of the idea. 'As long as safety and efficiency are our watchwords,' she said as soon as she could get a word in edgeways. 'And we'll need massive investment. Everything's worn out after the war – the track, the rolling stock, the buildings. The staff, too,' she added with a rueful smile.

'Aye,' her partner agreed, doing some nifty footwork to pilot them round two of their fellow dancers who'd had one drink too many. 'We're also seriously undermanned.'

Carrie looked thoughtfully at him. She hadn't been going to bring it up when they were both guests at Isa and Donald's wedding. It didn't exactly seem the appropriate occasion, but seeing as how he had mentioned it . . .

By the time she had finished recounting her tale of woe they were seated at his table, Anne-Marie listening attentively.

'So,' she said when Carrie had finished, 'they're happy to keep you on, but only if you agree to go full-time and do all the different shifts? Is that the position?'

'Yes. They're not asking all the women to leave like the last time. They need a lot of us. As Pascal says, we're seriously under*manned*.'

Thinking of the thousands of women whose labour had helped keep the railways running over the war years, she couldn't resist giving a teasing emphasis to the second half of the word he had used. Anne-Marie got it immediately, and rolled her eyes in sympathy. Carrie grinned at her, and went on.

'But they are making it very difficult for any women with children to stay on. I've made it clear that I'll do my best to be as adaptable as possible. I'm perfectly willing to do a longer shift occasionally and cover for holidays and sickness. And I'm quite happy to start in time for the morning rush hour.'

'Mrs Cooke keeps the children till it's time for school?' asked Anne-Marie.

'Yes. And she's ready to help out if I am covering for somebody else. All I'm asking is that, as a general rule, I can work a six-hour day shift Mondays to Fridays so I've got time to do my shopping and a bit of housework and be home for my children coming out of school in the afternoon. It doesn't seem such an unreasonable request.'

'It's not unreasonable at all,' said Anne-Marie with some passion. She turned to her new husband. 'Pascal, surely you can do something to help?'

Carrie understood immediately the conflicting emotions evident in his expression.

'Anne-Marie,' he said awkwardly, 'we really can't make special arrangements for women which could be seen as giving them an advantage over men.'

'What, like paying the same rate for the same job, you mean?' asked his wife pertly. 'Perish the thought!'

He made a face at her, and Carrie leaped in. 'Pascal, during the war we all worked whatever hours were asked of us, and were glad to do it. We were flexible then. Can the railway not be flexible now?'

'Carrie, no one's denying that the women did a great job under very difficult circumstances –'

'But now we're all supposed to be content to stay at home and stir the porridge?' queried Anne-Marie.

'You wanted to give up work!' he said accusingly.

'Aye, I did. I was fed up pulling great heavy levers and being stuck in a signal box for hours on end.' She laid a conciliatory hand on her husband's arm and fluttered her eyelashes at him. 'And I wanted the chance to minister to your every need, darling boy.'

'That'll be right,' he said ruefully.

'Poor lamb,' she said, and gave him a quick kiss. 'In my case, there was also a man coming back from the army who needed his job back – the particular one I happened to be doing. But Carrie's in a different position.'

Carrie leaned forward over the table. 'That's right. I'm not taking a man's job, Pascal. You know that. We're extremely short-staffed on the clerical side. And I'm not trying to make some sort of a point either. Part of me would love to go home and be a full-time housewife again, but I'd be broke if I tried to live on my widow's pension, and Archie and April would suffer. And,' she finished up, 'I like my job. And I'm good at it. You know that too.'

'Aye,' he said uncomfortably. 'I do.'

Anne-Marie was looking hopefully at him, clearly expecting him to come up with an instant solution, but Carrie knew Pascal was in a difficult position. As an NUR representative, he was duty-bound to protect his members, most of whom were male. He had to make sure they all got back the jobs they had left when they joined up and safeguard their interests during the transition to a nationalised railway network. Part of that was ensuring that male wages and salaries weren't threatened by the employment of too many women working – through no fault of their own – for a lower rate of pay.

'I'll ask for a meeting,' he said at last. 'You can put your case directly to management.'

'You'll go with her, Pascal,' said Anne-Marie, frowning a little. 'She is one of your members.'

'What? Oh, aye. Of course.' Reminded of his responsibilities, he put a hand inside his jacket and came out with a diary. 'When would suit you, Carrie? Did I hear you say you were taking the weans away over the summer holidays?'

'We're going up to see Mary and Douglas,' she said, and suggested a date in the week after the schools went back.

'Will you tell Mary and Douglas I was asking for them, Carrie?' said Anne-Marie.

'I'll be glad to.'

Trying not to be too disappointed by Pascal's obvious reluctance to help her, Carrie smiled broadly at Anne-Marie.

Pity she wasn't the NUR rep. She seemed more prepared to help than her husband did.

Neither of the children wanted to get undressed and ready for bed when they got home that evening. Anxious to admire themselves in their wedding finery, they began fighting over the space in front of the long mirror in the lobby. Exasperated, Carrie threatened to cover it with a blanket if they didn't agree to take turns.

'She's had much longer than me already, Ma. I should get the first shot.'

'People said I was pretty,' contested April. 'I need to look at myself to see if they were right.'

'They said I was handsome,' retorted Archie.

'Handsome is as handsome does,' responded his sister loftily.

Carrie's exasperation gave way to amusement. That was one of Florence's sayings. Both children had picked up quite a few of her and Isa's turns of phrase over the years. They weren't always entirely sure what they meant. In some cases – particularly when it came to Isa's utterances – that was probably just as well.

Her merriment had another source. Archie was a typical boy, forever coming home with the seat out of his trousers or a rip in his shirt caused by falling out of a tree or catching it on the wall he happened to be climbing over at the time. April wasn't much better. Seeing them take such an interest in their clothes and how they looked in them was a novel experience.

'My father wore a kilt, didn't he, Ma?' asked Archie. 'When he was in the Argyll and Sutherland Highlanders?'

'He did,' she said, standing behind him and placing her hands on his shoulders. In a year or two she would have to stand up on tiptoe to be able to do that. She met his eyes in the mirror. They were shining . . . and so like Matt's.

'Can I be a soldier when I grow up, Ma?'

'If you want to,' she said lightly, 'but I'd like to think there wouldn't be any wars left to fight in by the time you grow up.' She squeezed his shoulders. 'Haven't we had enough of all that?'

April piped up, using a word she'd just learned at school. 'But our Daddy *was* a gallant soldier, wasn't he, Mammy?'

Carrie smoothed the hair whose colour was the image of her own. 'Aye,' she said slowly. 'He never got the chance to do any real fighting, but he died saving two people. A mother and daughter like you and me, April. He was a brave man.'

And a complex and complicated one, she thought as she lay in bed before she went to sleep that night. She'd spent a lot of time trying to puzzle out why Matt had turned out as he had. She didn't think the way his parents had brought him up had helped, but she'd also gone over and over the mistakes she herself might have made. Could she have handled him better?

In the end, after a great deal of soul-searching, she'd decided the answer to that was no. She hadn't deserved what he'd done to her, hadn't – in that terrible phrase people used so unthinkingly – asked for it. He had loved her, but it had been a supremely possessive love. He had thought he owned her, wanted to control her. There had been some kind of a demon in Matt, which had pulled him towards the dark side of his nature. Carrie supposed that was what all the other women had been about. They hadn't seemed to bring him much joy.

Odd how different he had been from Ewen, although with hindsight she could see some tiny physical similarities. Apart from the wavy hair, they were more in the occasional gesture. There was something about the way both of them had laughed . . .

It was sad that such antipathy had existed between two

brothers. If circumstances had been different, might they ever have been friends? No, that was to live in cloud cuckoo land. Charles Campbell would never have acknowledged the relationship, let alone the existence of his second son.

She took the children to visit their grandparents occasionally, but they never stayed for long. As far as Carrie was concerned it was a duty visit, nothing more. That was sad too.

Her father-in-law was still a charmer – to those who didn't know him very well. Matthew had charmed her, she supposed. No, it was more than that. He had aroused her, and she had mistaken passion for deep and lasting love. Then circumstances had conspired to push her into marriage with him: her father's death, her mother's longing to see her settled before her own time ran out, Esther's opposition to Ewen.

'You were wrong about him, Ma,' she whispered into the darkness. 'You were wrong about both of them.' Yet how could she regret marrying Matt? He had given her Archie and April.

She lay on her back, staring up into the darkness. They had been funny tonight, admiring themselves in the mirror, although thinking about how Archie's eyes had shone when he talked about Matt didn't make her smile. It didn't help to realise that she herself was largely to blame for her children's evident hero-worship of their dead father.

She was all too conscious of the gap in their young lives. The awareness had grown keener during this past year when other children's fathers had begun coming home. So she had determined that Archie and April would at least have positive memories of their own. They would hear no criticism of Matthew from her lips.

And whatever his motives, in the end their father had given his life for others. That was surely something of which his children ought to be allowed to be proud.

There were times, however, when she feared she had gone

too far in the other direction. She was anxious too in case either of the children had inherited Matt's temper. So far there was no sign of it, but that didn't stop her worrying, particularly about Archie. He resembled Matt so much physically. What if he had some of his personality traits too?

Yet there had been strengths in Matt's character too: the way he had comforted her and helped her cope at the time of her parents' deaths, his cheerful encouragement of everybody in the time they had spent in the shelters during the Clydebank Blitz. He had been such an odd mixture.

She had experienced a maelstrom of emotions after his death. There had been anger, both against herself and him, so strong that the grief which followed it had taken her by surprise. She had thought it must be guilt, then realised what she was really grieving for: the promise their marriage had at first seemed to offer, the person he might have been if the flaws in his personality hadn't outweighed the strengths.

There had been guilt in plenty, of course. Carrie did know that the accident which had resulted in Matthew's death had been just that, but there had been months, perhaps even years, when she had tormented herself over her part in the events of that day.

She had turned them over so many times in her mind, agonised over every word she had said to Matt. Had she influenced his behaviour in any way, made him act in a foolhardy manner because he had thought himself betrayed?

It had been a long process, but she had come now to the conviction that the way he had acted during his last moments had been entirely in character. There had certainly been some cockiness in it – recklessness too – but that was the way he was. He had thought himself invincible. Nevertheless, he had acted with real bravery, rising to the occasion as he had at other times. It was the way she tried to remember him.

The guilt might have gone now, but it had done its job well. Florence had hit the nail on the head tonight, as she often did. That was what had made Carrie send Ewen away. She had told Florence she had no right to expect him to come back and try again. That was perfectly true. What she hadn't told her was how much she had hoped that he would . . .

Carrie let out a long breath. Real life wasn't like the pictures, of course. You couldn't always expect a fairytale ending. You could probably very seldom expect a fairytale ending.

'Oh, very philosophical,' she muttered crossly. Then she turned on to her side and told herself sternly to go to sleep.

Chapter 33

Laughingly declining to play yet another game of rounders, Carrie left the children on the green sward at the bottom of Douglas and Mary's large garden and walked slowly up through the neat rows of vegetables to join her hosts. They were sitting on the verandah Douglas had built on to the back of the railway cottage, Mary cradling the youngest member of the family in her arms. Her husband had a protective arm about her shoulders and was looking tenderly at his three-month-old daughter, sister to the two boys and one girl currently playing with Archie and April.

Carrie slipped off her shoes, enjoying the feel of the grass paths beneath her bare feet. She took in a deep breath of clean Highland air and looked around her admiringly. The setting of the line-side cottage was quite stunning, with wooded and heather-clad hills rising all around. The springy vegetation was beginning to acquire its purple hue, poised to decorate the autumn mountainsides with glorious bursts of colour.

She raised her eyes to the hill on the other side of the house, over the railway line. She and the children of both families had clambered up it yesterday, stopping when they reached the head of the narrow waterfall which trickled down it to wave to Mary and the baby, watching them from far below.

The Campbell family had only one complaint to make

about their holiday so far. On the train journey up, Carrie had promised the children a grandstand view of the highest mountain in the British Isles. She remembered it well from her previous visit, when April had been a babe-in-arms and Archie also had been too young to take in the spectacle, clearly visible from Douglas and Mary's back garden.

However, they'd been here for a week now and Ben Nevis had remained resolutely invisible throughout that whole period, shut away behind billowing white clouds. 'It's there,' she kept telling the children. 'It really is there.'

In contrast to the wild and natural grandeur surrounding it, the vegetable garden was a masterpiece of order and method. There was a large potato patch, lines of peas supported on sticks, rows of lettuce, carrot and beetroot. Carrie had forgotten how wonderful the fresh variety of the latter tasted, especially when you had pulled it out of the ground yourself before preparing it.

She'd been doing her best to help out during their stay, taking on as many tasks in the kitchen as Mary would allow and also lending a hand in the garden. Her hostess had made a token protest that she was here for a holiday, not to work, but Carrie had assured her that she was having a wonderful time. For one thing, she was revelling in getting her hands dirty again. It was an awful long time since she'd had the chance to do any gardening.

She was nearly at the house. She looked up again as she approached. Douglas and Mary and the baby were still in the same position, all cuddled together on a wooden bench padded with soft cushions. Carrie thought a little wistfully that she missed that sometimes: a strong shoulder to lean on. But she didn't grudge them their happiness, not one bit of it.

'The three of you look like one of those religious paintings in the Art Galleries,' she called.

Douglas looked up with a laugh. 'The holy family? No' us, I don't think.' He looked beyond her to the children at the foot of the garden. 'Have that lot worn you out? I'll go down for twenty minutes. Then they can help me get the supper.' He rose to his feet and came to meet her, extending a hand to pull Carrie up the open wooden steps of the verandah before clattering down them himself.

'You sit here and talk to Mary for a while. Although,' he added, throwing a very male look over his shoulder, 'I should have thought the two of you might have run out of conversation by now.'

'Never,' said Mary cheerfully. She patted the space next to her which Douglas had vacated. 'Come and sit by me, Carrie. Do you want a shot of the baby?'

Laughing at how the question had been phrased, Carrie turned and held out her arms, then carefully eased herself back against the cushions and put her feet up on the horizontal bars of the verandah.

'Och, you're a lovely wee bundle,' she told Mary's daughter, bending to gently nuzzle the tiny nose with her own. A pair of very clear blue eyes stared straight back up at her, and she laughed again and raised her head. 'We have talked quite a lot, haven't we? And late into the night. Is Douglas worried that I've been keeping you from your beauty sleep?'

Mary looked fondly at her youngest offspring. 'Sleep? What's that?'

'Aye, you've got your work cut out, Mary. Where do they get their energy from?' she asked, indicating the older children, now gleefully welcoming Douglas's arrival. 'April looks like a jumping bean.'

Mary gave her a slow smile. 'They take it from us, of course. Although I must say you strike me as being fighting fit yourself, Mrs Campbell. You've been running about there like a jumping bean yourself for the past hour.'

'Reliving my lost youth,' Carrie said cheerfully. 'This holiday's been a real tonic, Mary,' she said. 'We're grateful to you and Douglas for having us all. Especially with you just having had the baby.'

'It's no bother at all,' Mary said firmly, 'And it's been a break for me too. Douglas and I are just glad if we've been able to help you have a bit of a rest. You work hard, Carrie, holding down a job and bringing up the children single-handed. You make me feel quite lazy sometimes.'

Carrie looked at her in amazement. 'Lazy? With four children and this garden to look after? That's a job in itself.' Her gaze ranged over it. 'It's one I wouldn't object to having, mind you.'

Mary raised her arms above her head, stretched long and languorously. 'What's happening with your father's garden now? It was all turned over to vegetables during the war, wasn't it?'

'Yes, the railway horticultural society worked it more or less as an allotment for the duration, although it's looking a bit dilapidated now. It'll be a challenge for someone to turn it back into a real garden again, although it won't be the Gibsons.'

'Is he retiring?'

'Yes, but not till the end of next year. He's going to take us up to nationalisation, he says, then hand over the reins to someone else. I'll be sorry to see him go. He's been a good boss.'

'They've decided on the first of January 1948, haven't they? As the official date when we all become British Railways?'

'I believe so.' Carrie readjusted her hold on the baby, still reflecting on the current state of the garden at Partick. Like

Mary, she continued to think of it, however much she tried not to, as her father's domain. She knew he would have been one of the first to volunteer to dig for victory, but witnessing the alterations which had been necessary to turn it into a high-yielding vegetable plot had given her a few pangs of regret all the same.

Most of his carefully thought out and laboriously built landscaping had been removed. The drying green had been cultivated, of course, the small square of grass near the back door having to satisfy Mrs Gibson for drying her clothes now. And since you couldn't eat flowers, most of them had been dug up too, although they had kept the roses round in the front garden and the red hot pokers and marguerites at the edge of the grass round the back. Carrie had been glad about that.

Mary's mind was obviously running on the same train of thought as her own. 'And the rhododendrons are still there?' she asked anxiously. 'I don't think I could imagine the garden of the station house without them.'

'Me neither,' Carrie said warmly. 'Some wee man from one of those government committees did suggest they were taking up valuable growing space, but fortunately nobody listened to him.'

'You wouldn't mind taking on the task yourself, Carrie,' her friend observed. 'The garden, I mean.'

'I'd love to, but since they're highly unlikely to appoint me as the new stationmaster I don't think I'll get the opportunity,' she said wryly. 'I'm beginning to think I'll be doing well if I manage to hold on to the job I've got.'

'You'll manage. You're a fighter, Carrie. Look what you've come through already.' Mary coughed delicately. 'What with Matthew and everything.'

Carrie looked her in the eye. 'You never liked him, did

you?' She paused. 'Even before you knew what I've told you this week?'

Mary swallowed, clearly torn between an unwillingness to speak ill of the dead and a desire to answer Carrie's question honestly. 'There was something about him which always made me uneasy. Do you remember the night of your hen party? When he more or less ordered you home? I was really unhappy about that.'

'Maybe if I'd stood up to him then – right from the beginning – things might have been different,' Carrie said reflectively.

'That's you blaming yourself again,' said Mary sternly. 'I thought we'd agreed you weren't going to do that.'

'Easier said than done,' said Carrie, smiling at her. 'But you're right. We did agree on that.'

'And I really don't think you need to worry about the children,' Mary said, referring back to a conversation they'd had a couple of nights ago. 'April has the same kind of nature as you. She has a temper, but it's like yours. Quick to rise and quick to subside again. She doesn't bear grudges and she forgives easily.'

'Thank you for that character assessment of my daughter and myself,' said Carrie with a smile. 'And Archie?'

'He strikes me as being very even-tempered, and he reminds me an awful lot of your father. He's got that same dry sense of humour I remember Mr Burgess as having. And while we're at it, I don't think you need to worry about them hero-worshipping their father. I think that's natural – particularly at the ages they're at now. You can always decide to tell them more later. When they're old enough to understand.'

'I'm not sure I'm old enough to understand it,' said Carrie wryly. 'I still get confused trying to puzzle it all out. The way Matt was, I mean.'

'Maybe you should stop trying, then. Just accept it as something unfathomable and get on with your life.'

Carrie dropped a kiss on the baby's head. 'What a wise woman your mother is,' she said. 'It's been really great being with you, Mary. You'll let us return the compliment at Christmas?'

'We'd love to. Are you sure you can fit us all in?'

'Nae bother. You and Douglas can have my bed. This wee one can be in with you and the children and I can sleep in the front room. We can always spill over across the landing if it turns out to be too tight a squeeze.'

'How's that working out? They haven't all murdered each other yet?'

Carrie laughed. 'No. Fortunately Donald and Florence get on like a house on fire. The two of them sometimes gang up on Isa, as a matter of fact – but only in fun. Donald's got a really wicked sense of humour once you get to know him. And he and Isa have got their caravan now, so the lovebirds can get away occasionally if they need a bit of privacy.'

'Ah, love,' Mary said archly. 'They say it makes the world go round, you know.'

'Really?' Carrie was giving her no encouragement on this one. Unfortunately she didn't need any. Shamelessly using her newborn as a prop, Mary's eyes dropped ostentatiously to the bundle in Carrie's arms. 'It suits you, you know.'

'Mary,' she responded, 'I'm not sure if I should tell you this. It could come as a bit of a shock. I know you've had four children, but you may not have realised that it wasn't the stork who brought them.'

Mary grinned, and Carrie gave the baby a little pat. 'Before you get one of these,' she said, 'you need one of those.' Her hands being full of baby, she gestured with her chin to where Douglas was running around with the children. 'And I rather think that one – a particularly fine example of the species, by the way – is spoken for.'

Mary grinned again and threw a glance down the garden towards her husband. 'Aye, he's no' a bad lad.' Her gaze came back to Carrie's face. 'But there are other fish in the sea, Carrie.'

'And that's the best place for them,' she said smartly, 'unless they're wrapped up in newspaper and covered in salt and vinegar.'

She pulled a funny face, but Mary had stopped smiling. 'You're still young, Carrie, and you won't have the children forever, you know.'

'Don't you start,' she said gloomily, turning her head away and gazing out over the garden. 'I get this all the time from Florence.'

'I can't believe you haven't had any offers. You're an attractive woman.'

Carrie's head swung back round. 'I never said I hadn't had any offers!' she said indignantly.

'Only they haven't come from the one person you'd be interested in?' suggested Mary shrewdly.

For a house containing three adults, five children and one baby, everything seemed very quiet when Carrie awoke the next morning. Although it had to be extremely early, it was already broad daylight, the sun streaming in through the open curtains of the room she was sharing with April and Mary's elder daughter.

She tiptoed through to the scullery to get herself a drink of water, glanced out of the window, and stood for a moment stock still, arrested by the sight which met her eyes. The Ben had finally decided to show itself.

She opened the back door as quietly as she could and sped

out on to the grass. It was wet with dew, soaking her bare feet and the hem of her long nightie. She scarcely noticed, entranced by the view of the mountain. Ben Nevis looked almost like a piece of beautifully painted stage scenery. She felt as if she could stretch her hand up and slide her fingers down the back of it.

Even at this time of year the long plateau of its massive summit was decorated with patches of white: corries where last winter's snow had been preserved. Carrie stood lost in admiration. It looked so powerful: solid and strong, awe-inspiring in its scale and grandeur.

She felt as if she'd been given a gift, one she had better pass on to Archie and April before the day got much older. The sky was blue and cloudless now, but you didn't have to spend much time in the West Highlands before you learned how quickly the weather could change. Nevertheless, she stood a moment or two longer, savouring the moment and experiencing a strange feeling of content.

What had she thought yesterday – that she missed having a shoulder to lean on? But when had she ever had that? Certainly not since her parents had died. In a strange sort of way it had been the other way round with her and Matt.

She would have to be her own strength and support. She'd had enough practice at it, after all. And she would do as Mary had advised yesterday: stop trying to analyse it all. Perhaps you simply had to accept that to some questions there were no answers. You just had to get on with your life. And leave the past with all its broken hopes and promises where it was.

It was the future which mattered now – for herself and the children. If she was to provide adequately for them she needed to keep her job. She was going back home to fight for it.

She wasn't sure if the set-up was designed to be intimidating, but it would, she considered, be very easy to feel daunted by it. She was in the LNER's regional head office in Glasgow, in a huge and high-ceilinged room on the first floor. It could have accommodated a good-sized wedding.

It was elegantly furnished, if a little austere, all dark wood and polished floorboards. Her shoes had squeaked as she had walked across them, shown to an upright chair positioned in the centre of the room.

It faced a long table which ran almost the whole length of one wall. Like the boards under her feet, the dark and luxuriant wood of which it was made was polished to a high sheen. Behind it, backs to one of the three long and elegant windows which lit the space, sat four officers of the railway company. Pascal Sharkey had accompanied her to the interview, but they had seated him over by the door, out of her line of sight. To all intents and purposes Carrie was on her own.

'So tell us, Mrs Campbell,' began the chairman, 'why should we accede to your request in this matter?'

It was all very mannerly, but she could tell from his demeanour that he was expecting to deny that request. They were going through the motions, that was all. She had also just remembered who the person sitting on his right was.

It was the man who had turned her down for a job after her father had died, who had thought it so unreasonable that a woman should even put herself forward for a clerical job on the railway. He was unlikely to be a supporter of continuing female labour now that the crisis was over. She remembered how patronising he'd been, and thought she could see that same attitude on his face now.

She glanced at the two other members of the panel. Four of them to deal with one humble clerkess. A sledgehammer to crack a nut? Carrie straightened her shoulders. That's what they thought. She took a brown envelope out of her handbag, laid it on her lap and began to speak.

She talked for several minutes, putting her case cogently and succinctly. She had prepared it all in advance, written it out and then learned it off by heart. Donald Nicholson had listened to her, made some helpful suggestions. Then she had practised it in front of him and Isa and Florence a couple of times, made sure it sounded fluent but natural.

She reminded them of the long hours she had put in during the war, of how she had never failed to turn up for work even under the most difficult of circumstances. Neither rain, snow nor gale-force winds had stopped her from being at her post at the required time. She told them the evidence suggested that women workers, particularly those who were a little older, were extremely reliable in this regard. The man to the right of the chairman raised a sceptical eyebrow.

The gesture infuriated Carrie. It also strengthened her resolve. And she would deal with him in a minute.

'I'm not speaking only for myself,' she said. 'I know of at least eight other women in the same position. We're all widows.'

Interesting. That last comment had aroused a little flicker of unease. She opened her brown envelope and took out a letter. She had composed it and all nine of the women had signed it. She read it out. It argued that while the small concession they were seeking would cause very little disruption to the company and its operations, the resulting benefits would make an enormous difference to the lives of the loyal female employees affected.

'. . . *allowing us to raise our children without becoming a burden to the state or the community,*' Carrie finished. She'd been rather proud of that phrase. It ended by repeating what she'd said to Pascal when she had first asked him for help. '*We were flexible during the war. Can't the railway be flexible now?'*

She finished and looked up expectantly, suddenly nervous. There was a brief silence. Then the man to the right of the chairman spoke. She'd seldom seen such an insincere smile.

'Mrs Campbell, the company is deeply cognisant of the sacrifices you good ladies made during the war, but those were emergency conditions. Surely we all want to get back to normal now?'

'There are those of us who made greater sacrifices than others, of course,' she said evenly, looking him straight in the eye. 'Some of which make it rather difficult to get back to normal.'

She hadn't been going to bring Matt's death up, intending to present her case in an unemotional way, but it intrigued her that the unease she'd sensed before was now obvious discomfort. Her questioner coughed nervously and looked away. The man on the other side of the chairman shifted in his chair. They would have been briefed on who she was, of course. No doubt the accident enquiry report had been dug out of the files.

Perhaps they'd been expecting her to try and shame them into keeping her on. They weren't to know that wasn't her way.

Extracting several sheets of paper from the envelope, she stood up, walked over to the desk and laid them in front of the panel members. 'Copies of attendance records for myself and my colleagues for the past five years,' she said. 'There's also a reference for each woman relating to the standard of our work during that period. It's been provided by our respective stationmasters, who were all more than happy to do that for us. I'll let you peruse the information for a few moments, gentlemen. I believe it speaks for itself.'

Brisk and businesslike. That was the only way to be – the only way she might stand a chance of success. She resumed her seat, glancing at Pascal before she turned and sat down. He gave her a swift wink. That was all very nice, but she'd been hoping for a bit more than that . . .

The chairman was the first to finish reading. 'These are certainly very impressive,' he said. He lifted his head and his voice, projecting it to the back of the room. 'Mr Sharkey, do you have anything to add to what Mrs Campbell has told us?'

'I most certainly do,' came an enthusiastic voice from behind her. Carrie swung round in surprise. Pascal was coming across the dark floor, taking something out of his inside pocket. He had a brown envelope too, a bit fatter than hers. He came to stand beside her, resting his free hand lightly on the back of her chair.

'Firstly I'd like to back up everything Mrs Campbell has said. I've been doing some research of my own into the contribution made by our female employees both during the war and after it and I have to say that I'm very impressed.' He walked forward to stand in front of the long table. 'I'd also like you to consider this.' He leaned forward and laid his envelope in front of the panel. Somewhat bemused, Carrie watched as the chairman pulled out what looked like an awful lot of sheets of paper.

'It's a petition,' Pascal was explaining, 'in support of the argument you've just heard and with specific reference to the lady sitting in front of you.' He swung round briefly, threw Carrie a smile. 'It's signed by staff members of all grades, train crews and passengers. Mrs Campbell is a very popular employee, both with her colleagues and the travelling public. I've seen her in action, and I know that not only is she a most conscientious worker, but also that her genuine interest in the passengers and their concerns brings enormous benefits to ourselves. There's a sort of mutual respect and goodwill.' His smile grew a little grim. 'We're going to need as much of that as we can get as we make the transition to nationalisation. As we're going to need staff members like Mrs Campbell and her colleagues.'

It was a good job, Carrie thought, that none of them was looking in her direction at that precise moment. Brisk and businesslike? Fortunately she had managed to swallow the lump in her throat by the time they had finished reading and examining the petition. The chairman was smiling: a real, genuine smile.

When they were back outside she couldn't resist throwing her arms around Pascal's neck and giving him a kiss on the cheek. 'Thank you! I never guessed you were cooking up something like that.'

'Well, I think it was your arguments and the way you put them that won the day, Carrie, but I hope I helped a bit. Once I started looking into it I realised what an asset women workers are. I'm sorry if I seemed reluctant to begin with.'

'That's all right,' she said, beaming at him as they walked into the station concourse. 'You've made up for it today. And I'm really grateful.'

Pascal gave her a very rueful look. 'It's not me you should be thanking, Carrie.'

'Ah,' she said. 'I get it. Certain people used their powers of persuasion on you?'

'How did you guess?' he asked wryly. 'I didn't have a hope in hell of standing up to the blandishments of my wife and that smooth-talking father of mine.'

Carrie grinned, her eyes shining with the joy of success. 'Was the petition Anne-Marie's idea? She organised one before, of course.'

Pascal nodded. 'Aye. She told me that, said it had brought positive results. She insisted we had to try everything to help you. My father and I went round with the petition while you were on holiday.'

'Well then,' Carrie said happily, 'let's get on a train and go back and tell them both the good news.' She glanced up at the station clock. 'If we're lucky we might manage to catch your dad as he comes off his shift.'

Martin Sharkey's working day had been over for half an hour by the time they got back to Partick, but he had stayed behind, waiting for them under the canopy of the station buildings.

'Sure, you're not needing to tell me anything,' he said as Carrie stepped off the train, closely followed by his eldest son. 'It's written all over your face! I'm real pleased for you, m'dear.'

Carrie kissed him on the cheek too. He laughed uproariously, clearly delighted by the gesture. After she had thanked him several times and been told several times that she was entirely welcome, Martin informed her that he had a wee surprise for her. 'Something that might come in handy. Especially as you're going to be staying on here at the station. Would you be remembering a conversation you and me had about a month ago when you mentioned a notion you had to start up the station garden again?'

'Yes . . .' Carrie said cautiously.

'Well, look round the corner of this canopy here and see what the little people have left you.'

His benign smile broadened when he saw her delighted reaction to what she found. 'Two of my father's half whisky barrels! I thought they'd all been used for firewood!'

'I saved these two. Hid them at the back of the bothy. I've cleaned them up for you, but I'll not get the lads to put the earth in until you tell me where you want them put.'

'Whatever made you think to keep them?' asked Carrie, already working out where the tubs were going to stand.

He laid a paternal hand on her shoulder. 'I knew we'd be wanting to grow flowers again some day, lass!'

Chapter 34

Carrie was finding it harder than usual to bite her tongue today. She and the children were paying an afternoon visit to her parents-in-law, who now lived outside Largs in a pleasant sandstone villa overlooking the Firth of Clyde. It wasn't too far along the coast from Donald and Isa's caravan. In fact, they had travelled to Largs from there, having just spent a cramped but highly enjoyable few days of the Easter holidays with Mr and Mrs Nicholson, beachcombing by day and stargazing by night.

She'd rather have done it the other way round – got the duty visit out of the way first – but this last Saturday of the school holidays and her own Easter break had been the only day which had suited Shona and Charles Campbell. Allegedly.

Given that their lives still consisted of what seemed to Carrie to be an empty round of social engagements, she couldn't quite understand why they hadn't been able to see her and the children sometime during the previous three or four days. That would have allowed Archie and April and herself to get home to Glasgow earlier tonight. They could have had a relaxing evening by their own fireside before inevitably having to spend most of Sunday getting organised for going back to school and work respectively.

It was always like that, though. They had to fit in with Shona and Charles. It never seemed to be the other way round.

Since the visits were few and far between Carrie had decided to put up with that, reluctant to do anything which might lead to a severing of the children's connection with their grandparents. Archie and April had very few living relatives, after all.

One whom they met now and again was Roderick Cunningham. He'd had his own share of problems over the years, chiefly occasioned by his relationship with Josephine, but Carrie thought – or hoped at least – that things were working out now. Whatever his worries, Roddy always visited at Christmas bearing presents and unfailingly remembered the children's birthdays. It was always a pleasure to see him.

Visiting his sister's house could never be called a pleasure. Carrie did her best to be polite, even chatty, but it could be hard going. Knowing what she did now, she also found it difficult to stomach Charles Campbell's bonhomie. Sometimes it was all she could do to be in the same room as him.

He must have known that he had fathered a child. Yet he had allowed the mother of that child to be cast out without a penny, condemning her to a terrible life and a tragic death. During Carrie's first few conversations with him after Matthew's death and the enquiry into the accident she had been on tenterhooks lest he bring up the subject of his chance meeting with Ewen, but Charles seemed to have forgotten all about it.

She put that down to the selfishness and self-centredness which characterised her father-in-law's personality. His own account of the enquiry, a story he repeated interminably, revolved around the young female reporter who had interviewed him, and the article which had subsequently appeared in her newspaper.

He'd been particularly pleased with the photograph taken to accompany it. There was a framed copy of it on the small antique table which stood in the bay window of the villa's sitting room. Next to it, in a similarly ornate silver frame, stood a picture of Matt, handsome in his uniform. As far as Carrie could see, Shona seldom gave it a second glance, paying as little attention to her son in death as she had in life. Carrie herself was staring fixedly at his face at the moment, trying not to get angry at what her mother-in-law was saying.

Shona was riding one of her favourite hobbyhorses today. Since the Labour Party's election victory nearly two years ago it was always a variation on the same theme. The country was going to the dogs. Today she was expressing herself volubly on how lazy everyone had become since the war had ended.

It was all the fault of this socialist government. They were giving people ideas above their station, as well as far too many holidays. Why, they were even talking about introducing shorter hours in shops and factories! That was quite ridiculous.

Coming from someone who had never done a day's work in her life, Carrie considered it was also a quite breathtaking piece of cheek.

'Not that you get any real service in the shops these days anyway,' Shona went on. 'Service seems to be a dirty word all round. Have you any idea how difficult it is to get help in the house these days?'

Well, no, Mother-in-law, I don't actually. Seeing as how I do my own housework and always have done. And go out to work six hours a day. There was no point in saying the words out loud. Shona had little idea of what Carrie's life was like. No interest in the subject either.

'The trouble is that women of that class have far too many alternatives these days. Going into service isn't good enough for them any more. They'd rather work in a shop or an office.' Shona's cool eyes flickered over her daughter-in-law. 'I'm surprised you've continued to go out to work, Caroline. I was reading an article in the *Daily Telegraph* only last week which predicted a massive rise in juvenile delinquency due to children running riot while their mothers are at work. Young women today are so selfish, of course. And they set their children no acceptable standards of behaviour.'

Oh, it was hard not to rise to it! Carrie occasionally had daydreams in which she imagined telling Shona exactly what she thought of her, but in real life she knew it simply wasn't worth it. If she started, she probably wouldn't be able to stop, and that would certainly mean an end to the visits to Largs.

She glanced across at the children. They were sitting together on a small sofa in front of the empty grate. Charles had managed half an hour with them today before getting bored. He'd muttered something about having some business to attend to and had then disappeared. April was engrossed in one of the comics Carrie had bought on the way to the house, but Archie was looking solemnly at her and his grandmother. Carrie wondered if he'd been listening in. He looked a little worried, so she smiled brightly at him and let her mother-in-law's monologue wash over her.

It was a relief to be out of the house and into the clean salty air, happily marching the mile or so along to the town, duty done for another few months. Having left a little earlier than they actually needed to, they got to the station with time to spare, only to find that the next train to Glasgow had been cancelled. There was a wait of more than an hour till the one after that.

'What will we do?' asked April as the three of them walked back out into the street.

'We're going to get home even later than we thought,' said Archie.

'Well,' Carrie said slowly, 'that is a bit of a nuisance, right enough.' She paused, deliberately spinning it out. 'We could always have our tea here, of course. Give us something to do while we're waiting.'

Two pairs of eyes lit up. 'Chips?' asked April hopefully.

'Out of the paper?' ventured her brother.

That was breaking one of her own rules, the one about eating in the street, but it had been a boring afternoon for the two of them. They deserved a treat. Carrie gave in.

'Letting my standards slip,' she said mock-mournfully as they walked along the front enjoying their tea. 'I'll just have to hope that me letting you eat chips out of newspaper doesn't turn you both into juvenile delinquents.'

The comment went over April's head, but Archie gave her a sharp look.

'How long till the train now?'

'Five minutes less than the last time you asked,' she responded with a smile, lifting a hand to smooth the lock of dark hair which had fallen forward over her son's pale brow. The three of them were sitting together on a bench in the railway station, Carrie in the middle. On one side of her, knees drawn up and wrapped in her mother's protective arm, April was asleep. On the other, Archie was all too wide awake.

'Why do we visit here?'

'Because they're your grandparents,' she replied, but the days when he was satisfied with a simple and straightforward answer were over.

'And blood is thicker than water?'

'Is that something Florence says?' she asked, amused.

Archie nodded, then wrinkled his nose in perplexity. 'What does it mean?'

'Well,' Carrie said, 'I suppose it means that what connects

you to your relatives is more than what connects you to your friends.'

He digested that. She could see the wheels turning, and his next question didn't surprise her. 'Are Auntie Florence and Auntie Isa and Uncle Donald our relatives?'

'Nope. They're our friends. Very good friends.'

'Auntie Mary and Uncle Douglas aren't really our aunt and uncle either, are they?'

'No. They're very good friends too.'

Archie nodded in agreement. 'So in our case water's thicker than blood?'

Carrie laughed. 'I suppose it is.'

Tired of the subject, or perhaps simply satisfied to have worked out something which had been troubling him, he slid forward on to the edge of the bench and looked around. 'I like stations,' he said. 'And trains.'

'Do you?' enquired his mother fondly. 'So do I.'

'Then it's a good thing that you work for the railway,' he said solemnly.

'I would say so,' she replied, trying to match his seriousness. There was something else coming. She could tell.

'It's good for us too,' he said brightly. 'April and me, I mean. That's why we get free passes and privilege tickets, isn't it? We get to travel by train a lot, and we like that.'

'I'm very glad to hear it,' Carrie said.

'And you like your work, don't you?'

'Yes. Very much.'

'And when you're at the station we're either at school or Auntie Florence or Auntie Isa are looking after us. I mean,' he said earnestly, 'it's not as if we're *running riot* when you're not there.'

It was the exact term his grandmother had used. Touched, Carrie realised that he was offering her his support. What had

404

she done to deserve this wonderful child?

'Slide back in the seat,' she said. 'Have a wee rest. Are you too big a boy to want a cuddle?'

'Well,' Archie said confidingly, 'nobody knows me here, do they?'

She slid her spare arm about his slim shoulders. 'But we'll keep coming to see your grandparents,' she suggested, 'to be polite.'

'And so as not to hurt their feelings,' he replied. 'You should always try not to hurt other people's feelings.'

'Does your Auntie Florence say that?'

'No,' he said comfortably, cuddling in to her, 'I just know it.'

Carrie smiled. 'You know something else, Archie Campbell? You're a very nice person. And your mammy loves you.'

'I love you too, Ma. How long till the train now?'

'*Russell* lupins?' queried Carrie. The name wasn't familiar to her.

'Yes,' said the passenger with whom she was discussing the subject. He ran a business in Partick, travelling in by train from his home in Dumbarton. 'They're a new strain, came on to the market the year before the war broke out. Although apparently the chap who developed them had been working on them for years. Did it all on an allotment in York, I believe. His life's work – and a remarkable achievement. I think you'd like them, Mrs Campbell. There's a splendid selection of colours, and they're very sturdy.'

'They sound lovely,' she said. 'If you're sure you can spare some?'

'With the greatest of pleasure, my dear,' he said warmly, regarding her from under pepper-and-salt eyebrows of

405

luxuriant growth. 'Now,' he said, 'I know you don't like your flowers too regimented, but I was thinking that if you had a clump of them in the centre of each of your flowerbeds – at the back against the fence – it would add a pleasant unity to your overall design.'

'Mmm,' she said consideringly, surveying the bed they were currently standing in front of. 'You could be right.'

'Think about it anyway,' he said. He gave her a little pat on the shoulder. 'And keep up the good work. You've made a real difference here. Brightened up the gloom.'

Carrie smiled fondly after him as he strode off towards the Crow Road exit. He'd been one of the first to comment on her gardening attempts. She'd begun in a small way with the tubs Sharkey had given her the previous autumn, carefully nurturing the bulbs she'd planted in them over the cold and wintry months which had heralded the start of 1947.

Admiring the welcome splash of colour, the businessman gardener had promised to bring her some more bulbs towards the end of the year. When she'd acquired some other tubs and – with a bit of help from two of the porters – reinstated the platform flowerbeds, he'd brought her some cuttings out of his own garden to start off her summer flowers.

It had all kind of snowballed from there. An older lady who travelled regularly from her home in Westerton to do her shopping in Partick handed in a box of bedding plants. The marigolds in particular had done very well, growing bright and vigorously as a border round the central flower bed. Carrie loved their cheerful colour. They were so long-lasting too.

Other passengers had started taking an interest. She'd been given more cuttings from a very friendly couple who had an allotment. A previously rather shy middle-aged bachelor had begun discussing the plants and flowers with her, offering lots of helpful advice. She'd introduced him to the nice couple, had happily heard them trading invitations to look at each other's gardens.

A younger couple brought her some geraniums. Another man asked her if she'd like him to bring her the odd bag of manure. Carrie smiled, remembering how embarrassed he'd been, although anxious to convince her of the benefits of that particular fertiliser.

She needed no convincing now, she thought. Her beds and tubs were full of healthy soil which in turn had allowed the growth of tumbling plants and vibrant flowers. Morning rush hour over, she took five minutes to walk up the platform to review the situation. Although they were well into the autumn she was pleased to see that there was still plenty of colour in evidence.

The trailing blue and white lobelia in the whisky barrel furthest up the platform, to the side of the gate, was beginning to look a wee touch straggly. She'd give it a couple of weeks more, then plant some spring bulbs in there.

Horticultural tour of inspection finished, she walked smartly back to the booking office, deep in happy thought. If she managed an even better show next year perhaps they could think about going in for the best station garden competition, give Hyndland a run for its money. The next station along the line had a beautiful display this year, and the friendly rivalry between the competing stations which had existed before the war looked all set to start up again.

She'd need to do something on the other platform too. She glanced over at it as she came in under the canopy. So far she only had one tub of flowers there. She could do with some window boxes and plants around the station buildings too. She had some on her own windowsills at home from which she could take cuttings and was planning also on trying to raise a tray or two of seedlings next year, as much as she could find space for.

She passed through the booking hall. Its large windows would make it an excellent greenhouse. She would bring her geraniums in here before the first frosts. She was smiling as she went back into the booking office. If she mentioned to the people who now cheerfully referred to themselves as the travelling gardening club that she was hoping to go in for the competition, she'd probably be inundated with plants. The rivalry between stations extended to the passengers too.

'You look as if you're plotting something, Mrs Campbell,' observed the stationmaster.

'I am,' she said, and told him what it was.

'Well,' said George Gibson, 'you've certainly made a big difference to the station, and I can only wish you the best of luck if you do decide to compete for the title next year. I'll not be here to see it, of course.'

She knew he was looking forward to his retirement – he and his wife were moving to Stirling to be closer to their married daughter and her family – but she could hear the wistfulness in his voice.

'It'll be a wrench for you,' she said gently, 'leaving the railway.'

'Aye,' he agreed, 'but it's time to give someone else a chance. I've done my bit, I think.'

'Much more than that,' Carrie assured him. 'Through some very difficult years too. There's a lot to your job even when you're not coping with the effects of a world war.'

'You'll know that better than most, lass.'

Registering that *lass*, she realised that he must be feeling a bit emotional. He was usually so formal. 'Do you think we'll get an LNER man to take your place?' she asked brightly, pleased when she saw his face light up.

'Maybe. I know they have advertised it internally throughout the company, but I suppose it won't necessarily be the case. Not in this brave new world.'

He looked sad and she realised that however welcome the change was to many people, there would be others who would deeply regret the passing of the old railway companies and the swallowing up of the Big Four.

Coming in to see her three weeks later, however, Mr Gibson was in jovial mood, brandishing a sheet of paper. 'They've sent me a list of candidates for the job,' he announced.

Carrie looked up from her work. 'Anybody we know?'

'Yes,' he said brightly, and presented the letter to her. 'An old friend of ours. Look!' he said, and pointed out the sixth name on the alphabetically ordered list.

Chapter 35

She couldn't assume anything. It was four years since that bitter parting in George Square. Ewen could be married to someone else by now. He could have a child. And life did things to people. She knew that better than anybody. Circumstance and experience altered your perspective, made you look at the world in a different way. It was inevitable that he would have changed. He had also been to war. That had to affect a man too.

All the same, she had never forgotten his final words to her. *I'll always love you.* She remembered them . . . and she hoped.

She knew she couldn't expect a letter herself, but was surprised when one took so long to arrive for Isa and Florence. It contained a further surprise when it did. Ewen would be staying in a hotel when he came to Glasgow for his interview. Florence was upset about that, but Carrie did her best to reassure her.

'He probably feels bad because he hasn't written to you for so long. Doesn't want you to think that he's taking advantage of you.'

Florence spluttered. 'And how could he ever do that? The laddie's mair or less family, for goodness' sake!'

Another case where water was thicker than blood.

Ewen's visit would also be brief. He was arriving on a

411

Thursday, keeping his appointment at the railway company offices on Friday, and probably travelling back south late on the following Monday afternoon.

'South?' Carrie asked when Isa read this information out to her. 'Has he been working in London, then?'

'He's no' giving very much away here. Read it for yourself.'

She did. The letter was cheerful in tone, apologetic for not having been in touch for so long. He was, he wrote, very much looking forward to seeing them again. *It'll be a short visit, but I'd like to see everybody. You and Florence and Donald – not forgetting Bobby! Archie and April, of course. Their mother too.*

'*Their mother too*,' Carrie repeated wryly. 'That makes me sound like a bit of an afterthought.'

'No, it doesn't,' Isa said reassuringly, 'but you'll have to expect him to be a wee bit cautious, hen.'

'You think that's all it is?'

She'd had no chance of trying to hide her hopes from those sharp eyes. Isa gave her a swift hug. 'I know so. Once you tell him how you feel . . .' She winked conspiratorially. 'D'ye see what else he says? He wants us to go up to Glasgow to have high tea with him on the Thursday and be his guests at a supper dance in the Burgh Hall on the Friday night.' She paused for thought. 'If he's been working in London, how on earth did he know there's a dance on at Partick Burgh Hall next Friday night?'

One week later, Carrie stood in the foyer of a Glasgow hotel watching the man who had always been able to find things out walking towards her. Beside her, April was jumping up and down with excitement. Unable to contain herself any longer, the little girl ran up to him. Ewen's arms opened as wide as his eyes. 'My, how you've grown!' he cried.

412

Archie walked forward too, and then it was hugs and greetings for everybody. Ewen left her till last, extending a polite hand. 'Carrie,' he said pleasantly. 'How are you?'

There was a greater maturity about his face. No doubt his experiences in war-torn Europe had something to do with that. He would have tales to tell.

As though she were sleepwalking, she allowed her hand to slip into that well-remembered firm grasp of his. He looked as energetic as ever. He was saying something. Carrie had to struggle to concentrate.

'. . . introduce my bride-to-be to you.'

She turned and looked at the woman – a well made-up blonde, giving her a cool smile which made no pretence of reaching her eyes. Her hair hadn't always been that colour. Carrie remembered her as a brunette.

The prospective Mrs Ewen Livingstone was smartly, if a little flashily dressed. She was, however, wearing a smock under her coat. Ewen might not have a child yet, but by the looks of it he only had a few months to wait. Janice Muirhead was expecting his baby.

Chapter 36

'I'm not going to the supper dance tomorrow night, and that's final! You two can take the children if you like, but you can count me out. So stop going on at me, Isa!'

The children were in bed, and she was at her own kitchen table, Florence hovering solicitously at her side and Isa sitting opposite her.

'He's going to marry Janice Muirhead,' Carrie said flatly. 'That's all there is to it.'

'He hasn't married her yet,' Isa retorted. 'You could fight her for him. If you come to the Burgh Hall the morn's night.'

'Och, Isa,' Carrie said despairingly, 'she's carrying his child. And they've obviously been living together in London. You heard all those wee hints Janice managed to drop into the conversation as well as I did.'

'What the hell difference does that make?' said Isa impatiently. She made an exclamation of disgust. 'I could fair do wi' a fag.' She looked around as though she expected one to materialise out of thin air. 'Mind you, you would think the stupid bugger could have been a wee bit more careful. He's no' a boy any more.'

'Isabella Nicholson,' said Florence. 'Mind your language!' But the rebuke had been automatic. She sat down at the table and looked puzzled. 'There's something here that doesnae quite meet the eye. How has he no' married her already?

415

That's what ye would expect a man like Ewen to do.'

Isa looked at her as though she was soft in the head. She gestured across the table at Carrie. 'Because he wanted to see this lassie one last time before he made up his mind,' she said. 'To see if she had changed *her* mind. Why else?'

'If that's the case,' asked Carrie, 'why is he going out of his way to make sure he and I never end up on our own together while he's here? It was all of us this afternoon. It's all of us tomorrow night.'

'There's always the weekend, pet,' said Florence, frowning anxiously.

'When he's asked if he can take Archie and April out on Saturday and agreed they'll come to you for their dinner on Sunday.' Carrie threaded her fingers through her coppery hair. 'In any case, we all know Ewen's the last man in the world to desert a woman who's having a baby by him.'

Florence opened her mouth to say something, then closed it again. That argument was irrefutable.

'You're still coming to the dance,' Isa said. 'You're going to put on your glad rags and look your best. I'll do your hair.'

It was easier to give in. What did it matter really?

Half an hour into Friday evening, it seemed to matter quite a lot. Carrie had expected Janice to be all over Ewen like a rash, wasting no opportunity of showing off her ownership of him, but it wasn't like that at all. It was much worse.

There seemed to be genuine friendship and affection between them, and a good few private jokes. And although Janice was wearing an engagement ring, she certainly wasn't flashing it about.

She was friendly and relaxed with the children too. They had taken to her, as they appeared ready to resume their relationship with Ewen where they had left it off. They had known him for only a few short weeks several years ago, but they had never forgotten him. He had made an impact on them.

He asked Carrie up to dance fairly early on in the proceedings. Getting it over with, she supposed. The touch of his fingers, restrained though his clasp was, brought back far too many memories. She could barely speak, and was glad when he was apparently not very interested in making conversation either. Just as she was wondering how much longer she could stand to be in this polite embrace, he mentioned that he had been for his interview earlier that day.

'How did it go?'

'Not bad. They seemed quite impressed anyway.'

'Oh,' she said. 'That's good.'

They finished the dance in silence and when the music stopped he escorted her courteously back to her seat. Then he asked Janice up on to the floor. Donald led Isa out and a laughing Florence agreed to stand up with Archie. That left only Carrie and April at the table. She slid her arms around her daughter's waist, and the little girl leaned back against her in response.

Carrie's eyes kept finding Ewen, wherever he was on the dance floor. He looked a hundred times more relaxed with Janice than he had been with her. She pressed her lips gently against April's hair. This was awful. She shouldn't have come. The music stopped again, everyone returned to the table, and the band leader announced the imminent arrival of supper.

'But first,' he said, 'we all need to work up an appetite. Ladies and gentlemen, take your partners please for the Dashing White Sergeant!'

Ewen was still holding Janice's hand from the last dance. He looked across the table at Carrie. 'How about it?' he asked. 'For old times' sake?'

'No,' she said hurriedly. 'Take April.'

Janice sank down into her chair. 'It's too energetic for me, Ewen.' She laughed up at him. 'Especially in my condition.'

'You and April then,' he said, looking once more at Carrie.

'No,' she repeated, although she knew it was the height of rudeness to refuse his invitation a second time. 'Take Archie. Put April in the middle.'

Donald asked Florence and Isa to make a set with him. That left Carrie and Janice alone at the table. To Carrie's immense relief, the other girl excused herself and went off to the ladies' room. Almost everyone else was up on the floor, throwing themselves into the dance and concentrating on the intricacies of the steps.

Ewen was throwing himself into it too, laughing with Archie and April whenever any of the three of them made a wrong move. Carrie watched him hungrily, saw his energy and vitality, his strength and grace. He had all of those characteristics in abundance, both physically and mentally. He had laid them at her feet so many times.

Now, when she would gladly have thrown herself at his, he no longer wanted her. Her children were revelling in being with him, responding to his interest in them. She thought of how different things might have been. For all of them. And found she couldn't bear to look at the three of them together for one second longer. She turned away, glanced across the table and jumped. 'How long have you been back in your seat?'

'Long enough,' Janice said. She gave Carrie a bland smile.

'Will we all fit in round the table?'

'If we pull out both leaves,' said Donald in his slow voice, and set about performing the task.

'We'll need your chairs, Carrie,' said Isa as she went to help him.

418

Florence was busy at the range, looking for all the world like a benign witch presiding over a collection of cauldrons. 'And your good cutlery, pet,' she threw over her shoulder. 'We havenae got enough respectable stuff to go round.'

'We'll go and get it all now. Come on, you two,' Carrie said with a brightness she was very far from feeling. There didn't seem to be any way she could get out of being present at this meal. What excuse could she possibly offer?

After all, she had gone to the dance on Friday and allowed Ewen to take the children to the pictures yesterday. Naturally, Janice had gone too. Carrie had waved the four of them off and smiled cheerfully when they came home. She had even invited them in for a cup of tea. That had been politely declined, but she'd spent the rest of the evening listening to her children chattering excitedly about their afternoon out with their Uncle Ewen and – she supposed that one was inevitable – their Auntie Janice.

Archie and April took a chair apiece. Carrie took one as far as the landing, placed it against the wall between the two houses and turned to go back into her own to fetch the cutlery.

'Exactly what I need in my condition,' came Janice's voice. 'How thoughtful of you, Carrie!'

She put a smile on her face and turned to greet them. Janice was pulling herself up the last few stairs, Ewen behind her, jokingly pushing her towards the landing. She sank into the chair. Then Archie came out.

'Hello, wee man,' she said cheerfully, ruffling his hair. 'Are you needing my seat?'

'Go on in,' Carrie said. 'I've another one to fetch.'

'And the cutlery, Ma,' Archie reminded her.

Janice put a hand out to him. 'Be a gentleman, pet. Help me up.' She smiled at her fiancé. 'Why don't you give Carrie a hand, Ewen?' She put on a posh accent. 'Archibald will

419

escort me into luncheon. Won't you, kind sir?'

Archie giggled. Janice let him pull her up, pretending to need a lot more assistance than she actually did.

'May I take your arm?' she queried once she was on her feet. 'Because,' she confided to him, reverting to her own voice, 'I'm growing as big as the side of a house, Archie. I need all the help I can get to move about.'

He giggled again, and obliged.

In contrast to the hustle and bustle and frantic culinary activity taking place across the landing, Carrie's own home seemed unusually quiet. She was very aware of Ewen's silent presence behind her as she walked into the kitchen. Memories were flooding back of two other occasions when she had been alone in this room with him.

'There's the chair,' she said unnecessarily. It was the only one left at the table. Feeling the need to fill the silence, she said the first thing that came into her head. 'She's quite a character. Janice, I mean.'

Ewen smiled. It made his eyes crinkle, emphasising fine lines at their corners which hadn't been there four years ago. 'Oh, she's that all right,' he said warmly. He walked forward, putting his hands out to lift the chair. Then he stopped.

'What's that?' he asked, his attention obviously caught by a small picture hanging on the wall between the range and the box bed.

'Oh,' Carrie said, wishing he hadn't noticed it, 'just a big postcard, really, but I got Donald to frame it for me. Archie and April bought it for me this summer. They thought I might like it.'

He was walking across the room to have a better look. 'Why, it's Oban, isn't it? The view out over the bay?'

'Yes.' She crouched down to open the cupboard where she kept the canteen which held her good cutlery. 'We had a day trip down there in the summer, while we were staying with Douglas and Mary at Fort William. You remember Douglas, don't you?' She extracted the wooden box, then stood up and closed the cupboard door with her foot. Ewen was still standing with his back to her, gazing at the little picture.

'Oh, aye,' he said absently. 'Oban Bay,' he murmured. 'With Kerrera in the foreground and Mull of the Mountains in the background. Lovely photography,' he observed.

'Yes.' She wished he would pick up the chair. Then they could go.

'It's very tasteful,' he said. He turned at last, and smiled at her. 'Guaranteed not to provoke an attack of the screaming abdabs in the middle of Oban High Street.'

She rested the canteen of cutlery on the table. She was sure it hadn't been so heavy the last time she had lifted it. Ewen was still smiling at her.

'I can remember that day we had there so well.' His face lit up further. 'And the train journey back. "*Faster than fairies, faster than witches, Bridges and houses, hedges and ditches*",' he quoted softly. 'Do you remember the boy at Tyndrum who was clambering and scrambling?'

'It was a long time ago,' she managed.

'Twelve years,' he said.

'A long time ago,' she repeated. She hoisted up the box of cutlery, made sure she had a secure hold of it.

'Aye,' he said slowly. 'We were both very young then.' He walked across to the table, lowered his eyes to the chair.

A dismissal then. A relegation to the days of their youth. He looked up at her. 'Are you happy, Carrie?' he asked softly. 'Is life good?'

'Yes,' she said. 'I'm happy. My life is very full.' That last was true, at least. Only she had a feeling that from now on there was going to be a yawning chasm at the very heart of it.

'I'm glad,' Ewen said. 'I'm really glad to hear that.'

'They'll be wondering where we are.'

'Aye,' he said, and began carrying the chair towards the door. He paused to let her go in front of him. 'After you,' he said politely.

Carrie pushed the crocus and daffodil bulbs into the earth, rose to her feet and cleaned the dirt from her hands and her trowel. It was a sunny day, but there was an edge to the wind this Monday morning, a foretaste of the cold and dark months ahead. The snell breeze blew a strand of hair across her face, making her eyes water.

She made her way back down the platform. Funny how something as small and fragile as a bulb could survive through the cold and dark of the winter. Carrie was trying very hard not to think about how she was going to do the same. She was trying very hard not to think about a lot of things.

Something her father had once said came back to her, floating down out of the ether. Over the years, she had often been aware of his presence in this place where he had spent so much of his working life. *Dangerous occupation, thinking. Probably why lots o' folk try to avoid it altogether.*

'You were dead right there, Daddy,' she said sadly. Quietly, but out loud. Just in case he was listening.

There was a sharp tap on the ticket window. Putting her coat on before going home at the end of her shift, Carrie turned to see who it was. If she hadn't been so obviously getting ready to leave she would have come up with some excuse. As it was, good manners forced her out into the booking hall.

'I thought you and Ewen were going back to London today,' she said.

'I'm meeting him at the train. I wanted to have a word with you before I left.'

'Janice . . .'

'Please, Carrie,' the girl said quietly, with none of her usual brashness. 'Just walk up the platform with me for a wee minute.'

When Janice stopped outside the back garden of the station house, it crossed Carrie's mind that she had come to gloat. If Ewen got the stationmaster's job, his bride would be mistress of this little kingdom – but somehow that didn't fit in with the girl Carrie had got to know again over the past couple of days. And when Janice spoke she could hear nothing of that sentiment in her voice.

'The garden needs a lot o' work, eh? To get it back to how it was before the war. Ewen would enjoy getting stuck into that,' she observed. She turned and smiled, a wry twist of the lips. 'Whereas I personally would hate it. You used to help your daddy in the garden, didn't you?' She glanced down at the half whisky barrel at her feet. 'Have you been planting something?'

'Bulbs for next spring. That's when they'll sprout.'

'A bit like myself.' Janice patted her stomach and laughed. 'It's great when the baby starts moving, isn't it? You know you've got a real wee person in there.'

Carrie couldn't take much more of this. 'Janice, please say what you've got to say and let me go home. My children will be waiting for me.'

That wasn't strictly true. At the moment Archie and April were both still in school. They were going straight to their aunties' house afterwards, Florence having declared she would cook the tea for everybody tonight.

'To give you a wee rest, hen,' she had said, not bothering to hide her concern at her young neighbour's pale face and listless demeanour.

Janice moved towards a bench placed against the fence, under the rhododendron bushes. She waited till Carrie, all unwilling, had joined her.

'You know Ewen and I have been living together for the past couple of months,' she began.

'So I gathered.' Carrie knew she sounded stiff and disapproving. She didn't much care.

Janice gave her an odd little glance, knowing and sophisticated. 'Nobody gives a damn about that sort of thing in London, you know. Certainly not in the area where Ewen's been living. He has this little service flat near the station: one room and a tiny kitchen. There's one bed,' she said precisely.

She *had* come to crow. Carrie slid forward on the wooden seat, poised for flight. 'I'm not interested in your domestic arrangements!'

'You should be,' came the calm reply. 'How else would I know that he talks in his sleep?'

Carrie felt the breeze on her cheek, sensed the distant vibration of the next train about to pull into the platform. Very slowly, she turned her head and looked into the face of the woman sitting next to her. What she saw there was mischief rather than malice.

'He murmurs your name. Sometimes *Carrie*, sometimes out in full: *Caroline Burgess*. I've been getting a bit fed up of hearing it, to tell you the truth,' Janice added lightly.

The train was approaching round the curve of the track, crossing the bridge over Dumbarton Road. The engine stopped opposite where they sat, and the driver lifted his hand in greeting. Janice waited until he had started up again and pulled away.

'They've offered him the job. Someone came in person to the hotel this morning. King's Cross have said they would release him immediately, but I think he's going to turn it down. Because you're too good an actress.'

Carrie took her eyes off the retreating train, and turned once more to Janice.

'I saw the way you looked at him on Friday night,' the girl said softly. 'When you thought nobody was watching you.'

'I don't understand,' Carrie said. 'You're engaged to him, you're expecting his baby. Why are you telling me all this?'

Janice spoke very clearly. 'The baby's not his. There are several possible candidates. Well,' she admitted, her expression growing rueful, 'quite a few actually. Unfortunately Ewen's not one of them.'

'What?' Carrie's heart had begun to thump violently. 'Does he know that?'

'Oh, aye,' said Janice blithely. 'He rescued us, you see. Walked into this club in London where I was working. For some not very nice people. They didn't want anything to interfere with my earning potential,' she said carefully, her hand going protectively to her stomach. 'But I'd already decided I was keeping this one. Ewen helped me get away from them.'

Carrie pondered that for a moment. 'He couldn't save his mother, but he managed to save you?' she suggested.

'That's about it,' Janice said cheerfully.

Carrie was studying her face. No malice. No distress either. 'Don't you love him?' she asked. 'Doesn't he love you?'

'We're fond of each other,' Janice said equably, 'but that's as far as it goes. We gave each other comfort at a time in our lives when we both needed it. That's all.'

'So why has he asked you to marry him?'

'Because he's a gentleman.' She grimaced. 'Although he knows very well that he hasnae exactly ruined my reputation single-handed. And,' she added carefully, 'because even

425

someone as strong and as determined as he is gets tired of pushing the same rock up the same hill.'

Carrie raised her face to the sky. 'I'm scared, Janice,' she said at last. 'How can I be sure that he still wants me? He hasn't told you in so many words, has he?'

'You don't think that he might be scared too, Carrie?'

She lowered her head again. Janice was smiling at her. 'You'll have to stick your head above the parapet this time,' she said. 'How often did he do it for you? Go on,' she commanded, giving the sleeve of Carrie's coat a little tug. 'If you're quick you'll catch him. He's along the road. Where you would expect him to be.'

Carrie stood up. 'You'll not get mixed up with those people again?'

Janice was still smiling at her. 'No. London's a big place, but I'm planning a move to the coast anyway. Somewhere nice and healthy for the baby to grow up. Somewhere I might stand a chance of finding a decent man, a nice chivalrous one who'll feel sorry for the young widow and her baby. Wasn't it sad that my husband survived the war, only to be run over by a bus in Kensington High Street a couple of years afterwards? And a week before I gave birth too.'

Carrie laughed, liking her. 'You're a survivor, Janice.'

'Oh, aye, I'm that, all right.' The mocking eyes grew shrewd. 'I used to envy you so much, you know.' She gestured with her head to the garden behind them. 'Living in there with your father and mother who loved you. But you've paid your dues since then, I think.'

'You could say that.'

Janice reached out, curled her fingers around Carrie's wrist and gave her hand a shake. 'Well then,' she said, 'go and grab yourself some happiness. Before it's too late.'

* * *

'Did you climb over the wall, or did you come in the grown-up way?'

He whirled round. He'd been standing with his back to the gate, looking up at the sky. 'What are you doing here?' His attitude was anything but welcoming.

'Janice sent me.'

'Oh?' He was wearing a raincoat, long and unbuttoned. He thrust his hands into the pockets of his trousers, pushing back the light-coloured folds.

'She and I have been having a very interesting discussion.'

One fair eyebrow went up, but Ewen contented himself with another one word answer. 'Really?'

'She said they'd offered you the job, but that you might be going to turn it down.'

'Aye. I might.'

Carrie glanced around her, at the old graveyard in which they stood. 'You came here to think it over?'

His chin went up. 'What's it to you?'

She reminded herself she had no right to expect this to be easy. 'I think you should take it. You'd relish the challenge.'

'Maybe I'm fed up facing challenges.' His eyes were a cool grey. 'Maybe even someone as stupid as me eventually realises when he's pursuing a lost cause.'

'Don't call yourself stupid,' she said sharply. 'You were never that. Not even when you were a wee raggedy boy out there on Keith Street. And,' Carrie enquired, 'are you absolutely certain that the cause is lost?'

He took his hands out of his pockets and two hesitant steps towards her. Then he stopped. 'There's times when I still am that wee boy,' he said. 'Lots of them.'

'I know,' she said softly. 'I know.'

Something flashed across his face then, but he recovered himself quickly. He stood where he was, making no further move towards her. He'd been hurt too many times, and he was wary. So it was up to her. Time to stick her head above that parapet. She took a deep breath.

'I'm going to tell you something, and then I'm going to ask you a question. You can say yes, or you can say no.' She took another breath. 'I love you, Ewen Livingstone. Will you marry me?'

He stared at her. She was too late. She'd left it too long, thrown his love for her back in his face so often it had evaporated. Cast to the four winds, it had vanished as though it had never existed at all.

Ewen took a step forward. 'Are ye no' supposed to wait till it's a leap year?'

'Is that one of your pieces of useless information?' she asked. She wanted to laugh. She wanted to cry.

He took another step. Then one more.

'I think we've waited long enough,' she said breathlessly, looking up into his face. 'Don't you?'

'Way too long,' he growled, and bent his head to kiss her.

Chapter 37

'You didn't need to come and see me off,' Janice said.

Ewen contradicted her. 'Of course we did. Here, I got you some magazines and fruit for the journey. Now,' he said briskly, 'you'll remember to eat properly? Get all the vitamins and minerals you need?'

'I will. Thanks for these.' She took the magazines and fruit from him and stuffed them into the small bag at her feet. He'd already put her case on to the train. 'I'll send your things,' she promised.

'There's not that much,' he said. 'My books and a few other bits and pieces, but tell the people at King's Cross to contact me and I'll arrange to pay the carriage at this end. The room's paid for the next six weeks. Will that do you, or do you want me to send them another month's rent?'

Janice shook her head. 'No, that's more than enough. Oh!' she said suddenly. 'I'd better give you this back.' She began tugging at the engagement ring.

Ewen's hand closed over hers. 'No, no,' he said. 'It's yours, lassie. Sell it if you like.'

'Only if I need to,' she said. 'Otherwise I'm going to keep it to remember you by.' She reached up and kissed him on the cheek. 'Thank you for everything you did for me.' She looked across at Carrie. 'Is it all right if I give him a hug as well?'

'Be my guest,' she said gently. She'd been hanging back to

allow the two of them to make their farewells.

Over Janice's shoulder, Ewen's eyes were far too bright. 'Good luck,' he said huskily. 'Especially when the baby comes.'

Janice gave him one last squeeze, then let him go. 'She'll give you one of your own,' she said. She held out her hand, and Carrie came forward.

'Will you write and let us know how you get on?'

'Probably not.'

Carrie looked into her eyes, and sighed. 'I suppose you're right, but we'll always remember you, you know.'

'I should bloody hope so. Cupid's little helper, that's me. You'll look after him?' Janice asked. 'And let him look after you?' She gave Ewen a smile. 'He likes to do that.'

'Oh, Janice!' Carrie threw her arms around her neck and embraced her. Janice hugged her back. When they separated, both of them had tears in their eyes.

'Would you look at the state of us! Him, too.' She gestured with her thumb towards Ewen, once more looking decidedly moist-eyed. 'Well, I'd better get aboard.'

The door was slammed behind her, and Janice leaned out of the window to say a last goodbye. Her final words were for Carrie. 'You'll enjoy giving him a wean. He's all right in that department. A lot more than all right. Know what I mean? Take it from one who knows.'

Ewen Livingstone – stationmaster designate – blushed to the roots of his hair. The final whistle blew, and Janice threw them both a wicked grin. 'Have fun, my children.'

'In the name o' God,' said Isa in exasperation. 'Where on earth can your mother have got to? She's more than two hours late.'

'Aye,' said Florence, 'the meal's going to spoil if she's no here soon. Away down to the street and see if you can see her coming, children.'

Ten minutes later, April came pelting through the half-open door of her aunties' house, giggling furiously. Archie was hot on her heels, clutching his neck and making exaggerated faces as though he were about to be sick.

'Heavens above,' said Florence, grabbing April as she ran helter-skelter into the kitchen. 'What's going on?'

'Come and see! Come and see!'

Isa went storming out on to the landing, preceded by the children and closely followed by Florence, Donald and Bobby. 'Where the hell have you been, Carrie?' she began. Then she saw what was happening down on the half landing and her face broke into a wide, broad smile.

Ewen was braced against the narrow stone sill of the long windows which lit the stairwell. He sat with his legs apart, and one of them was providing a seat for Carrie. He was grasping her waist firmly with one hand. The other rested on her knee. She had her arms coiled about his neck.

'They won't stop kissing!' said April in delight.

'It's disgusting!' exclaimed her brother in accents of horror.

Ewen took his mouth off Carrie's and grinned at him. 'It's allowed, Archie,' he said cheerfully. 'We're going to be married.'

The landing above them was a sea of smiling faces. Even Bobby, front paws up on the banister, was wagging his tail. With a supreme effort of will, Isa managed to replace a grin with a ferocious scowl.

'Is that right? And where, might we be so bold as to ask, does Mr Ewen Livingstone think he's staying until the ceremony takes place?'

'In there?' he said hopefully, pointing towards Carrie's front door.

431

Isa responded to that with a snort of derision. She turned to Florence. 'You're going on your holidays,' she announced. 'To Carrie's house. You,' she announced, jabbing a finger at Ewen, 'are lodging wi' Donald and me for the duration.' She sniffed magnificently. 'This is a respectable close. We're having no shameless and unseemly behaviour in here!'

Epilogue

His hand on the bolt of the platform gate, Ewen paused and turned. 'I suppose I'd better go.'

'I suppose you'd better wipe that smile off your face before you do. No one out there's going to respect your authority otherwise.'

'Aye, it took me a long time to work out that was your father's trick. Soft as butter really, wasn't he?'

Carrie's own smile grew sad. 'Ewen,' she said hesitantly, 'this job took its toll on him, you know.'

His eyes softened. 'I'm a different personality to him.' He reflected. 'A bit harder, maybe. If anyone gives me a mouthful, they know I'm quite capable of giving them one back.' He slid his arm about her, gave her shoulders a reassuring squeeze. 'I'm sure he's looking down on us from somewhere, you know. Giving me a helping hand now and again, chuckling when I make a mistake.' His generous mouth quirked wryly. 'I'm not so sure I'd like your ma to be watching over us, mind.'

'She'd have come round to you.'

'You think so?'

'I'm sure she would have. Come on now. Duty calls.'

'One more kiss?'

'You've had lots already,' Carrie said sternly.

'Who's counting?' he asked, and added a few more to the tally. Carrie gave him a shove. 'Go,' she said. 'You can have all the kisses you want when you come off duty. The trains have to run on time, remember?'

He looked fondly at her. 'Always the stationmaster's daughter, aren't you?'

'Now I'm the stationmaster's wife.'

'So you are,' he said. 'So you are.' He dropped a kiss on her nose. '*The stationmaster's wife*,' he said consideringly. 'Possibly my favourite words in the entire language. Apart from *Caroline Livingstone*, that is.' Swinging her round in his arms, he laid a large but light hand on her stomach, splaying his fingers out over the bump. 'Going to put your feet up this afternoon?'

'Certainly not,' she said, although her intended briskness was being sabotaged by the soft little kisses he was dropping on the side of her neck. 'There's gardening to be done.'

He lifted his head and heaved a theatrical sigh. 'I suppose it's just as well. If you're out in the garden, I won't have a hundred passengers asking me where you are or if you're keeping well. Giving me presents and wee bits of flowers and plants to pass on to you. Hoping that you're putting the station in for the best garden competition again. You might as well still be on the payroll.'

'I know,' she said happily.

'Don't do any of the heavy stuff then,' he said. 'I'll get Archie and April to help me with that this evening.'

'Donald can help too,' she reminded him. 'They're all coming round tonight.'

'So they are. I'd forgotten. Are Florence's knitting needles still in danger of catching fire?'

Carrie laughed. 'You mean the several dozen matinée jackets she's making for the baby?' She lifted a lazy arm, found his jaw and traced the line of it with her fingertips. 'You've got to go back to work, Mr Livingstone.'

He sighed, and allowed her to turn around. 'Carrie . . . Archie and April are happy about the baby, aren't they?'

'Are you kidding? They're over the moon. Apart from arguing constantly about whether we're going to have a boy or a girl, of course. No prizes for guessing who wants what.'

Ewen smiled. 'Maybe we should let them choose the name,' he suggested. 'Would that be a good idea?'

'We're there ahead of you,' she said. 'And they actually agree on one point.'

'Which is?'

'Both their names begin with the first letter of the alphabet, so they think it would be nice if the baby's did too.'

'Fine by me.' He thought about it some more. 'In fact, that's a really nice idea. Have they anything in mind?'

'So far Archie's come up with *Andrew* or maybe *Alan*. *Alexander* is also in the running. What do you think?'

'All good names,' he said. 'And if we have a girl?'

'Oh,' she said, 'April and I have already decided. We thought we'd go for *Anne*. After your mother,' she added unnecessarily, for his reaction was there in his face for her to read.

'Hard, are you?' she enquired a few moments later.

He lifted his head from her neck and gave her a sheepish look. 'I don't know what I did to deserve you.'

'Och, Ewen,' she said tenderly. 'You do.' She patted his broad chest. 'Be off with you. Go out there and give 'em hell.'

He couldn't resist one last kiss, leaning over the fence and cupping her face between his hands.

'You're happy, then?' she asked.

His eyes were like a Hebridean sea: deep, full of quiet power, as constant and enduring as the mountains and rocks.

'Happy?' he repeated, and the sun came out and turned the grey waves a warm blue. 'Lassie,' he said, 'I'm delirious with joy!'

Our Kid

Billy Hopkins

It was on a Sunday night in 1928 that Billy Hopkins made his first appearance. Billy's tenement home on the outskirts of Manchester would be considered a slum today, but he lived there happily with his large Catholic family, hatching money-making schemes with his many friends.

When war came, and the Luftwaffe dominated the night sky, Billy was evacuated to Blackpool. There he lived on a starvation diet while his own rations went to feed his landlady's children – 'I might as well be in Strangeways!' But even the cruel blows that were to be dealt to the family on his return to Manchester would not destroy Billy's fighting spirit – or his sense of humour.

Nostalgic, sad and funny, OUR KID recalls an upbringing and an environment now vanished.

OUR KID, originally published under the author name Tim Lally, was warmly acclaimed:

'How wonderful to have a book like this. A book . . . that pulls readers back to that different world . . . A glimpse of a lost reality' *Manchester Evening News*

0 7472 6153 9

HEADLINE

The Ties That Bind

Lyn Andrews

Tessa O'Leary – the only daughter in a family of fatherless boys, when her mother dies she's her brothers' lifeline to survival. So for Tessa the privations of war are just another battle to be fought for a young woman who was born fighting . . .

Elizabeth Harrison – oppressed by her shopkeeper mother's snobbish expectations, it seems the coming war offers an escape from her family's emotional ties – but at what cost?

The Ties That Bind – the unputdownable story of two young girls in the slumlands of war-wracked Liverpool, bound together by a friendship that surmounts disaster, poverty and heartbreak . . .

'A great saga' *Woman's Realm*

'A compelling read' *Woman's Own*

'Gutsy . . . a vivid picture of a hard-up, hard-working community' *Express*

'Spellbinding . . . the Catherine Cookson of Liverpool' *Northern Echo*

0 7472 5808 2

HEADLINE

Any Old Iron

Lynda Page

Kelly McCallan has more than her fair share of
worries. Her mother is dying and needs constant care;
her father has returned to Leicester from the Second
World War but is an emotional wreck; and her
brother, Mickey, has turned to a life of crime that is
putting the whole family at risk.

Kelly's boyfriend, Rodney, and his sister, Glenda,
know that she's scared of what Mickey might do next.
But they turn a blind eye to her fears – with disastrous
consequences for them all. When Kelly has lost
everything she holds dear, she and Glenda pick up
the pieces and start again. And one man, in particular,
is there when Kelly needs him most: Alec Alderman
– a kind and gentle rag-and-bone man. But Alex has
problems of his own . . .

'If you want an enthralling saga, read Lynda Page'
Martina Cole

'You'll be hooked from page one' *Woman's Realm*

'Full of lively characters' *Best*

0 7472 5505 9

HEADLINE

Stay as Sweet as You Are

Joan Jonker

With the face of an angel and a sunny nature, Lucy Mellor is a daughter who'd make any parents proud. But her ever ready smile masks a dark secret. For while her friends are kissed and hugged by their mothers, Lucy only knows cruelty from the woman who brought her into the world. Her father, Bob, tries to protect her, but he is no match for a wife who has no love for him or his beloved daughter.

The Walls of their two-up two-down house are thin and Ruby Mellor's angry outbursts can be heard by their neighbours. One day, Irene Pollard, from next door, decides she can no longer stand back, so she and her friends take Lucy under their wing. But sadness remains in Lucy's heart because, despite everything, she still craves a mother's love . . .

'Hilarious but touching' *Woman's Realm*

'You can rely on Joan to give her readers hilarity and pathos in equal measure and she's achieved it again in this tale' *Liverpool Echo*

'Packed with lively, sympathetic characters and a wealth of emotions' *Bolton Evening News*

0 7472 6111 3

HEADLINE

If you enjoyed this book here is a selection of other bestselling titles from Headline

ANGELS OF MERCY	Lyn Andrews	£5.99 ☐
A LIVERPOOL LULLABY	Anne Baker	£5.99 ☐
THE RIVER FLOWS ON	Maggie Craig	£5.99 ☐
THE CHINESE LANTERN	Harry Bowling	£5.99 ☐
RICHES OF THE HEART	June Tate	£5.99 ☐
TOMORROW THE WORLD	Josephine Cox	£5.99 ☐
WHEN DAY IS DONE	Elizabeth Murphy	£5.99 ☐
THE WAY THINGS WERE	Hilda McKenzie	£5.99 ☐
SWEET ROSIE O'GRADY	Joan Jonker	£5.99 ☐
NELLIE'S WAR	Victor Pemberton	£5.99 ☐
A THIRSTING LAND	Wendy Robertson	£5.99 ☐
KATIE'S KITCHEN	Dee Williams	£5.99 ☐

Headline books are available at your local bookshop or newsagent. Alternatively, books can be ordered direct from the publisher. Just tick the titles you want and fill in the form below. Prices and availability subject to change without notice.

Buy four books from the selection above and get free postage and packaging and delivery within 48 hours. Just send a cheque or postal order made payable to Bookpoint Ltd to the value of the total cover price of the four books. Alternatively, if you wish to buy fewer than four books the following postage and packaging applies:

UK and BFPO £4.30 for one book; £6.30 for two books; £8.30 for three books.

Overseas and Eire: £4.80 for one book; £7.10 for 2 or 3 books (surface mail).

Please enclose a cheque or postal order made payable to *Bookpoint Limited*, and send to: Headline Publishing Ltd, 39 Milton Park, Abingdon, OXON OX14 4TD, UK.
Email Address: orders@bookpoint.co.uk

If you would prefer to pay by credit card, our call team would be delighted to take your order by telephone. Our direct line is 01235 400 414 (lines open 9.00 am–6.00 pm Monday to Saturday 24 hour message answering service). Alternatively you can send a fax on 01235 400 454.

Name ....

Address ....

....

....

If you would prefer to pay by credit card, please complete:
Please debit my Visa/Access/Diner's Card/American Express (delete as applicable) card number:

Signature .... Expiry Date ....